TRIBES

G.W. MORGAN

CONTENTS

The Enlightenment Protocols: Tribes.

I'll start by declaring this, Tara Fatimah Bittrich remains the most exotic woman I have ever met. That's saying quite a bit after the travels I've had. She is a singularly outstanding woman. I don't say that just because she's from another planet either. Yes, that's right. Tara Bittrich is from a planet called Comar, in a stellar state called Denestri. Denestri is part of a trans-stellar league here in our galaxy called the Commonwealth of Stellar States.

Tara Bittrich is a Recondo operative, a scout in their Common Stellar Fleet. She and the unit she is a part of discovered us in November 2013. That's right. They found us.
So much for SETI. Don't make the mistake of calling Tara or any other Commoner an 'alien'. Especially to their face. 'Foreigner' is okay, but not 'alien.' Not that anyone of us would know it if we talked with a Commoner. How do I know all this?
She and other Commoners have told me, and I believe them.

I'll tell our story in the book, 'Commoners of Draken'.
In brief, Recondo Master Sergeant Tara Bittrich came into my life one cool November morning in 2013 and has never left. I became her surrogate and offered her my home to establish the first of a network of transit points and safe-houses for the Recondo Planetary Surveillance Teams that followed her. The operatives fanned out across the globe and conducted a 'due diligence reconnaissance' of our people, as part of what is called a 'tribal enlightenment assessment'.

From Nov 2013 to Dec 2014, they talked with our people. They walked our streets, read our books, watched our movies and television, and listened to our music. They learned our history, our economic systems, our politics, and our religions. They collected what the reconnaissance world calls their Essential Elements of Information for their Common Senate back home.

I met Commodore Gaven Webster Morgan through Tara. It was at that first meeting he asked me to present this series, 'G.W. Morgan's The Enlightenment Protocols' to audiences here on Sol-Earth. With the Commodore's permission, I decided to use 'G.W. Morgan' as a penname.

If there is an overarching theme to this series it must be this. Despite what many here may think, we Sol-Earthers are unique only in the fact we are exactly average. I'll tell you about that later. Further, we are not as horrible as many of our tribe believe. There are many, many human tribes. Some are older than we are, many are younger and are still developing. Other tribes, like us, are just beginning to reach out beyond their terrestrial bounds. Some tribes are better behaved towards one another than we are, others are much worse.

G.W. Morgan's The Enlightenment Protocols are the Commoner's stories. You may find some of their place-names a little difficult to pronounce at first, and some words or phrases may look and sound familiar but may have a foreign context. You will find no direct references to us, except in key calendar equivalents I inserted. The reason for this is the Commoners didn't know we existed until recently. Otherwise, you will find the Commoners and their contemporaries are indeed NOT alien to us. In fact, we are very, very similar.

The Commoners left a few monitors and re-transmission buoys behind when they left, but the bulk of Task Force Draken was enroute home to the Commonwealth by December 2014. Their Common Senate will debate, about us. At some point, they will vote on whether or when Commoners will return and open diplomatic and commercial relations with us. It's been a few years, but I hear things are looking pretty good.

A Message to the Earthers of Sol.

I am Commodore Gaven Webster Morgan of the Commonwealth of Stellar States Fleet, now retired. My home is in the stellar state of Sperieus in the Nursery Crescent region of our galaxy. Under my command, Task Force Draken discovered your tribe and successfully conducted due diligence reconnaissance of your galactic sector, AEWX-0449. I led this mission over a time period equivalent to your Sol-Earth Common Era year 2014. That is roughly equivalent to our common stellar year 771CE. As a result of this surveillance, the Senate of the Common Stellar States has scheduled the first debates to consider the enlightenment of the Sol-Earth tribe, with a non-Aligned trans-stellar political status.

Earthers, there have always been two types of human tribes in our galaxy. Those who have recognized the existence of other human tribes are called 'enlightened'. Those tribes who, for various reasons have not, we call 'unenlightened'.

Enlightened tribes communicate and trade with one another as non-aligned political entities or as members of any one of the several trans-stellar leagues, such as our Common Stellar States, our close contemporary, the Valerian Monarchy, or our most significant adversary, the Sacorsti Alliance.

Enlightenment is a seminal event in the history of any global population. While not an end in itself, enlightenment is a transition of a world's tribe into the community surrounding them. Accepting the universality of Man and the similarity of tribal development between worlds, at least in our known galaxy, is perhaps the greatest challenge a newly enlightened tribe must face.

Many tribes have achieved global unity resulting from contact with trans-planetary and trans-stellar neighbors. Global prosperity through commerce has followed in most cases. In contrast, others have suffered invasion and conquest at the hands of aggressors they never knew existed until it was too late. The tribes of Sacor and their Alliance of Stellar Republics have practiced such aggression many times.

Earthers, non-Aligned planetary tribes make their own way in trans-stellar politics and trade within the central and outer metropolitan regions. As a league of stellar states, Commoners subscribe to and defend the five universal freedoms; thought, speech, association, assembly, and enterprise. The Valerian, Patruscan, and Asigi Leagues all recognize compatible canons of human rights. Unfortunately, the Sacorsti canons of conduct are incompatible with basic human rights. There have been wars between us. Fortunately, the fourth such war has recently ended on terms very favorable to us.

'Tribes' opens amid the closing days of the fourth Alliance War. As the final battles raged, and negotiations filled diplomatic back-channels, the former Alliance Senior Lieutenant Nadia Tinor, and her valiant crew took advantage of the confusion to make a daring escape from Sacorsti tyranny. This set events in motion that led ultimately to Operation Dragoon, the mission that brought my force to your region and Task Force Draken's discovery of your Sol-Earth tribe and your neighbors in the regions you call the Centauri group and Tau Ceti. This remarkable woman, Nadia Tinor, and her intrepid crew, are fully deserving of the highest praise.

G.W. Morgan, Retired Commodore,
Commonwealth Stellar Fleet.

Tinor's War.

Aboard the Aglifhate Research Vessel Retnec, berthed at the Y-31 Shipyard, an Alliance support depot orbiting the planet Carillon in the Vega Stellar Republic. Deciem 15th, 468 of Pygan's Common Era.

The guard keyed the incorrect code sequence for the second time. Chaffing at the delay, Shafiran Defense Forces' Senior Lieutenant Nadia Tinor stood fidgeting with her headset and data pad just behind him. They had one last chance, or the entire cryogenics lab archive went into security lockdown.

"I have the access code here on the work order, Private. Stand aside, I'll do it."

The guard shook his head.

"That's against regulations, madam."

Nadia had to let him try again. If he failed again, as she expected, they would be trapped there in the archive stacks. The security technician on the bridge would have to unlock the system. She put her headset on and adjusted it to be ready to call for assistance.

They had less than a day before *Retnec* set to the nearest outbound gravity wave and there was still much to do in other areas of the ship. Rumors abounded within the shipyard and on Carillon. She had heard there was desperate fighting in the nearby Vighandis stellar region and *Retnec* had been ordered to retreat to safety.

Nadia knew trans-stellar communications were steadily degrading, and the priority for civilian newscasts had been downgraded. Sub-Commander Giles vin Nedman, the ship's executive officer, had said their occupation force moving into Vighandis had stumbled into a huge Commonwealth force that no one knew anything about.

'It was an ambush,' he had said. 'The Commoners were waiting for them, and now three full phalanxes may be trapped, nobody knows for sure.'

This time, the guard keyed the correct sequence.

"I've got it, madam."

In the Vega stellar group, they were just 130 trans-stellar astronomic units away from Vighandis. *Omens,* Nadia did a quick mental calculation. *With the reactors at 85% output and riding the regional gravity waves, that's just a 5-day transit from here. Those forces have to stand.* She had heard reinforcements had gathered in the stellar group called Bavat, which lay a one-day transit between Vega and Vighandis.

The storage unit was the last section of *AGRV Retnec* that needed to be unsealed after her refit. They both heard the rush of stored atmospheric gases being pumped into the lab storage compartment, as the darkened lock status above the manway illumined a flashing green. It then steadied, and after a moment, went to blue. The manway lock latch disengaged, the seal released, and the manway slid open.

Tinor stepped through the manway and down the short ramp to a metal grate deck.

"Mr. Warrick, can you hear me?"

'Loud and clear, Lieutenant,' her chief engineer's voice crackled in her right ear from his station, three decks above in auxiliary control.

She walked along a short corridor into the cryogenic storage compartment and stood there at the entrance for a moment. Several ranks of shadowy men and women, suspended in translucent, cylindrical stasis pods filled the dim compartment. Color-coded piping attached to the power units snaked across the deck, under the grating, to labeled tanks mounted to the bulkheads. She turned around and was relieved to see the guard had remained at the open manway at the head of the ramp.

"Are you nervous, Private? They're just sleeping."

She heard the click of the intercom.

'I've heard the scientists call them ice-sickles, madam. They're over three hundred fifty years old now,' he said.

Nadia heard him trying, but failing, to sound authoritative. She answered him with a calm assurance.

"That's what the manifest says, Private."

'These people here aren't like the ones on deck five, madam. These here didn't get their heads fixed first.'

"That's true. They weren't implanted when they were put under." Nadia didn't have to look at the manifest to know that. Her headset optic lit her path through the gloomy aisle as she turned to move deeper into the compartment.

'If they wake they could kill us,' the guard's voice sounded ever more plaintive. 'They say people like these can become as strong as three men if they're not awakened properly!'

"Well, I don't know if that's true, Private. With the gas flow rates they've been getting all these years, these people won't be awake anytime soon. Don't worry."

'Yes, madam.'

Nadia heard the intercom click off. She keyed her headset microphone to whisper mode and spoke softly.

"I'm in now, Warrick. He's back by the manway. He's not following me."

'They're superstitious. Go straight ahead to row five. Turn left and go to junction node five four. The nodes are at gaps in the deck grates. Record the positive and negative flow rates from five four, to eight four. But the nodes at six four and seven four are the critical standards. Understand?'

"Understood."

Nadia learned long ago to trust her warrants and artificers, the senior section technicians. Ernesto Warwick, chief Alliance engineer aboard the 425 year-old ship, told her a year ago to be patient. He told her to wait for this day, and all her doubts would be erased. Vin Nedman had hinted at the same thing when he issued the work order.

Working her way along the narrow, grated walkways, Nadia quickly located Junction Node 54 and made the necessary notations on her data pad. She followed the piping under the deck grates to each of the next three nodes in rapid succession, paying no attention to the sleeping occupants.

"The readings are holding steady so far, Warrick. They're in the eight three range."

'That's good, madam. I'll set the parameters here and we can re-route the monitoring functions from the bridge, down here to auxiliary control.'

"Which adds to our daily task list, Warrick."

'We are here to serve, madam.'

Nadia heard the old warrant chuckle through her earpiece. She looked around at the environmental indicators attached to supports at intervals around the compartment.

"We've still got some heating and grav fluctuations on the boards down here, Warrick."

'I see them on the readouts up here, madam. They're within their nominal ranges. They'll steady up once we power the mains when we get under way.'

"We've got nothing holding us back from launching on schedule on the morrow, Warrick. Then seventy hours for shakedown, before a nice cruise to Sacor the Second."

'Then what, madam?'

"With this war, who knows? But definitely home leave. Shafir is only six days transit from New Laconia, Warrick. You should come with me to Alboa. I know some very nice matrons there."

'Matrons? Are you saying I'm old, madame? I'm only eighty-six. I like 'em young and lively.'

"I'll keep that in mind, Warrick," Nadia said smiling, working her way between pods following the winding deck grating. "The science teams won't start work until we get to New Laconia. We can use those ten days of transit time to wire their stations in our area."

'Will do, madam. And their mess deck ready rooms as well.'

"We've still got a lot of work to do."

'Work is good for the soul, madam.'

Nadia grinned at Warrick's sarcasm while recording the rates at the 84 node and tabulating her data.

"Complete, Mr. Warrick. The maximum variance is eight three point eight at node seventy four."

'Good, madam. That's right where it's supposed to be. We'll lock them in manually when you get back up here. Don't get lost coming out. Just turn around and come out the way you went in.'

"Will do."

Retracing her steps, Nadia looked into the sleeping faces of each pod's occupant as she passed. Their facial features, visible through the suspension gel, and the vismask administering what the techies' called '*dream gas*', were not what she had expected. The manifests only listed their pod and corresponding manifest number. Yet, the data plate on their power mounts identified them by name and seal date. They were all clad in the same gray, gravwear torso suits, 2nd Pygani Century versions of the 5th Century style she wore under her fatigue duty uniform. They floated, suspended in viscous, pale blue cryogenic fluids that massaged their body's muscles to prevent atrophy.

Nadia stopped at Pod 74, the one vin Nedman spoke of in a hush in his billet. The diminutive, long haired woman didn't look much older than Nadia herself. Translating the Laconian language data plate, she stood close enough to touch Alexandra Marena, the last freely elected president of the old, neutral-pacifist, Shafiran stellar state. The woman who was alleged to have betrayed and abandoned her people for the non-pious Commoners.

In school, Nadia had been taught Marena had lived out her days in luxurious exile, among their enemies in the Commonwealth. Nadia's family had been one of many quiet skeptics since she was a little girl. The story was part of the carefully constructed, and well-maintained lie Warrick exposed to her and that vin Nedman had all but confessed. The seal date at the base of her pod confirmed she had been trapped right here, in stasis for over three hundred fifty years.

President Marena's stasis pod stood just steps away from the similarly podded scientist in number 64 who, it was now clear to Nadia, had put her there, Doctor Salezar Ben-Ali. These two, and 173 others had been sealed in this compartment since the time of the first Madonna.

"I've found her, Warrick," she whispered. At that second, the war that had raged within Nadia Tinor's soul ended. The legend was true. Her grandfather's familiar image smiled in her mind's eye. *Papa Silas was right all along,* she thought. *'The first martyr is not dead.'*

'Keep moving. Don't dawdle,' Warrick's voice crackled. 'The atmosphere in there is still a little unstable. You sound light-headed. Are you alright?'

Staring at the truth in front of her erased all of the doubts and confusion that had plagued Nadia since her first sight of this ship, eighteen months ago. Now she knew, her entire life had been a lie. *The Sacorsti and our government have been lying to us for generations,* she thought. *We're no better than implanted levies to the Sacorsti. I've been a fool!* "Yes, yes, right. I'm alright, now. I'm coming out, Warrick. I'll meet you back up on the drive deck."

'Warrick out.'

Nadia gave the woman one last look, fixing her image in her mind, then moved on. She wanted to cry, but she forced herself not to. Everything she had learned to love and cherish; her family, defending her people's way of life, their history, had just crumbled to dust. She was numb, there was nothing left. Nadia was certain of what she had to do now.

    We must escape. It's the only thing to do. No matter what the cost.

*

Near the moon Karel of the ice giant Alfreya, in the disputed Vighandis Stellar Group. First month, 29th day, in the year 770 of the Common Stellar Era.

    Commonwealth fleet task forces surprised the invading Sacorsti-led Alliance phalanxes and pushed them away from the Vighandis habitable zone planets. The Alliance units then found their lines of communication to the neighboring Bavat stellar region had been cut off by the arrival of still more Commonwealth fleet units. The Alliance forces were trapped in the Vighandis outer zone asteroid fields and were being pummeled from every direction.

    The Commonwealth hunters hid their fewer numbers. Their ships stalked the ionized clouds bordering the outer zone asteroid fields. They jammed the Alliance communications where they could, while projecting false imagery and electronic signals to mask their own movements and signals. They scanned the thick fields with passive sensors while their scouts probed ahead amid the herds of rocks and dust.

    The *Commonwealth Destroyer Hanson*, led six ships of Destroyer Flotilla Five. They crept within the decelerating fold of a planetary gravity wave inbound towards the star Vighandis. Their position near the outer giant blocked the Alliance force's last escape route back towards their bases in the Bavat Stellar Group.

    Red ship symbols appeared on the tactical plots in *CD Hanson's* command information center. The low-key tone of reports, orders, and acknowledgements belied the rising tension. That disciplined cross-talk on her bridge and the bustle of activity it generated, kept the destroyer's crew of 800 alive and alert, and the flotilla dominating their sector of the battle area.

    "Spot report, commander, from scout charlie-six," a signals tech called out. His alert took priority, momentarily silencing crewmembers nearby. "Three destroyers, bearing Vighandis one niner five. Direction, six three down. Distance, one six seven; speed m-six, AC/DC factor, four point three. No IFF. Kritt and Shafiran

10

drive signatures, definitely hostile. Scouts request immediate suppression and fighter support."

"Looks like we're just in time," the commander said. She swiveled towards the bombardment support officer.

"Confirm and loose your interdiction bombardment."

The officer pressed his earpiece to hear better over the chatter in the Command Information Center adjacent to the bridge. He nodded and pointed towards the situation plotter.

"Confirm, confirm, target designation zero one three bravo. From target reference point zero, zero four, shift one five left, zero three down, out one seven."

Even though outnumbered by their Alliance enemy and stretched thin, the Commoners held the initiative and kept the pressure on.

*

Commonwealth scouts made sure their Alliance counterparts never lived long enough to pass on information to their phalanxes. That first part of their job left Alliance Falcon scout ships as sparking wrecks and their crews as drifting bodies in remote areas of the outer asteroid fields.

Penetrating the Alliance reconnaissance screen line, eight pairs of Commonwealth Fitter scouts flittered among the rocks one-half million kilometers forward of *CD Hanson*. They reported their detection of another enemy breakout attempt, then began the deadly dance, maneuvering to locate and delay the main enemy force.

"Petra, standby torpedoes. Target the leader!"

The sergeant piloting Charlie-Six re-scaled his multi-dimensional tracking plot to get a tighter picture on the approaching drive signatures of a trio of destroyers 13,000 kilometers to his front. The two-decked, triangular enemy ship's apex mounted 47.5cm mag-rail gun turrets angled towards his two tiny Fitter scout ships. He knew his scout ships' drives had been spotted through the thinning wisps on the extreme edge of charged particle clouds bordering the asteroid field.

His gunner locked onto the leading vessel and half squeezed the launch lever. The range finder flashed green.

'Clear to Engage - 13,089.4 kilometers'.

"Target. She's rolling to port, target is flatting. Towards us! She's trying to turn away. Solution is green, Sarge."

"Missile Alert!" his scanner operator shouted. "Two, make that three, three Talons inbound!"

"Loose Torpedo…" the sergeant ordered. He launched distractors and made vapor. "Juke, Seven," he shouted into the mike glancing over his shoulder out the lamalar, in the direction of his sister scout. "Get back into the clouds!"

"Torpedo awaay!"

The Mark-8 torpedo shifted polarity to match that of the scout ship. Sliding from the starboard launch tube, its inertia carried it 20 kilometers before its drive unit kicked in. The weapon accelerated, constantly shifting polarity as it streaked across the prevailing gravity wave.

"Torpedo two standing by."

"Loose number two."

"Torpedo awaay!"

**

"Commander, *CD Hauser* reports additional destroyer contacts," another tech announced. "Two separate groups, lead group is four destroyers. Cross bearing is Vighandis two seven…correction, Vighandis two niner by Alfreya three four six. Direction four-eight low, out eight-three. Distance one five zero; speed m-eight, AC/DC factor two. No IFF, madam. Shafiran and Kritt drive signatures, confirmed hostile."

As the tech continued her report, scanner operators in the CIC transferred the new contacts from their screens. Their data reflected immediately in the holograph plots on the bridge, and in the battery direction centers controlling the gun turrets.

"Second group is one battle cruiser with three destroyers. Bearing Vighandis one seven true. Direction niner three level. Distance, one-niner-five; speed m-six point three, AC/DC factor four. No IFF. Sacorsti and Astarene drive signatures, confirmed hostile. Madam, *Hauser*, and the frigates *St. George* and *Asbury* are engaging now, now, now!"

The commander sat forward in her chair. "Tell *Hauser* we're coming. Nav/Pro, increase to flank. Helm, vector two one seven, approach Karel from the ice giant's southwest. Give me an ETA, Nav/Pro! Get the vespids in there to support the scouts, Lieutenant Karl!"

"Roger that, Commander," the liaison aboard from the flotilla's escort mini-carrier confirmed from his console. "I've got three elements inbound, ETA, six minutes."

"Bombardment, I want interdicting SK on both those groups!"

"ETA to Karel insertion is two zero minutes, madam," the navigation/propulsion officer announced with a perfunctory calmness. The Commander turned to him and gave the young officer a grinning nod.

The bombardment liaison reported. "Arak BDC is adjusting on groups two and three from TRP zero, zero nine, madam."

"Very well. We've got the bastards boxed in! Signal the flotilla, Battle Stations. Engineering, engage battle overrides. Go to ninety percent on your reactors. Helm, give me a new Karel ETA."

"Battle Stations!"

The 'Reactor Inhibitor - Battle Override' klaxon sounded, the interior lighting throughout the destroyer went to battle red.

"Commander, *Bombardment Ship Arak* signals TRP zero, zero four Shot. Time of flight is zero three minutes," the bombardment liaison reported.

"Very well." The commander nodded in approval.

"Charlie Six, this is Eagle, get small, get small, immediate suppression SK and vapor, SHOT! Time of flight is zero three mikes, Oscar is inbound from your starboard in zero six, acknowledge, over."

Her senior signals petty officer transmitting the alert to the scouts reassured the flotilla commander they would know help was on the way.

**

"Acknowledge that Wen," the scout sergeant ordered his signaler/observer. He worked his controller, maneuvering his craft in anticipation of the bombardment's shock wave. His gunner's voice filled his headset.

"Torpedo target in three, two, one, impact!"

The scout's first torpedo struck the lead Alliance destroyer dead amidships on her exposed underbelly. The discriminator in the gunner's sighting binocular suppressed the blinding flash as the 285dcb warhead punched into the armored outer hull. The destroyer's Talon anti-ship missiles went stupid and fail-safe

13

detonated when their guidance beam severed. The destroyer visibly staggered under the impact as the scout's second torpedo struck directly under its starboard apex gun ball turret. The gunner clearly saw large pieces of armor plating tear away, spinning from the stricken vessel. Its Shafiran drive signature wobbled in their targeting screens.

Two torpedoes from Fitter Charlie-7 struck home on the Kritt destroyer echeloned to port of their mate's target. The close release of a Mark-10 anti-ship guided missile from their overwatching Fencer mother ship raised sparks on the second destroyer as the two scouts made vapor. The pair thrustered up-angle, spiraling into a thick bank of cloud. Tracking the target and the first missile, the Fencer's second Mark-10 self-corrected and found its' mark, releasing within centimeters of the Shafiran's portside gun turret.

*

"New ETA to Karel insertion is eleven minutes, madam," *CD Hansen's* navigation/propulsion officer reported.

"Very well. Signals, order the flotilla. 'All batteries engage as your turrets bear.' Advise the cruiser. 'We are engaging a Bavat-ward breakout attempt, have launched my vespids, request vixen bomber support.' Attach our current plot update."

"Yes, madam."

*

Detonating Talon missiles and kinetic bursts from the Sacorsti destroyers' mag-rail launchers rocked and shook the Commoner scouts as they weaved and dodged back into the clouds with no asteroids for cover. Their only protection was their speed and their pilot's maneuvering skill. Seconds later, the destroyers disappeared in vapor from their own projectors. It was of no protection however, as massive vapor clouds blanketed them, followed by the deadly, wobbling shock of 72cm SK projoes from the *Bombardment Ship Arak*, 450 million kilometers, 3 stellar astronomic units behind the scouts.

*

Kinetic shockwaves jolted Alliance ships, dissipating their inertia. Silhouettes of ships flashed amid the SK wobbles of detonating projoes. Turret rings fouled with fragments and debris impacts. Shockwaves vibrated sections of ships' outer and inner hulls. That overpowering grating noise resounded through whole

14

sections of ships, drowning out klaxons and yelled commands. The initial salvo's shockwaves weakened and shoved armor plating. Successive detonations buckled outer hulls and ruptured vessel inner hulls. Compartments leaked and decompressed, some steadily, giving their terrified crews precious seconds to evacuate and seal them off. Other compartments decompressed suddenly, violently propelling crewmembers, consoles, ammunition, and hundreds of tools and objects into the void.

*

The starboard Alliance destroyer never detected the stubby vespid fighters boring in on them out of Vighandis' glare, nor did they see their incoming Mark-10 salvo. The destroyer's Shafiran crew never got off a shot. She staggered and pitched wildly under the impacts. Her inertia dissipated in an instant. She dropped to the speed of the local gravity wave she was riding when struck. Dead in the void, the destroyer's carcass would ride that wave forever. Her aft section and starboard drive nacelle began to glow bright white, then blue, extending forward to her amidships.

"Her reactors imploded. They're cookin' in there," Charlie 6's sergeant lamented.

"Better them than us, sarge," the gunner grunted.

*

Aboard AGRV Retnec.

Lieutenant Nadia Tinor was the senior ranking Alliance of Stellar Republics officer aboard *Retnec*. The command crew and the scientists aboard were all Sacorsti, several were from high Homostoioi Gentry families. The security detail was of their working class Periolaikoi social order recruited from colonist families on Carillon. Tinor and all the *Retnec's* engineering systems, maintenance, supply services and most of the technical crew were selected Periolaikoi and helots from various worlds ruled by Sacorsti colonist clans. Like all the stellar systems in the Alliance, her native Shafir had supplied the Sacorsti with professional technicians, soldiers, and levied servants for generations.

The Sacorsti will call us mutineers. They'll label us deserters. My own people will call me a traitor. So be it. She heard the click of the intercom.

'Are you almost finished down here, Madam Lieutenant?' The guard sounded more composed, more sure of himself.

15

"I was just verifying the timing of the flow rate exchanges between the gas lines, private," she answered.

"Everything is nominal. I'm coming out now."

'Very well, madam.'

Warrick was right, she thought, *we don't enlighten the heathen, we conquer and enslave them.* Seeing President Marena for herself was just what Tinor needed to combat the constant fear of discovery, or betrayal over the long months of her conspiracy. The proof that she, Nadia, was in fact the tyrant's instrument was here, aboard this ship, evidenced by the Sacorsti's own labeling and recordkeeping.

Her Papa Silas had always said. 'The first martyrs are not dead. The heroes our schools taught us all of, are villains.' *Yes, Papa, you were right. Just like you were right about the codes.*

'The racial codes are a Sacorsti farce to keep the Shafirans, and all the peoples of all the Alliance States, divided and subservient to them.'

Damn them! Damn them all to hell!

Outrage at the thought of her people's stolen history rushed to fill the vacuum in her soul. That outrage swiftly boiled into fury. Yet once again, training and discipline stopped Nadia from acting before she was ready. Her rage fueled a new sense of resolve. She felt a new sense of duty within her. A duty to expose the truth, even though that meant defecting to the Commonwealth. She owed it to Papa Silas and, to the old Shafir that Alexandra Marena represented. There were still final safeguards needed.

Nadia was a battle-seasoned veteran, she knew fear was natural. *You're scared means you're alive.* Still, she had not felt anxiety like this since the night before she left home for university, almost twenty years and too many battles ago. She knew the path she planned lay filled with both unknown dangers and opportunities. She closed her data pad and after taking one last look around, worked her way out of the pod ranks to the main aisle.

"Do you know who these people are, Private?" she asked, ascending the ramp towards the guard.

"I'm not allowed to speculate on the activities or cargo aboard the vessel I am assigned to guard, madam."

He had recovered his nerve and conveniently forgotten he had been very chatty a few minutes before.

Nadia was sure she smelled urine.

"We're scheduled to set to the wave in twenty-three hours, Private. Consider yourself fortunate." As the tall, brown-haired Homostoioi officer spoke, his green eyes stayed fixed on the clearly terrified guard. "Chief."

"Yes, sir," the Strelski chief snapped.

The executive officer spun around towards the security chief, pointing at Vickers. "This woman gets ten days penal servitude. Effective immediately!" He turned towards the sergeant of the guard. "Sergeant, disarm Private Vickers. Have her secure her equipment and report to the helot master steward within the hour."

"Yes, sir." The sergeant stepped forward, she pulled Vickers' weapon from its holster and cleared it.

Vin Nedman nodded back towards vin Patrice, stabbing a finger at the guard. "Every latrine, and every trash chute. She's used to hard work. Every dirty helot job there is aboard this ship, chief. She gets it. Understood?" vin Nedman commanded.

"Yes, sir," vin Patrice's response was not as enthusiastic as vin Nedman wanted.

"Would you prefer her being set out of an air lock for insubordination, chief?"

"No, sir," the man shot back, bracing up. "I'll see to her being properly punished as you direct, sir. If you'll excuse me, I'll see to it personally."

"The sergeant will take care of that. What about this urgent matter of an unauthorized weapons shipment you brought me down here for?" The XO planted his fists to his hips, glaring at the security chief.

"I, I, must apologize, uh, for that, Sub-Commander. I've checked the regulations, and Ensign Regal is correct, sir. 'All Aglifhate Collective level vessels will have sufficient small arms and ammunition aboard for designated crewmembers to reinforce the security force to repel boarders'."

Nadia gestured for another gathering cluster to disperse. Ensign Regal sent the techs following her back the way they had come. Crewmembers, again went on their way. Sub-Commander vin Nedman rolled his head and eyes towards the ceiling, then down and along the emptying corridor.

"That's a blinding flash of the obvious, chief," the XO sneered. "We've been at war for four years. It's a good thing you called me and not the captain," he snorted. "Very well, dismissed, chief."

CWO vin Patrice thumped his clenched right fist to his left breast in gladial salute. Sub-Commander vin Nedman returned the man's salute smartly and turned towards Nadia. The Strelski warrant officer strode off along the corridor, angrily gesturing for the sergeant and the dejected Vickers to follow.

"Is our cargo secure, lieutenant?" vin Nedman asked her.

"Yes, sir. All secure, all readings are nominal, the technical staff can take over at any time."

"Very well. You can brief me later. Report to my billet after the dinner sermon. We're done here, I'll be on the bridge."

"Yes, sir!" Nadia clicked her heels and gladial saluted. She and Ensign Regal held their salutes until the XO dropped his return salute and strode away towards the command lift.

Nadia turned to Ensign Regal. "I don't want to know what brought that on, Lucy. But I know you're going to tell me anyway."

Still wearing her surface duty, class B uniform with all her authorized awards and decorations, the older woman shook her head. "It was as though he was looking for something, madam. He wouldn't let us off load. I explained to him, that this was routine, and that you would control the armory access," She said, shrugging her shoulders. "He just wouldn't believe me."

The two women saw Private De'Molay admiring Regal. The ensign's gold pip rank insignia were in sharp contrast to the four rows of service and campaign ribbons above her left breast pocket and the silver combat vessel boarding action badge below her right breast. They ignored him.

She and Nadia turned towards the deck lift, a short distance along the corridor opposite of the command lift, in the same direction Chief vin Patrice went. Private De'Molay followed them at a respectful distance.

"Well, go ahead and get them stowed," Nadia said. "I'll set the access codes from the drive deck when you lock the arms rooms."

"Yes, madam."

"What about the class-A and B rations and med supplies?"

"Three basic loads, madam. The fourth is due in on the shuttle at twenty-thirty hours."

"Good. I want us fully provisioned when we set to the wave. But don't miss sermon, Lucy. You could get away with skipping a few as an enlisted. But you're an officer now." Nadia tapped her friend's epaulet.

"And a lady," Regal snickered.

Bright blue Vega, and her light reflected from Carillon, illuminated the shipyard outside the corridor's lamalar panels they walked past on the way to the lift. Neither Nadia nor Regal spoke of it but the lack of activity around the berths surrounding the main station, the gantry and maintenance platforms, and the antenna fields were sure signs of their recent defeats to their experienced eyes.

Maybe even De'Molay can see it, Nadia thought.

"Look at that, madam," Regal spoke softly, nodding out the lamalar. "Every day there are fewer shuttles and maintenance sleds in the yard. It looks like they're not doing any work at all."

"I know," Nadia replied in a hush. "You can still see battle damage on those Kritt destroyers in the central berths. I haven't seen any progress on them since they were towed over."

"The yard master schedule of repairs has slowed even further over the last few days, Lieutenant."

"I hadn't heard that. That means they've lowered our priority for fuel and spare parts."

"Not us here aboard *Retnec*, madam," Regal said loud enough for the guard to hear. "Our supply train to the station, and down to the surface is running full tilt." She made a sweeping gesture towards the planet. "Wide open, madam," she chuckled. "This is the Madonna's ship! Whatever we ask for, we get. Usually within a day or so."

They stopped at the Y-section, where the laterals branched off along the Alpha towards the amidships shuttle bay and the deck lift.

"Well, I'm sure you've things to take care of, Ensign. I'll see you at sermon."

"I'll be there, Madam Lieutenant, body and spirit." Regal grinned and gladial saluted. Nadia returned her salute and turned to step into the lift with De'Molay.

***

The Vighandis battle area.

Supporting another breakout attempt, Alliance crewmembers aboard the Sacorsti battle cruiser stayed at their posts fighting two battles. One against the Commoners to their front and flanks, the other at their stations. Bathed in sweat, they fought the overpowering urge to vomit from the odor of burnt wiring and insulation mixed with burnt flesh, urine and loosed bowels.

Petty officers relayed orders to secondary systems operators and brought technicians forward to repair over-loaded primary systems. Marines and deck officers helped medicos carry smoking corpses of electrocuted shipmates past frantic secondaries and tertiaries assuming ever greater duties.

"Commie frigates, sir! I have multiple contacts, center bearing three-four-five degrees, two-zero degrees down, range one-zero-five."

"Incoming Bombers off the Starboard Bow! They're Locked On To Us!"

A wall of SK wobbles erupted just in front of the cruiser and its two surviving escorting destroyers. Shockwaves rocked the vessels, shattering antenna, breaking radar and particle locks and severing communications.

*

Another salvo of SK and vapor projectiles blossomed in front of and within the Alliance formation. Super-heated ionized clouds merged into a blanket, blocking their lidar and thermal viewing. The approaching Commoner bomber crews locked on to the enemy ships' drive signatures. The bombardment forced the Alliance surge to a crawl, at wave speed, setting them up perfectly for their torpedo run.

"Group, this is six lead. Six-four, you take the closest destroyer, six-eight, attack the escort on the far side. Everybody else follow me to the cruiser. Stay above 'em, break past me after you launch. Watch out for each other's shock waves! Rendezvous at checkpoint bravo."

Covered by the frigates' guns, missiles, and torpedoes, the vixen squadron accelerated and bored in on their quarry, targeting their ordinance loads. There was no one single launch command, the individual vixens reached their respective launch points within seconds of each other. All 14 craft ripple launched their entire racks of individually targeted torpedoes and heavy Anti-Ship Guided Missiles into the stalled Alliance formation.

*

Negotiations continued as fighting raged in the Vighandis outer regions, via tele-conferences between the Sacorsti Trans-Stellar Alliance and the Commonwealth of Stellar States. The two Foreign Offices communicated through diplomats from the Asigi Collectives and the Patruscan Trans Stellar League, from their embassies on Sacor II-New Laconia within the Alliance and, on Saluri-Demeos in the Commonwealth.

***

Y-31, aboard Retnec.

When they returned to Deck 3, Private De'Molay took his station in the well-travelled 3-Alpha corridor outside the Auxiliary Control Unit. Nadia stepped through the open manway and, seeing Warrick standing at the cryo-storage monitor panel joined him there. Others of the auxiliary unit, Martin, the auxiliary helmsman, and the navigators, Ensigns Prine and Jackson acknowledged her with a wave or a nod from monitoring stations around the compartment.

"So you believe me now, madam?"

"I never doubted you, Mr. Warrick. But I'm glad I know now where to look. You're right, those junctures are critical."

"Eight years, I've been caretaker on this ship, madam. The systems warrant before me had it for fifteen. It's a good ship, just needs lookin' after is all."

Retnec's senior Alliance warrant officer reminded Nadia a little of Papa Silas, he had the same smile. He told quaint stories of his boyhood on Malaren in Tantori, which often left him melancholy. Warrick had no family left, but he knew more about *Retnec's* systems than anyone alive. Warrick dedicated his time to teaching Nadia, the officers, the systems artificers and every other Alliance crewmember and helot aboard.

Entering her data from the bio-storage, after verifying it with Mr. Warrick's, Nadia and everyone in the compartment and the corridor heard De'Molay's outburst.

"Hey Catamar, treat that techie you're guardin' there well. He's very special. His sister is the one I told you about. I planted my seed in her for eight hours before I came on rotation. Yeah,

25

thinkin' 'bout that nice piece of Karelian ass is really gittin' me through the day."

Nadia and Warrick heard De'Molay's accent change noticeably.

"Yo' family did real good, Jander, raisin' a good swallower like her fo' us!"

Returning under guard, as usual, from the command tower, senior power systems artificer, Mica Jander, had to pass De'Molay's station in the corridor and endure his abuse to walk through the manway.

"I was afraid of this," Warrick whispered, nodding towards Jander. "They're trying to provoke him."

Nadia turned to see Jander's contorted face as he entered the compartment.

"Is it true brown girls got black pussy, man?" the other guard asked, joining in De'Molay's fun.

"It sure is. But it's hot pink inside."

"She be a screamer, De'?"

"The first time up the ass, she was. But by the THIRD time I plowed dat brown pussy, she was a real moaner."

"Yeah?!"

"Yea, man. Ah gives her the rude awakenin', afore I let her go dis' mornin'."

Jander headed directly to his station, he hung his data pad on the charger and started transferring its data.

"Rude awakenin'? What's dat, friend?"

"Man, you a virgin or sumpthin'? I wake up with a hard-on, so I turns over onto her. When dem eyes snap open, I gots her pinned down see and slides betwixt them thighs. I jam ma dick in and ah'm poundin' me some jist wakin' up pussy, friend. Den I turns her over. I gits all dat hair just a-bouncin' AGAIN, Jander. I had yo' sistah's ass just a-jigglin' AGAIN, Jander. Heh, heh. I tell ya, Cat! She all a-moanin'. She be a good piece a meat, man!"

"I bet you had dem titties just a-rockin', huh? Yeah man, you a real stud, De'!"

"Yeah, she moans real good, now. Who'd you git?"

"Nobody yet, I ain't built up de' points. But I got ma' eye on 'dat white Genoese bitch on deck five."

"Which one?"

"Da ginger girl, green-eyed Greene. I hear ol' Jander heah done tapped dat tight little ass his very self. Ain't ya' Jander?"

"Oh, Curly Top! Yeah, I'd like sum o' dat me self. I'll summon her for you, man. We'll train on her. But I get her ginger pussy first."

"Much obliged, De'. You be a good friend. She can swallow me while you be a-sticking her pussy good. I'll see ya later."

"Later, man, we'll git her."

Warrick finished his input and made some notes on his data plate. Nadia, Warrick and the others all knew the hatred Mica felt for the guards. All they could do was watch him clench both fists to his chest. Jander's arms and shoulders shuddered as the man suppressed a desire for something much more physical. He appeared to want more than anything to strike out at something or someone, so Warrick was cautious walking over.

"Are you up for a game of cribbage after sermon, Mr. Jander?" The old warrant patted the young power systems artificer on the shoulder, squeezing a little, as if to say everything will be alright.

Jander exhaled heavily, forcing himself to relax. "I'd like that, sir."

"Good. After we get past the captain's inspection and do a full power up, you will have earned a good beating!"

"Will you join us tonight, Mr. Prine?"

"I can't, Jander. The captain has summoned me to service her tonight." The slender ensign looked around to ensure the Strelski guard wasn't nearby. "She's a lot to handle."

"You'll live, mister," Warrick chuckled, he glanced toward the manway, and back to Jander, his face darkened. "Mica, how is Anika?" he whispered.

"She'll be alright," the man answered softly, with his head down in shame. "He didn't beat her, at least."

"He'd have been punished if he had," Warrick assured him. "She did the right thing, boy. It would have been worse for her if she had refused him."

Prine leaned in close, nodding towards De'Molay.

"That Waffen Strelski pig outside summoned her too, Mica?"

"He sure as hell did. Not even a week after those two corporals," Mica whispered.

Nadia stepped a little closer and listened sympathetically. The Sacorsti were uneven in applying their racial codes, but the summons could fall on any person of non-Golden skin, Periolaikoi or helot. The Madonnas, since Indira vin, had only made it illegal for Homostoioi to take Golden-skins in the levies. Though there were certain customs, and some measure of mutual respect between the Homostoioi class clans and the Periolaikoi clans they controlled, regardless of skin tone, neither non-Golden Periolaikoi nor Helot had any rights the exclusively Golden Homostoioi of Sacor II were legally bound to respect.

Nadia, as well as everyone else had known all their lives, man or woman, a Homostoioi could summon anyone, from a levied slave to even a person's spouse, if they fancied. Giles vin Nedman had told her the new Madonna had extended those, and other historic Homostoioi rights, to certain Sacorsti Periolaikoi clans, including those on Vega-Carillon below.

Giles had summoned Nadia shortly after he reported aboard, he wasn't the first Homostoioi officer to do so. But he wasn't like the others. She was fortunate with him. He earned the respect of the Alliance crew and was feared by the Sacorsti. He was one of the few primary tier Homostoioi who had actually served aboard Tantoran destroyers in combat against the Commoners, instead of aboard the big Sacorsti battle cruisers. Regal had advised her to be cautious, but Giles was tall, ruggedly built and handsome, though not brash and bombastic as primary tier Sacorsti Homostoioi tended to be. Giles was an historian with a brooding, introspective nature that Nadia admired.

The second time he summoned her, they took surface liberty together on Carillon and went sightseeing, he even gave her presents. Giles told her of his boyhood and family on New Laconia. He spoke proudly of their old Laconia heritage and their role is uniting the 14 original worlds of old Sacor, before the great migrations. Nadia told him of her family, about Papa Silas and growing up on Shafir-Alboa. When they returned to the ship, Giles recommended to the captain the Alliance crew be allowed access to the trans-stellar links to keep up communications with their families from the crew lounge aboard ship. The captain approved his recommendation without hesitation. Nadia was sure that was when she had fallen in love with him. Both Warrick and Regal approved when she told them she had stopped taking contraceptives after his second summons.

Nadia and the others noticed Technician Martin scratching the back of his head, standing near his helm station. In the corner of her eye, she saw Private De'Molay stepping in front of the manway to make his routine survey of the crew's activities. His taunts of Jander must have restored his confidence after the incident with Vickers. He looked smug, checking the time on his wrist pad, apparently impatient for shift change.

"Martin, are you set?" Nadia asked.

"All set, Madam!"

"Still, Warrick, I'm going to ask the captain to consider an escort for the calibration cruise."

"You can, Madam, but it'll be a waste of resources. The most critical time for a ship of this age is the first day out of the yard. She'll either go, or she won't."

Nadia nodded, turning towards the manway, she stopped short, pretending to be startled by the guard's presence. "Oh. Private, you can inform the security chief and the bridge that the drive deck is ready for inspection."

De'Molay nodded. "Yes, Madam Lieutenant." He raised his wrist pad, but apparently thought better of it, and walked over, out of sight, towards the wall intercom down the corridor instead.

Nadia turned back towards the others; her eyes wide with excitement. She silently mouthed the words,

"I saw her! She's beautiful! She's an interbred...," She looked around, then leaned closer. "...and so is Ben-Ali, they've modified his image in the history books."

Jander's eyes went wide. His head and shoulders raised as if a great weight had been taken off him. His face broke into a broad grin, he clasped his hands and shook them together. Warrick smiled, the corners of his eyes crinkled like Papa Silas, then he nodded to Jander. There was to be one final meeting with the other leaders.

***

Sermonal Hour. Deck 5, main mess hall, AGRV Retnec.

"All matter under heaven is the creation of Pygan. As Pygan's chosen, we, the Great Goldens of Sacor the Second must carry the burden of the administration of Pygan's material worlds." The Morale Officer on Board, Lt. vin Lurel, began every sermon the same way.

Artificers Mica Jander and Camea Greene joined Technicians Martin and Anika Jander sitting with Mr. Warrick at the right of the sixth row of tables, right of the aisle, among the assembled enlisted crew. The Sacorsti Periolaikoi crewmembers, except Waffen Strelski Private Leticia Vickers, filled the rows of tables between them and the Homostoioi MOB's portable lectern, which she had positioned in front of the main entry.

Sporting a bruised face and bandaged lip, Private Vickers sat sullen and disgraced with the maintenance helots in the rear. Only the anchor watches on the bridge and the reactor pods were excused. Lt. vin Lurel was the only officer present, the rest of the officers and the researchers assembled in the ward room for their own group sermon.

The assemblage raised their right clenched fist to shoulder level. "Enlighten the heathen in your sight and in your hearing to the truth of Pygan, by word, by deed, and by the gladius. Huzzah!" they replied in unison.

The crew lowered their fists and sat at attention, awaiting the next quote of the Prime Canons and another standardized affirmation.

"Shipmates, the evidence has remained unassailable since the Time of Pygan's Knowing." Lt. vin Lurel shook two fingers of one hand towards the ceiling as she spoke. "Every evolutionary study from our joint scientific efforts, including Doctor Ben-Ali's trans-stellar research aboard this very ship, has confirmed the racial-tonal-ethnic balance and hierarchy."

As vin Lurel stepped away from the lectern, the familiar, life-sized, golden-skinned image of the famous Shafiran scientist emerged from the holo-pad. Scanning the room, her green eyes fixed on Jander as the image dropped.

"Senior Artificer Jander, you will stand and define the natural helot."

Jander stood to attention and turned to face the bulk of the crew. His 12 years' experience in the Shield resonated through the mess hall.

"Shipmates, the earth toned base races, the whites, blacks, the reds, and yellows are the natural helots. They are deemed by Pygan to be the beasts of the human race. Helots are by nature fit only for manual labor, under the supervision of we middle toned Periolaikoi, the browns, and the olives."

"You are Karelian, Mr. Jander, of the medium brown race. Are you not?"

"Yes, Madam Lieutenant," Jander answered, staring straight ahead over the heads of the crew.

"And Karelians serve the Aglifhate as full Periolaikoi?"

"Yes, Madam Lieutenant. We Karelians conform to the Sacorsti Canons. We require all Periolaikoi to dedicate themselves to controlling the helots placed in their charge. We work to free the Goldens of the Homostoioi to lead us all to the blessings of Pygan's Conformance."

"You may be seated, Mr. Jander." Lt. vin Lurel clasped her hands together, smiling and nodding in approval. "Your patriotism is an inspiration to us all."

She raised her right clenched fist to her shoulder.

"Periolaikoi!"

The crew all knew what was coming next.

"Lust not for the pleasures of the flesh or material reward!"

The crew raised their fists and answered in unison,

"Rather, submit two thirds of thy wealth, thy concubines, and the fruits of thy levies' labors to succor our Gentry and the Aglifhate. Huzzah!"

One hand remained up in the second row, left of the aisle, catching the MOB's attention.

"Yes, Private De'Molay, you have a question?"

De'Molay stood and scanned the assembled crew, he sneered towards Jander; then turned to face the MOB.

"Madam Lieutenant, if helots are unfit by nature for technical work," he waved an arm back towards the mixed races of Alliance crewmembers. "Then why are they here, among the browns and olives of the Alliance crew?" The other golden-skinned guards and command crew nodded and murmured in agreement with his question as he sat down.

"I can answer that, Madam Lieutenant." Jander sprang from his seat, raising his hand at the same time. He startled everyone, except the black-skinned Mr. Warrick and the white Technician Martin seated next to him.

"Madonna Indira vin's primary appeasement to the Alliance, dated Noviest thirtieth of the year one seventeen, allowed each republic to establish their own variant to the racial codes upon the Aglifhate's approval," Jander said, staring at the back of De'Molay's head. "The text of the appeasement affirmed the Sacorsti cannot accomplish their primary tasks without us! Exceptional helots can overcome their natural limitations with proper guidance and training."

Jander sat back down, contempt for De'Molay plain on his face. Sacorsti who had turned around and the MOB all saw the smirks, grins and nods of affirmation among the Alliance crew.

"That is absolutely correct." Lt. vin Lurel spoke up quickly to defuse the situation. "Mr. Jander has provided your answer Private De'Molay. Mr. Warrick and Artificer Greene, you are excused for your survey."

"Yes, Madam Lieutenant," Mr. Warrick said. He and Camea Greene, got up and quickly exited the mess hall as the MOB continued her lecture.

"For our main topic this evening, The Aglifhate Chamberlains have codified the next twelve of Madonna Nicholla's appeasements to all Periolaikoi. This is good news for all of you. I shall explain each in detail."

*

On the command deck, CWO vin Patrice watched the sermon with the captain on the monitor in her stateroom next to the bridge.

"I like that fellow. Jander. Good solid fellow," the captain said, lowering the sound.

"True enough, madam. He's a fine physical specimen as well. But he's too close to Warrick though. In my opinion," vin Patrice said from his swivel across the console from the captain.

The captain turned towards him. "You needn't worry about Warrick. I'll transfer Jander to the bridge before we depart for New Laconia, he'll be closer to you." She gave the man a sly look and started to undo her long, brown hair. "I've heard his sister is quite popular among your guards."

The security officer smirked. "Humph, as soon as that damned appeasement to our Perios was announced, the troops jumped at the chance to summon their fancies. Three men in a row asked for her. What could we do? Either one of them would have made a good informant. He's close to Warrick, Tinor and the Shafiran crewmembers. She's close to Greene and the rest of the Karelians. But they're embittered now."

"You don't have enough undercovers among the Helots, Shamus?"

"None I would trust out of my sight, madam," vin Patrice gestured towards the monitor. "And the surveillance systems aboard this ship are antiquated, even by second century standards. Madam, none of the officer's or warrant's billets are monitored."

"The people who serve aboard this ship have always held the Aglifhate's highest security clearance, Shamus, you know this. Our surveillance systems don't need upgrades. Your new recruits seem vigilant enough. But what about this incident with this guard and Lieutenant Tinor?"

Chief vin Patrice expected this; he was relieved she hadn't mention his questioning of Regal's weapons delivery. "If you mean Vickers this morning, madam, I can't see the XO's reasoning for humiliating the girl that way. To sentence her to work as a helot, in front of helots. It elevated them. I could see it in their eyes."

The captain raised a hand slightly to calm the man. "I won't comment on the executive officer's handling of discipline aboard this ship. As far as the summons, I want no worries about any of the crew, Shamus. Before we depart for New Laconia, requisition a score of levies for your guards. Deny any further summons for crew members."

"Does that include the executive officer, madam?" vin Patrice snorted. "He's been banging Tinor since he reported aboard."

The captain softened her voice, but she locked vin Patrice in her stern gaze.

"You will respect the sub-commander's clan prerogatives, Warrant Officer."

"Yes, madam."

"We are all Gentry, Shamus."

"I beg your pardon, madam, but you know, the primary tier families have always used their position of benevolence to curry favor with the Periolaikoi and the Helots against low tier Homostoioi, like us."

The captain waved off his seditious comment. "We must continue to placate vin Nedman and the others. He is of a first tier family, many of the others are primary tiers as well."

"And those damned scientists too?"

"Yes. Especially young Comidas, Shamus. Assigning him to the cryogenic team was a peace offering to the Borigai. Nicholla actually admires him and wants to work with him. After all, he is a direct descendant of Indira vin."

"He's a snot-nosed brat, madam. He actually stopped a guard administering on the spot punishment of a mess boy. He threatened to flog the guard himself if he ever struck the boy again!" he said. Visibly angry, vin Patrice sat forward in the swivel towards the console, then leaned back and crossed his legs at the knees. "Madam, he even shook hands with and spoke directly to that helot," he huffed in indignation and leaned forward again, planting both feet to the carpeted deck. "A high Homostoioi like him. Disgraceful." His hands flung out and upward in frustration and slapped to his thighs. "It's a good thing the Alliance crew doesn't know who he is."

The captain smirked. "What level is your Clan on New Shalla, Shamus?"

"So low we don't count, madam," he answered. "We may as well be Perios ourselves. We have three families on retainer, they handle about three score and ten helot families on our farm."

"That's interesting, Shamus. What do you farm?"

"Fish, madam," he announced with a proud grin.

The captain's head tilted, one of her eyebrows arched, she didn't understand the word.

"You call them aquane."

"Ah, yes. I can't imagine you as an aquanary."

"Me?! Oh no, madam. I'm the fourth son. It was the Clergy or the Shield for me."

"Yet you chose the Strelski."

"The Aglifhate Enforcement Bureau chose me, madam. No one volunteers for this type of work, not anymore."

The captain nodded. "My clan ranks in the five hundreds on New Mandan, Shamus. My family is low in the clan order, as well. Like yours, we have no say beyond our vote for our

Assemblage Representative. Yet, we prosper. I prospered to command of this ship, by knowing whose ass to kiss and when, or whatever else. We can never raise our clan station, Shamus. We can, however, raise our own."

She wagged a finger at him. "Understand, Shamus. We need vin Nedman now more than ever. His Barony clan ranks above the Gentry Ngier and Borigai. If the Madonna's rule is ever challenged, we will need his protection. The Borigai are asserting Nicholla may be mad. There are persistent rumors she attempts to channel the spirit of Indira vin. The Borigai hate the notion of another vin Ngier attaching herself to their great ancestor."

The captain watched the look of confusion come over the security chief's face.

"Madam, I don't understand." The Strelski officer's eyes narrowed. "Do you think there will be a coup attempt?"

"More like a counter-coup, Shamus. And Nicholla is aiming to stave it off by appeasing the Borigai with young Comidas. Our orders now, are to deliver this laboratory to her by Janus sixth. That's just three weeks away. She intends to apply the Shafiran doctor's genius to our modern technology."

"Why the urgency to move, madam? Surely the science teams can work from here."

"No, they can't. We've been monitoring the shipping that has passed within range of our extended sensory and ranging pods to calibrate the systems," the captain said. "Since we lost the Trudan six months ago, there has been a dwindling number of commercial ships in this area, whether arriving from other republics, or transiting Vega, towards Bavat and the front in Vighandis."

"Yes, madam. I am aware of that," vin Patrice said.

"Do you know why that is, Shamus?"

"No, madam," he shook his head. "How could I?"

"Of course not. Scheduled maintenance of the regional supernet buoys and beacons has been drastically cut. Shield Operations has had to deploy almost all of our service and support assets from here to Bavat to support the offensive in Vighandis. The gaps in wave data coverage here grow larger every day now. Without that data, Shamus, communications transit times are increasing and commercially or militarily efficient trans-stellar vessel transits will soon be almost impossible."

The security chief still didn't understand.

"This war is lost, Shamus. Mathilda's forces were defeated and forced out of the Vighandis habitable zone," the captain said.

He sat there, as if in shock.

"I knew things weren't going well, madam," he said, trying to collect himself. The AIM reports have said nothing remotely like that." A hint of skepticism colored his tone, his voice broke. He fidgeted in his swivel again.

"I knew that was why they attacked there again after three years. After Trudan, we had no other choice, we all knew that. None of their bulletins. There, there has been no communique from headquarters, madam," his voice steadied, he began to regain his composure.

"Ngier Nicholla vin Flavius controlled the information ministry under her aunt's reign, Shamus. She knows how to manipulate public perception," the captain said.

"And Mathilda commanded the Strelski," the warrant officer said with a nod.

"Without the Trudan, we can no longer supply this region with uniform grade reactor fuels. Strict rationing has been imposed, all across the Alliance, Shamus." She leaned forward. "Three months ago, the Madonna called on the Asigi and the Patruscan Leagues to mediate cease fire negotiations with the Commonwealth."

"I've heard rumors of peace talks, Madame. We've had fuel shortages before. The new Maderan fields in Tantori will resolve those..."

The captain held up a hand to interrupt him. "The Tantorans have defected."

"What?! Madam Captain!"

"It's true. Three weeks ago. They've severed all relations with us and the rest of the Alliance and have declared an armed neutrality. This war will be over before we reach New Laconia." She looked downcast. "We should never have tried to occupy the Vighandis planets, Shamus. They are too close to the Commonwealth," she lamented.

Crestfallen, vin Patrice opened his mouth to speak, but the captain continued.

"Somehow, the commies knew Mathilda's forces were concentrating in Bavat, Shamus. Some Periolaikoi traitor most likely. Mathilda has had the operations staff purged, but the interrogations have yielded nothing. That's why we accelerated the reactivation program and our move to a safe anchorage in the Sacor the Second region. First however, we must report to the Madonna on New Laconia, no later than the sixth."

Vin Patrice pondered that for a brief moment before he spoke.

"I understand now, madam. This ship is a critical asset, now for political reasons regarding the Shafir, with the Tantorans gone. We would be stranded here, out of contact with the Madonna. Half of our destroyer force here is in repair dock. We're defenseless and vulnerable."

"Vega is well within range of a Tantoran strike force, Shamus. They may know who and what we have aboard. They would use this ship as leverage with a Shafiran resistance, against us."

"Tinor is Shafiran, madam. And Warrick, Warrick is Tantoran. Shouldn't we remove them, or at least restrict their access. Tinor was in the archival cryogenic storage compartment just today."

"The cargo status work order, yes, vin Nedman told me. We'll replace the Alliance crew after we reach New Laconia. In the meantime, Tinor is a decorated veteran, Chief, like Regal and Jander. She has enlightened heathen wogs in four campaigns before this war."

The security officer nodded in acknowledgement.

"She's an arrogant pain in the ass, I know," the captain continued. "But, the Baron has tamed her. She is a graduate of Quislier University on Shafir-Alboa, so she's loyal, of that I have no doubts. And Warrick," she snorted. "All Warrick knows or cares about is this ship."

"Very well, madam. So when the people learn we have lost the war…"

"The people will never learn that, Shamus. The Aglifhate Information Ministry and the Alliance media make sure of that. We have never lost any war." The contempt in the captain's voice held a hint of sadness.

"That explains the appeasements," vin Patrice snorted. "Particularly towards these so-called New Egalitarians. They will ensure she retains popular Periolaikoi support."

"Low Gentry will benefit as well, Shamus." The captain didn't stop there. She knew more about her security chief's pastimes than he thought. "After Nicholla's next round of appeasements, Shamus, you'll be able to summon both Janders for yourself if you like." She leaned towards him with a sly grin. "Do your duty to our race, first. Impregnate the girl, then you can change the boy's attitude."

Vin Patrice cast his eyes to the deck as he shook his head. There was no sense denying he preferred men. Still, his Homostoioi duty was to breed inferiors out of existence.

"The Madonna is moving too fast, Madam Captain, in too many directions. You know this. The Barony will never stand for it."

"Nonetheless, Shamus. Nicholla intends to employ as many, let's call them distractions, as possible over the next few years. The people will take them and run. The Barony may not like it, nevertheless, as usual, we'll never hear of it," she assured him.

The Strelski chief shrugged. Then he looked at her with a gleam in his eye. "Once we arrive at New Laconia, Madam Captain, you and I will be close enough to Nicholla to hear everything."

The captain smiled and nodded, then thought better. "As long as nothing we hear has anything to do with Borigai Indira vin Ngier." She stood and stepped away from her console towards her wardrobe, unfastening her fatigues. "Fix us a drink, Shamus. The inspection went well. We'll set to the wave at the tenth hour on the morrow, for a quick shake down. Then we can finally get away from this, Carillon cesspool, and back to civilized living."

"Yes, Madam," he answered. He stood and walked towards her bar.

"I suppose it's different for a happy bachelor, Shamus, but my husbands are waiting for me on New Mandan. I must say I am anxious to see them both. On the other hand, life at court on New Laconia will be much more interesting." There was a hint of gaiety in her voice, vin Patrice saw her dance a little behind her changing screen in the reflector above the bar.

"I'm sure Madam has not been completely bored here. I personally found it rather relaxing." He walked over to set a half-filled tumbler of mash on the table next to the screen.

"Oh, of course not. These Carillons are nice boys, then again, my favorite is aboard. He'll be reporting after dinner."

"The auxiliary navigator? Prine? An excellent choice, Madam."

The captain stepped, bare-breasted, out from behind her changing screen and picked up the tumbler. She raised it in toast towards vin Patrice, took a short sip and she set it back down. The Strelski chief admired his attractive commander's ample breasts and well sculpted figure, but he didn't stare.

"I thought you would approve of him. Use helots and levies for another year, Shamus. Vin Nedman has done his duty, Tinor is pregnant." Nude, she leveled a forefinger at him. "You need to make some babies as well. Afterwards you can have any man you desire, openly."

"I didn't know about Tinor, madam," vin Patrice sighed. "But in all honesty, I'll believe that appeasement when I see the Aglifhate codify it." He raised his tumbler in toast towards his voluptuous captain and drank half his mash in a single gulp. He stepped to the console and slid the monitor's screen to the ward room and turned the volume up a little.

The captain's presence in her small shower activated the unit. The screen closed, warm water sprayed from scores of small nozzles imbedded in the shower walls, gradually heating up. She raised her arms and spread her legs and let the now steaming water cascade onto every part of her body from all directions. The pulse setting allowed her time to soap and scrub-sponge between four surges at the massage setting.

Bathing quickly, she then shifted the water nozzle control to air-dry. A continuous flow of warm, soothing, forced air replaced the water pulses, drying her hair. She sponged herself dry, then brushed and pinned her hair to regulation and put on a fresh uniform for dinner.

*

Warrick kept watch on the corridor through the small window in the manway as Camea Greene sat working the panel at her console in the Deck 5 main laboratory's darkened administrative office.

"Did you hear that about the Tantorans, sir?"

"Yes, I heard it when she first got the report. It makes no difference to me. They sold me to the Sacorsti when I was a boy."

"One thing I still don't understand, sir."

"What's that, daughter?" he asked.

She smiled at that. Manipulating the signal return, to clear some of the fog.

"How is it the Strelski never knew of these reflector recorders, sir?"

He glanced her way before turning back to scan the corridor. "I've been caretaker aboard this ship for eight years, daughter. The old fellow I replaced told me about the surveillance systems first off. He told me quite a few things about this ship and about the people they got on ice here. As soon as I heard they were activating her again. I disabled all the reflector units except the captain's, the XO's, vin-Patrice's and those scientists. Then I wiped all evidence of them from the ship schematics here and at the surface depot."

Greene shook her head, grinning.

"I'm closing and dating this file and starting a new one, sir. I'm keeping these recordings spread out across the archive," she said.

"Good job, Camea. Don't fill any storage unit. We can retrieve them later." He turned to scan the corridor.

"Complete. Sir, if anything happens to me, before we get away. Everything is stored in files under the letters of my name."

"Nothing bad is ever going to happen to you again, daughter. I'll make sure of that."

"Thank you, sir," she blushed a little and smiled. She had forgotten how, until she came aboard *Retnec* and met Mr. Warrick. The old man calling her 'daughter' helped.

"I still have a bad feeling, sir. Anyway it's my name spelled in Genoese, with a K and a Y, not a C and an E. I just thought you should know."

Warrick turned from the small window in the manway towards her and smiled.

"I'll remember that. The corridor is clear, we can leave now."

*

In the ward room on Deck 2, Nadia took her usual seat near the galley and the steward's entrance along with the Alliance ensigns Prine, Jackson and Regal.

Sub-Commander vin Nedman had opened the sermon in the same prescribed manner as the MOB did with the enlisted crew. Then his lecture took a strategic turn. He keyed up a holographic view of the forward battle areas around the Bavat and Vighandis stellar regions.

"The campaign in Vighandis shows all the signs of winding down, ladies and gentlemen," he said. The image shifted to a tactical map of the planetary groupings within the Vighandis heliosphere. "Our forces there are currently consolidating their gains. However, they've had to pull back from the habitable zone to shorten their lines of communication with Bavat."

Nadia, Regal and the other Alliance officers saw the front line trace, representing the forward line of battle, lay closer by several stellar astronomic units, to the Vighandis heliopause. The line had moved back, towards their assembly area in the neighboring Bavat stellar group. Something about the three neat blue ovals depicting three defensive zones merging into one didn't make sense. They were bunched up, much too close together, in a dense asteroid field between the orbits of two of the star's outer gas giants. Nadia knew better than to interrupt the session, so they could get it over with. One of the new bridge officers, however, raised her hand. Nadia recognized the annoyed look on the XO's face.

"Lieutenant vin Krelo. What is your question?"

The young officer stood. "Sir, where are the enemy forces? The Egalitarians are saying the commies have our forces surrounded and cut off from Bavat."

The exec bristled at the inexperienced officer's derision of an enemy Nadia knew he respected and feared. *The Egalitarians are probably right,* Nadia thought. *But the Captain and vin Patrice are listening.*

"Be careful where you get your information, Lieutenant. I won't tolerate defeatist propaganda aboard this ship."

Every officer in the wardroom braced in their seat as if the XO's stern rebuke was directed straight at them. Lt. vin Krelo stood there, shaken.

"Yes, sir! I meant nothing by it, sir. I, I was..."

"Take your seat, Lieutenant," vin Nedman cut her off and turned away. He faced for a moment towards Nadia and the

Alliance officers at the back of the wardroom, then around towards the other Sacorsti.

"All the indications are, the Commoners have withdrawn from Vighandis. Admiral vin Flavius is consolidating her forces in preparation for a swift advance into the habitable zone. The admiral is one of the most brilliant strategists in our history, ladies and gentlemen. She ranks with the great Golden Valerian strategist, Castrada Vida, in tactical innovativeness. I'll show you why." His next display was exactly what Nadia and Ensign Prine needed.

"Admiral vin Flavius has five full phalanxes with her, the bulk of our fleet. Three, you can see are in Vighandis itself, and two are in reserve in Bavat. Three phalanxes are supporting the Quislier Line in the Shafir. Now that the Tantorans have rejected Piety, the admiral has brilliantly re-deployed the Home Phalanx. As you can see, she has shifted destroyer divisions to protect Sacor the Second and the convoy stream of our people from Tantori into Astaran, at least for now.

"Only small covering forces remain on the Patruscan and Asigi frontiers. One division of five destroyers remains to secure Vega and the surrounding systems. The Shield is stretched thin, ladies and gentlemen, from here to the OMR outer frontiers. The Commoners don't know that. We have to do our part. That's why we're moving this vital asset to New Laconia in the Sacor the Second stellar group."

Nadia half-expected a question about the Tantorans, but she knew no one would dare. *That means any credible pursuit is weeks away, good. Just one more thing to do.*

Vin Nedman dropped the display. He pulled a seat over in front of the holo-pad where he could see the entire group. Nadia's seat was almost directly in front of him down the length of the room. He moved on to his next topic.

"Since the Lieutenant brought up the Egalitarians, you all need to understand. The Madonna is working mightily to curb their excesses. Their rhetoric does more harm than good. The AIM always provides reliable source links to their reports, the Egalitarians' sources are dubious, at best. There are some indications, ladies and gentlemen, they are financed by the Commoners' Central Intelligence Directorate.

"The captain wants me to assure you all, the Madonna's newest twelve appeasements will go a long way towards stifling the Egalitarians. I've distributed them to your data pads. We'll go over them briefly here now but learn them in your off-duty hours in case any of your crew have questions."

Nadia only half-listened to the XO as he went on. *He's doing his part. He's just confirmed how right the Egalitarians are.* She didn't care anymore about the Madonna's new appeasements.

There was an ever increasing stream of formerly contraband communications and goods flowing across all the borders, except the Quislier Line defending the Shafir from the Maians and especially the Poians of the Commonwealth. Yet, the constables, confused by this new Madonna's last round of appeasements, had done nothing to stop it. Since the appeasements, even Commoner goods and devices the government banned before, had become commercially available if one had the crowns. The legislators loudly debased the commoner's music and literature from their pulpits, but the constabularies seemed not to care who bought what since the previous announcement just three months ago.

The Egalitarians' editorial media and the Patruscans, said the Shafirans should not hate the Poians or any of the other Commoners. They claimed the Poians were not the war mongering guard dogs of the non-pious, industrial capitalist Commonwealth the Information Ministry made them out to be. Some had even blamed the Shafirans, Nadia's own people, for starting the Great Defensive Conflict. The one the Patruscans and the non-Aligned tribes called the Second Alliance War of 415 to 417 of their Common Era. They said before that war, the Shafir and Poia were strong friends. Papa Silas said the Maians and Poians were primos of the Shafir before the Acquiescence.

Before beginning work on this ship, Nadia only knew of the Wars of Stellar Conformance, and the Great Defense. The campaigns of enlightenment she had fought were all minor affairs against unenlightened wogs. *We brought them death, destruction and slavery from the stars. I can't call them wogs anymore. They were human beings just like me.* Then another dispute with the Commoners, allegedly over Vighandis, erupted into a full scale war with them. Nadia had never heard of any of the so-called, Alliance Wars, until she watched some contraband Patruscan cinemas vin Nedman bought on the underground market.

Nadia, Warrick, Jander, and all the others knew the Appeasements were lies. Everything the AIM and the government said was a lie. Nadia and the others were no longer content to live the lie. But they didn't know what the truth was. Vin Nedman and Warrick only knew some of it. Now, at least, Nadia had seen their truth. Just as Papa Silas had said all those years ago.

The first martyr is not dead. My school days hero is, in fact, a villain. The racial codes are a Sacorsti farce!

They were all committed now. In just a few hours, she and her mates planned to break away and escape, with this ship towards the creative self-interest of the Commonwealth, where the Egalitarians say the Individual is sovereign over the State.

** **

The captain and vin Patrice joined the officers in the wardroom, as dinner was being served, a few minutes after vin Nedman's benediction. Tinor watched the Strelski security chief smirk in contempt at her recommendation. He stood behind the captain but said nothing. Neither did vin Nedman or any of the other officers in the wardroom. It was the captain's decision; vin Nedman only gave the captain advice when asked, and she never did.

"I gave you Warrick because he is the best there is, Lieutenant. You listen to him. If he says the most critical time is the first day out of the yard for a ship of this age then that's all there is to it! We will always be within nine hours of any search and rescue unit. No, Lieutenant," the captain said. "The Shield needs every warship to win the battle in Vighandis. *Retnec* has no need for an escort. Not yet."

The captain's haughty dismissal of Nadia's suggestion of an escort for the shakedown cruise circumnavigating the Vegan Stellar Republic, sealed her fate, and that of the command tower crews. Standing at attention before the captain, Nadia gladial saluted her. "As you command, Captain."

She's right, Nadia thought, *in her praise for Warrant Officer Warrick.*

*

Near the Alfreyan moon Norvah, nearest the Vighandis habitable zone.

'All turrets, rapid fire. Sacorsti battle cruiser target zero three. Loose as your guns bear.'

Symbiosis among the gun crews was a direct result of the Commoners' cultural mindset of constant challenge and practice. It had been paying off across four bitter years of war. Every member of each of the twelve gun crews pushed themselves to be just a bit better today than they were yesterday.

The *Commonwealth Battle Cruiser Shin Tao's* magnetic railgun battery turrets were locked onto the Sacorsti battle cruiser targeted in their direction center multi-plots. Their data translated directly to fire control computers on each of the guns of the cruiser's four battery turrets. In the turrets, gun layers confirmed the data on their mag-rail launchers to data from their direction center;

'Gun two, check and set, lay shows green; Confirm load and lock!'

'Load and lock!'

The oblong, 1.5 meter long 68cm projectile slid into the breach well. The interrupted screw breach mechanism swung shut behind it, rotated to starboard and locked. The locking breach automatically unlocked the barrel blanks, just forward of the projectile.

'Load and lock confirmed; panel shows green. Barrel blank is unlocked!'

'Target is laid, launch magnetos show green, STAND BY!' the gunner yelled over the crew intercom to ready the next projoe.

'Loose!'

At the upper amidships Battery Control Officer's command, twelve gunners depressed their right safety foot pedals and squeezed both trigger handles.

*

Another ragged volley of twelve 68cm high speed programmable fused anti-ship projectiles lanced out from *Shin Tao*. Observers aboard her supporting destroyer, *CD Bagley* were awe-struck as kilometer long tongues of light stabbed outward from her dark, roughened hull. Twelve illumined projoes streaked across the void. In seconds, a tight pattern of sparkling SK wobbles split the distant blackness.

**

After taking three more crippling hits, no one aboard Aglifhate Battle Cruiser 018 could recall who actually gave the order to abandon ship. The command bridge was a sparking ruin. The ship's intranet was fouled and her targeting radars inoperative. None of the surviving bridge crew witnessed their commander's last moments while they were being battered from three sides. No one was sure if he died of a stroke or heart failure or a failure of his evac suit. They only remember passing, among others, their Commandante's lifeless body, seated in his command chair, as they scrambled past towards their escape pods.

The battle cruiser's sensory arrays were shot away, all her gun turrets out of action. Her self-defense gun launch controls stood abandoned. More than half her crew lay dead or incapacitated, her decks slick with blood, her corridors filled with the screams of wounded and the stoic moans of the dying. On every deck, survivors fought both fires in interior compartments and decompressions in outer compartments. No one paid attention to who was who in charred, blood-spattered evac suits. Everyone, whether homostoioi, periolaikoi, helot or levy, looked just like anyone else in the smoke, noise and confusion. People were shoved by others into escape pods with a score or more others and launched, by someone, into the void.

The mechanical voice overpowered the cacophony aboard, reverberating in Sacorsti-Laconian throughout the ship.

"Sacorsti battle cruiser, registration number five nine four zero one eight, this is the Commonwealth Destroyer Brewster, off your starboard amidships. Heave to and prepare to be boarded! Strike your transponder and power down your reactors or we will shoot. This is your only warning!"

*

46

Bridge of AGRV Retnec, 9:56am Deciem 16th, 468PCE.

"Sub-Commander, anchorage operations reports our transponder is active as of zero nine fifty six hours, this date." The primary communications technician's report signaled the culmination of the *Retnec's* 2-year refurbishment.

"Very well," Sub-Commander vin Nedman answered from his second tier station of the crescent shaped amphitheater bridge. He stepped away and walked down the central ramp, surveying the crew at their stations. He stopped at the base level, next to the captain, seated in her command chair and clasped his hands at his back.

"Signal from the lead tug, Sub-Commander," the secondary communications technician announced. "Both tugs have disengaged, sir. We are clear of our berth and free to navigate."

"Flash signal our gratitude to the tugs and to the yard master," the captain ordered.

"Yes madame."

Three tiers of technicians in high backed swivels monitored their station consoles that curved around the extended sensory and ranging multi-dimensional plot table in front of the command chair. The captain sat proud and erect, surveying the bridge crew going about their duties. The application displays on her side mount panels at her left and right armrests showed blue for fully operational. She nodded in approval at each status update and vin Nedman's smooth control of their departure.

"State your power systems status," vin Nedman commanded.

The head-setted Petty Officer in the center of tier two starboard scanned across her panel. "Reactor power is at sixty-seven percent. Escape burn capacity in four minutes, Sub-Commander."

"Exactly on schedule, Madam Captain," Vin Nedman said.

"Excellent, Commander. Carry on."

The XO nodded and turned towards the lower left tier console bank. "Helm. Status."

"Sir, No course given," The helmsman reported. "We are maintaining Carillon's rotational speed of zero point four six three nine kilometers per second. We are currently riding the neutral region of the planet's L six C three gravity wave band."

"Very well, stand by for course. ESR, raise the plot."

The slate grey surface of the octagonal table at the center of the bridge, in front of the command chair illuminated. The Carillon planetary group octagonal grid map rose to eye level with the captain and the first tier consoles and populated.

The *Retnec's* vessel symbol lit up in the center of the display. Iridescent variations around Carillon's real time image, and her four moons, indicated their relative motion, showing current and intensity shifts in their magnetic fields. The active stellar finder arrow icon at the top center of the projection angled in the direction of the star Vega. The primary arrow oriented towards the singularity at the galactic center, the secondary arrow towards Sacor II.

"Warrant Officer vin Patrice, what is our security status?" vin Nedman asked. With no prompt answer, vin Nedman turned around, facing aft and up towards the security station in the second tier aft. "Chief!"

Warrant Officer vin Patrice stood focused on his panel and those of his three surveillance technicians and again, did not respond.

"Power-up complete, Sub-Commander, all reactors are at eighty-five percent," the bridge engineering chief announced.

"Very well."

"My, my panels show blue and secure, Sub Commander, but..."

Noting the change on his console, the helmsman dutifully announced the status deviation, despite the stammering security officer. "Sub-Commander, the ship's orientation is Vega zero eight-six by Carillon two-seven one, zero-niner outbound, AC DC zero point zero one three. No course given."

"Stand by on course!" The captain spun around in her swivel, her face an angry grimace. "What is the issue, security?"

"Uh, Madam Captain, all our systems are routing through auxiliary control. I don't understand why."

"We're a Collective level vessel in wartime, Chief. They're monitoring to be able to take over at any time. We've been through this before," Vin Nedman snorted. He turned to the captain. "The Tantoran frontier is less than seventy trans-stellar astronomic units away, madam."

"Yes, quite right. Are we blue for security Mr. vin Patrice?"

The warrant officer waved his technicians to carry on. "Uh, Yes, Madam Captain. Security is blue."

The captain nodded to vin Nedman to continue and spun back towards the ESR plot.

"Expand the plot," the XO commanded.

The ESR plot extended outward and populated. Carillon, Vega's second habitable zone world, shrank away to its orbital position, surrendering to the blue/white F type star. The photonic display included the three lush, green, habitable zone worlds and their variety of moons, the six outer giants with their retinues of satellites, the two hellish, inner worlds and the major asteroid fields.

Color coded triangular symbols indicating orbiting planetary stations and stellar stationary platforms, including the republic's three shipyards appeared. Navigation and communications buoy symbols lit up. Finally, contoured lines representing the flow of gravity wave bands emanating from all the major celestial bodies rose and intertwined.

Basking in the moment, the captain smiled and tilted her head up towards vin Nedman. She made a grand, sweeping gesture towards the multi-plot. "You may indulge yourself, Sub-Commander."

"I thank you, Madam Captain." vin Nedman nodded and cleared his throat. "Helm, set course for the southeast heliopause region by way of the gas giant Mantilla."

"First course given, Carillon time, tenth hour, thirty seconds." the helmsman answered and touched an application on his panel. "Ship's chronometer is active."

Noting the distinctive colored wave pattern on his center panel, he set his vessel's position and laid the course. The ship's position and velocity established, the helmsman highlighted the giant on his navigation propulsion screen and input its parameters.

A bright orange dashed line appeared in his screen beginning at the vessel symbol at the center of the display and reached out to the northwest of Carillon, relative to the parent star, Vega. The line coiled twice around the inner habitable world, Paramus, indicating two orbits and an orbital shift. It then extended out and down to the southeast towards Mantilla.

"Recommend initial heading, Vega three one five degrees, accelerative factor four."

"Make it so."

"Thrusting to port eight-five, up one-six, out two niner three. One point eight on the main. Standing by on maneuvering thruster banks one and three."

"Power the main," vin Nedman commanded.

"Engaged. Burned. Off."

Carillon began to noticeably recede in the bridge's forward and starboard lamalar panels as *Retnec* deftly slipped into the Carillon CV93D outbound wave and accelerated toward the bright, barren moon, Navarh, above the planet's north polar cap.

"Captain, shall I activate the lower decks' lamalars?" vin Nedman asked.

"Captain, I would recommend against that," vin Patrice interrupted in protest. "The prohibition against allowing levies to view planetary departures."

"We have no levies aboard yet, madam," vin Nedman advised.

"True, not yet. Nevertheless, Sub-Commander, we will have, in a few days. No sense starting out with bad habits." She put a hand on one hip and leaned to her right, looking up at vin-Nedman on her left. "Besides, the crew has work to do, no need for distractions. This is a research vessel, not a pleasure cruiser."

The XO nodded. "As you command, Captain."

After a few moments, as Carillon and the Y-31 shipyard faded into the star field, the captain stood from her swivel and looked around the bridge in satisfaction.

"Who has the first watch, Sub-Commander?"

"Lieutenant vin-Krelo is standing by to take the con, madam," he replied instantly.

"Very well, you and Mr. vin Patrice are free to make your rounds, sir. Be sure to give my regards to the science team. I'll join them for breakfast on the morrow."

"Yes, Madam Captain."

"Lieutenant vin Krelo, you have the con. I'll be in my stateroom."

"Yes, Madam Captain," Lt. vin Krelo answered.

The bridge engineering officer left her swivel in the forward quadrant and walked down the port ramp towards the central plot and the command chair. Sub-Commander vin Nedman stepped to the left to let the captain step down off the swivel's platform base to the deck. She strode up the ramp behind her and turned onto the second tier towards her stateroom manway.

"Attention on the bridge," vin Nedman announced. "The captain is departing." At their stations, the bridge crew continued their work despite the announcement of the transfer of command.

"Chief, I'll start at the reactor pods, I suggest you visit auxiliary control first. I'll meet you in the deck four mess. After that I want to check on the researchers."

"As you command, Sub-Commander."

**

Sub-Commander vin Nedman's billet. Deck 2, 2:13am Deciem 17th, 468PCE.

"We'll change the plan. We'll wait. No, Giles. There's got to be another way." Nadia buried her face into her lover's chest. Her arms tightened around him, pulling their bodies closer.

"Shhh. Hush now," he said softly. He stroked her long, black hair, and caressed her back. "It's too late now, Nadia. We could never be free if I came with you. My billet here isn't monitored because of my Clan privilege, but the Commoners would never trust me completely. We would be under constant surveillance between their debriefing and verification sessions. They would come and take me whenever they please and keep me for as long as they please. What would that be like for our child, Nadia?"

"I'll stay here with you," Nadia sobbed.

Giles sat up in the bed. He lifted her chin gently and looked into her tear-filled eyes.

"No." He brushed her hair from her face and gently kissed her forehead, then her cheeks, then softly touched his lips to hers. He sat up again and looked her in the eyes.

"You would never be allowed to see our child, Nadia. Homostoioi are to be raised by Homostoioi." He let go of her and turned to sit on the side of the bed. Nadia sat up and gently stroked his back. Giles sighed softly, he put his underwear on and walked over to his console. Opening a drawer in its desk compartment, he retrieved two sheets of flexmet, and a small data disc. Nadia saw both sheets were full of writing. She watched him fold the flexmet and with the disc and flexmet in hand, he walked back over and sat on the bed in front of her.

51

"This is not just about us, Nadia. You are the love of my life. But my people cannot go on like this. We've conquered more than enough territory to resettle all of our people. We continue on because of our greed. We use you and the others to impose our will on wog worlds. We say it's in the name of our religion. But we have shaped our religion to fit our desires, Nadia. You asked me once about the Commoner's five freedoms. Do you remember?"

Nadia looked at him and nodded. "You said you didn't know. That's when you said there was someone aboard who could explain them to me. You meant, you meant her?"

"Yes," he nodded. When you are safe, wake the Marena woman and ask her. Ask her what our people did to her and to your ancestors. Your people deserve to know what really happened, not what we've told your government to tell you. Give the Commoners this ship, Nadia. This Madonna is crazy, the Barons all know it. And Ben Ali can still be held accountable for his experiments in a trans-stellar court."

He got down on one knee in front of her. Nadia edged closer to him. He placed the folded letter and disc in her hand. Nadia wanted to read it, but her eyes stayed locked on his.

"I love my family, my Clan and my people, Nadia. We reached out to survive, in the beginning. Then we saw how easy it was to conquer. We must maintain central control, but we cannot sustain it all. Surface infrastructures on too many worlds are crumbling because we take technically trained people in the levies. Every one of our terra-forming efforts on class two worlds has failed. People on too many worlds go hungry because we take their harvests to feed other people in camps on barren class two rocks.

"The data disc contains the directory of the Barons who have had enough of our expansionist policies. The Commoners don't fund the Egalitarians, Nadia. We do. This disc contains the funding links for the Egalitarian movements in all of the Alliance republics and Sacor the Second. The CCID will know what to do with it. The letter is for you, and our child."

Nadia started to speak, but Giles raised a finger to silence her. He stared into her eyes taking her hands tight in his.

"I'm the only one who can justify my presence on the bridge now that we're underway, Nadia. You know this. You've only got a narrow window of opportunity. Both of Jander's devices are in place. I've seen them, I know they'll do the job. No one on the command deck or deck two must survive, Nadia. That's why you must strike before the guard shifts change. Regal, Warrick and the others need you to lead them.

"Once you're away, the captain will log as much information as she can, but without environmental or the life-pods, her only hope will be that someone eventually finds us. By that time, well, you and your people will be long gone." Giles' smile and his unflappable logic made Nadia grin. He pulled her closer and wiped her tears.

"Did you talk to your brother?"

"Yes," Nadia answered.

"Did you warn him?"

"I reminded him of a story our grandfather told us about his great-aunt Denisha. The expression on his face told me he understood."

Giles vin Nedman stood and looked down on her. Nadia suddenly felt the urge to cover herself as Giles' face hardened.

"It's time for you to go, Lieutenant," he said in his firm, commanding tone. "You have serviced me well. Go ye forth and bear my seed."

"Yes, my lord Baron." Nadia wiped the last of her tears. She got up from the bed and collected her underwear and uniform. Neither of them spoke as she dressed. Sub-Commander vin Nedman watched her brush and pin her hair up to regulation. Nadia slipped the letter and the data disc into her cargo pocket and left her summoner's billet.

*

Near the Alfreyan moon Nipron, in Vighandis.

Commonwealth Battle Cruiser Indomitable controller's steady monotone filled the Vortex flight lead's headset. 'Delta one, this is Oscah five. You have ten plus daggers inbound your position, passing checkpoint two-three, distance one-two eight thousand, intercept and delay, over.'

"Roger Oscah. Break, Delta flight this is Delta One, we got trade inbound. Combat pivot on my command, post pivot vector is ... Nipron-one, one six, by Alfreya two six; at m-twelve. One zero plus daggers inbound at one-two eight thousand. Go passive on sensors, acknowledge." Delta flight acknowledged their leader.

"Combat pivot starboard eight zero, up seven zero, roll right three zero ..., ready..., ready..., pivot."

The six vortexes port bow and starboard quarter thrusters fired at 100% for 0.13 seconds. Delta flight pivoted, rolling to starboard and pitching up on their central axes, changing direction 140 degrees. The ambio-fluid in their flight helmets and suit inner liners adjusted its pressure, maintaining trans-stellar average pressure on the pilots' bodies. The fluid supported cerebrospinal fluids cushioning the pilots' brains inside their skulls and suppressed endolymph fluid wave action in the semi-circular canals of their inner ears. The fighters wing rolled left over right and accelerated, angling upward 70 degrees relative to Vighandis.

"Delta flight this is Delta one, four minutes to intercept; combat pivot to port after we engage; watch your fuel! Rendezvous at checkpoint one six; there's no telling what's behind them."

'This is four, we'll know soon enough.'

*

The commander of CBC *Indomitable* was concerned, the dagger fighters were only the lead element of what appeared to be a division-sized breakout maneuver.

"What's *Cabrera's* status, Colonel?" he inquired of his executive officer.

"She's moving at flank speed from X-Ray, she's a good twenty minutes from launch range, Commodore."

"Dammit, that flight's gonna get chewed up if we don't get some support in there. Get the rest of the squadron over there! Have *Mastodon* bring interdiction fires on that cruiser, tell them to come up on Delta's frequency, give Delta One priority of fires."

"Yes Sir!"

"Commodore Kinson, *Cabrera* says she is monitoring Delta One, they say they are ten; that's one zero mikes from launch."

"Ten minutes? But how?" the wing operations officer asked. "Wait, oh yes sir, *Cabrera's* carrying vespids with super-cruise," he informed the Commodore.

"Keep Delta One informed."

"Yes, sir."

CBC *Indomitable's* controllers received Delta Flight's 'Tien Lien' on the 10 dagger combat patrol leading a cruiser and three destroyers attempting to break out of the pocket. Delta flight's six vortexes cut the enemy force off before it reached the southern Vighandis-Alfreya Y6EM inbound wave where the asteroid field begins to thin near the moon, Alfreya-Nipron. Controllers listened

54

gravely as Delta Flight went to active sensors and launched. Their missile salvo destroyed three daggers from below and starboard.

*

The merge of the two groups of fighters put Delta flight between the Alliance survivors and their cruiser. The Sacorsti cruiser's signature illuminated in the vortexes' sensors and was transmitted to CBC *Indomitable's* CIC. Delta flight's second combat pivot put them on their opponents' six o'clock position and another dagger was claimed by a particle seeking missile before the survivors could themselves pivot.

"They've got the wave-gauge Delta, blossom out!"

The flight leader ordered Delta flight's two sections of three to form three sections of two to attack the daggers from multiple directions. Running with the inbound wave, the daggers also split into sections. The lead two daggers angled toward the flight leader and her number 2. Closing to gun range, they loosed two long bursts of 30mm auto cannon from their noses and wing roots.

On the downward, buffeting against the wave, Delta 1 spiraled her craft right over left to avoid illumines, sliding behind an icy asteroid. Cannon shells blasted sparkling fragments off the opposite side as the daggers streaked past, weaving to dodge debris.

"You ok, Blu?!" the flight leader saw her number 2's IFF on her right rear, but she needed to hear his voice.

'Right with ya boss, they overshot!'

"Pivot one-eighty now, now!"

The two vortexes thrust about, lining the daggers' drive nacelles in their sights; Delta 1 loosed an AIM-3 particle seeker at the starboard dagger. Delta 2 loosed two short 60mm cannon bursts enveloping the port fighter. Blu's prey shuddered in the detonation field, sparks and vapor engulfed the fighter, the pilot ejected. The ejection cocoon buffeted from the debris as it inflated. Delta 1's target broke right and tried to pivot but he was too late. The missile caught up with him, detonating between the nacelle and the port stabilizer.

"Oscah five this is Delta One, I need immediate suppression bombardment support, checkpoint two three to checkpoint two one! One battle cruiser with three destroyer escorts;

55

bearing Alfreya one five zero degrees; course, Vighandis one seven zero degrees. Speed m-five estimated, over!"

'This is Oscah five, India-Sierra shot, time of flight zero three mikes. Deploy your Sammy for bombardment direction. Whiskey three says stay defensive, help is on the way, over.'

"This is Delta One, you don't have to tell me twice, dropping Sammy. I'm gonna be busy, out."

The flight lead released her surveillance drone to take station as a marker beacon for the void bombardment platforms to lock onto and adjust from to forestall the capital ship threat.

*

Delta 5 and 6 were in a tight spiraling duel with two daggers running on an Alfreya-Nipron inbound wave with the four fighters drawing ever closer to its mass. The two pairs of opponents pirouetted, canopy to canopy. They alternately extended ten kilometers laterally and closed to within five hundred meters of one another, each bent on gaining a firing solution on the other. The red line of the hot-deck around the moon, shone brighter with every microsecond in Delta 5's visor and canopy interface, but the dagger gradually edged behind her with each spiral. The fifth dagger hung back, then swung out in a climbing turn well to starboard away from the merge. It circled the four ship spiral looking for an opportunity to streak in from abeam. The dagger saw an opening and made its' move.

*

Holding at wave speed, among the asteroids, Delta 1 regained her situational awareness. She found her elements and took control of the fight.

"Three, four come right, break Takeo's spiral and take out that loner!"

'One this is three, Tien Lien. Break, pivot one-five on me, Lester. Ready, ready, pivot.'

'One This Is Five, I, I Can't Shake This Guy, One More Spiral and He's Gonna Get…'

"Five! Five! SKI!"

'Ski's hit!'

*

Delta 6 was out of options and things were getting worse, spiraling with one dagger, he tracked a second approaching on lateral, and now the dagger that shot Delta 5 was rolling in on him

56

from below his left. Delta 6 rocked, shuttered and sparkled from exploding cannon projoes from the right side and his lower left. Delta 6 slip-pivoted to port with the wave with his entire starboard thruster bank, breaking out of one of the streams of exploding shells. He up-thrust hard over, inverting his vortex and slipped out of the second. Lining up on the lateral approaching loner, he loosed a long 35mm burst into the dagger, shattering the light fighter.

'TAKEO, BREAK!'

Delta 6 instinctively pushed his stick hard left, firing his entire starboard thruster bank.

Delta 1 saw Delta 6's vortex buck from the shockwave of a Talon missile. Pieces of metal flew off the craft. She clearly heard cockpit alarms blaring in the background and static distortion of Takeo's desperate transmission.

"My, my field generator's hit, I'm losing mag field, I, I need help!"

'Hang on T, we're here, thrust right!' Delta Three loosed a stream of 60mm into the climbing dagger's unarmored fuel cells, exploding the Astarene. Its second Ajax missile spiraled off towards the moon and failsafe detonated. Delta 6's spiraling dagger broke out on the inner half towards its cruiser but was intercepted and destroyed by a missile from Delta 2.

"One, I see Five...she's out...I see... cocoon, I got...tone...her, One."

'I see her, Takeo. Switch to stellar battery, do an emergency reactor restart.'

**

Delta 1 and the rest of Delta converged and circled the damaged Delta 6 and Delta 5's cocoon.

'One, this is four, I'm picking up inbounds! Two zero plus forming up around the cruiser. They're gonna break this way!'

"Roger four, There's still two somewhere close, Delta, assume defensive weave, center on six. Takeo, stay close to Ski. Break, Ohana this is Delta are you monitoring?!"

'Roger Delta, we monitor, whiskey friends following, be advised sweetheart is inbound, red friends show ETA your position zero five mikes, over.'

Her operations officer's voice came through reassuringly over her headset. "Roger Oscah, Break, Delta, keep your eyes out for the rest of the squadron, we got a white bird inbound and vespids in five. Keep the weave tight! Keep your eyes open."

**

Watching the highly visible 'White Bird' close on Delta 5's cocoon, Delta 1 pushed her defensive screen out to give the shuttle a clear zone to work, keeping only the damaged Delta 6, trailing vapor, but with an intact mag field, on a close orbit. She had seen the enemy perform the same maneuver; she knew they would respect it.

*

Indomitable Ambulance Shuttle 03 kept close behind Echo and Fox Flights of 808 Squadron as they arrived to support Delta. But IAS 03 did not want to get too close. In the shuttle's cargo bay, the pilot's voice came over the IHEA suited medico sergeant's headset as the deck separated.

'I got cocoon beacons lit up and locked on,' the shuttle pilot announced to his SAR team. 'We don't have much time, Vaughn. We're in the moon's main inbound and accelerating. Watch out for the debris flow.'

"I know. Launching now, follow me close."

The sergeant nosed the boarding sled down and forward, clearing the lower cargo bay. He canted the handlebar steering thruster control down and left and fired the main thruster. The open, 3-meter long sled closed rapidly on the cocoon.

"One hundred fifty meters to close, ready grapnels, Smitty."

'Ready, Sarge.'

"One hundred meters, seventy, forty, braking, twenty, grapnels, Smitty." Troopers Smith and Gale launched their lode lines towards the bright orange cocoon, the mag-grapnels attracted and securely attached.

"Got it! Retracting now. Close up, shuttle, I'll reverse into you."

'Good work, Vaughn. Haul that one in, there's two more over to the left,' the pilot responded.

"I see 'em, they look like Astarene colors."

'Shafirans.'

"Duke, you wanna waste time going after prisoners!" IAS 03's co-pilot interjected. "Their own people are closing fast."

58

"You know the order, Madina. Pilot prisoners are high priority; besides, they see us making an effort they'll do the same for our people."

"Are you sure about that?! Just seems like a good way to get killed or captured ourselves. And those people are desperate!"

"We'll risk it. Nobody deserves to be left out here!"

***

Mutiny.

AGRV Retnec, drive deck. 7:13am Deciem 17th, 468 PCE.

"Man down! Guard! Get in here, quick! We need you!" Ensign Jackson's yelling brought the guard to the auxiliary control manway. Taking in the scene, she instinctively stepped in to help the ensign lift the helmsman up off the deck. She didn't see Ensign Prine hiding behind the support column. Prine brought the heavy two-handed spanner down hard against the back of her neck, sending her sprawling across Martin and knocking her helmet off.

"Seal the manway," Martin said, shoving the unconscious auburn-haired woman off of him.

Jackson stood and stepped back. In a fluid motion she checked the corridor and slapped the manway control and lock panel.

"Is she dead?" Prine asked, standing over the prostrate guard.

"We'll worry about that later, sir."

Prine jerked himself back to reality, with the spanner in one hand, he reached down to help Martin disarm and manacle her.

"Secure that spanner, sir. She's a big girl. Help me drag her to the alcove."

**

At 7:15am, the first explosion aboard *Retnec* wrecked the command tower's reactor bank. Chaos erupted on the bridge as the lights went out. Environmental controls failed; the internal magnetic field collapsed. All functions routed, by default, to auxiliary control on the Drive Deck.

On Deck 2, between the Command Tower and the Drive Deck, compartments sealed as electrical arcs blocked the Alpha corridor. Of the bulk of the security platoon, those not fighting the fire in the main corridor, were trapped in their billets and compartments, unable to breach any of the manway or corridor locks.

*

In Auxiliary Control, Martin and Ensign Prine sealed off the decks and compartments throughout the ship according to the takeover plan, and wrist pad communications with Nadia, Regal, and Warwick. Ensign Jackson disabled the vessel's transponders.

AGRV Retnec 'went dark', disappearing from the Y-31 anchorage's ESR scanners.

*

The application displays on the captain's side mount panel winked out one by one. She stood from her command chair, bracing herself against the ESR plot table to halt her forward momentum. The table's celestial plot disintegrated when its photon containment field collapsed. Frantic, the captain looked around the bridge for answers, as systems shut down all around the command center.

"Signal the drive deck, actualize auxiliary control," she ordered.

"We have no intercom, madam!" a crewmember, searching for a source of the outages, called out from under a console panel.

"Launch the emergency beacons! Log our position, Lieutenant."

"We have no power, madam. All our systems and controls are inoperative."

"The deck is sealed off. We can't get off the bridge!"

"Madam Captain! We, we've been sabotaged!"

"Tinor! That traitorous bitch! And Warrick!" vin Patrice shouted. Holding onto the deck railing, he lost his fight to stay upright in the diminishing gravity. "I'll see them hang!"

"Abandon Ship! To your escape pods. Lieutenant vin Krelo, secure my logs."

"Yes, Madam Captain."

"No! Madam Captain." Giles vin Nedman sneered in the dimming light of the command center and bridge. "None of you are going anywhere. You're all staying here, with me."

"Nedman! No! Have you gone mad?!" vin Patrice and frantic bridge crewmembers thrust themselves at the XO to stop him, but they were too late. He was already in position. Sub-Commander vin Nedman plunged the three manual override control levers downward. The bridge crew, and security crews on Deck 2, all heard the dull metallic thuds of disengaging papoose clamps, followed by the rushing release of propellants from the evacuation tubes.

"The life pods are jettisoning!"

"Kill him!"

*

Deep Observation Post 297 in the heliospheric northwest of the Chein Stellar State, in the Commonwealth Administrative Zone. 02-02 of 770 of the Common Era.

The bored technician stared at his monitor from the stand counter a few steps away. The vessel's symbol blinked on his screen as he munched his compact lunch and savored the last sips of juice before stepping back to his swivel. Just three more hours before his shift ends and he can catch an HG cinema in his billet after dinner, something swashbuckling.

The enhanced light-time imaging technician enjoyed a surprisingly routine, comfortable life, beneath the dwarf world's icy surface. The last eight months had certainly been interesting enough, but he looked forward to rotating back to Eatoni-Priame in four more Common months. He had often wondered who those people were, aboard the *Retnec,* and what they were planning to do with the old ship. But that was someone else's job back on Priame or even on Saluri-Demeos.

He suddenly stopped chewing. He stood there, mouth agape, staring at the screen.

"What the hell?" Intrigued, the technician stepped towards his console.

"What's the matter, Neal?" his symbiot asked, turning from her own console.

The technician remembered his cup, he turned to set it and his lunch down on the counter without taking his eyes off the alert flashing next to *Retnec's* vessel symbol. The empty cup and compact hit the floor, he didn't care. The technician checked to ensure his monitor was recording and pressed his comms link.

"Mr. Ronyn, you should come down here. I need you to see this!"

*

The Vighandis Pocket; deep inside the Alliance defensive perimeter.

A palpable aire of despair and defeat rose amid the doubt and confusion on the bridge of the Alliance phalanx's flagship. Crewmembers monitored their symbiots' stations giving each other time to fully don and seal their evacuation suits' gauntlets and semi-rigid hoods.

The steady stream of bombardment reports, of mounting damage and casualties in the phalanx had become a flood. Deep in the asteroid field, dense clouds of rocks and dust speckled their forward and port lamalars. The ice giant, Alfreya, lay to starboard, partially obscured through the fields. In every direction, the bridge crew saw fleeting glimpses of short streams of green-blue outgoing and red incoming illumine SK projoes flash across the frontal boxes of their perimeter defenses at the edges of the asteroid field. Knowing that up to ten non-illuminated projoes bookended each illumined round heightened the crew's anxiety.

"Commander, Third Division reports enemy bombardment is increasing in intensity!" The secondary signals technician stood at her console, shouting to make herself heard over the confusion.

"*AGBC Fifty-nine* reports her drive is out, her bridge and two gun turrets are damaged and inoperative, sir! Commandant vin Marcelle is transferring his codes and ciphers to *AGBC Thirty-two*."

The signaler pulled the hood of her evac suit over her head and tucked stray strands of her hair under it, away from her face. She tapped the suit's wrist pad and activated the visor. Her face plate's black, tear drop shaped, binocular visor contrasted sharply with the steel gray suit.

"Acknowledged! Tribune…"

"I heard. That's all my cruisers, everyone has damage, even us!" The Tribune swiveled his command chair towards the primary signals officer. "What response from Admiral vin Flavius?"

The Tribune reached down between his feet and opened the small compartment under his command chair. He pulled the gray metallic evac suit out and stood, to begin donning it.

"Nothing, sir. We've lost all tactical and comms feeds back to Bavat, Tribune. Colonel Ahmadi's transports are failing to respond as well. We're getting bombardment reports from all the divisions and the other two phalanxes, sir!"

"Tribune vin Waxnar! Tribune Galeio's cruiser transponder is being interrupted at its source! *AGBC Shalla* is being boarded by Commonwealth marines! They're reporting close combat on her command and engineering decks!"

The flagship commander turned anxiously from the plot to the Tribune. "We're surrounded!" he exclaimed.

Facing the multi-plot, and fastening his evac suit, the Tribune stared at the map and operational graphics, searching for a way out of the trap.

A few of the command center crew saw the silent, sparkling wobble of still another Commonwealth bombardment salvo distorting portions of the scene in the forward lamalar. But everyone looked up as another star-bright burst of light erupted in the distortion. Imploding reactors, heralding the death of another one of their ships, illuminated the command center for a long moment before fading.

*

Vectored in by signals intelligence from their cruiser, the squadron of stub-winged Commonwealth stealth vespids whipped off the ice giant's outer moon and penetrated the fragmenting Alliance defense perimeter undetected. The squadron took the acceleration off the southern pole of the giant and closed on their quarry. The twelve stealthers activated the false transponder projectors in their electronic counter-measure pods and defracted within point-blank range of their quarry's transponder signature.

*

"ALERT! I have multiple small contacts! Center bearing Alfreya one-eight-zero, approaching our starboard beam. Range one-one-zero-zero kilometers, closing rapidly sir!"

"Identify."

"No IFF! Targets are hostile! Range one thousand kilometers and closing!"

"Close defense weapons free!"

"Launch the ready fighters. Where's the combat patrol?!"

"Contacts identified! Commonwealth vespids, thirty plus, range nine hundred kilometers! They're Locking Radars!"

*

"One, three and five take the forward destroyer. Two, four and six follow me to the cruiser. Concentrate your fire on the port landing bay and drive nacelle. Take it to 'em!"

Without waiting for an acknowledgement, the squadron leader banked his craft up and to the right, aligning his targeting pipper on the center of the starboard launch bay door. The vespid's stub wings extended from the wing roots along the fuselage, exposing the fighter's missile pods.

Concentric circles of the weapon sight flashed from red to amber at 900 kilometers, then to green at 700 kilometers. With his right thumb on the selector switch, his fingers wrapped the controller's trigger and squeezed. He released the trigger then squeezed and released it again.

Each trigger squeeze launched a laser-guided Mark-20, heavy anti-ship missile. The guiding laser pulses struck the hangar bay door within centimeters of one another. The missiles streaked out of the vespid's launch tubes as he ripple fired numbers three and four. Brilliant orbs of illumine projoes arced in from the cruiser and the destroyer off her starboard bow, detonations enveloped the advancing Commoners.

Caught by surprise, the cruiser's close defense batteries fired wildly. Holographic and electronic projections giving the impression of three times their number drew the Alliance fire. None of the attacking vespids were effectively illuminated by the Alliance defense tracking radars or hit by the uncoordinated firing.

The squadron leader's HUD flashed the top silhouette of his craft, indicating the launching of two Mark-20s each from his port and starboard weapon's pods. The muffled whine of his engines and his own rhythmic breathing accompanied the streaking and flashing brilliance of the incoming defensive fire all around him and his squadron.

One-one thousand, two-one thousand, three-one thousand…

*

Racing ahead at three times the vespid's speed, the missile salvo slammed into the comparatively thin armored door. The first of twenty-four 130dcb warheads detonated sixty centimeters from the flexing armored curtain. Its shaped charge shoved a focused 24cm diameter, 390db kinetic wave into the door, denting the relatively thin plate. The missile's high-density fragments scoured and gouged its smooth surfaces. Missile after missile slammed into the door, buckling it.

The hammer blows blasted scabs of white hot metal off the door's interior, sending them hurtling through the launch bay.

Pelted by debris, the inboard magnetic shield generating pylon just behind the bay door collapsed, taking down the inner magnetic shield and decompressing the launch bay. The ruined bay door crumpled outwards under the impact of internal atmosphere, fighters, shuttles, carts, equipment carriages and crew, spewing through the gaping bay door into the void.

*

Closing his wing pods, the squadron leader banked hard right and climbed to avoid debris surging out of the stricken Alliance cruiser. Leveling, he winged right over left, inverting to maintain a visual with her. He marveled for a brief second at the brilliant blue, orange and white flashes of secondary explosions of ammunition and fuel biting deep into the ship's portside mid-decks.

Twisting his head and torso in his seat, he scanned all around searching out his squadron detachments, regaining his situational awareness amid the sparkling detonations. His headset was alive with exultant cheers and victory howls.

"Maintain control, leaders," he barked. "Make your run, go dark and break for the rendezvous. Jimmy, bank and spread. Guns, guns. Take the heat off the other divisions."

'Gotcha, Major, swinging wide at your five.' His wingman's transponder lit up in his HUD. He heard his voice loud and clear in his headset. The major lined his craft up on a 100mm close defense turret and its supporting automatic gun turrets, his targeting sight locked on. He flipped his selector to mixed guns. The projectile convergence zone pipper lit up, he squeezed the trigger. The vespid's 40mm chin mount and its two fuselage mounted 30mm rail guns each launched a twenty projoe burst into the main turret. Sparkling detonations engulfed the main gun turret and two of the three supports.

In the corner of his eye he saw explosions, fragments and wisps of white vapor rising along his wingman's line of fire. Illumines streaked across the front of his craft, more arced in from one of the escorting destroyers. His vespid buffeted from shockwaves. Fragments peppered the craft sounding like rocks pounding a metal building. Below him, the cruiser visibly shuddered from the combined impacts of his follow-on vespids' missiles.

"Wing over right and pivot southeast, Jimmy. Let's get the hell out of here!"

***

AGRV Retnec.

The mutineers cleared the Drive Deck and Deck 4. The scientists were caught by surprise and taken prisoner. Most of their technicians also surrendered. All of the maintenance helots cooperated. But Mica Jander was shot dead during the take-over of the reactor pods on Deck 5. Infuriated, the well-coordinated mutineers closed in on the Sacorsti. In a running gun fight, they herded the survivors through the last remaining open corridors down to Deck 6. There, 16 Sacorsti, mostly guards, sealed themselves in the amidships shuttle bay, just as Mr. Warrick predicted.

It was a mistake borne of desperation. They were trapped, with no access to the shuttles and no way to control the outer bay doors. Tinor and Ensign Regal stood at the bay systems control console, overlooking the bay through the thick lamalar panel. Over the intercom, she gave them a chance to surrender.

"Everyone knows this war is lost. The Commonwealth has cut off our Trudan fuel supply. The offensive in Vighandis is broken. The Tantorans have abandoned the Alliance, they've gone home. Come with us, I guarantee you fair treatment!"

'Never!'

'Traitor!'

'You and your family will burn in hell, Bitch!'

Nadia recognized De'Molay's voice. She saw him on the monitor standing near the middle of the bay, shaking his fist up at them in defiance.

They were all milling about in confusion, between the two shuttle craft. She saw Vickers aiming a battle rifle towards the control booth. Several of the others had rifles and side-arms pointed at her and towards the manway, expecting the mutineers to make a final rush at them through it. Nadia saw the guard sergeant desperately working to unlock a personnel hatch on one of the cargo shuttles. It would do them no good. Regal had already changed all the shuttle access codes. Both crafts' hatches were security sealed.

Enraged, Nadia had no intention of sending anyone in after them. She reached across the panel for the outer door

67

actuator. Ensign Regal stopped her with one hand and pressed the large red actuator herself with the other.

It was quick. The shuttle bay door raised just a few centimeters before the entire bay de-pressurized. The rush of escaping atmosphere from the bay overpowered the refugees' screams through the intercom. They were blasted through the narrow gap between the rising door and the deck. The impact and pressure of ejection tore their bodies apart, spewing human wreckage into the void. The two shuttles' magnetic deck clamps held firm. The bay door failsafe engaged at 10 centimeters. It dropped back into place sealing the breach, but not before most of the blood and bodily fluids along its base had vaporized.

Nadia and Regal shared a look of simple acknowledgement. Then Regal winked and nodded, she turned to the console and keyed the applications to re-pressurize the bay and run a systems diagnostic. Nadia knew she didn't have to say anything. She raised her wrist pad to transmit.

"Where are you, Mr. Warrick?"

'Deck five. The reactor banks are secure.'

"I'll meet you back up on the Drive Deck."

'Yes, madam. Are you alright?'

"Yes, Mr. Warrick. I'll be fine. Break. Martin, change course immediately! Start your pattern."

'Will do.'

Martin changed course to ride the trans-stellar band wave SV39G. The high-speed wave put maximum distance between themselves and any immediate search and rescue. It also took them well away from the base of the Alliance destroyers scheduled to rendezvous with them at Y-31, and escort them on the voyage to Sacor II - New Laconia.

Nadia needed time to think. Jander was gone. Though disillusioned with his people, Giles vin Nedman had steadfastly refused to abandon them. He was trapped aboard the dark, disabled command tower, being taken far off course, unable to communicate. Nadia could only hope they had killed him quickly, instead of letting him live only to freeze to death or suffocate in a few days along with themselves. Nadia and her crew owed Giles everything. *The captain and vin Patrice will torture him for spite*, she thought. *Knowing it would hasten their own demise, but he had deliberately stayed away from any of our planning for just that very reason.*

Nadia followed Camea Greene's team hustling a group of prisoners, including the MOB, Lt. vin Lurel, towards the central billets where they would be stripped down to their gravwear and searched. She touched the cargo pocket of her fatigues, feeling the form of the letter and data disc Giles gave her before she left his billet. There would be plenty of time to read it, and mourn, later. She rubbed her belly and thought of their child, then she moved on.

Papa, Madam President, we can never be pacifist again. But our children can be free again!

She walked slowly along the corridor, past ceramic deck panels blackened and gouged by fragments, which would have to be replaced to maintain a uniform mag field within the ship.

**

Tinor entered auxiliary control, now the ship's primary command center, as helot crewmembers carried the big guard's manacled corpse out. She ignored the pounding echoing from beyond the upper access to Deck 2. *Just a little while longer.*

She was relieved to see Mr. Warrick returning after securing the reactors during the takeover. Visibly shaken by Jander's death, he had a bitter scowl on his face. But he had imposed his will, and an aire of something akin to normalcy quickly settled in everywhere he walked aboard the ship. But not quite. Pounding resounding through the bulkhead from the command tower decks grew louder. They were wasting time.

"Let's get this over with, Mr. Warrick."

"Yes, madam." Warrick moved past her, taking station at propulsion. Entering his override command code, status levels rose across the panel board and turned blue.

"Drive main units are online, Martin. Deflection thrust one five three, down one eight."

"Deflection thrust one five three, down one eight aye, Chief."

The steady bludgeoning continued, accompanied by a new sound. Warrick recognized the distinct, grating buzz.

"The Strelski have gotten hold of a plasma drill from the fabrication shop annex, madam. High time they thought of that. But they're too late."

Warrick transferred propulsion to Martin at the helm and walked over to the upper track to the command tower papoose lock panel. He armed the papoose lock emergency releases and without hesitation, turned all eight manual handles to the right.

*

Eight sets of explosive bolts fired around the ship's outer hull, shattering the Deck 2 papoose joints with the Drive Deck's superstructure. Thrusters pushed the superstructure down and to the right, away from Deck 2's eight sparking tails of severed conduit clusters.

*

The pounding ceased on the Drive Deck. In his heads up display, Martin saw Lt. Tinor's reflection remotely detonating the second explosive charge within Deck 2. Jander's second charge destroyed the orphaned tower's navigation mainframe, and its stellar collector controls.

"Vector is laid. All my panels are blue, madam."

"Very well, Martin. Engage main drive."

"Engaging." Tears streamed down Martin's face. *I'm free! Thank you, Mica.*

*

In zero gravity, no one trapped aboard the two crippled upper decks felt the jolt as the superstructure disengaged. They were slow to notice as the tower and Deck 2 set to a slow counter-clockwise rotation as it dragged across the outer hull of the upper drive deck.

"They're leaving us, Captain!" the bridge helmsman shrieked, gesturing wildly towards the lamalar.

"They're abandoning us!"

Shamus vin Patrice thrust his way past crewmembers to reach a lamalar as if going after the main vessel. Most of his detachment, and all the technical division chiefs were isolated on Deck 2 below them. The entire command crew floated here with the captain. Altogether, 197 souls wailed and prayed, when through frosting lamalars they saw the remaining four main decks of their ship disengage from them, change course, fire the main, and thrust away.

"Plot our present position, and their heading, Lieutenant. Quickly!"

70

"Yes, Madam!" Lieutenant vin Krelo pulled herself along the bulkhead towards the log stowage. The light was dimming, and it was already getting cold. She knew they should not have strangled the traitor, vin Nedman, so quickly. Whatever he knew of Tinor's plans died with him in vin Patrice's rage. She felt the vibration of the second explosion on Deck 2 before anyone heard it.

*

Tinor watched the navigators, Ensigns Prine and Jackson, realign their fixes and raise the ESR plot of their region of the Alliance of Stellar Republics. Warrick unlocked the inner shutters on the entire ship, the extended ranging lamalar panels went active. Illumination from the nearby Krunae Nebula flooded in. The harsh service lighting compensated, softening, as if in surrender.

*

The scene gave Josiah Martin the sense of a real bridge, and a sense of hope.

"Say your helm status, Mr. Martin," Lt. Tinor commanded.

"Madam, we are presently traveling at a meron factor of eight on the Alpha-nine trans-stellar outbound. Our accelerative, deccelerative factor is eight point five three on the accelerating curve." Martin kept his hands and eyes steady on his panel.

"Very well. Mr. Prine, state your plot."

The navigator extended his photon rod and highlighted the grid location of a point on the outer edge of the Vegan stellar heliopause. He linked the image to Martin's heads-up display to keep him oriented.

"We are forty three degrees, left outer deflection from our original course since our mutiny..., since we took control..."

The old warrant steadied him. "It's alright, boy. We know."

"I'll, I'll be alright. We are ...now, at twenty-two point five hours from shipyard departure. Since we went dark at twenty-one hours, and haven't communicated or launched a beacon, Search and Rescue will assume we have lost power and are adrift. They would account for inertia and extrapolate our course, curving with the plasma shock towards Vega. So they would start their search about here, madam." Prine pointed to a region four stellar astronomic units to the right of *Retnec*'s flashing vessel symbol.

Martin listened intently. *Hmm, still too close.* He wanted to know everything that was happening. *I want to learn.* He kept focused on his panels first, then the HUD, as Prine continued.

"Madam Senior Lieutenant, we are on a base course to intercept the E-four singularity downward outbound waveband, at a point three kilo-parsec downslope of its aphelion curve." Prine raised the photon rod, following the curve of the high speed trans-stellar wave.

"This will avoid a costly breaking maneuver to ride the curve, madam. It'll save fuel and prevent our being slung out irrevocably into the trans-galactic void."

Prine highlighted their projected route along the wave patterns, while Jackson, Prine's symbiot, expanded the plot to known galactic scale.

"From the point of wave insertion, madam, we will be able to ride it into the southwest spiral region, at approximately eight, to eight point-five kilo-parsec from the singularity, on the zero or lateral plane."

He highlighted the base course to the low left region of one of the only recently better defined spiral regions of the galaxy.

"This will place us at the lateral plane in sector AEWX-zero-four-four-nine. The E-four wave is constant at AC DC-one point nine beyond the eight kpc line."

"What's there in the sector?"

"Three stellar groupings, madame," Ensign Jackson answered.

"Are there any known habitable worlds there? Any known human tribes?"

"Unknown, madam. We'll get better definition and maybe pick up some electronic transmissions, if any, as we draw close."

Prine pointed out the center stellar group. "For now, madam, it's simply a point at which to make an orbital shift and change direction."

"Very well. I guess it's not important. But you never know. How long is the transit?"

"With an eighty-five percent reactor output, madam, this route should place us in the sector by Augusia twenty-sixth, four sixty-nine."

The old warrant grunted. Nadia saw him scowl, he had bad news.

"Use Commonwealth time from now on, Ensign," Nadia softened her voice, correcting the navigator.

Martin smiled hearing that.

"Yes, madam. Our arrival date is ...Oh-one eleven of seven-seventy." Ensign Jackson shifted the plot, bringing the known Commonwealth Administrative Zone frontier in line with sector AEWX 0449.

"There is our problem, madam," she said. "Once we reach the turn point, we don't know how far it is to the Commoner's frontier."

Nadia stared at the plot and absent-mindedly rubbed her belly. "Once we make the turn. We'll slow down and use active scans. We'll try to find one of the sentinel buoys," she said. "It'll help them find us, instead of our looking for them."

"Yes, madam."

"What's our status below, Warrick?"

"Kenner, the bitch that shot Jander, managed to bleed off two-thirds of the fuel from reactors five through eight before we found her. Camea killed her before I could."

The Strelski operative's final act wrecked the navigator's computations. Hearing this, Martin felt a sudden foreboding. *Everything I've hoped for, now in jeopardy over the loss of a few kilos of reactor fuel rods. But Warrick always has a plan.*

"Due to the fuel loss, madam, we can now only make eighty percent to deliver m-fifteen. At one point nine wave speed, that's only m-twenty-eight point five. That will add one month to the voyage." The engineer leaned forward with a gleam in his eye. "But, if we reduce the ship's power consumption by twenty-five percent. I can deliver m-twenty. That'll guarantee m-thirty-eight on the wave."

After some rapid calculations the navigator spoke up. "That would put us in sector approximately Sestiembre tenth, uh, pardon me, fifteen eleven of seven-seventy, madam."

"Five months to reach the turn. And then, who knows how far to reach the Commonwealth? What would we have to disable to achieve the twenty-five percent reduction, Mr. Warrick?"

The old man's answer was stern and immediate.

"Cut the power to the bio-storages, madam. They draw forty percent of deck five and thirty-two percent of deck six's power just to maintain the stasis pods."

"Without them we have nothing to offer the Commoners."

"The pods have battery packs, madam, the chargers are off the main grid. And we still have the backup data in the library servers."

The weight of command, of mutiny, and of murder already showed on Tinor's face. She had the fate of her fellow mutineers, now deserters attempting to defect, as well as the helots on her shoulders. She wanted one less thing to worry about.

"Set guards here and on the reactors, Mr. Warrick. Ensign Jackson, get on the intercom, have everyone else gather in the mess hall, the prisoners too. We need them, but they don't have to know that yet."

"Yes, madam."

"Martin, stay steady on this bearing for another hour, then locate a subduction for us to power down in. You and the guards can listen on the intercom."

"No worries, madam. I'm with you all the way!"

The helmsman never took his eyes off his screens or hands off his panel. His view of the swirling magenta and cyan clouds of the nebula in the left upper quadrant of the deck's active lamalars wouldn't change for two days.

"Now hear this, now hear this…"

**

The mess hall on Deck 5 filled quickly. Warrick peeled off ten to guard central Deck 4 and aft Deck 5.

"Lieutenant, we can only hope everyone is as steadfast as young Martin," Warwick quietly cautioned Nadia. "We've got a long way to go. Some of them will have a hard time bearing up under the stress."

"Yes, I know. We are going to have to watch everyone carefully."

Warrick looked around the mess hall and the corridor one more time before raising his wrist pad.

"Alright Camea, bring them in."

The prisoners were shuffled up the corridor from the billets and forced to their knees in the mess hall's main aisle. Nadia was worried. There were too many eager hands, and not enough weapons to suit her in case things went badly. But shipboard parole is an ancient tradition. Even with two decks gone and the fifty helots, *Retnec's* four remaining, 213 meter diameter circular decks and, one rectangular 180 meter drive deck is too big a ship, with too many systems for the 172 of them to operate for months on end without relief. The cryogenic and medical technicians could stay alive if they cooperated.

*

Nadia's Papa Silas was sentenced to three years labor at a re-education center on Shafir-Belfin just for mentioning Alexandra Marena's name and offering a blessing for her soul in public. The government released Papa when Nadia was nine years old. From then, until she left for university at eighteen, she would defy her parents when they, and her two brothers were asleep. Nadia crept into the cellar apartment her parents consigned Papa to. She would make him tea, then sit quietly on the side of his bed and listen to his stories of the old Shafir of his grandparents' time. Papa always warned her never to repeat them.

The Health Ministry said he was cured but told her parents to report any unusual behavior to the social workers when they made their monthly parole visits. The social workers told young Nadia the same thing. No one in Nadia's family reported Papa's stories.

Nadia stood on a center table so all could see and hear her. She spoke openly as a free egalitarian, a free Shafiran, for the first time in her life. She had thought before about preparing a speech but dismissed it. Instead, the Senior Lieutenant candidly explained their situation to her fellow mutineers. At the same time, she offered their prisoners a chance to live.

The majority of the crew were Shafirans, true to their nature, discussion broke out.

"Those are our brothers and sisters in those tubes, Lieutenant! Cutting the power would kill them!"

"They're living dead, they have no memories, no personalities. They're just vegetables!"

"Show some compassion, Lieutenant," the helot, Nash, from the corridor incident with Private Vickers, spoke out. "They've been experimented on enough, let them die!"

"They're no one's brothers and sisters anymore!"

Technician Anika Jander sneered at the prisoners; her uniform spattered with her brother's blood. "I say wake 'em up and put these people in the tubes!"

75

Tinor knew the grieving Karelian woman was the wrong person to be holding a weapon on the prisoners. Even though she had watched De'Molay being ejected from the shuttle bay, and her other two summoners were trapped aboard the command tower. However, neither she, nor Mr. Warrick, could do anything about it at the moment.

On his knees, his wrists and arms bound, one of the surviving researchers interrupted the debate. A young scientist whose previous rebuke of a Strelski guard, had stopped the beating of a helot crewman, who, in the melee, had saved his life. Nadia and Mr. Warrick knew who he was, none of the other mutineers did.

"They're not vegetables," he shouted, shaking his head in denial. "They don't all have implants. You make it all sound so diabolical. We were helping them!"

"Comidas, NO!" Lt. vin Lurel shouted in panic.

"Shut up, bitch!" Nadia barked.

Artificer Greene jabbed the muzzle of a battle rifle into the hated officer's back. She glared down at her, then up to Nadia.

"We don't need this one, Lieutenant. Just say the word."

"No, Greene. There's been enough killing for one day. But I may change my mind about her on the morrow. Talk, scientist!"

The young prisoner looked around at vin Lurel and his mates. He saw the fear in their eyes. He knew what they were afraid of even more than for their lives. He was no longer afraid of the same thing.

"Deck five holds Ratabi test subjects. The Ratabi had no natural immune systems in those days. Our research on those subjects helped developed a series of thyroid hormones for them. Deck six holds the Shafiran doctor who led the project, Ben Ali, and his staff. The Marena woman, and other government officials are there as well. They've been in stasis since the second war with the Commonwealth. You can cut the power mains. None of them will die as long as each pod's backup batteries can be recharged every ninety hours."

Nadia was relieved to hear him speak up. She knew the other prisoners knew him and would follow his lead.

"Don't believe him, Lieutenant. We've been working on this ship for almost two years and no one has ever confirmed she's in there."

"Who else would it be? We need to keep those tubes intact and functioning, Lieutenant. At least we know Ben-Ali and his research team are there." A mutineer lab technician joined in, backing up the scientist.

As others had their say, Ensign Prine took Warwick's cue and got close to Jander. He was able to comfort her somewhat and got the weapon from her.

"You're Shafiran, Lieutenant," a Genoan technician said. "You know Ben-Ali has to pay for his crimes. But we have to confirm whether Alexandra Marena, and maybe her cabinet members, are in there too!"

"But how can we?" someone asked from across the room. "We don't even know what she looked like?"

"I'll wager they do, Lieutenant!" the lab technician stared at the prisoners.

Tinor looked down at the old warrant. "It's time they knew, Mr. Warrick."

The room hushed. Warrick's word was beyond question.

"We have confirmed it," Warrick announced. "The Shafiran President and several of her cabinet members are alive, and in stasis aboard this ship. Just as the boy says."

"She's an interbred, Shafirans," Nadia continued. "So is Ben-Ali, and many of the others. They needed to separate us by skin tone to control us. They levied and sold off the interbreds first."

The Homostoioi prisoners let go a collective moan, all except the young scientist. The mutineers were all stunned, especially the Shafirans.

Besides Nadia, there were forty-three Shafirans among them. Ernesto Warrick was the sole Tantoran aboard, the rest of the crew a mix of Genoans, Vegans, and Karelians. It was impossible to determine who was from where simply by their physical appearance. Only their grav-balance underwear was different, being manufactured from the earth of their home worlds. Unless Nadia knew them personally, she had always had to refer to the personnel database if there was any need for such trivial information.

The very mention of the last freely elected leader of the Shafir was like a stab in all their hearts. Generations of subjugated people on scores of Sacorsti-ruled, Alliance home worlds had silently prayed for her soul.

In the Shafir, the very mention of her name was punishable by imprisonment, and even levy since the so-called Great Conformance, the despised Shafiran Acquiescence more than 350 years ago. Far from being blamed, President Alexandra Marena was revered as its first victim.

The cinemas and literaries approved by the Aglifhate's AIM and Shafiran Information Ministry's entertainment branches always said Alexandra Marena was a traitor. All the history books said she looted the Shafiran treasury and fled to Poia with half her cabinet, after the Duma, the Shafiran stellar state legislature, overruled her veto of then-Interior Minister Quislier's proposal of Conformance to the Sacorsti Aglifhate in 114PCE. The Duma impeached her and named Quislier Premier, not President.

The Shafiran Information Ministry said she then tried, and failed, to launch a counter-revolution from Poia and Mai. This, Nadia had always been taught, caused the Great Defensive Conflict of 114 to 116 PCE. The Great Defense pitted the fledgling Shafiran Defense Force and the Alliance Shield, against the combined strength of the Poians, the Maians, and their Commonwealth allies. Yet her Papa Silas had said the Shafir had no armies or fleets before the Acquiescence and no Shafirans actually fought in the Great Defense that followed.

Marena did manage, the media said, to instigate the counter-revolution in the Questri-Shontor Binary State after they conformed. She was also able to use stolen Shafiran gold and platinum to pay Commonwealth mercenaries, under the hated Praetor Kratari, to invade, and subjugate both the Questri-Shontor, and the Trinovan Stellar Union.

The Patruscans and the Egalitarians said President Marena was regarded in the Commonwealth, and the other Leagues, as a tragic figure. They claimed she disappeared the day of The Great Conformance, and presumed she was devoured by a beast she thought she could pacify.

The legend was true, the first Madonna, Indira vin, spared the deposed president from the levy markets all those years ago. To solve the mystery of President Marena's disappearance could spark revolution in the Shafir that could spread across the Alliance. But, they all knew, first, they had to escape.

"We're going to circle wide, around the outer edge of the Outer Metropolitan Region. This is a long-range vessel! We can approach the Commonwealth from a non-threatening direction. Mr. Prine?"

"Ah. Yes, madam," The navigator cleared his throat and spoke up. "We will approach the Chein-Haeun territory from its far southwestern regions."

Nadia continued. "The Chein are said to be the most fair-minded of the liberon Commoners. They will grant us asylum in exchange for the living bodies of Salezar Ben-Ali and his staff, and research data."

Crewmembers around the mess hall looked at each other, nodding in agreement.

But what would become of the martyred president? Nadia wondered.

"You! Scientist!" Tinor demanded. "What's your name?"

The young scientist knew his days were numbered. His pedigree could not help him. In fact, his pedigree put his life in danger. Perhaps his honesty would keep him alive a little longer. He held his head erect and responded clearly. "Comidas, Borigai Comidas vin Ngier."

"Of the Borigai Clan?! Oh My God. He's part of the Sacorsti Royal Family!"

"Be quiet, Jander! What are your orders, Madam?"

"Thank you, Mr. Warrick. Take the pods off line. Bring the reactor power to eighty percent." Tinor said looking around the room, speaking to everyone. "Plus, we'll reduce power consumption everywhere we can, we may need a reserve." She drew her hands close to one another to illustrate what they all already knew.

"We've got a narrow window of time to put maximum distance between ourselves and the few destroyers in this sector, people. The anchorage's loss of our transponder signal will trigger an immediate search. We've got to be smart. We've got a lot of veterans in this crew; we're going to need all our skills to avoid detection and slip away."

"I know this region well, Madam Lieutenant," Ensign Prine added. "So does Jackie, there are lots of subductions to hide in between here and the OMR frontier. If we can cross into the outer metropolitan region before any of the ships from the Quislier line get there, we've got a good chance of making it all the way."

"That's right ma'am." Ensign Jackson endorsed him. "Our light-time imaging systems are better than those aboard any of our warships." She turned, speaking to the others. "We can scan the sprint routes between subductions."

Ensign Regal advised them all. "We'll have to shut down all but the most essential systems to not leave any discernable trail. Supply division will start a survey straight away, Madam."

"Outstanding, Regal, get your people to work on that, shut them down as you go."

Jackson spoke up again. "One other thing, Madam. We have to mark but avoid navigation and retransmission buoys and census stations along the routes. Any one of them will register our passing."

Nadia knew what that meant. "Did you all hear that?" She looked around the room. "That means no news or contact with anyone in the CMR. We'll be completely in the dark about what is happening around us."

"Everybody got that?" Warrick barked.

"Yes, Chief, Yes, Madam."

"Right then, Mr. Warrick, secure the prisoners in the billets until we figure out parole duties for them. But take our scientist friend, Comidas vin here, and put him to work on the pods. If anyone in those pods dies, he dies too!"

"Yes, Madam!"

The old warrant gladial saluted his commander and set about imposing her will. Nadia looked around at her shipmates nodding in agreement. Two of them helped her down off the table. The crew parted, letting their leader pass as she walked out of the mess hall.

"You stay with me, boy! Linus, bring your section. You stay here too, Jander. Camea, take the rest of these people back to the billets and post guards on them. Keep the MOB separate from the others. The rest of you, get back to your stations. Move It!"

Tinor left the mess hall, turning left along the corridor to the lift to return to the drive deck. She needed to rest, her billet was behind her, but to close her eyes meant to think about Giles, and Jander. These senior engineers and technicians were all needed. Tinor had to parole them. Lt. vin Lurel was another story. *She's a threat, as long as she's alive.* It was going to be a long voyage to freedom, and she had to keep their best bargaining chip, their cargo, safe.

As her shipmates moved past her, most moving back to their stations, and Greene's section hustling prisoners away, Tinor was still not certain if all of the Strelski had been identified and jettisoned. The risk of even one undercover operative managing to get a signal back to the Aglifhate would result in every one of her crew going out of an airlock themselves. Worse, were the Strelski to discover their desertion too soon, their families back home could be arrested and levied, or even crucified. Tinor, Warrick, and their fellow mutineers, were confident that at least for the time being, they were not being tracked by any long-range surveillance. They were wrong.

****

With all the attendees accounted for, league constables closed and sealed the entrances. The mag-seal doors merged into the sterile, windowless chamber's bare walls. The pale green tint in the chamber's illumination signaled they were secure and could speak freely.

"You've known that ship has been activated all this time and we're just now hearing about it? What have you been doing?!"

Well known for his aggressive political nature, Joachim Boyars launched his attack straight away. "How long have we been using the DOPs to spy on them? Why wasn't I briefed about this during the Senator's, er, the Chief Executive's campaign? I have an Admiralty level one security clearance now."

Boyars was an arrogant, hot tempered former political consultant, who, in the minds of the admirals and senior senators present, had too often confused his title with his actual authority. Neither Senator Morales nor his 'little errand boy' had a need to know during Morales' long-shot campaign. His stunning election victory however, had changed all that.

After a month of contentious confirmation hearings, the agenda for the new Commonwealth Security Advisor's first joint conference was supposed to be about Vighandis. The committee chairs of the Senate Foreign Affairs, Intelligence and Military Affairs Committees, their ranking members, and the Combined Fleet Chief of Staff and his principal deputies for operations and intelligence were in attendance. But it abruptly changed within the last hour with updates from the fleet operations situation room under Blue House, tucked away in the hills north of the city.

More than half the conference attendees were dismissed from the outer chambers and told to report back to their offices. The few staffers allowed in, took seats in the lower rows, close to their bosses seated around the crescent shaped table at the base of the amphitheater conference room.

"That was nothing personal, Joachim, just standard procedure," the intelligence committee chair assured him.

"DOP two nine seven traffic is classified Top Secret 'Need to Know'. You and your senior aides have been vetted for general site information and all traffic. Admiral, would you orient Mr. Boyars quickly, please."

"Yes, Senator."

Sitting next to Boyars, the chief of staff keyed up a regional map of the Chein Stellar State on the data pad imbedded in the table in front of him.

"Sir, the image you are about to see, and its narrative is the original deep observation post mission statement. It's still relevant today. You should see this before we start the actual briefing."

The multi-plot rose from its base in the floor before the conference table. The room lights dimmed to compensate.

A distinguished-looking gray-haired gentleman in a 5th century style suit, identified as a past Senate Cosmographic Studies Committee Chair sat in a thick swivel, framed by shelves of leather-bound literaries, behind an old-fashioned polished wooden desk. The man leaned forward and crossed his arms on the desk as he began to speak. Still fuming, Boyars sat quietly and listened. The senators present exchanged subtle glances, knowing that was very hard for him.

"Life Search Enterprises, Ltd., of Chein-Caironia is constructing several Deep Observation Posts under contract from the Commonwealth Cosmography Directorate and are orienting them to probe outward toward the spiral arms of the galaxy. Each DOP has been tasked to chart magnetic fields and scan stellar systems in their sector from seven to fifteen kilo-parsec from the galactic center.

"Making maximum use of continual improvements in Enhanced Light Time Imaging, and other electronic and spectrographic detection means, these observation posts are designed to search for evidence of technological tribes capable of achieving the Enlightenment Protocols."

The image faded and was replaced by a default map of the Commonwealth Administrative Zone as the Combined Fleet Chief of Staff began his briefing.

"DOP two nine seven is unique among the others, Mr. Boyars, in that its' observation arc scans across sixty percent of metropolitan Alliance territory. Including all of the Sacor the Second stellar region."

Boyars swallowed hard. His eyes widened in amazement. The admirals and senators expected another of the rhetorical rants he was notorious for. This time however, he sat and listened.

"Though not originally designed as an intelligence gathering platform, its value to our operational intelligence about the Alliance increased to the point, early on, where its precise location was removed from all but the most highly classified CMR/OMR census maps. Great care has been taken, sir, even before this war, to ensure no military operations were conducted without a deception plan to hide any reference to DOP two nine seven information."

The senate intelligence committee chair leaned towards Boyars and interrupted the admiral.

"Joachim, DOP two nine seven is totally inaccessible to the Aglifhate's forces or Strelski operatives, if its existence is even known. CCID has maintained a listening and observation post there since the third war."

"That long? Over ninety years?" Incredulous, Boyars looked around the room.

Stone-faced, the admirals to his left and the senators to his right looked back at him, waiting for him to process what he was hearing. Finally, he nodded and turned back towards the graphic. Taking her cue from the senator, the Director of Central Intelligence explained her agency's role.

"The DOP maintains its original function, sir. The Life Searchers still conduct their deep scans as the contract requires. My people's listening post sifts the station's ELTI data for strategic information. In addition to military movements, we monitor ship and void platform construction statuses and civilian news and information; including industrial activity, commercial trends, and certain business transactions.

"My directorate established a closed network of retransmission buoys connecting DOP two nine seven with our regional station at the Chein-Medio depot, and then on to headquarters on Eatoni-Priame, sir. The listening post reports twice daily via encrypted, hyper-wave burst transmissions, carrying batches of Alliance intercepts and drive signature telemetries."

"ELTI?" Boyars was not sure of what he had heard.

"Enhanced Light-time Imaging, sir," his primary aide, Mrs. Allen, reminded him from her swivel just behind him.

"Oh, oh yes, of course."

"To be frank, Mr. Boyars," the chief of staff said. "We intercept, decode, and translate their transmissions often before their colonial governors and phalanx commanders acknowledge receipt of them."

Boyars harrumphed. "That's not what I'm upset about! Vanger's people said absolutely nothing about this during transition. But I understand now. Let's get on with this." Boyar's expressions reflected the deep concern his boss, the new Chief Executive, Edgar Morales, held for this new development.

The chief of staff gestured towards Vice Admiral Pol, his J-2, Deputy Chief of Staff for Intelligence, handing the briefing over to her. The multi-plot shifted to the Vegan stellar region in the Alliance of Stellar Republics.

"Mr. Boyars, ladies and gentlemen, DOP two nine seven first detected work in the Vega-Carillon Shipyard Y-Thirty one, on a drive signature later identified as the *AGRV Retnec*, eighteen months ago, in oh nine of seven sixty-eight. Of course, the fact that this vessel was active again perked a lot of ears here in my office, in the senate intelligence committee, and the previous administration's security advisory staff.

"Readings indicated the drive and other sections of the vessel had been magnetically sealed for a considerable time, and the yard was having trouble synchronizing the power-plants. Our concern grew when telemetry data noted *Retnec*'s departure from Y-Thirty one and, after twenty one hours, departing the Vegan Stellar Republic."

"Twenty one hours? They're really taking their time."

"We believe it's on a shakedown cruise, sir. After being sealed for so long," the chief of staff advised.

"I see."

Pol continued. "*Retnec*'s signal pulse surged, yesterday, at sixteen fifteen hours, Demeos Central Time. That indicated an energy release of some type. We assume it was an explosion. The vessel lost some of its mass and abruptly changed course. A second energy surge, or explosion, was detected in *Retnec*'s wake, and after three hours, the somewhat smaller vessel slowed to wave speed and powered down for several hours."

"What is it doing now?" an intelligence committee senator asked.

"As of a little more than an hour ago, the vessel has changed its course and speed several times, but has, so far, maintained a base course of thirty one degrees relative to the galactic singularity." The admiral expanded the plot as she spoke. "If *Retnec* does not radically alter course within one hundred hours, at its present speed, sir, it will penetrate the known galactic barrier into the trans-galactic void."

"What are your estimates?" the intelligence committee chair asked.

Boyars looked around towards his primary aide. She nodded, and he turned back again, listening as the possibility of the unescorted *Retnec* being sent on a multi-millennial journey to another galaxy was briefly discussed. The fleet operations senior astronomer however, set the matter to rest.

"Our first analysis, ladies and gentlemen, of gravity wave current interactions along *Retnec*'s extrapolated course, showed a possibility of the vessel catching a singularity downward outbound gravity wave at one of two points. These are the eight kilo-parsec line, or the nine point five kilo-parsec line, and riding either into the southwest spiral region, at approximately eight to eight point five kilo-parsec from the singularity, on the zero or lateral plane."

"So what?" Boyars leaned back in his swivel.

The astronomer expanded the HG image, overlaying two dashed routes the vessel might be taking. The extrapolated routes intersected at a point on the map that clearly illustrated the meeting's importance to all the attendees, except the security advisor.

"Oh, my Lord!" His assistant blurted out, surprising Boyars.

He turned and leaned towards her again. She whispered in his ear, gesturing towards the plot. Boyars nodded after a second or so. The senators and admirals all knew of the widowed Mrs. Hollandia Allen. The real brain in the CSA's office. The security advisor's advisor from a major strategic think-tank in Morales' and Boyars' home state, Denestri.

Shortly, Boyars straightened, turning back to the front. "I understand. Continue, please," he said.

The chief of staff nodded, and the astronomer carried on. "This will place the vessel arriving at the galactic lateral plane somewhere in sector AEWX zero-four-four-nine. As you can see, the region is on plane with the Chein Stellar State, though well beyond the Commonwealth's strategic rear. No known vessel or probe has yet been sent towards this southwest spiral region, sir. The AC-DC-delta is only one point nine at that distance. Singularity based gravity waves are slow and steady in the outer galactic regions, and just beyond."

Boyars stroked his bearded chin, his brow furrowed, reflecting the gravity of the situation. "How much time do we have?"

Mrs. Allen began jotting notes down on her wrist pad. The intelligence chair held up a hand to interrupt the astronomer.

"I'm sorry, Mrs. Allen. No notes please. All *Retnec* briefings are 'For Eyes Only'. We'll send an official brief by courier."

Boyars put a hand out towards his aide, acknowledging the senator's admonishment. She nodded, folded her hands and sat back as the astronomer continued.

"We've estimated *Retnec*'s arrival in that sector to be the twenty-first day, of the seventh month of seven seventy CE. That's approximately one hundred thirty days at maximum Alliance reactor output, or one hundred ninety days at eighty-five percent. That arrival date estimate is zero one, of the ninth month of seven seventy CE. These dates, sir, are based on the vessel taking the E-four singularity downward outbound wave at the eight, to eight point five kpc wave line series."

Mrs. Allen's head tilted. One of her eyebrows arched as she gave the astronomer colonel a quizzical look, as if expecting more, but the officer appeared to be moving on.

"What about the nine kpc line series?"

"Yes. The nine to nine point five kpc series was discounted, ma'am, on closer scrutiny. As the edge of the wave extends beyond the galactic rim, it would be impossible to break free of."

The assemblage collectively nodded. Boyars and Mrs. Allen exchanged another quiet conversation. Their heads close, the chief of staff noticed her hand movement seemed to reflect changes in her demeanor towards Boyars. She seemed to become more of a teacher than an executive assistant. After a moment, the two sat up and faced the plot.

"What are the Sacorsti doing about it?" Boyars asked.

Admiral Pol tapped her data pad and took over. The multi-plot shifted to a tactical map centering on the Vegan Stellar

Republic. The region closest to Boyars and Mrs. Allen, Vighandis, Bavat and on towards Vega illuminated, populating with red ovals. The vast majority were within the Bavat and Vighandis heliospheres. To Boyar's right, fronting and above the senate committee chairs, lay the former Alliance Republic of Tantori, now a well-armed and well equipped non-Aligned stellar state, highlighted in yellow.

The southeast of Tantori's heliosphere lay dangerously close to the Vegan support facilities in the rear of the Alliance Fleet in Bavat and Vighandis. Another large group illuminated in the Shafir, to the chief of staff's left and well above Vega. Boyars nodded, recognizing the Quislier Line, the heavily fortified sector of Shafiran heliopause fronting Commonwealth Poia, Mai, and Chapuri.

Well beyond and slightly above Vega, in front of Boyars, but on the far side of the projection, lay Sacor II, the former Genoan stellar republic, and yet a third large red oval grouping. Finally, small packets of red triangles began appearing at various points along the trace of the Sacorsti Alliance Administrative Zone that fronted the Commonwealth.

Pol shifted the plot, scaling in towards Vega again. Five red triangular symbols appeared to be moving in echelon left along the northwest of the Vegan heliopause moving towards the north, relative to Vega. The admiral tapped her data pad. The *Retnec's* symbol appeared, moving north by northeast, relative to the singularity at the center of the galaxy. The vessel's track showed its weave, halt and sprint maneuvers had taken it well out into the trans-stellar void between Vega and Tantori and away from both.

"Mr. Boyars, the enemy is currently showing little reaction to the *Retnec's* maneuverings. As of last hour's update, the pattern of destroyer drive signatures we've been tracking nearest Vega, in the middle of the plot there, sir, is compatible with a search pattern along the outer heliopause, towards Vega."

"A search? No pursuit?"

"None so far as we can tell, voice and data intercepts takes generally one and a quarter hours longer at these distances, sir. That's due to inconsistent retransmission buoy maintenance on their part. There may be orders being transmitted at any time. The phalanxes in Shafir, here, behind their Quislier Line are the closest to Retnec's present position and extrapolated course. But that could change at any hour. "

"Where's their vaunted Admiral, uh, what's her name, the Madonna's sister? Mathilda."

"We have her flagship's drive signature in Bavat, here, sir, orbiting the second habitable zone planet between the phalanxes staged to support the forces in Vighandis. We believe she's aboard."

Vice Admiral Oshermeyer, the J-3, Deputy Chief of Staff for Operations, spoke up on Pol's cue.

"Those Vighandis phalanxes are isolated, sir. You can see there, by our third and fifth fleets. Second fleet is positioned to reinforce if we detect any movement out of Bavat to relieve the Vighandis phalanxes."

The foreign affairs committee chair interrupted. "They won't move out of Bavat. The Sacorsti have agreed to the Patruscan hold in place demand outside Vighandis. They won't reinforce the pocket, but they won't order them to stop trying to break out either. That actually strengthens our hand on the issue of prisoner exchange. Additionally, what they don't know is, and this doesn't leave this room," he waved a hand around towards the attendees in the amphitheater. "Except of course the CE and Privy Council, Joachim."

The senator cleared his throat. "The Patruscans, with Asigi endorsement, have asked the Valerians for direct military assistance in policing the cease fire and protecting their observers. As of the start of this meeting the Khan has conditionally acceded to the request, pending an agreement on the demarcation lines the Valerian Armed Forces are going to police. Madonna Nicholla is going to get quite a surprise."

The chief of staff smirked. "And there's not a damned thing she can do about it."

The intelligence committee chief grinned and nodded, then gestured for Admiral Pol to continue.

"Didn't G.W. Morgan predict that in the hearings with some ridiculous time line?" Boyars asked. He and Mrs. Allen exchanged nods.

"Yes, sir. Yes he did. He predicted the front-line trace of zero nine zero one VET," Admiral Pol responded as the plot extended outward.

"Of this year, seven-seventy."

"Yes, sir."

"Humph. Where'd he get that?"

"I really don't know, sir. I could find out."

"Don't bother, Admiral, he's delusional. Continue."

"Yes, sir." Pol cleared her throat. "There is considerable movement of Sacorsti civilian and military transport out of Tantori, towards Jodar, in the east, ah, relative to the singularity, sir. Others appear to be vectoring towards Krittar and Astaran, in the west, here. Strangely, not towards the Sacor two group itself."

Mrs. Allen reached out and tapped Boyars; another whispered conference began. Boyars nodded, then they both sat up.

"Assuming *Retnec* is running from the Alliance," Boyars held up a hand in caution. "Not saying it is. What could we do to help it get out of the Alliance Administrative Zone without tipping our hand?"

The intelligence committee chief smiled. He gave the military affairs chief's arm a subtle tap and made a surreptitious nod towards Mrs. Allen.

"Admiral?" Military Affairs asked.

The Chief of Staff tilted his head towards Admiral Oshermeyer. They spoke softly and gestured towards the plot, before Oshermeyer spoke.

"Sir, we could rattle the Shafirans along the Quislier Line with a few demonstration exercises on our side." He shifted the plot to the two opposing, heavily militarized heliopause regions. He rotated the image, placing the region directly in front of Boyars, Mrs. Allen and the Senators.

"This blue region on the left is our Poian Stellar State. The upper left octodrant near Poian Gas Giant three is under continual Shafiran surveillance from asteroid strongpoints along the line and their patrols on their side of the demarcation line. They've been quiet there since we secured the Trudan. But, in the past, any activity there of destroyer flotilla size or larger has drawn an equal response on their part."

He highlighted the Shafiran gas giant, SGG-6 planetary group across the short trans-stellar gap from PGG-3. "Here around SGG-six. With the Trudan gone and the loss of access to the Madera fields in Tantori, sir, they would be hard-pressed, fuel-wise to respond to say, task force-sized maneuvers between Istria, the Istrians' Decia-Ponte group of stellar stations, and PGG-three."

Admiral Pol grinned. "We could refight some of the Second war battles for a few days. That would fix all the supporting phalanxes in place. It could cause the entire SDF to go on full alert, sir."

"And the phalanx in Sacor two? What about it?" Mrs. Allen asked.

Oshermeyer shook his head. "If it's ordered to move against the ship, ma'am. There's really nothing we could do to stop it."

Boyars had seen enough, he gestured for the plot to scale down. Admiral Oshermeyer brought it back to a small scale of the overall region.

"When I brief the chief executive, he's going to want your assessments of what *Retnec* may be up to in our rear as soon as possible. What else can we do about this?"

The chief of staff was more ready for that question. He exchanged glances with the military affairs committee chair and keyed up the combined fleet's current tactical disposition. The image showed the unit symbols of the bulk of the fleet deployed in and around the Vighandis region. Smaller units were scattered, seemingly at random, around the Commonwealth Administrative Zone. Boyars and Mrs. Allen could see there was nothing random about the deployments.

The military affairs committee chair spoke for them all.

"Pending the CE's authorization, the chiefs have decided to alert Task Force Draken at Pirieus-Tresium, here, that's depot nineteen, to move to DOP two nine seven."

"Draken?!" Boyars sat bolt upright. "That's Morgan's bunch, isn't it?"

"Yes, Morgan is in command. Draken is re-fitted and preparing for deployment readiness exercises, Joachim. Afterwards he can march administratively to Chein and jump off from near DOP two nine seven with a firm fix on *Retnec*."

"Can't you replace him? The boss hates his guts!"

"There's no justification for relieving him, Joachim," the chair warned. "Now that the Maranon investigations are over and done with. It's Morgan commanding Task Force Draken, or a storm of shit in the press, especially in the Nursery Crescent news media for relief without cause. They love him out there."

Boyars harrumphed in frustration. The highlighted military map symbol of a fleet task force, labeled Draken and crowned with two Xs, stood out at the depot station just 60 trans-stellar astronomic units away. He could only shake his head in resignation.

"Damn. Alright. But he needs a clear directive. No more of this open interpretation nonsense like Trudan bleeding over into Maranon! Hot pursuit, my ass. I still say it was his road to a permanent Praetorship is what it was."

The chief of staff suppressed a chuckle at Boyars' inference. Mrs. Allen tapped her boss' arm before she spoke.

"What exercise is this you spoke of, Senator?"

The military affairs committee chair smiled and nodded at her. "It's our standard procedure. All our task forces conduct unit level exercises before they deploy."

"A shakedown cruise? Like you believe Retnec was doing?" she asked.

"Ah, yes," the senator chuckled. "Quite right,"

"Well, I think we can forego a practice," Boyars chortled. "This Retnec, whatever it's up to in our rear has to be stopped. That's our first priority!"

"I respectfully disagree, Joachim," the senator said. The intelligence and foreign affairs committee chairs, the other senators, admirals and senior staffers all looked up, focusing on the two. Boyars fidgeted. The senator continued. "The Task Force Liberty law requires a PDRE before any unit is declared operational. Additionally, without one, a task force-sized sortie beyond the CAZ at this stage in our negotiations with the Sacorsti would raise too many eyebrows. We can't afford to give any indication we know anything about their movements or about *Retnec*."

Boyars saw the knot of senators behind the three committee chairs nodding in unanimous agreement.

The chief of staff lifted his data pad and checked the status reports of his commanders down to the battle group level. He found Gaven Webster Morgan's activity schedule and leaned over to show it to Boyars.

"Morgan is on Degoa-Earth, on a student panel discussion at the Academy as we speak. He'll be shuttling over here this afternoon, sir."

Boyars' head jerked up. "He's still here?! In the Capital District?!"

"He returned yesterday, sir," the admiral said. "I sent him home the day the hearings ended. To rest, sir."

He sat back in his swivel and gestured to Admiral Oshermeyer, who nodded and began to scribble notes on his data pad.

Boyars grunted, casting a twisted grin. "If I had my way, he'd have gotten a nice, long, rest, at a new home. Stanleyville Correctional for twenty years would've done nicely," he quipped.

No one found the remark humorous.

"How long will he be here?"

"Just long enough to receive his orders, sir. I'm sending him to Andolusia for his task force PDRE. Afterwards I've slated him for ready response status."

"Hmmph," Boyars snorted. "The entertainment mogul, part-time soldier who wanted to buy his way to being named Praetor-for-life gets to go pay homage at the grave of his idol. Well, good. I don't want to see him, neither does the CE. How long before he can get after *Retnec*, or at least get that fleet or task force, get those warships and troops away from this capital? My God, Pirieus-Tresium! How close are they to us here? Three days?!"

The military affairs committee chair saw Mrs. Allen roll her eyes behind her boss before she leaned forward and tapped his arm. His rant vented, Boyars swiveled round and listened for a moment. The chief of staff gestured to Admirals Oshermeyer and Pol to be ready with an answer. Oshermeyer nodded at his boss. Finally, Mrs. Allen raised her head.

"Colonel, you said *Retnec* reaches AEWX oh four, four nine, in our ninth month?"

"Uh, yes, ma'am," the astronomer answered. "By our best estimate.

"And the DOP is continuing to track them?"

"We've got their drive signature archived. Any of the DOPs can track her now and vector our ships to an intercept," Admiral Pol said. Mrs. Allen saw the CCID Director nodding in agreement.

"How long will it take Commodore Morgan to reach the sector from Chein?" she asked. Boyars sat quietly, as all the others' turned their attention to Mrs. Allen.

"Three months at the outside, ma'am," Admiral Oshermeyer answered. "That's at an approach march velocity and laying standard markers along the way. They can do it in two months at flank speed, laying battle markers."

Boyars turned back towards Mrs. Allen but said nothing. He swiveled back again and stroked his chin in thought, his head and eyes making furtive movements, taking in the plot.

"What do we know of the region?" Mrs. Allen asked. "Is it inhabited?"

"There are three stellar groupings there, ma'am," the astronomer said. "One is a tri-stellar grouping. The DOP has detected industrial pollutants in most of the habitable zone planets' atmospheres in all three stellar groups. There's evidence of electronic transmission capability from some of those worlds. Most of which emanates from the center system, a solitary G2V. That's what we call a main sequence white to yellow star, based on its surface temperature."

The astronomer saw Boyars nodding in understanding.

"And the third?" Mrs. Allen asked.

"Another G type, ma'am. A yellow dwarf, about twenty percent smaller than the one in the center."

She nodded.

"All the groupings are enclosed by debris discs, ma'am. But the center star is imbedded in a massive dust, comet and asteroid cloud that includes a score or more dwarf outer worlds. We've detected four ice or gas giants, within the middle heliosphere, with three class A or B worlds in its habitable zone. There may be at least one small world in the inner zone as well."

The image sharpened, concentrating on the center stellar group.

"We focused on this group, ma'am, because we detected the majority of the sector's electronic emissions from the three-world habitable zone. It is protected by an inner asteroid barrier and the inner-most gas giant. That inner giant is also the largest in the entire sector. We haven't detected any celestial transits or mining activity anywhere in the sector."

94

Boyars perked up as the image zoomed into the larger G2V star in the center, displaying its habitable zone. He pointed a finger at the grouping, interrupting Mrs. Allen's line of questions. She calmly sat back.

"Does Jamison know about this? Or Hanash?"

"No, Joachim," the intelligence committee chair spoke up. "We leave it to you to brief the CE and the Privy Council. I don't put up with back channels. You know that."

"I know, Senator. But that man has ears in the walls. I don't want Morgan turned loose on any more poor unenlighteneds," he exclaimed. "That's just what Hanash and the fundamentalist party is going to lobby for. We've already got the damned Maranon mess to clean up, and now Vighandis."

"What about Morgan's commanders and staff?" Mrs. Allen asked.

"His chief of staff, his sergeant major, and his cruiser battle group commanders are traveling with him, ma'am. The battle group master chiefs and operations officers as well. The bulk of the force's personnel were put on block leave when they stood down after Maranon. They're due to muster in ten days. The ships' crews at their shipyards, the marine regiment and the aviation wings at their surface depots and exo-dromes. The marine regimental headquarters and several quick reaction and specialist units have reported in already."

"I understand." Mrs. Allen mused for a moment, before she spoke again. "Does his task force still have a Spetznax-Recondo cohort assigned to it?"

"Yes, ma'am," the chief of staff responded with some surprise. None of the senior senators were surprised Mrs. Allen knew of the special action regiment's existence.

"Spats-what? Recon-what?" Boyars asked, looking around in confusion.

"I'll explain later, sir." Mrs. Allen tapped his arm and turned back to the admiral. "Did the commodore, staffers and the recondos who testified at the hearings get any leave to rest, Admiral?"

"Yes, ma'am. I made sure of that. As I said, I sent them all home, the day the matter concluded."

"Oh, he's had enough rest alright," Boyars chortled. "Enough to openly contradict you, Admiral and the Chief Executive in that Galen interview."

"Be that as it may, Joachim," the intelligence committee chair answered. "Morgan was right, again. We did over-estimate their fuel reserves. And we completely missed the Egalitarians gaining control in the Tantori legislature and their defection."

Boyars sat back and folded his arms at another elder statesman's quiet rebuke. Mrs. Allen tapped him again and a longer hushed conversation ensued between them. Admiral Oshermeyer and the chief of staff exchanged data pad notes, beginning the process of putting a mission statement together for the military affairs committee chair's review. Whispered conversations continued in pockets around the conference room.

Senators and admirals could not fail to notice Mrs. Allen's forceful knife-edged gestures of emphasis and Boyars' immediate head nods. After a few moments, she and the security advisor sat upright in their swivels, the side conversations came to a halt as he cleared his throat to speak.

"I'll brief the CE. Let Morgan play his war games before he sets to the wave. Give him enough time to get to that region beyond Chein, grab *Retnec* and get the hell back here. But no more." He stabbed a forefinger into the air for emphasis.

"I don't want any word of this getting to the press. Tell Morgan to keep his big mouth shut too, Admiral," Boyars commanded, asserting his new found authority as the Chief Executive's representative on matters of league security. "He is to restrict his information to his immediate staff and no further, not even those pirates you call battle group commanders. At least not without authority from me, er, I mean the CE."

The chief of staff's head and eyes rolled. His right hand dropped from the conference table to his hip as he swiveled towards Boyars.

"You're being vindictive now, sir. You shouldn't restrict a commodore's ability to communicate with his subordinate commanders." He looked past Boyars to the senators for support, but, this time there was none.

"My side won the election, Admiral. It's important, for political reasons that Morgan's supporters in the fundamentalist party don't find out about the unenlighteneds in that interception area."

"Commodore Morgan has no political affiliations, sir," Admiral Oshermeyer asserted with a scowl. "Not with the fundamentalists or anyone else. I've known that man almost thirty years. So has Admiral Pol."

Pol nodded, seconding the operations officer. The chief of staff lifted his left hand slightly to stay his senior staffers.

"Will there be anything else, sir?"

Boyars' confidence rose with the chief of staff's acquiescence. "Yes. I want daily updates on *Retnec's* location and status sent to Mrs. Allen here. And on Task Force Draken's activities and schedules. What have you got to defend the DOP if necessary?"

The chief of staff turned to Admiral Oshermeyer. "The *Stone* is on ready reaction, correct?"

"Yes, sir," a stoic Oshermeyer replied.

"Work up the operations order, Admiral. Have the Fleet Destroyer Flotilla, *Karen L. Stone the Second* proceed at best speed to deep observation post two niner seven and report to the CCID station chief for further orders. Have Morgan report to the situation room as soon as he arrives from the D E."

"Yes, sir."

The chief of staff turned back towards Boyars and Mrs. Allen. "Admiral Oshermeyer will have an initial operations order prepared in a few hours for your review, Senator, Mrs. Allen."

The military affairs committee chair simply nodded.

"If it's no inconvenience, Admiral," Mrs. Allen said with a smile. "I'd like to work directly with Admirals Oshermeyer and Pol, to observe your planning process."

"I'll see to it, ma'am."

"Good." Boyars rapped the conference table with a knuckle. "We're done here." He abruptly stood and gestured towards a surprised Mrs. Allen.

"One other thing, sir," she said. The senators and admirals watched her tone turned cold and impatient. As a strict tutor would with an impudent student. Boyars stopped in his tracks and sat back down. They had another hushed conversation, in a moment, Boyars sharply nodded again.

"Ah, yes," he said. Boyars turned towards the chief of staff. "Admiral, who is heading the media group assigned to Task Force Draken?"

"Uhn, give me a moment, sir." He turned to summon his Fleet Media Affairs officer over. The colonel scanned his data pad and turned it for the admiral to see.

"Capella Metropolitan Gazette of Poia-Istria has the duty for the Zone of the Interior, sir. Ah." He took the data pad himself and scrolled further. "Apollodoris J. Mortimer has two journalists and videographers with him."

"Just three journalists for an entire task force, Admiral? What would Praetor Kratari have said about that?" Boyars quipped.

"It makes sense, sir," Mrs. Allen said. "The bulk of media attention is on Vighandis. With the war winding down, the public is focusing on the troops coming home. The team's senior journalist is Poian, yes, but from Vizio, they're very close to Morgan's people in Chapuri. In fact, he's the one who coined the moniker, 'The Commodore'." She turned towards the officer. "Is he not, Colonel?"

"Uhn, yes, ma'am. I believe he was."

Boyars eyes narrowed again, he nodded towards the media relations colonel. "I know you. You anchored for some network in Borealis. Harper, right?"

"Harkness, sir. Yes. The Lysander Harkness Report. I'm a reservist, sir."

"Ah, good. We all have to do our bit."

Another tap from Mrs. Allen brought another hasty, murmured conversation. She made repeated gestures towards the reserve officer amid Boyars furtive glances at him. This time however, the audience was treated to a further display of his assertiveness.

"You're my assistant, Holly. She can help, but I expect you to handle it. Whatever you have to do, you do it." Boyars stood again and faced the chief of staff.

"I know A. J. Mortimer too. A nice cozy news media setup in the Commodore's favor. Well, I'm sorry ladies and gentlemen, but I'm asserting my authority in fleet-media relations in accordance with the War Canons."

The assemblage exchanged surprised glances.

"On my authority, I'm assigning Maria Hardesty of Denestri Information Group from Denestri-Comar as senior media embed to Task Force Draken. A. J. Mortimer and the others can stay, but Hardesty and the DIG will be the Draken's primaries until I say otherwise. Is that clear?" He scanned the room, looking past the glares of Admirals Oshermeyer and Pol and Colonel Harkness. No one in uniform could object to the security advisor's executive authority.

"Thank you, Admiral. Mrs. Allen will be the point of contact with my office on this matter from here on. "Keep a tight lid on our 'Praetor', Holly. Keep that maniac on a short leash."

***

Deadlines, Despots and Demigods.

Student Union in the Old Main, Commonwealth Leadership Academy, Degoa-Earth, Commonwealth Capital District. 03-02 of 770CE.

A young man stood on the right side of the auditorium, near the front, and asked the question Morgan had been hoping for. "Commodore, do you believe the Tantorans will reach out to us or one of the other leagues now that they've broken away from the Alliance?"

Commodore Gaven Webster Morgan leaned back in the comfortable, low-backed swivel. He exhaled audibly as he looked up into the ceiling in thought for a moment before he answered. His microphone picked it up.

"Yes. Yes I do. At some point in the future, I think we will be able to put our past behind us and do business. The Tantorans are a very talented people. They build good ships. I understand their economy is a bit shaky at the moment, with the breakaway and I'm sure there's going to be some turmoil as they readjust. They've been under Sacorsti domination for over five hundred years, so I would expect their foreign policy to be fairly tentative for a few years. The Patruscans and the Valerians, I'm sure, would be more than willing to establish ties with them."

"What about us, sir?" The superintendent, seated next to him in her role as moderator for the discussion asked.

The quiet young couple in the middle of the auditorium's third row, again caught Morgan's attention as they had from the very start of the session. They had applauded only half-heartedly compared to the much more animated applause and laughter from the more than a thousand students and faculty around them, after different answers or some of his more humorous quips over the last 50 minutes.

"I think it would be best if we wait a bit. We should let them decide to come to us. That's just my opinion of course, Madam Superintendent. I should probably leave foreign policy to the experts though." He smiled and flippantly waved the final comment off as it drew another burst of laughter from the audience. The young couple, however, merely exchanged glances. The man tilted his head and said something in the woman's ear that made her nod in apparent agreement.

100

The superintendent nodded and gestured towards the next member of the audience selected by one of the floor moderators. A young woman on the far left near the back row stood next to the moderator and spoke into his microphone.

"Commodore Morgan, I'm sure I speak for many of us here when I say, I want to apologize to you for the shabby and unprofessional treatment you and your officers received at the Senate Maranon hearings."

Applause rocked the auditorium. Morgan and everyone on stage was taken by surprise at the sudden outburst. Fully two-thirds of the audience leapt to their feet in a cheering ovation. Humbled and flushed with gratitude, G.W. Morgan looked around the stage at his and the superintendent's staff. His face a broad, beaming grin, he raised a hand slightly. In an instant, the auditorium hushed, and people took their seats.

"I, I thank you, miss. I thank you all, for your support," he said. "We here, my officers and I, Superintendent Faltea, her staff and faculty are all servants. We serve John Q. and Jane A. Commoner. That includes you. I personally strive to remind myself of that fact every day."

More applause erupted, Morgan smiled as his head lowered and turned the superintendent and back towards his officers before he continued.

"Regardless of what certain senators may believe about my business affairs or my clan, ladies and gentlemen, my officers, the men and women who command those stout ships and those good marines;" G.W.'s use of that celebrated term evoked another intense barrage of applause. "These officers are dedicated professionals. They are not non-conformists, and they are definitely not pirates or mercenaries."

Morgan's face hardened; he raised a forefinger for emphasis. "Awarding prize monies for captured ships and installations to these men and women and the troops under their command is one of our most ancient and honored traditions, ladies and gentlemen. Practically every Commoner tribe has carried the tradition over from their own pre-stellar histories. The rhetoric on that score during the hearings was just that, rhetoric. Its purpose was to make their utterers look good to the uninformed. Well, from your reactions and others I've seen and heard in the news, John and Jane Commoner rejected it out of hand."

The audience's applause told Morgan they heartily agreed with him. Still, the center couple sat stoic. One of the floor moderators angled their microphone towards an older gentleman, a few rows behind the quiet couple. The superintendent recognized the associate professor of political ethics as he stood.

"Professor Pa'are, if you please."

"Thank you, madam. Commodore, do you see Mr. Morales' election and the election of Statist majorities in Denestri, Camarone and other stellar states as the latest threat to Praetor Kratari's reforms? And if so, would a new Praetor, such as yourself, sir, have the constitutional authority to check a power grab within a Stellar State?"

Morgan chuckled at the suggestion. "A threat to Kratari's reforms? No. The notion is just the latest weak challenge to Kratari's reforms. I perceive it as the latest in a long line of attempts to ascribe rights to a government, beyond its enumerated authorities. For example, governments already have an enumerated authority to levy taxes, albeit limited to type and scope. A government is a body of citizens, hired and drawn together for the purpose of administering our civil infrastructure. By definition, they are collective entities, and cannot be ascribed individual rights. The Statists want to interpret the Constitution equating a government's authority to levy income tax to that of an individual's right of enterprise. That's a siren call, because neither the size of the levy nor the scope of any such interpretation would end there."

Professor Pa'are nodded and joined in the applause to Morgan's answer.

"And professor, I think that permanent Praetor issue is dead," he said. "The whole concept of a Praetorship is predicated on the Commonwealth being in a dire set of circumstances, derived from either an internal or external threat to all, or a majority of our tribes. Fortunately, that set of circumstances did not materialize, thanks to the actions of the battle group commanders and troops of Task Force Draken and the rest of the Common Fleet." Morgan waved his arm to his left and rear, towards his cruiser commanders. The gesture drew another round of applause.

"To my mind, that makes the constitutional amendment question moot. But to answer your question directly, a Commonwealth Chief Executive or a Praetor would not have the authority to interfere with the internal affairs of a stellar state, unless and until those affairs posed a substantial threat to the rest of the Common States."

Morgan smiled as the professor nodded in agreement.

"Just between us, professor, I'm mighty glad I audited the political ethics curriculum when I was stationed here some years ago. Good course," he said, tapping a forefinger to the side of his head. "It stuck."

The comment drew chuckles from around the room.

"One thing though, at least occasionally, some of our elected representatives at the stellar state and league level forget that they are but stewards of this great estate we call the Commonwealth of Stellar States. They are hired by the masters, John Q. and Jane A. Commoner, to manage the estate. We give them the power to regulate, but we control those regulations with mandatory, third-party, effectiveness evaluations. We give them the power to levy one tax on our consumption, but only one, and only on our consumption, and we cap that levy at a total of fifteen percent. Even in our darkest hours, Commoners, only once, has that rate even approached eleven percent!"

Thunderous applause filled the auditorium again.

"We keep the majority of that tax revenue at the municipal level, where it most benefits us, Commoners. We apportion the remainder upwards via a diminishing scale through the levels of government. Every master, every one of us, Commoners, every John and Jane pays his fair share to support our infrastructures through which we all trade and communicate across the known galaxy in real time, regardless of our separate calendars."

He shifted in his chair looking across the audience. His hands made small, open gestures as he spoke.

"We Commoners are the masters of our manors, we collectively enforce the five individual freedoms, thought, speech, association, assembly, and enterprise. We achieve symbiosis while being creative in our own self-interest. We all prosper because we, the Commoners, control our government's power to tax. Our government servants receive exactly what they enumerate in their legislative budget processes, no more, no less for their fiscal periods. And we keep close watch on them through an aggressive, objective, accurate and timely news media that is beholden to us for their livelihoods."

G.W. was enjoying this. He found he had stood and was walking along the stage. All the while using his hand gestures to stress one point or another.

"Sometimes, some of our politicians, not only at the league level, but at every one of the five levels of representation gets a notion into their heads to assume the role of master. But to do that they need to control news and information, and they need a permanent, uninterrupted power source, fuel, as it were. For a government, that means an unlimited flow of money. And there are only two ways to get it. Confiscate it through taxes on income, from whatever source, without appropriation, or counterfeit it."

He talked his way back to his chair. Superintendent Faltel was smiling.

"The Individual is sovereign over the state in the Commonwealth of Stellar States, that's why there's a hundred and sixty-one of us; encompassing three hundred thirty-six worlds." He waved an arm across his front, arcing across the applauding assemblage. "Five thousand six hundred seventeen independent, yet cooperative nation-states, city-states and provinces. All of them represented in this room."

Applause filled the room again.

"The comments made about me during the hearings reference a coup d'état, and permanent military dictatorship were election year political red meat, nothing more. We all know from our own global tribes' histories that no good can come from government being our master and we, Commoners, its working servants."

G.W.'s right arm rested across his lap, his left elbow atop his right hand. His left hand, however, continued to keep time as he spoke.

"Across the five levels of representation, from the Municipal Mayor and Council to the trans-stellar Chief Executive, Privy Council and Senate, our governments administer our police and public safety, our armies and our fleets, but they belong to us, the Commoner, not to the State. It's for that very reason that we in the Common Fleet affirm in our commissioning or enlistment oath to defend the Commoner and support the Constitution, in that order. We stand and affirm alone, in front of our mates, our officers and our families. The hearings brought the facts out, and common sense prevailed, at least for now."

G.W.'s closing comment drew more applause, and this time a hint of animation from the quiet couple. On his left, in the corner of his eye, Morgan noticed his chief of staff, Colonel Debra Rivas checking something on her wrist pad just before she leaned over to whisper in his ear.

"Admiral O wants to see us at Ops straight away when we arrive on Demeos, sir."

"Okay, Debra." Morgan turned and spoke softly to the CLA Superintendent. "Looks like duty calls, Natasha. Vince Oshermeyer wants to see me at Blue House."

The superintendent had heard Rivas. "We can wrap up now, Commodore. It's been a great success. The kids so love these Informals."

"I do too actually," Morgan answered grinning. "No lecture notes to prepare. No exams to grade. Lovely. Lovely."

The superintendent stood and announced the closure of the session. Abruptly, the quiet man raised his hand. Seeing his hand go up, Morgan pointed him out for one final question. The floor moderator nearest him stepped back over in the young student's direction and directed the microphone towards him.

"Thank you. Thank you, Commodore for taking my question."

"My pleasure."

The young man smiled, the young woman with him produced a PtC and began recording her friend and Morgan's interaction.

"Sir, I followed the constitutional amendment process until it was tabled by the Senate committee and the Maranon hearings with great interest." He gestured towards his friend. "We both did. Sir, during the entire time, no one directly asked you this question. Sir, would you accept a Praetorship, if offered, and further, would you hold the office for life?"

Morgan smiled a little and stroked his chin in thought for a moment." The auditorium hushed.

"You know, son, you're right. You are the first person to ask me that question directly. I'll say this. Hypothetically, of course. If offered the Praetorship for life," he smiled broadly. "I'd take it. I'd keep the Gladius and name my estalon Hercules as heir-apparent. I would rule by decree from astride his back. But," he held up a forefinger for emphasis. "Every day, the Commoners would know who is really in charge, when they see me cleaning his stable."

The auditorium erupted in a loud, long burst of laughter and applause.

"We've got about twenty minutes to make it out to the exo-drome, sir," Colonel Rivas whispered with a wide grin.

"Okay, Debra, let's get rolling."

As the assembly concluded, Morgan's primary staff and commanders stood from their chairs to attention, the assemblage stood in ovation when he gladial saluted his fellow commoners. Class cheers thundered throughout the venerable student union when he dropped his salute and gave the room one of his characteristic hand waves as he led his staff off the stage.

"Creator's blessings on you, G W!" someone yelled over the din from somewhere in the audience.

"You too!" Morgan shouted back with a broad grin and another wave.

***

Arrivals terminal, Popularum City Municipal Exo-drome, on Saluri-Demeos, Commonwealth Capital District.

The sign above the gantry portal reading 'Welcome to Demeos' in five languages changed to another set of five at ten-second intervals. The portal's embedded sensory suite scanned each debarking shuttle passenger. The gate steward and her assistant stood at their podium across from the portal and verified each passenger's recognition features with the Degoa-Earth to Saluri-Demeos shuttle manifest as they emerged into the concourse. Her screen framed each Commoner's image and data in green, or blue for foreigners. From her console, she updated their reservations and itineraries as needed and, where necessary, their immigration and customs information. The woman's smile brightened as Maria Hardesty stepped through the portal.

"Welcome back to Demeos, Miss Hardesty."

"Oh, thank you, Angelina!"

Maria Hardesty wasn't surprised at being greeted by name at a Demeos exo-drome arrival gate. Not anymore. She had come to know many of the Polaris Shuttle Service flight crews and terminal personnel during her frequent capital district visits.

"Uhn, a moment please, Miss, Miss Hardesty, ma'am," the steward's assistant hesitantly asked. The young man wore the company white button down shirt with a bright red company tie, crisp blue trousers and highly shined shoes. He stepped tentatively forward with a hard cover literary in hand. Maria blushed a little, seeing it was a copy of her first bestseller.

'Miss Hardesty, may I have your autograph?" he asked presenting the open literary and a stylus.

Her vibrating wrist pad caught her attention as passengers streamed by noting the scene. Three of whom having had the young man's experience during the four hour flight across the Capital District.

'Waiting for you here at Baggage Claim. There's been some changes in your assignment that I think you'll like. Mason.'

Damn, he could've just sent a POV and driver. Why did he have to come himself? She wondered. She hated that part of being a journalist for the DIG. Looking the man over in front of her, she enjoyed this part of her being an author.

"Have you read it?" she stared up at the tall, slender steward.

"Yes M, Miss I have, cover to cover."

Maria smiled seeing the pages were in fact, well thumbed, with certain key passages highlighted or underlined. "You really did!" she exclaimed. "I'd be happy to sign this for you, uh, Trainee. Is that your name?" she jokingly asked.

Passing passengers witnessing the exchange applauded, others recorded the remarkable event. The 'Dragon Lady' autographed a literary copy and posed for photos without peppering a person with questions about, 'Never Let the Bastards See You're Scared!'

**

Jordan Mason, the DIG's managing editor for governmental affairs greeted Maria in his usual crisp, efficient manner.

"Any other luggage?" he asked as he took the larger of her two bags and set it in his utility roadster's back hatch.

"No, Jordan, just these two and my side bag," she answered, tapping the slender case containing her data pad, recorder and personals. Maria put the smaller bag in next to it and the rear cargo hatch slid closed.

She admired the POV's smooth angular lines and deep sheen as Mason led her around to the passenger door just then sliding open. It slid shut as she settled into the forward passenger seat. Mason came around and climbed into the operator seat, the door slid shut, activating the vehicle. The engine purred to life; the controller extended to a standby position in front of him.

"This is one of the new Zephyrs isn't it?" Maria asked, looking around the spacious interior. Four of the vehicle's six passenger seats were folded away in evidence of Mason's preparations.

"Yes."

"The company treats you well."

"Actually it's my wife's, she's a nurse," he admitted in his matter-of-fact tone. "I stopped at home to pick it up. I was coming to get you in my roadster, but I thought you may have more baggage. A simple precaution," he said.

"I travel light," Maria quipped.

Mason cracked a smile at that. "Pharsus, the Philmor Arms, River Street lobby entrance, command."

"Complying, music?"

"Yes, Pharsus. Travel track, command."

"Complying."

A children's ditty accompanied by a plinking keyboard filled the interior at a conversational level. Mason quickly switched it off, smiling. Grippers closed over their shoulders and hips, securing Maria and Mason in their seats.

"Wife and kids, Jordan," Maria chuckled.

Mason adjusted the sound track manually and found more appropriate, grown-up music.

The Zephyr signaled its intention, pavement nodes recognized the vehicle's signature and interacted. Linked through the nodes to other vehicles, it merged into traffic in the travel lanes departing the terminal.

"So what are these changes in my assignment, Jordan? I've picked up some leads about Maranon I want to follow up on," Maria said.

"Oh, really? At the archives?"

"No," she answered. "Whatever they have there is locked up tight." Her voice tinged with a hint of both frustration and optimism.

Exiting the exo-drome outer perimeter and accelerating towards the 160kph highway limit, the Zephyr merged with

Motorway 6 north-bound traffic towards the capital district. Cypress trees lining the curving north-south highway flashed past. Beyond the trees, to the east, green cultivated fields zipped past their panels, bordered by alternating patches of the snow-capped Taunus Mountains' forested foothills and valleys. As the cypresses passed into the distance behind them towards Saluri's ever-brooding face, more of Popularum City's skyline came into view through the hills ahead.

"I caught the Deputy Fleet Historian coming out of the archives a few days ago. I got a line on two marines who were called to testify at the Maranon hearings. They're assigned to some special unit I never heard of."

"What unit is that?" Mason asked.

"Something called Recondo. Have you heard of it?"

"No. That's a new one. Probably something ad hoc they threw together at the last minute."

Trees on the west screened pastoral farms and vineyards that dotted the plain from south-bound traffic along the Motorway. Beyond, the Ayoette Canal and Lake Ayoette's crystal waters shimmered in Macillus' light. As usual during the drive from the exo-drome to town, Maria caught fleeting glimpses of Zip Line mass transit cars and heavy lorrys emerging between tunnels through hills along the rail-links between the surface POV and light lorry lanes.

"It didn't sound like some scrapped together outfit. He made it sound like it's been around for a long time. It has something to do with a unit called Spetznax."

"I've heard of them, trained killers, middle-of-the-night raiders. Istrians from Poia mostly. Been around since the second war."

"Hmm. Some hush-hush outfit for Morgan and his gang to play with. Assassination squads maybe?" she quipped.

"Not even Morgan stoops that low, Maria. That's our board of governors' kind of talk. But they are definitely a raiding force though. You'll be able to follow up when you get back from orientation."

"Orientation to what?"

"The Fleet. You're taking over the Task Force Draken media embeds."

"What?! When did you decide this?"

"I didn't. The Board called a couple of hours ago. Jo Boyars threw his weight around in some briefing with the Admiralty this morning. He nearly blew a gasket when he heard A. J. Mortimer was leading the team deploying with Morgan's task force."

"Good old Apollodoris Jefferson Mortimer. I'm replacing Morgan's biggest cheerleader?"

"Not exactly, you're taking over the team."

"How does A. J. feel about that?"

"Do you care?"

"Hell no," she snorted with a grin. "Hey, wait a minute, I'm a politico. I'm not a military journalist. I've never been a Fleet embed."

"That's what I said when the Board called me. As it turns out, same with Mortimer. You'll both have to go through training before you report to the task force."

"Basic training, Jordan!"

"Just ten VET days of it, actually. Structure of the fleet, basic vessel familiarization, uniform and equipment issue, that kind of stuff."

Maria huffed. "Weapons training, IHEA suits, evacuation suits, and Creator knows, Fleet history. Marching around, calisthenics. All that, *'No more Task Force Libertys'*, all that, *'Karen Stone Up'* nonsense!"

She folded her arms in a huff, looking out at the countryside giving way to Popularum's suburban sprawl. The POV slowed below the 112kph municipal limit. Light industrial facilities, mixed with two and three story merchants fronted tree-lined, residential side streets.

Advertisements in the pavement nodes located the Zephyr's signature and alerts for several made it through the preference filters. They queued up on both side panel windows. Maria ignored them; Mason tapped the third icon on his panel.

A GWM Cinematique corporate logo filled the multi-vision viewer panel in the center of the dashboard. The image morphed into a scene of two women in 5th Century Commonwealth Marine deck duty uniform dueting a still popular 300 year-old song to the rousing accompaniment of a crowd of marines.

'Reach in your soul for the answer.'

'Find it. Have faith it'll pull you through.

"Get on your feet!" Mason softly sang the next verse in chorus with the women, surprising Maria. She smiled and couldn't help joining in. They sang together. The POV lowered the cinema trailer voice-over's volume to conversation level. Mason waved the volume back up a little.

'Get up and take control.'

'Get on your feet!'

'Stand up. Make something happen.'

'Get on your feet!"

"I didn't know you were a Karen Stone aficionado."

Lowering the volume, Mason smiled. "It wasn't her song, she just liked it so much. Nobody knows where it came from."

"Probably a Dopper," Maria said.

"A Dopper? What's that?"

"That's what the people at the archives call those broadcasts the deep observation posts have been picking up and translating since they first started operating."

"Oh," Mason said, nodding. "Never heard of that term, but Earthers are like that, always making up words."

"Is that a Saluri dig, Jordan? From you?"

"It just slipped."

"We're Denestri, Jordan," Maria scolded him, turning her seat towards him. "We're not Salurian or Degoan, and that war was almost a thousand years ago."

"My wife is Salurian, It's their home world overhead. It's a constant reminder," he said with a shrug. "You live here long enough; you pick up a few of their prejudices. Especially this time of year, with the planets at perihelion. Anyway, I don't know any veteran who hasn't had *'Get on yer feet'* or *'Make something happen'* yelled in their ear at least once. You'll get used to it. Hell, you already know how to *Karen Stone Up*. *'Never Let the Bastards See You Cry'* is a great literary, Maria. You'll handle the fleet. I see your sales are up again. It'll be what, your third best-seller? Congratulations."

"Well thank you, boss," she said grinning, with a nod towards him.

The trailer morphed through a series of scenes depicting the heroic 5th Century marine corporal, Praetor Kratari and Commodore Macksey. Iconic scenes of the great trans-stellar conflict flashed and faded.

'See her as they did. See G.W. Morgan's 'The Praetor and the Second Alliance War', coming soon to theaters near you!'

The image faded as the Zephyr merged onto the Capital Avenue in the diplomatic quarter. The municipal areas gave way to colonnaded brick and marble buildings separated by parks and tree-lined avenues with ornate hotels and walled diplomatic compounds. The Zephyr slowed to District limit, 40kph. As usual in the Capital District, crowds of consular employees bustled about among the shops, cafés and sidewalks taking advantage of clear skies in Macillus' warmth, under Saluri's sad eyes, after the daily, mid-spring morning shower.

They all knew, like Maria, Jordan or any Commoner or foreigner stationed here, the swirling, multi-colored, radioactive clouds of Demeos' dead mother world, Saluri, was the reason the seat of Commonwealth government, the House of the Thousand Flags, was here.

"Your flattery is noted. So, what access do I get?"

"Virtually unfettered," Jordan answered raising a forefinger for emphasis. "Remember though, operational considerations will always have priority. You'll coordinate all your journalists' activities with the task force chief of staff. Some colonel named Rivas. The basics are in the briefing packet. Your team has unfettered access to the crews."

"What about my access to Morgan?"

"That's the virtually part..."

"Operational considerations always have priority..." she answered for herself in unison with Mason.

"I can assign Mortimer, ah, I mean my team anywhere I want?"

"It's your team, Maria. A Common Fleet task force has at least twenty ships. The admiralty attaches smaller units to make them as big as they need to. Counting battle cruisers, troop transports, destroyers and all, Morgan normally commands at least fifty thousand troops."

"More than enough to secure this capital if he wanted. And so damned close."

"There you go again."

Maria raised a hand, tempering her rhetoric. "I know, I know. He's no coup d'état threat, like Boyars and the rest of Morales' cronies in the Senate claimed in the hearings. But," she paused and sighed. "I don't trust him. He bribes his way to being recalled to active duty. He shoots his mouth off about, what was it? 'Re-Re-organizing' the fleet, in the middle of the war. The admirals all peed their pants and gave him want he wanted. And then off he goes," she vented, making a flippant gesture into the air. "To the rescue, saving our collective asses in Trudan."

Jordan Mason knew well his star investigative journalist's frustration. He knew better than to interrupt her as her mind churned through the remarkable chain of events leading to what had turned out to be the decisive campaign of the current war. The last shots of which, they knew from the morning news were being launched at Alliance forces trapped in Vighandis at that very moment.

"I just don't get it, Jordan!" She sliced the air in front of her with a knife-edged hand gesture.

"So if he broke the Alliance's back in Trudan, why go to Aletia-Maranon? No one had ever heard of Aletia, Jordan. The Maranites weren't enlightened!"

"That's not true, Maria." He took a chance. "They'd been invaded and occupied."

"Well, alright. But by so few Kritt troops. Why bother? And the admiralty. He had them so frazzled they practically danced in the streets when they announced it. So if it was so momentous, why the information blackout?"

"For the sake of the Maranite people, they said," Mason offered.

"My ass." Maria waved the thought off. She folded her arms and gazed out the panels at shops and city traffic. "Maybe they're hiding something."

"Did you talk to the Embeds who were assigned to Task Force Draken at the time?"

"No. That's another thing, Jordan. They're all retired! At generous pensions in exchange for their silence. According to Marcel."

"Who's that?"

"Oh, the fleet historian, deputy historian rather."

"First name basis?"

"I fucked him twice," she chuckled. "I'd better be."

"Say no more," Mason grinned, shaking his head.

"Oh, but there's plenty more," she turned to him to continue her recitation of facts.

Mason watched her in admiration, her eyes squinted, her black and silver bangs shifted with her crinkling brow. She was on the hunt. He loved it.

"I got those names, those marine recondo whatevers, Bittrich and Romanov, and a couple of ships, *Condor* and *Yulan*."

"Never heard of *Condor*, but *Yulan*. That's a transport. I remember, it's part of Morgan's task force. The war is still going on, Maria. A lot of the crews and marines that were there are probably still with the force."

"Good. Good. I'll track those lowlifes down and get the scoop on Morgan's dirty deeds on Maranon, while he's doing this next mission. What is it anyway?"

"Damned if I know. The Board was really tight-lipped about that. Just that they wanted you there."

"So when do I have to be, wherever this orientation is?"

"You can take a couple of days to relax. You, A. J. and the rest of your crew will report to Gabb'es-Sestria reception station on the tenth. Then you'll join the task force at depot nineteen in Piraeus on the twenty-third."

"Piraeus, the beast's lair. But Gabb'es? Really? We Commoners pay good coin, training our armies in the resort capital of the Commonwealth. Sweet."

"Not Sestria, dearie," Mason smirked. "Sestria is the outermost of the habitable zone worlds there. The sixth. It's temperate, but cold. It's nowhere near as lush as the main planets. They say Sestria and its moons is the perfect place to train Commoner infantry. Perfectly miserable."

"And you're a veteran."

"Whoa, I'm a Denestri Stellar State Guard veteran. I was patriotic, but I wasn't a fool. The Common Fleet is the last refuge for most of the ner'e do wells, Maria. Their ships are old, and dirty, this is what people tell me. The crews, they can be pretty rough. So you watch yourself. Stay close to the officers."

"I hate you, Jordan."

***

'You have got to get this situation under control, Admiral,' an angry Edgar Morales boomed. His pacing HG image gestured at the video monitor with Commodore Morgan's frozen image on its screen in his background.

'The cease-fire negotiations are at a critical stage. And now I've had to inform Senators Jamison and Hanash of the *Retnec* situation and those tribes in AEWX oh double four nine. They're livid that I didn't inform them sooner.'

Joachim Boyars' image uncrossed his legs and shifted his body in the arm chair in the background.

'How dare they burst in here like that, sir! Haranguing and lecturing you! It was totally disrespectful.'

'That's not important now, Jo.' Morales waved the thought of an informer off. 'And now this! Admiral! Did you hear what this madman Morgan is saying?!' 'He has the unmitigated gall to use that CLA forum to demand the Gladius! AND THEY'RE CHEERING AND BLESSING HIM!!'

"Mr. Morales, I assure you, this video is a fake!" the chief of staff responded.

'What are you saying, Admiral?'

"I saw it myself on MV at lunch, sir. I called him direct on his shuttle frequency. He related to me the full question and his complete answer. He said he was illustrating the absurdity of the question by being absurd. I tell you, sir, Morgan has been the target of a deliberate smear. Someone obviously edited his flippant answer to that hypothetical question, sir."

'That's the most ridiculous thing I've ever heard, Admiral,' Boyars' image said. 'Whatever he was trying to do, it didn't work,' he chortled.

Mrs. Allen closed her PtC and walked back to the chair across from the Admiral's desk before she joined the HG conference.

"Mr. Morales, I've just spoken with Superintendent Faltea. She, her deputies, and Morgan's senior officers were with him the entire time. They remember the question and the Commodore's answer."

CE Morales stopped pacing. He looked at her and folded his arms.

"The news media has been duped, sir. I have no doubt of that. The couple involved are not CLA students, sir. They had guest passes from a community college on Treluna Province."

'Are they sure, Holly? It's only been four hours since it appeared in the trans-stellar web and the Eatoni Middays are already running with the story. Two of the Borealis evening editorials have asked us for statements.'

"Yes, sir. Faltea said the constables are aware the two were using counterfeit identities. Academy Security matched the pair to Gaylord District Municipal Constabulary files over on Treluna, sir. They both have fairly extensive records. It's a matter now for Capital District Constabulary here. The District Prosecutor is filing a non-bailable warrant request for political disinformation, sir. Constables will pick them up for questioning in the meantime."

The Chief Executive looked visibly relieved.

'That man is drawing the very oxygen from the room of every committee meeting in the District, Admiral. The safest thing for us and for Morgan is to get him out of here, before he really does say something stupid. I don't care how you do it, Admiral. But send him back to Tresium, TONIGHT!'

The CE's image dropped. The admiral stood and walked away from his desk. He sighed, casting a sullen look at Mrs. Allen, and gestured towards the office door.

"We'll take my lift-tram down to the situation room mezzanine, ma'am."

"Lift-tram?"

"Yes, ma'am. The situation room itself is fifty meters below the surface and is offset quite a distance from this building. For obvious reasons."

He looked tired to her. It had been a long war. He appeared ill at ease in his uncertain new role with her and Boyars. He was receiving little or no support from the Military Affairs Committee and, worst of all, he was rapidly losing the respect and loyalty of his senior deputies, Admirals Oshermeyer and Pol.

"Understand, Admiral." She looked at him in sympathy, and in expectation of a little herself. "I'm only doing my job."

"Of course, I do understand. It's Boyars who doesn't," the admiral huffed. "And that Morgan has always been a giant pain in my ass! I never thought he wanted the Praetorship. He wants my job! But he's not going to get it. I'll retire him. For good this time!"

The admiral cleared his office in quick strides, but nearly walked into the door that barely slid open in time for him to pass through. His secretary and aide lifted their heads and sprang to their feet as he and Mrs. Allen walked past them.

"Sir, Commodore Morgan and his staff are in the situation room, as you ordered."

"Yeah, yeah. Tell Oshermeyer we're on our way down," he mumbled, passing through the outer office to the lift.

**

"Mrs. Allen has been working with us in developing Oplan Dragoon, Commodore," the chief of staff said, introducing her to Commodore Morgan.

"I'm glad to finally meet you, Mrs. Allen, I've read a good deal of your work with the Colonial Institute," Morgan said smiling, shaking her hand. "My chief of staff, Colonel Debra Rivas."

"A pleasure, Mrs. Allen," Rivas said, shaking the statuesque woman's hand.

"My Command Sergeant Major, Chester Morris."

"Ma'am," CSM Morris grunted. He shook her hand, looking down into her stern grey eyes.

Mrs. Allen turned back to Morgan. "I'm very glad to meet you too, Commodore." She was as tall as he was. They eyed each other, each watching the other's movements like prize fighters in the opening seconds of a match.

"Before we begin, Admiral," Mrs. Allen interrupted, clearly taking charge. "I'd like to ask the Commodore a question if I may."

"Certainly, ma'am," the admiral said.

She turned to Morgan as she took the swivel on the chief of staff's left, Admiral Pol's usual seat. As they took seats around the inactive multi plot, Morgan and his immediate staff flanking him, all noted with interest how the admirals had all acquiesced to the security advisor's executive assistant. So did Morgan's battle group commanders settling into seats in the gallery above.

"At your service, ma'am," Morgan said.

"Thank you, Commodore. If you please. Can you tell me how it is you come to the conclusion the Valerians will demand a cease-fire line based on, what is it?" She tapped her wrist pad and squinted. "Oh nine oh one V-E-T. What reason would the Valerians

117

have to want to push the Sacorsti so far back? That's their original start line from Bavat."

"That's exactly right, ma'am; and there lies your reason."

"I don't understand, Commodore."

"Simple, ma'am. Admiral, may I borrow your map?"

"Be my guest. Raise the Plot. Respond to Commodore Morgan's direction."

The holographic image illuminated, blossoming to the Common Stellar States Administrative Zone default.

"Thank you, sir. Raise the Trudan to Spice Alley to Vighandis front line trace of zero six hundred hours, zero nine of zero one of this year, void equivalent time."

The alignment of Alliance and Commonwealth forces facing one another across the three battle theaters before the Alliance's latest, unsuccessful incursion filled the image. The image depicted Commonwealth units in blue, Sacorsti and Alliance forces in red.

"Display the southwest of the Valerian panhandle region and the corresponding region of the Tantoran heliosphere. Display the trans-stellar grav wave pattern across the entire region."

The HG morphed in compliance. Mrs. Allen, the Admirals, and the gallery attendants above, all sat in rapt attention.

"Once you see a pattern, Mrs. Allen, ladies and gentlemen, you can't just un-see it. It'll jump out at you every time." Morgan picked up the photonic tracing rod at his swivel and traced the grav wave pattern. "A cease fire line there will push the Alliance hard up against Bavat and Vega on their side, ma'am."

Admiral Oshermeyer saw it straight away. Looking around the mezzanine. He caught sight of CSM Morris' smirk. The admiral folded his arms and put a hand to his chin. His fingers covered his grin as he shook his head. Admiral Pol looked across Mrs. Allen and the Chief at him, then at the plot, then to Morgan, she got it. Morgan nodded at her.

"It opens a direct, high-speed trade route, protected by our presence in Vighandis on our side, from Eysamon into the heart of a six-world advanced stellar state, with tremendous economic potential, ma'am."

"Unbelievable. It was right in front of us all the time," Pol said.

Neither the chief of staff nor Mrs. Allen had the faintest idea what the others all saw. Morgan raised the photon rod and highlighted the Ostari-Eysamon depot in the Valerian panhandle, then dragged the rod across the map directly to Tantori. Mrs. Allen got it.

"That's a direct transit wave, straight to Tantori," she exclaimed.

"Not a single accelerative fly-by is required off any other heliosphere, ma'am, coming or going from Eysamon in the Valerian panhandle to Mynos in Tantori," Morgan said.

It was only then the chief of staff nodded in understanding.

"That's why the Valerians are assisting the Patruscans," Mrs. Allen huffed.

"I couldn't think of a better reason, ma'am. I'm sure they suggested it to the Patruscans."

"Of that, I have no doubts, Commodore. It opens another route for them to the Trinovans in the north and the Asigi in the southeast."

"The savings in vessel transit fees alone means good profits to all concerned, ma'am," Morgan quipped, retracting the photon rod.

"What do we get out of this?"

"The opportunity to not shoot at someone for the first time in four years for starters, ma'am. In-roads to the Tantorans ourselves in due time. A permanent chasm between the Sacorsti and the Shafirans on one side, the Kritt and Astarene on the other. More of the minor Alliance states like Vega and Bavat and even Karel can be exposed to CCID Freedom of Information broadcasts."

"Well, thank you, Commodore. I've learned something. I'll be quiet now."

Morgan smiled, nodding towards her. "My pleasure, ma'am. Transfer the plot."

The HG morphed to the default CAZ map, awaiting its next command.

"Good," the chief of staff said. "Now, Commodore, I'm assigning you to conduct Operation Dragoon. First however, we need to discuss your PDRE requirement. I'm sending you to Lucainus-Phuong, for your PDRE, its enroute to your jump-off point for your mission."

"Phuong Battle School, sir? Yes, sir." *Lovely, lovely.*

Morgan thought for a second. "Admiral, in that case, I request my primary evaluation to be the battle group forced entry into Phuong-Yeuin range," he announced.

Oshermeyer and Pol both saw G.W.'s ploy for what it was, they watched in silence as their admiral walked into Morgan's hasty ambush. The chief of staff sat back in his swivel. His head tilted back, his mouth open, his eyes went wide. He blinked and shook his head in disbelief.

"You're asking to commit professional suicide, Commodore. As well as sacrificing one of your group commanders. You've selected the toughest pre-deployment test in the Common Stellar Fleet!" He shook his head. "No one has ever done that battle task to standard, Commodore! Not the Lucainans themselves, and they built it! Not the Istrians, not even the Valerians that have visited Phuong."

Admiral Oshermeyer exhaled heavily, seated on the chief's right, across the plot table from Morgan, Colonel Rivas, and Command Sergeant Major Morris. He shook his head as he keyed his panel. The HG morphed into the Lucainan moon training area. The frontal oblique aerial view of the notorious Phuong-Yeuin seaside battle village came into view. The image moved slowly from south to north along the dreaded, twisting, 18 kilometer long, 'Happy Valley', from the exo-drome and on up steep bluffs into a sprawling town.

"The Battle School standard requires you to seize the exo-drome and the town within fifty hours, while sustaining no more than twenty percent casualties, Commodore."

Admiral Pol and Mrs. Allen looked on, listening. Oshermeyer leaned forward. "No one has done it without sustaining less than thirty-eight percent. It's a go or no go scenario, G.W., if this is your primary, the entire Task Force has to be rated non-deployable if that one Battle Group sustains more than twenty percent casualties!" Oshermeyer said. He had done his part.

"It'll be an opportunity for Stefan and the marines to excel," Morgan quipped. "Eh, Sergeant Major?"

"That's a hard row to hoe, suh," Morris grunted.

The chief of staff pointed at the most experienced soldier around the plot, nodding his endorsement. Task Force Draken's Command Sergeant Major, Morgan's 'avenging angel and right arm', folded his arms, squinting, in deep thought at the slowly rotating image. No one spoke as he craned his neck and head, getting a good look.

Admiral Pol spoke up. "Kratari's old cavalry unit is part of the opposing force in that scenario, Commodore." She nodded towards Mrs. Allen as she spoke, including her in the conversation. "There's a lot of unit pride involved in being 'undefeated on their home turf', as they say."

Morris waved an arm towards the different terrain features in the plot. "Ah ain't sayin' it cain't be done, Admiral." His arm fluoresced in varying colors in the photonic stream. "You see what I see, Commodore, Colonel?"

Morgan, Colonel Rivas and the others followed his arm along the photonic map board.

"Lovely. Yes," Morgan said with a sly grin. "Stefan can handle it,"

Colonel Debra Rivas shrugged; trepidation clear on her face. "No pressure, sir."

"Yes Admiral. My command battle group, led by *CBC Draken*, will show the Fleet how it's done."

*

It was Commander Phillipe Stefan's turn to sit, eyes wide, his mouth agape, shaking his head in disbelief. He and the other cruiser battle group commanders watched from the gallery above. The other two commanders could only shake their heads and his hand in macabre gestures of congratulations.

*

Mrs. Allen did not like what she was hearing. "Help me to understand this. If one of your groups fails this, this, forced entry exercise, your entire task force is declared non-deployable? Well that's just ridiculous. I won't stand for it, Admiral. This mission is too important!" She stopped herself, remembering the secrecy admonishment. "Humph." Then she realized what Morgan had done. She turned towards the chief of staff. "Can't you waive that requirement, Admiral?"

The admiral saw he had been hoodwinked. "Not without raising more questions than it's worth, ma'am." The full impact of what was happening was just hitting him. "Mr. Boyars' restrictions tie my hands."

The chief of staff fidgeted, rubbing his chin in frustration, looking directly at G.W. Morgan.

121

"Commodore, your request is denied. Your Task Force will seize and clear Phuong-Yeuin and the Phuong-Alpha asteroid station as supporting operations for your primary evaluation. That will be, the interception, board and seizure of a suspect vessel. You may assign your battle group missions as you see fit. You must accomplish each task within the Battle School time and proficiency standards. However, your units' casualties must not exceed the overall Fleet average per battle task."

Morgan's response was a foregone conclusion.

"May I ask the reason for this, Admiral?"

The chief of staff turned to Mrs. Allen with an 'I told you so' look on his face.

"Damn," Mrs. Allen muttered. "Alright, tell him. But clear the room first."

The chief of staff gestured to Admiral Oshermeyer.

"Commodore, I'm going to have to ask you to have your battle group commanders and sergeant major wait in the lounge."

Now it was Morgan's turn to be stunned. Oshermeyer's and Pol's stern looks told him he had no choice. Turning and looking up into the gallery, he tilted his head and nodded. Without a word, the three commanders, their master chiefs and operations officers stood and left the gallery, sealing the outer door behind them. Morgan grabbed Chester Morris by the arm and stared defiantly at Mrs. Allen.

"I can brief my commanders, but my right arm stays with me."

Mrs. Allen leaned forward to speak, then thought better. She nodded and gestured towards Admiral Oshermeyer.

"Task Force Draken will proceed administratively to a region no closer than two stellar astronomic units of DOP two niner seven's outer beacon line. Upon arrival, TF Draken will rendezvous with, and attach the CD *Karen L. Stone the Second* group.

"You will coordinate with CCID personnel at DOP two nine seven and determine the best possible course to intercept and capture the *Aglifiate Research Vessel, Retnec*, somewhere in sector AEWX zero-four-four- nine, no later than the first day of the tenth month of seven seventy CE, void equivalent time."

Stunned, Morgan's eyes went wide. He leaned back in his

swivel and looked to Mrs. Allen. Her face betrayed nothing, then she gave him a, *'Yes, it's true,'* nod.

"TF Draken will return to the Commonwealth Administrative Zone with all research, data, and crew aboard *Retnec*. You will take appropriate action in the event *Retnec's* movement to the CAZ proves impractical.

"Additional instructions relative to reconnaissance of unenlightened technical tribes located in the region will follow in separate orders under the code name Dragoon two."

"Well I'll be damned," Morgan muttered.

The admiral cleared his throat before continuing, noting the chief of staff's nodding approval.

"No discussion of this mission order with subordinate commanders is authorized, until such authority is issued by the office of the Chief Executive. Prior to such authority, ALL, repeat, ALL information and orders will be classified 'Top Secret, Close Compartmented'. What are your questions pertaining to your orders, Commodore?" Oshermeyer concluded.

Morgan cleared his throat, exchanging glances with Rivas, Morris, Pol and Oshermeyer. "Well I'll be damned."

****

The Citadel, Sacor II-New Laconia.

The Madonna retired early for the night, alone. That made the guards nervous. They knew what that meant. Sentinels at their posts watched their sector, and only their sector. On the ridge above, deep in the Teurel fortress, no one in the Ready Reaction Platoon billets made jokes about her lovers. The inactive shift could claim the ignorance of sleep.

None of the 120 Waffen-Strelski marines of the Madonna's personal guard shift tonight wanted to see her gyrations or hear her ranting. The less they knew about her visitations the less likely they were to be accused of revealing them. The guards knew, they themselves would not be punished for such a crime; that would be too easy. The guard's family would suffer instead.

In the Citadel's security station control room, the platoon leader on duty contacted her commander while her three Gefreiters turned their monitor and headset volumes down. They reset their viewers to thermal around the Madonna's bed, and motion detection only for her chamber doors, walls, windows, conduits, and ducting.

"Is Her Majesty down for the night, Lieutenant?"

'Yes sir, Her Majesty cued the Madonna Legacy, and is reading. She sent for tea. She is a-bed now, with a night light. Her Majesty's vital signs, and chamber environmental settings are nominal, sir.'

"Very good, keep me informed."

'Yes, Captain.'

The captain switched his intercom to the central monitoring station in the Aglifhate Gallery. "Status, Lieutenant."

'They are still debating, Captain. It seems the Egalitarians are refusing to compromise on that private enterprise reform bill. They can't adjorn for the night without a decision.'

"Damn them," he sneered. "How are the others behaving?"

'The Grand's have them under control, sir. It's gotten heated, but the gallery is civil. I don't think anyone wants a repeat of last week.'

"Especially us, Lieutenant! Have those additional medicos arrived yet?"

'Yessir, I've staged their ambulances at all the side entrances.'

"Very good. Keep me informed."

'Yes, sir.'

The company primae ventinar knocked twice before entering her commander's office. She handed him the Teurel's nightly prisoner status. All were alive. They had been fed, bathed and bedded down. Prisoner Number 1A's status was unchanged relative to the suicide watch. He signed the document and gestured to his senior non-commissioned officer, his right arm, to sit awhile.

"We can relax for a little while, Ventinar. We may pass a peaceful night."

Standing and stretching, the captain walked around from his desk, over to the recess and poured himself another cup of jave'. He gestured to his primae ventinar to offer her one. She declined.

"No thank you, sir, I just killed a cup. How do you think she's taking the news, sir?"

The captain sighed. "I don't know, Ventinar. It's not this Madonna I worry about." He patted his tunic and trouser pockets before realizing he had left his pack of tabas on his desk.

"You mean the other one, sir?" The primae ventinar saw them, but the pack in her tunic was closer. She took it out and offered her commanding officer a tabacanoid, they both liked the same brand.

"Yes. The other one," the captain growled, but then shrugged in resignation. "Since that ship disappeared, one word from her, and the Madonna could start the fight all over again."

"You don't really believe the spirit of…"

The captain raised one hand, cutting her off. "No. Of course not. But it doesn't matter what we believe."

He took a heat stick from his pocket and touched it to the end of the tabacanoid's black cellulose wrapping. He inhaled and puffed twice. Nodding in gratitude, he slipped the stick back into his pocket.

"Be careful how you say things, sir."

He exhaled a thin wisp of canibinized tabacc smoke. "Yes I know, Ventinar. But if the Strelski is listening, I wouldn't be surprised if they felt the same way. We only lost a war. They lost Indira vin's ship!"

The captain walked over to the darkened alcove and gazed out the lamalar panel that encased an ancient arrow slit. Sipping the hot, black liquid, he sighed again. Looking down from the fortress' east battlement tower towards the Citadel, he scrutinized the dark, wintry mountain scene around it with an infantryman's eye. His rifle platoons, with specially trained scout canines, rotate around the clock patrol duties of the estate's outer perimeter. He searched the woods for any sign of one of them and found none. His pride in their proficiency shifted to the practical.

At least out there, they're above suspicion, if any word gets out.

*

Protected from disturbance by her guards, Madonna Ngier Nicholla vin Flavius relaxed and let her tea soothe her. She sat up in her bed, with the journal containing the 'Legacy of the Patriarchs and Matriarchs' open to the modern era on the journal's left pad. She added blank pages on the right pad to make her own entries. The winter wind howled outside her windows, snow swirled through the Citadel courtyards, gardens, and the ancient battlements beyond. She could see the great fortress from her bed through the lamalars' open shutters.

The Teurel stood illuminated on the ridge above her, where it had guarded the Citadel, this former palace of Castallaian Emperatori for 2,900 years before the Sacorsti claimed it, almost 400 years ago. The Teurel was still a fortress, but it's more practical contemporary purpose was as a prison. Undesirables from the former Madonna's government were still kept there. As well as, despite the official statements, the former Madonna herself, Prisoner 1A. She scrolled the left pad to the opening chapter and read Baron vin Hutiar's opening endorsement.

'Genoa-Castallanus was conquered by the Astaran Collective with Sacorsti and Tantoran help, just after the Astarene acquiesced to Conformance and Co-Prosperity, within our Alliance of Stellar Republics. I have found the Genoans useful in their own right, and have elevated them to Alliance status, equal vassals to the Realm as the Astarene.'

The Madonna sipped tea, scrolling past parargraphs of the 5th Century First Baron's awards of bounties and privileges, pardons granted, and continental levy quotas. She stopped at vin Hutiar's most famous declaration; the one she highlighted for inspiration the night First Baron Ma'alese presented her this journal and endorsed her ascension over her predecessor.

'In this year, 159PCE. I rename the star Genoa, Sacor II. Castallanus is renamed New Laconia and shall be the capital of the new Sacorsti Stellar State, as part of the Sacorsti Migration.'

But the migration is still incomplete. She reminded herself. She sycnhed her stylus to the blank page and began to write.

'Every patriarch and matriarch since the fourteen Sacorsti global tribes became one people have expanded the realm, they have sent more people to safety. By Pygan's Will, ours by right of conquest, we have enlightened the heathen on our new colonies to serve us. At last, the goal is within our grasp. Now, as Sacor enters her tertiary and final stage of supernovae evolution, my science collective has informed me that metals have begun to form in her core. Soon, the creation of iron will kill her.

She softly repeated her family shaman's teachings. "We Sacorsti have waited for generations to worship the day we catch our first glimpse of our mother star's implosion. By Pygan's Will, we will continue to fulfill our destiny. Someday soon, Sacor will fulfill hers, spreading precious metals and all the building blocks of the next eon of life."

She wrote on. 'The old Sacor home worlds' surface temperatures grow less tolerable with each passing year. Only Palaren and Sartis remain temperate and populated to any great degree. But, soon, that will no longer matter, the last of our great golden-skinned tribes, and the seed herds of our primary beasts will be gone from there.'

The Vighandis worlds were perfect. She sighed, taking the teacup to her lips and finding it nearly empty. She savored the last warm drops, then reached for the small kettle on her nightstand and refilled the cup.

It had been a long and difficult day, but less so than the previous two weeks. Nicholla vin Flavius had spent most of her time, up until yesterday, in her apartments adjacent to the Shield General Headquarters, and the Aglifhate Central Situation Room.

'There is nothing more I can do in foreign policy, the war is over,' she wrote. Her thoughts of the last days turned more and more to calming domestic chaos.

'The Gentry and the Periolaikoi need distraction. I will give the people games. I will give them toys and luxury goods. I must turn our focus inward. I will re-direct our industrial capacity to planetary infrastructure improvements. I must complete the migration. But it may not be enough.'

There is discontent, and rabble-rousing everywhere, she thought. *I give them appeasement after appeasement and still they grumble, still they demand more. Ingrates! What would Indira do? What would you do, mother?*

She paused for a moment to compose her next thought before continuing.

'The roots of growing unrest among the Periolaikoi, lay in their growing awareness of the higher living standards and conditions outside the Realm. Led by their increasingly influential New Egalitarians, their desires for greater reductions in tithes grow with each passing day. Some have gone as far as to demand reductions too severe to contemplate. The Egalitarians are cleverly manipulating public opinion by calling for raises in Periolaikoi take home wages to, if not on a par with the Leagues, at least on a par with the wealthier non-Aligned States.'

My reforms of the Implications will adjust Periolaikoi tithes yet again. She mused. *I will have the AIM announce I have begun considerations to replace Periolaikoi tithes altogether with an income tax system, similar to the Homostoioi tax code, but that's all I need say. There's no difference between the two, but they don't know that.*

'Maintaining the Shield's offensive capability and completing the migration weigh heavily on the economy. Fuel prices have skyrocketed with the Trudan gone. The vassal republics must all rely on locally produced fuel instead of a uniform trans-stellar refined grade. I am forced to order rationing of uniform-grade reactor fuels and other strategic and industrial minerals for defense.'

'The Barons and the Aglifhate authorized Aunt Sofia's meticulously planned second offensive to seize all of Vighandis to proceed, as we had no other choice after the Trudan and Aletia twin disasters. The drive has failed, and three phalanxes of the Shield are trapped, taking heavy damage and casualties. My Shield!

'We have promised not to reinforce the Vighandis phalanxes in exchange for more time to locate and buy back Commoner prisoners of war from their masters. Once the ceasefire goes into effect, those phalanxes will have to suffer the humiliation of being given just two VET days to withdraw from the region. Worse, they may only travel under escort of the Valerian Fleet. Mathilda must get as many ships as possible out of targeting range of the commie guns in the time allotted. But the Valerians have stated their intent is to escort her ships on to assembly areas in southeast Bavat.'

My poor dear sister is beside herself with rage, she thought.

'On my orders, Mathilda, aboard her flagship, remained at Bavat-Fera as the offensive began.' *And if not for my explicit repetition of that order, directly to her, Mathilda would have charged forward with her supporting units and been ambushed and trapped in the Vighandis Pocket along with her leading phalanxes.*

She shed a tear as she wrote. 'Tribunes vin Waxnar and Galeio are confirmed killed in the pocket in reportedly incessant commie bombardments.'

I cannot afford to lose my only sister as well. The first quarter of the Clan, the Borigai, Aunt Sofia's family, is still powerful, they thirst to reassert themselves. The best of those ragamuffins is aboard Retnec. If he is still alive.

'The traitors' trail has gone cold. Indira vin's legacy has been stolen just at a time when dear sister Mathilda has so few resources to mount an adequate search. Six days past Sabbath last, Deciem 31st, 468PCE, a Junilean freighter happened across what turned out to be the *Retnec*'s command tower. The captain's final log entries named the leaders of the conspiracy and gave the ship's position when the mutiny occurred, and the drive/research section's initial heading.

'Searches are underway throughout the Shafir, Karel and here in Sacor II for crew families. To date, Strelski records indicate the key conspirators are orphan wards of their various states, sold to our colonial administrators. The balance of the remaining crew are Vegan and other helots of, as yet undetermined origin.'

Setting the journal pad aside and turning off her light, she lay back and gazed out the lamalar at the wintry scene. Thick clouds slid by, hiding Triesta, New Laconia's solitary moon. She watched the swaying silhouettes of the conifer trees covering the ridges leading up to the Teurel. Their black forms contrasted against the dark gray sky as she drifted off to sleep.

**

Citadel Security Station Control Room.

"Lieutenant, Her Majesty's vital signs are shifting. Pulse, respiration, brainwave activity are all elevating, ma'am," the grefeiter monitoring the inner sensor ring announced from his station.

"Her Majesty's thermal image is moving tangentially, ma'am," the gefreiter monitoring the middle ring called out. "Her Majesty is agitated, thrashing, ma'am."

"Any activity in the outer ring?" the lieutenant asked perfunctorily, considering every option before stating the obvious.

"Negative activity in the outer ring, Lieutenant," the gefreiter at the station replied without taking her eyes off her screen.

The lieutenant buzzed her commander.

"She's starting to settle down again, ma'am. Vitals are stabilizing…vitals are decreasing."

'Yes, Lieutenant what is it?'

"It's started, sir. She has arrived!"

'Turn off all audio recordings, Lieutenant, muted or not, and no visuals on her! Turn off everything except her vitals!'

"Acknowledged, sir. Will do!" She gestured to the gefrieters to turn their monitors off.

*

They are of weak resolve, your chamberlains. You must strengthen their faith, daughter.

"Yes, mother. They are despondent with our losses. Three first born daughters and five sons within the chamberlains were reported killed or missing in Vighandis as of yesterday. We cannot even recover their ships. The Asigi terms require us to withdraw within forty-eight VET hours of the cease fire. There has been little word of the *Retnec*. They fear all is lost."

I will hold their children to my breast as Pygan holds me to his. Tell them, my child, their children shall service me as I service Pygan. Do not let their grief become defeatism that demoralizes the Gentry, daughter. You must retain control of the mass media.

"I understand, mother. But the terms we've agreed to require us to allow the Egalitarian press."

Then you must control the Egalitarians, and the Chamberlains in the Aglifhate as you controlled the AIM.

"But, mother, how can I control the Egalitarians? They reject every word uttered unless one of their own verifies it."

The tools of the Shafiran will allow you to bring some of their own under your influence, daughter. But be prudent and circumspect in your use of them. Let no one discover your true purpose. Approach each individually and bring them to you. This will take time, but you are young, and your enemies will soon tire of such stringent enforcement of the terms. Just as they have before.

"Yes, mother. We have found the command tower. The logs have given us useful information on the traitors."

You have done well, daughter. When the fleet returns, deploy them to defend our realm and find Retnec. They will flee towards the Commonwealth by a clandestine route. The Shafiran and the others will be safe. They are too valuable to the traitors. We will be able to locate it once we have our ships back. In the meantime, you have enough of the devices for our immediate needs. Do you have them still?

"Yes, mother. I have only verified they are still active; I have not touched them."

Excellent. They are small enough that you can inject them yourself, place one on the inside of your fore nail. Use the summons if you must, but you are as beautiful as you are wise. Lower their inhibitions, seduce them. One scratch at the base of the cerebellum will inject the tool to make them yours. The tools are self-propelled and will work their way

130

to their target areas within a day. Speak alone with each chamberlain and the most influential egalitarians, beginning with their media elite.

"Yes, mother. Mathilda and I will retrieve your property. I have hanged the Yard Master, his deputy, and the Strelski Area Commander for their incompetence! But what shall I do with the Shafiran doctor and his people? What shall I do with them when he has completed his work?"

Send them all back to oblivion. Your descendants may need them again.

"I understand, mother."

You have done well, my child. But the migration of our people is still incomplete. It is the others who have failed, not you. Give the Asigi and the Patruscans all your cooperation. Lull them to sleep again and they will send the Valerians home. We will deal with the Commonwealth again in Pygan's good time. Rest now, my child, I will send you the image of the first Egalitarian you must control.

"Yes, mother."

*

"Her Majesty's vitals are spiking again, Lieutenant. She's leaving."

****

131

Legio Patria Nostra. (The Legion is my Fatherland.)

The Sunshine Lounge, Redfordsville, on Piraeus-Tresium. Task Force Draken's Depot. 60 TSAU from the Commonwealth Capital District.

"So, did you talk to her? When is she comin' in?"

"Yeah, this morning. She's enroute now. Her liner docks at Ouiester Station here the day after tomorrow."

The club was about half-filled with patrons, most were in the main lounge. The lights and music volume was conversational there and where Rick Anders and Sam Proudfoot sat at the Cisco Street entrance bend in the club's famous oval central bar, dubbed the 'Hippodrome'.

Though the rest of the fleet and all civilians were always welcome, the decor throughout the Sunshine Lounge left no doubt the establishment catered to Commonwealth Marines. Replicas of each branch insignia and the heraldic crest of every regiment flanked by info plates represented all of the combat, combat support, and combat service support branches of the force. New patrons were easily recognizable, strolling along, reading each illumined panel. Regulars knew they could access the regimental histories, battle honors and campaign descriptions in HG at their booths.

Every wall held framed photos of marines, individuals, groups of mates, squads, platoons, and cohorts. Thousands of candid shots of marines at work and at play, in and out of uniform, morphed through looped cycles in the active frames. The revered, Heroes' Hall, leading to the restaurant adjacent to the lounge held photos and portraits of legendary marines dating back to the First Alliance War.

Deeper in the lounge, the club Jock was hot on his game.

'Welcome Commoners, to the land of sunshine, your home away from your home away from home.'

The jock saw everything through the lamalars and the monitors in his booth above the ballerum in the center of the back lounge. He kept the music volume fixed at party level on the ballerum and on the club dancers' runways and out back towards the Kushiro Street patio. Customers adjusted volumes themselves in their lounge booths and in the adjoining restaurant.

Multi-colored strobes and illumes shimmered throughout the comfortably lit lounge, but it raged with the beat along the

132

runways. HG of titillating, scantily clad exotics or seductive, elaborately veiled gyrias stage dancers, ballgames, or other sporting events blossomed from the center tables of booths controlled by patrons in each. A hint of incense and tabacanoid occasionally escaped a booth's filtration system. The booth happas emitted no smoke or flame, and most people swallowed their own. The few who didn't, watched their silvery white columns rise straight up into the ceiling particulate scrubbing filters.

"Richard, I'm telling you, as your medico, and your friend. If you love her, tell her."

"No!"

"Why not?"

"She wouldn't believe me. She'd think I'm just trying to get between her legs," Fusilier Corporal Richard Anders lamented into his brew. Most people called him Rick or 'Lil' Rick', only his mother and Sam called him Richard. He took a long swig and set the mug on the bar. He turned to Medical Sergeant Samantha Proudfoot with a forlorn look. "Like I do every girl she introduces me to."

"Don't you flash those puppy-dog brown eyes at me, Richard. I know you," she said grinning. "Plus, you got good moves, boy. You can jam with that three-bar. I don't know about the other folks in the 'Tribe', but you, 'Lil' Rick', you're gonna be a star!"

Anders blushed with the compliment, he started to say something, but Sam held up a hand to cut him off.

"Let me finish. I know Teri too. She's my home girl." She took a sip from her mash and a drag of her cirillo. "I tell you this, Richard. She's a devout Vestal. She's the same age as you. If she's not married by the time she's thirty, she'll take the veil. Then what are you gonna do?"

Rick shrugged and shook his head, then took another swig. 'Doc Sam' watched him with a seasoned eye, she took a drag on her cirillo and exhaled before downing her mash.

*

'In the land of sunshine, the staff is the hottest, the brew is the coldest, and the sounds are smokin'! Put your hands together, ladies and gentlemen, and give a warm welcome for the lovely Miss Anya on the center stage. The smokin' Miss Deidra on the south stage, and stunning Mr. Juan on the north stage. Don't forget to show some love for your lovely wait staff, and your hard-working bar staff! Now let's rock, Commoners, to the magic sounds of Diva Reginaah! 'Don't Hate Me 'Cause I'm Beautiful'. Oh BaBae!'

Around the club, patrons watched dancers on the runways, cheering and tipping the ones that were up. Other dancers strolled the aisles, showing themselves off between sets on the stages. They smiled and pranced, making their purses jingle, enticing new customers. Brothelers led patrons away to entertain them in private suites upstairs.

*

"Tony, can you give us another round here, when you get a chance?" Sam asked over her shoulder.

"J double K sour mash and a Simpson brew. On the Waay!" the retired assault gun platoon sergeant turned pleasure house owner and bartender answered.

"You know, Sam, I've never even kissed her," Rick admitted.

"I'm not surprised, she's family," Sam snorted. "Every woman in the cohort is your sister. And every man is your brother."

Anders sighed, he smiled, nodding his head in agreement and lifted a fist. "With different mothers." Proudfoot tapped her fist to his. She set a silver 10-credit coin on the bar to cover the round and gestured to Tony to keep the change.

"And don't you forget it, young buck!" The husky, silver-haired bartender added, setting a fresh brew and a mash in front of them. He slid the coin back towards Sam and planted his hands on the bar rail, taking a wide arm stance in front of them. She let it lay, and with Rick raised her tumbler to him. He stood there smiling, framed by the wall-mounted Commonwealth Marines shield emblem next to the large painting of a second war-era Anthar assault gun behind him.

"That's the way it is," Sam said. "And besides, you're too busy, nailing all her crewbie girlfriends."

"What can I say? They come on to me. Almost as soon as she walks away."

"They know she's looking for a wife for you. Those women know she's a vestal and you two are family. They know the rule."

"I hate No-Cop."

"No you don't. You love Teresa Faisal. If either you or Terri were crewbies or zoomies, you'd have hooked up when you first met. I knew that the first moment I saw you two together at Repple Depple."

"Faisal? Corporal, Third Cohort, Second Batt? Right?"

"That's right, Tony."

"I know her, she was in here right after y'all got back from Maranon." He looked around in recollection.

"Oh yea. Reserving the patio for a wedding reception. Next week, now that I think about it. Uh, Peres. Sound familiar?"

"Cooper Peres and Sara Coyningham. Coop's in our platoon. Me, Terri and Coop all went through basic together."

"When you learned about No-Cop it broke your heart, didn't it?" Sam remarked, nodding her head.

Tony chuckled. "Good old No-Copulation between cohort mates," he snorted. "Been around since way before Kratari." He shook his head, reveling in nostalgia. "You and that bunch o' noise-makers of yours want a stage and sound support that night?"

Rick's eyes lit up. He looked up with a grin, nodding in gratitude. "Thanks, Tony. We'll rock the house, I promise." He hoisted his mug and took a hardy pull.

Tony winked and nodded. He whipped the bar towel out of his hip pocket and wiped a section of the bar.

"I'll tell you something else," Sam said. "That ass wipe, Batiste scared her."

Hearing that, Rick swallowed hard and set his brew down. His mood instantly soured. "If I ever see that son of a bitch..."

"Don't say it, Corporal," Tony advised.

Rick didn't want to hear it.

"He put her out of his POV, Tony. Way out on Carder Rock Creek Road, when she wouldn't give him any. She walked damned near the whole way back to Depot. I had already signed out. I didn't hear about it till I got back."

"What the fuck? Who is this ass?"

"Some provost at the LEC, real dickhead."

"Batiste. Tall, light-skinned fella? Lots o' hair?"

"He talked a lot of trash about being a combo's manager before the war. He blew a bunch of smoke in her face about landing a recording contract for her after she gets out."

"I know him," Tony snorted. "Likes wearing drover hats and viper skin boots, got some line about being some kind of special operations constable."

"That's the guy," Sam nodded. "I hear he carries an old slave choke chain in one of his boots all the time. He claimed he took it off a dead slaver when his recon ship boarded a slave transport during first Vighandis."

"His right boot. He's a cook," Tony snorted. "In the LEC battalion mess. I hear he's done shit like that before, lots of times as the word goes, but no one has ever pressed any charges. Fatima, my night baker, she used to work with him." Rick and Sam shared a look. "And that slave choker shit is a crock o' shit," The old soldier announced. Their eyes locked on Tony.

"He's never been anywhere but Sestria for basic and here at Depot. He was born here on Tresium, just like me. That chain's Sacorsti alright, it's a canine collar. He bought it at a scrap auction. Just like I bought those lamalars on the squad booths. But like I said, youngster, you watch yourself." Tony leaned in close. "Without that chain he's nothing. But if he gets that thing swinging and connects with you…" he pointed an index finger at him. "You're going down and he'll be standing over you, kicking the shit outta ya with those blunt-toed boots."

Rick looked down at the bar. Sam saw the uncertainty on his face. She rapped his arm and winked at him when he looked up. "There's always a way," she said with a conspiratorial smile. "It may take some planning, but there's always a way."

Tony nodded. "Detailed planning, youngsters. Swift and aggressive execution. But you gotta ask yourselves, then answer, if those chevrons you've earned are worth avenging your sister's honor."

Rick's eyes narrowed. Tony knew what he was thinking. He had said his piece.

They sure the hell are. Rick thought.

Tony looked up towards the Cisco Street entrance and waved hello to a group of marines walking in.

"Heyah, Tony." A tall, lanky man strode in from the bustling street at the head of several robust men and women. His fiery red hair, was cut much shorter than regulation. Sam Proudfoot admired his dragoon high and tight, flat-top haircut, where the sides and back of his head were completely shaved. He was wearing denims, running shoes and a dragoon logo'd sport shirt.

"That you, Lang?!" Tony quipped. "I heard you was dead."

"It takes more than a few SK barrages to kill old Smithton Lang Junior, Tony. But that wife o' mine shure tries real hard."

The eleven dragoons behind him were all dressed more or less the same as the lanky leader. All but two of the men sported the same haircut. The two youngest looking sported longer, regulation haircuts. Four of the women in the group had one side of their head or the other shaved. The rest of their hair fell loose about their opposite shoulder or hung pony-tailed. One young woman had her hair pinned to one side giving the impression of a shaved opposite side. The stern looking woman bringing up the rear, was the exception. Her black hair was as high and tight as Staff Sergeant Lang's.

"We're gonna grab a Squad Room. Set us up will ya? I got three cherries to break in."

Tony nodded, counting and recognizing the veterans and replacements with Lang.

"Clipper time! A proud tradition! First haircut as a dragoon has to be by your mates. Three cherry-busters, brews for seven and two super mashes. On the Waay!"

Anders and Proudfoot exchanged nods and a wave or two of recognition with the dragoons as they passed on their way to an upper level corner booth with a lamalar that offered a panorama of Cisco Street traffic. The three awed replacements gawked at the surrounding décor. The scene only served to heighten the look of trepidation on their faces, anticipating what was to happen to them upstairs.

A floor host moved gingerly past them, unhooking the chain holding a triangular 'Squad Room' placard that guarded the short spiral up to the booth. Lang's squad climbed the spiral, taking seats around the server and HG as one of them switched the unit on.

"We'd better grab our booth before someone else does, Richard," Sam said. She stood from the bar seat with her tumbler in her left hand and her cirillo between her fingers. She picked up the silver credit Tony had refused and dropped it into one of the 'Marine Orphan's Support Fund' tip containers strategically positioned on the bar and proudly returned Tony's gladial salute.

They walked around the curve in the bar, where Sam unhooked the chain at the spiral of another 12-seat Squad Room street-view booth opposite the dragoons. Anders pulled his PtC from his pocket before walking away from the bar. He scrolled through his contact list and found the one he was looking for and sent a pulse. Staff Sergeant Theophilus Mixon buzzed him before he reached the booth.

"We're all set, Sarge. Doc has a squad booth. They're jammin' the beat here. Where are you?" he asked.

'We're parking now. We're right outside. How's the crowd?' his squad leader's image asked.

"It's a good mix of civvie mamas and dudes here. Hurry up, there's a bunch of dragoons here too. Regimental pathfinders, Lang and Mainworthy's section in fact. They're gonna gum up the action."

'We're coming.'

"Sweet. Gotcha' covered."

The first come, first served Squad Rooms were special. Larger than the floor booths, their lamalar panels, were actual vessel components purchased at auctions of scrap parts from captured Alliance void vessels. Tony and his employees enjoyed their patrons' speculations on what type of vessel they may have come from and how much they went for. In the Squad Room, a whole squad or crew relaxed, hoisted a few rounds and just watched the world go by on the streets and the club's main level below for a couple of hours without being seen, except for Tony's security cameras, as long as they maintained their bearing. Antonius Malenkov, Platoon Sergeant, retired, Commonwealth Marines, held squad leaders responsible for their troopers' conduct.

*

SSgt Lang sent his people on up the spiral, he and Tony stood chatting at the bar when SSgt Mixon and the rest of Anders' squad came through the same Cisco Street entrance.

"You're a true liberon, Tony. Equal service to everyone. I see you even let block-headed, old bastards like Lang in," Mixon grunted. "Or is it that times is just hard?"

Lang, pathfinder section leader in the Regimental Reconnaissance Platoon stopped in mid-sentence. He stood erect, stepping back from the bar, he dropped his chin to his chest. Tony stood erect on his side of the bar, he turned to face Mixon and folded his arms. Nearby patrons, staff and one of Lang's dragoons descending the spiral heard him and looked around. SSgt Mixon's squad slowed down coming through, also surveying the scene. Corporal Anders, coming up to meet the squad, stopped short and looked around, taking everything in.

Still facing the bar, Lang slowly rolled his head to the left. His eyes narrowed to slits, staring at Mixon.

"Who da fuck you callin' old?"

His slender body's minimal movement belied the explosive power he was well known for throughout the 7th Regiment. Mixon, a fusilier squad leader in 2nd Battalion's 3rd Cohort and the Regiment's Pugilism Master advanced a few steps, clearing the entrance and bar seats for a clear shot at Lang. He halted and squared bow-on, his eyes locked with Lang's slits.

"You. Bitch."

Mixon's fusiliers stopped and squared behind their leader. To their right, more of Lang's dragoons descended the spiral. Above, the Jock stood by on the fight alert to the Constabulary and aligned a charged net, just in case. But Tony appeared unconcerned.

Mixon advanced, Lang didn't move.

Anders eyes went wide as more dragoons came back down the spiral and squared off, facing his fusiliers. He recognized the stern, short-haired woman, Sergeant Mainworthy, hanging back, grinning down at him.

Mixon got into Lang's face, their emotionless eyes still locked. Their forearms thrust upwards and crossed.

"Brotha Blood!" They broke into wide grins and heartily hugged one another. Mainworthy turned around and went back up the spiral.

Lang chuckled. "Let's be clear, you're older than me."

"Hush that talk! How's ma sister? I know I don't call much. Ma said y'alls doin' okay. I figured y'all was busy makin' babies."

Mixon turned towards Lang's confused dragoons.

"You're old assed section sergeant is my brother-in-law." The dragoons relaxed.

Keeping one arm around Mixon, Lang pointed to him, turning to the fusiliers. "He paid me to date her. You can imagine what I thought she looked like."

"She was just shy, that's all."

139

"Shy my ass. Y'all gone back upstairs," Lang shooed his people away. "Grown folks need to talk."

Mixon turned to Anders. "Take charge, Corporal, I'll be there shortly."

"Roger that, Sarge."

Anders led the squad away, the lounge relaxed and the brothers sat down for a round of J Double K with old Tony.

"How many cherries you got this time, Smitty?"

"Three. You?"

"Four. Worse, I got a new Lieutenant."

"Sorry to hear about Brothers, he was a good man, a good officer."

"Yeah, Bennie was pretty broke up about it, but there was nothing anybody could do."

Tony nodded in sympathy. "When your numbers up troopers, it's up."

Lang lifted his tumbler. "To Ensign Denny Brothers."

Mixon and Tony clinked their tumblers to his.

"To Ensign Denny Brothers," they replied in unison. They downed their mash and set their empty tumblers upside down on the bar.

"Everybody reporting in okay, Sergeants?" Tony asked, changing the subject.

"So far. I haven't heard of any problems, we still got a few more days before muster."

"Why are you back early, Smitty?" Mixon asked.

Lang chuckled, rolling his head. "Pathfinders, Theo baby. First in, Last out. It's a staged recall, all the recon units and some of the other specialty platoons mustered a week ago."

"Old School, I like that," Tony chuckled. "I heard everything turned out okay at your boy's hearings."

"G.W.'s follies? Did you watch any of that, Smitty?"

"Nah. Too busy makin' babies. Is he back?"

"He was here a few days ago," Tony said, filling the two in on the latest scandal. "But according to the news, he's raisin' hell over on Degoa-Earth."

"What's he done this time?"

"Some nonsense about demanding the Gladius so he can convert Blue House into a stable."

The sergeants burst into laughter.

Commodore's Barge, Fleet Depot 19 liaison shuttle, LS-1. Departure plus three hours, enroute from Saluri-Demeos to Piraeus-Tresium.

"Where ya been, Moe? I thought you was bagged out." Master Chief Zoupre' asked CSM Morris from across the mid-deck galley as he entered the open manway.

"Signals shed on the flight deck, had to send a message back to Demeos Provost Marshal Desk. G.W. wants them to track down one of your vortex drivers."

"One of mine?"

"Yep, Mitchell Pulke."

"Delta Squadron's commander. Okay, yeah."

"Yep, boss wanted me to put a bug in his ear to come see him after he reports in."

"He's an officer, but he's still one of mine, Moe. What'd he do?"

"Oh, nothing. G.W. was impressed when he planned our fighter sweeps in Trudan. He wants to pick his brain about Phuong."

"Oh, yeah. He's a hell of a strategist and an historian. Stefan says he's one of the best operational minds around. Says he's gonna go a long way."

"Expect the boss to pull him up to the three-shop."

"How's G.W., Moe?" He handed Morris a steaming mug of java as the other battle group master chiefs gathered round. With the stewards on shift working back in the galley, the NCOs were alone in the dining area.

"Asleep finally. Thanks for this. I need it." He hoisted the mug in toast and took a refreshing sip and gestured for his NCOs to join him at a booth. Holding the mug in both hands, he closed his eyes and sighed heavily. Then rolled his head and shoulders, feeling the kinks crackle loose as he walked the few steps over and sat down.

"Aren't you going to tell us anything, Moe?" Chief Maynard chided.

"Cain't do it, Manny. G.W.'s got orders to keep his trap shut about it from the CE himself. That harpy, that Allen woman, she's forty klicks of bad road. That think-tank she works for has some pretty extreme Statist ideas. Her appointment to League

Security Advisory staff is a payback for their support of Morales' campaign."

"So what does that have to do with us?"

"Politics, Chiefs. Our worst enemy."

"They're still hung up on the Praetorship?" Chief Kibir asked in a huff. "We all heard G.W., that issue's dead."

"It's dead to G.W., and to us. But to Morales and his cronies, like that Allen woman and to a lot of senators, like Jamison and Hanash, that's a tactic. A smokescreen."

"Say you don't want something while you're scheming to get it." Zoupre' nodded his head.

"You got it, Zoop." Morris took another long sip of java, after letting it cool a little.

"Typical."

"I saw the batman panel showed Rivas' stateroom going dark as I was coming up. Your people tucked in?"

The three Master Chiefs all nodded.

"Good. Its twenty one thirty, get some sleep yourselves. G.W. wants to do a talk-around about the PDRE at ten hundred. We'll have Hix and Mackenzie on the HG from their depot. He wants to hit the ground runnin' when we get to Tresium to kit everybody out and set to the wave on the twenty-sixth."

Master Chief Zoupre' shook his head and snorted, slapping his thigh. "Damn, Moe. That had to be one for the grandkids. Stefan was still shook up when he bagged out. He said he saw his career flash before his eyes when G.W. said it'll be an opportunity for us to excel."

The NCOs got a chuckle out of that.

"I can imagine. Almost got me too," Morris admitted. "I figured out pretty quick what he was up to, so did Oshermeyer. He had to find out why that woman was there, taking over."

"And I suppose y'all got an ear-full," Kibir said.

"And then some. But like I said, focus on Phuong. It's gonna be a cast-iron bitch, even with the fleet average on casualties. Especially Happy Valley, Zoop. We still got a lot of veterans, but we got a lot of new folks. It's gonna be a good chance to train 'em up."

"Gonna be a lot of eyes on us."

"And G.W. wants to give 'em a real show. Let's make it happen."

Maria Hardesty's apartment in the Philmor Arms, Popularum City, Saluri-Demeos.

Maria set her talk-pad on the living room floor so she could chat with her sister's blossoming HG image at eye-level. After searching through shipping boxes delivered before she returned from Degoa-Earth, Maria removed the generations-old woven metallic sarape from its small storage tube.

"Doreen, this itty-bitty thing is gonna stretch to fit me? I'm small, but not that small."

'It'll fit. It fit me. Mother said it fit her, everyone Zinnia says it fits, it fits.'

"Oh well," Maria conceded. "When Aunt Zinnia is on her wavelength with the Omens, there's no arguing with her."

'Sweet pad there, sister girl,' Doreen Hardesty Munroe said, looking around the apartment. With a chubby infant on her knee, Doreen's seated image leaned forward, her head turned to see into other rooms. 'Nice view out the bedroom windows. Take me in there."

"Oh, maybe tomorrow, the room is a mess. If Papa comes in and sees it he'll hit the roof."

'How much are the rents there?'

"I really don't know. The DIG pays for it. It's a transient apartment. I just make sure I get it when I come here."

After emptying the contents of the third box she sat in frustration on the lounger in the living room in front of her sister's image. "Are you sure you packed it?"

'Yes, I'm positive. Everything is there. Aunt Zinnia put the novena in the box with the boots.'

"Oh! With the boots!" Maria sprang to her feet, dashing through Doreen's image towards the bedroom, startling her sister.

'Don't do that!' Doreen protested. "That's rude," she said rotating the image to follow Maria.

"Sorry. I left it in there exposed to the air!" Maria shouted over her shoulder. "I hope it hasn't dried out, Zinnia would kill me!"

A flurry of clothes and shoes flew past the open bedroom door in front of Doreen's image as two older women joined her at the kitchen table.

"Ah ha! I found it," Maria said, exiting the bedroom in triumph. "It's still sealed!" She stopped short seeing her mother Zara, and her mother's aunt Zinnia come into view.

"Mother, Great Aunt Zinnia, when did you come in?"

'We've been out back, dearie,' her mother replied.

'You've got the novena, good,' the older woman said, pointing to the cloth bag Maria was holding. "Swallow two now and put four in your bath water when we're done talking. Wear the dress and be sure to eat meat tonight.'

"Yes, Aunt Zinnia. Mother, I'm not sure I'm ready for this."

Zara admonished her. 'It's your time dear, the Omens are certain.'

'Tis now the Ides of Tauroun, child. The last quarter of the new moon. You will meet your true love this night.'

"Yes, Aunt Zinnia, but you're on Comar, and I'm on Demeos. Mother, explain to her, we're five hundred TSAU apart."

'I know that!' Great-Aunt Zinnia scolded them all. 'I'm old, not senile!'

Maria grinned as she opened the package and examined the six small, black capsules in it. She picked two out and dutifully put them in her mouth and swallowed them.

'Your mother and Aunt Zinnia have been chanting to the heavens for three days now, little girl.' A handsome, distinguished looking man with thick, black, silver-sided hair boomed as he stepped into the image with a java cup in hand. 'The neighbors are thinking they've gone bonkers.'

The muscular man's close fitting deep blue shirt and bright red tie spoke volumes to Maria. Her father set the cup down and draped the dark blue jacket of his business suit over the back of the chair. He leaned over and kissed Doreen's baby on the head and sat down at the table.

"Good hunting in court today, Papa. How are you?"

'I'm set to take them down. I'm fine, now that that Malcolm fella is out of my little girl's life and she is about to find a real man.'

"Oh, Papa, not you too. I thought you didn't believe in magic."

'I just didn't understand it was pheromonal,' Theodore Hardesty, Esq. Counselor-at-law, said with a grin. 'Aunt Zinnia said Malcolm would make you a great writer, and he did. After he... well, that's over. You just never let that bastard see one credit of your royalties! Ya hear me?'

"Loud and clear, Papa."

'Now if Aunt Zinnia says that novena stuff and that dress will fetch you a real man and me another grandchild, go get it done.'

"Doreen's aren't enough, Papa?"

'Three from each of you will be just fine.'

'Ha! One more, and Josef and I are off the hook, eh, papa?' Doreen laughed, patting her father's shoulders.

"Ooh, you people. Mother, how will I know if it works? Some man I don't know isn't just gonna walk up and jump me is he?"

'Child, don't be silly,' Zinnia answered, cutting Zara off.

'If one does, little girl, you know what to do!'

"Yes, Papa. First kick to the balls, second to the head, then run like hell."

'That's my girl.'

'You listen, Maria. The Creator's Omens didn't pick Malcolm,' Zinnia's image said. 'Your scent will attract your man. He will fill your eyes, you will see him as no one else does. You will sweat, you will be short of breath, and your heart will pound. He will teach you and you will teach him. The Omens say your man has courage. Your man has intellect and refinement.' She paused and held two fingers of one hand up, looking off into space. Then she leveled her eyes at Maria. 'Your man has no lineage.'

"No lineage? What does that mean, Aunt Zinnia?"

'Don't worry about that, Maria. Do as Zinnia says and trust in the Omens, to keep you from hurt, harm and danger.'

"Yes, Mother, I'll do it. I'll call tomorrow. I'll be here for two more days before I have to leave for fleet orientation in Gabb'es."

'Okay dear. You watch that Morgan and don't let him get away with anything.'

"I will. I'll call you tomorrow. Bye now."

'Bye.' The HG faded.

Maria got up and went to start the bath. She had only walked a few steps when she stopped and returned to the lounger to pick up the novena bag she left behind.

**

Lieutenant Commander Mitchell Pulke and Aviation Senior Warrant Officer Drago Mise arrived early for their dinner reservation at the capital's renowned restaurant, 'Nicky's On the River'. They were happy to wait in the salon from where they stepped out onto the Grand Veranda. The broad, marbled patio, renowned for its meticulously sculpted hedges and potted plants extended completely around the manor house at the top of a small rise on the north side of the river, across from Nadrew Park. Looking down the gentle slope of the manor's manicured south west lawn and gardens they watched water craft cruising the river and the vehicle and pedestrian bridge traffic.

*

Maria Hardesty took advantage of the warm evening and took the river walk to the Reynier Bridge across the Ayoette River that bisects the Philmor District. 'Nicky's on the River' was a good place to get a good meal while catching up on the league gossip. Everyone came to Nicky's, even the Chief Executives, Privy Council members and Supreme Magistrates from time to time, as well as many senators and diplomats and their staffers. Most took the, 'Who's Walking and Talking with Whom', route through Nadrew Park to the bridge to give journalists and other watchers of goings on in the capital a glimpse into upcoming events.

Saluri dimmed as Macillus set. Demeos' five sister moons grew prominent. So too, did the Hatu stellar group. As dusk fell, the group were the brightest trans-stellar objects in the sky, just nine TSAU away during this perihelion month. Degoa was easily identified, left of her blue parent star and surrounded by seven moons, the closest, being Degoa-Earth. The soft evening aura brought on a sense of peace Maria found just a little strange, given the history of the Twin Tribes. Her reverie was broken, with the laboring voice behind her along the walkway as she ascended the stone steps to the Grand Veranda.

"Hardesty, Maria Hardesty. Wait a minute!" A breathless man demanded catching up to her. "I want a word with you!"

She stopped and turned, looking down on him. "Apollodoris Jefferson Mortimer," she quipped as he stopped at the base of the steps, leaving two between them.

"You're going to have to get in better shape than that to survive basic training, A. J.," she chuckled.

146

"Funny. Ha, ha. I suppose you're pretty damned proud of yourself, taking my task force away from me. What political strings did you pull this time?"

He stepped up to her as she spun and they continued, side by side, up to the veranda and across to the main lobby.

"Now, wait a minute, A. J., I had nothing to do with that. I'm as surprised as you. I only found out a couple of hours ago. I'm sure you knew about it before I did. Capella Metropolitan has its spies everywhere."

"We need 'em to keep you Diggers in line. Alright, so what happened, Maria? You're no military journalist."

"Neither are you," she snapped back. "We both have to report to some hell-hole in Gabb'es I had never heard of until today.

"The fleet main reception and training center on Gabb'es-Sestria."

"Yeah whatever, I hear it's a nest of vipers and ner'e do wells."

The manor steward at the main entrance bowed slightly, touching his right hand to his left breast as he did so, in the traditional Saluri greeting.

"Miss Hardesty, it's so nice to see you again.

"Hello Cesare'."

Good evening, Mr. Mortimer. Service for two tonight?"

"Uh, well. Yes, Cesare'," A. J. answered. He turned to Maria and shrugged. "We have to talk anyway. You know, coordinate."

"Okay, why not? But you're buying."

"Well, I'll be...oh, alright. I'll have fun explaining that on my expense report.

"Easy. Dinner for your boss," she quipped with a sly grin.

"Your table will be ready in twenty minutes, Miss Hardesty, Mr. Mortimer. Would you care to wait in the salon?"

"Yes, that will be fine, thank you," Maria said, winking at a grimacing A. J.

The steward gestured towards a server, who bowed deeply, rendering a salutation. She gestured the two to follow her down the ornate, Bursuq Hall towards the salon.

"Come along A. J., I'll buy you a drink to salve your soul."

"So, spill it. How'd you do it?"

"Like I said, A. J., I had nothing to do with it," she said with a hint of impatience.

"Okay, okay. If there's one thing I know about you, you're not a liar," A. J. huffed. "So, where do you want me?"

"As far away from G.W. Morgan as possible."

A. J. stopped short for a second, with his mouth agape, then he stepped up, catching back up to her again.

"So you can get another shot at him, eh?"

"The third time's the charm, as they say."

"Okay, it'll be fun to watch."

"Your hero's going down this time, A. J."

*

Mitch Pulke saw the silvery-green image crossing the bridge. The image became a beautiful, long haired woman walking from the bridge towards the veranda steps to the main lobby to his right. The simple sarape she wore alternated between shades of silvery blue and forest green at different angles in the varying light. She stopped and turned when a taller, heavy-set man ran up to her. They then continued together up towards the lobby.

"If every bar has its own personality, Mitch. Then this place is schizophrenic," Drago Mise said, standing next to him. Drago turned, looking around at the staid, paneled salon, just inside the tall, ornamental glass doors separating it from the veranda.

"You'd never know there's a casino and ballerum down one hall and a fancy, five-star restaurant down the other."

"Pretty snazzy, huh?" Pulke answered, swirling his tumbler in his hand to warm his mash. "Been here a long time."

"So what's so special about the Hall? What is it again? Brususq?"

Bursuq, Hans Ibn Bursuq."

"The grav balance underwear inventor?"

"Right."

"So, all those other portraits are folks his descendants sued for stealing his patents?"

"It certainly was a bunch, wasn't it? I tell you Drago, This place reeks of money and power. Industrialists, financiers, academicians, diplomats and politicians all mixed up together."

"So what are a couple of poor-asses like us doing here?" Mise asked with a grin.

148

Mitch winked and cocked his head Mise's way with a proud smile. "We deserve it." He hoisted his tumbler in toast to his shipmate. Mise clinked his tumbler to Mitch's and they both took a short sip. The night was young. Mise stepped into the salon to get a good look.

Waist-coated stewards moved silently about, carrying serving trays of drink refills and finger foods for patrons in their areas from strategically placed wheeled carts. Polished wood shelves of literaries rose from waist level almost to the ceiling. The thick carpets and classical furnishings centered on high backed, four-legged, upholstered and leather chairs facing one another in groups. Everything in the room's décor was designed to easily keep conversations close, quiet, and confidential. He stepped back towards Mitch and turned to face the river and gardens.

"You think any of these folks realize the war's still going on, Mitch?

"These people? You'd better believe it. They know more than we do."

"Like when it's gonna end?"

"Probably," Mitch answered between sips. "Mark my words, Drago. I give it two weeks, three, tops."

"You sound like Morgan now."

Both men chuckled.

"If they bag Nasty Nicholla's sister in Vighandis you can bet she'll pack it in," Mitch added.

The open veranda doors gave them an earful of a couple, including the beautiful woman Mitch saw walking up, being led into the salon from Bursuq Hall and being seated near other small groups and couples.

Several people recognized the Nursery Crescent firebrand, Capella Metro Gazette's Apollodoris Jefferson Mortimer from Poia-Vizio, but practically all, including Mitch Pulke and Drago Mise recognized the Dragon Lady, Maria Joanna Hardesty of the Denestri Information Group from Denestri-Comar. The celebrity journalists however, had their own concept of what quiet and confidential conversation meant.

*

"It's that attitude of his that gets on my last nerve, A. J., you've spoken of it yourself many times. There's something about that self-aggrandizing, '...never say anything you don't want The

149

Creator to hear...' thing," Maria said. "That's what actually gets him into hot water with the Admiralty, and with us, time and time again. Except you Nursery Crescent types, obviously. To us Centralis, it always seemed he forgets the second part of his own adage. The part about, '...that way you have two choices; speak the truth, and damn the consequences, or manipulate the truth, and suffer the consequences.' He could add a third choice, keep his mouth shut, and avoid the consequences."

"Nice oratory, Maria, but it doesn't inform John and Jane."

"Well how about I make it plain. He says he doesn't want the Gladius, 'the constitutional amendment question is dead', he says. Then not three breaths later he goes off on some rant about naming his damned estalon his successor? What the hell was that all about?"

"He was illustrating the absurd by being absurd, he said so, Maria."

"Should've kept his big mouth shut." She picked up a glass of wine from a serving tray before settling into her seat. Maria leaned in close to A. J. and whispered in his ear. "There's more to Maranon than they said in the investigations." A. J. gave her a curious nod as she sat back in her chair and continued in what passed for her conversational tone.

"The Budget Committee got the military appropriations through in time. The compromise in it expands the fleet a little, but it keeps the admirals and commodores in their positions without adding any new ones."

"The expansion is unprecedented in itself, Maria. Every faction got something."

"Except Hanash, A. J., life search is still in the hands of the military, when it is clearly time to privatize. The DOPs have been contractual since they were conceived, but surveying their output isn't? And Jamison," she snorted. "Jamison didn't get even half the fleet expansion he wants." She sipped her wine. "Thank the Creator's Omens."

"Are you bragging, Maria? Or complaining."

"Neither. Both. Shut up," she said playfully, reaching for the finger food. "Look, neither the Chief Executive's cabinet, the Admiralty, nor a sizeable block within the Senate, including the Privy Council particularly cares for Morgan right now."

"Of course not, he's been right every time, and they've all been flat out wrong."

"It's actually funny sometimes," Maria said, between bites of a breaded fowlon nugget. "You've seen them individually, those senators, senior officers, and Morales' staff are, at best, as frightened children with wet pants whenever one of us in the press mentions Commodore Gaven Webster Morgan. Or, at worst, they despise him as a political opportunist," she said finishing the nugget and reaching for a bread finger.

"He didn't bribe the Military Affairs Committee to recall him to active service, Maria," A. J. exhaled in exasperation at the premise, waving a vegetable crisp, before popping it into his mouth.

"Okay, okay, that finally died away when he first went into the Trudan," she conceded. "Only to flare right back up again with the revelation of a movement in the Senate to recommend him for direct command of the Combined Fleet as Praetor, with all its attendant executive, and judicial powers, as well as key legislative powers from the Common Senate." She sat back, sipped her wine and crossed her legs.

A. J. summarized the DIG mantra for his smug colleague.

"And the conspiracy theorists in the central states are rife with speculation that Morgan himself engineered the movement." He pointed at her, then turned the palm of his hand upward, directing his commentary towards her network rather than towards her personally. "Again, allegedly through bribery. But they used the impact of the Trudan and Aletia campaigns to compel the constitutional amendment. Right?"

"Go on."

"Well then Morgan engineered himself almost out of a job. The battles in Trudan and Aletia actually eliminated the emergency and the need for an amendment. And now the cease-fire could be agreed upon at any time, just as Morgan said it would."

"His plan worked too well, A. J," Maria sneered. She made her famous, 'peering into a crystal ball' hand gesture, mocking some of her own network's more extreme Anti-Morgan views.

"The Military Affairs Committee is still very impressed with G.W. Morgan. Just not enough to commence a constitutional amendment process to legitimize a Praetor without a clear and present emergency. The simple fact is, 'The Commodore' is too successful in his present position. So the issue had to die. But how?"

"That was easy, Maria. The budget committee made no mention of any such process within any of the compromise appropriations bills. Regarding the fleet senior ranks, the Privy Council pressured Morales to accept the Military Affairs Committee recommendation to retain the present fifteen admirals, and twenty-three commodores on active duty in their present stations."

"Ha! Including Morgan?"

A. J. nodded. "Including Morgan. Commanding his current task force."

"That really must have burned Morales' ass! He hates Morgan," she chuckled. With that, her mood quickly darkened. A.J. saw it in her face. Her voice lowered, turning somber.

"That man has a score of warships and thousands of ground troops at Piraeus-Tresium anchorage. That's just three days from here. It's a dagger pointed at our throat."

"That's a lot of hooey, Maria. Morgan has no need to stage a coup. A third of the stellar states would give him the gladius for his business acumen alone from before the war. Another third will back him since Trudan. For three years our politicians and admirals floundered around. The war dragged on, and our economies suffered. Morgan did what he said he was gonna do and restored the trans-stellar grade T two H, H-E three flow from Baktimur."

"Well, Denestri leads the third that is not so easily swept off its feet."

"I tell you, Maria. The man's a genius."

"My ass, A. J. Well, perhaps an evil genius, but if you ask me, he's got people looking out for him. He's just too damned lucky."

"That's nonsense."

"Nonsense, really? Well, A. J. Mortimer, let's look at the facts. One, he's born into the Morgenash Clan of Moktar-Sandor. Damned near royalty right there.

"Ah, but he was born in Chapuri, not Moktar. And the family moved to Sperieus before he was five."

"Yes, certainly. Where they somehow miraculously become one of the richest families in the whole stellar state! Care to explain that, A. J.?"

"Prosperity is the natural outcome of the five freedoms, Maria."

"Bravo!" A rather large, bearded man endorsed A. J. from across the salon, where he and others overheard them, including Mitch and Drago.

"Hear, hear." A woman on the opposite side of the room raised a slender glass in toast.

"Does that prosperity include doing business with Alliance states? Hmmm?"

"That's a low blow, Maria. You know as well as I do, after twelve, in some cases fourteen hundred Common Era years of trans-stellar commerce, through war and peace, clans have no commercial respect for state boundaries, throughout the central and outer metropolitan regions."

"And nowhere is that more prevalent than in the Sperieus and Chapuri dome of the Nursery Crescent," a man in business attire said, standing to leave the salon following a host towards his party's dinner table.

The man's jacket sported a Persean stellar state flag lapel pin above a bronze Common Stellar Senate tertiary senator's button. He and the two younger members of his party bowed slightly towards Maria and A. J., the senator touched his fist to his chest as he did so, then strode away, with the others close behind him.

"Additionally, Maria, while those rumors may contain a grain of truth, it is also true that there are no direct ties to Morgan, or his immediate familial, or GWM Enterprises business interests."

"It's true, as well, of many hundreds of other clans, Miss Hardesty. A young man seated with two older women near them said. "Our clan has major interests in the Patruscan League and non-Aligns between us in Serianis and Karel in the Alliance. We have to purchase access to Karelian navigation buoys to transit our ore ships. The war hasn't changed that."

The matronly woman seated next to him tapped his arm. "Very good, son."

*

"See what I mean?" Mitch whispered to Drago out on the veranda. "C'mon, let's get closer."

"Sure, Mitch. Maybe some of it will rub off."

"You never know."

They walked slowly into the salon towards open seats near the doors, but close enough to hear.

"Do you smell orchids?"

Drago sniffed the air. "Nope."

A host stepped over and presented his tray, offering them fresh drinks.

*

"Okay, okay. Morgan was commissioned an ensign in the Sperieus State Guard after graduating from the Sandoran Military Academy, right?

"Correct, class of seven eleven. He graduated third."

"The Sandoran Academy, not the CLA."

"So what."

"The SMA has a purely military curriculum, no political ethics. And the Sandorans have a history of military takeovers."

"Not since Moktar joined the Commonwealth," A. J. shot back. "And that was almost five hundred years ago. Nice try, but, no score."

"Alright. So as a reserve officer, he's free to make a fortune of his own at the head of GWM Enterprises. Right?"

"Right. The company bought, upgraded and operated, three trans-planetary pleasure liners and two resort stations, catering to Sperien miners."

Maria leaned forward, pointing her finger at A. J.

"Remus Morgend was the Chapuri primary senator at the time. He pushed several retroactive Comfort and Morale provisions of the Deep Void Minerals Management Act of seven thirteen CE through the Senate. Remus Morgend, G.W.'s uncle. Now c'mon, who would dare say the good senator didn't know his young nephews' stations were based within ten days liner voyage of every asteroid mine and refinery from Sperieus to Chapuri and their Spice Moons?"

"That's an interesting point, Maria."

Exchanging glances, Mitch and Drago munched finger foods, sipped their drinks and listened.

"So then what happens, A. J., hmmm? By seven twenty, he turns his ambitions towards trans-stellar tourism and sight-seeing. That is, until the *LL Bright Star* gets captured by Junilean pirates, remember that?"

154

"Well I don't remember. You're not that old either, Maria. Are you?"

"Shut up," she snorted. "The accounts state they were captured while viewing the Astaran Nebula from well inside the CAZ, between Perseaus and Prosean."

A. J. saw an opening, he leaned forward and stabbed two fingers towards his colleague. "G.W. lobbied his legislative connections, calling in several favors to be reassigned to Task Force Hermes, Maria. It was his participation in the punitive expedition to Junile in Encephalon to rescue the passengers, vessel and crew that made him a commercial and media celebrity and, I might add, prevented his company's financial ruin."

"Well la-de-dah. He was only a middle level centurion on the task force operations staff, A. J. His GWM Enterprises information office ensured the public, and millions of potential investors knew he was there."

"It worked out for the best, Maria. The expedition was successful. The *LL Bright Star* took to the wave again in twenty three, along the same route, with a full complement of passengers and crew. G.W. himself was aboard, accompanied by a number of the rescued passengers, at his expense, along with as much media fanfare as he could get."

"Not to mention two private military company frigates as escort."

"He's no fool."

"The man is nothing if he is not a showman, A. J. Did you know GWM Enterprises copyrighted that quote of his afterwards? The one that became the recruiting slogan: '…thank The Creator, the Commonwealth could give us stout ships, hot pilots, and a few good marines to get the job done!' You still see those ads. So what's he do next? He sells their fleet of liners, but not the pleasure stations and branches into media-vision and cinema entertainment."

"Yes. He bought the first of three Moktari studios from his Moktar-Sandor cousins in twenty-four. But he wasn't involved in the day-to-day, Maria. G.W. kept a strategic hand in, but he left the routine operations of GWM Enterprises to his senior employees while he remained on active duty with the regular fleet for the next twenty years."

"Then what?"

"Is this a test?"

"I'm your boss."

"Okay. Nothing much really. G.W. resumed full time control of GWM Enterprises. The company continued to thrive but was never without controversy."

"Such as?"

"I see. This is indeed a test. Okay, boss," Mortimer smiled. He picked out an aperitif from a host tray before continuing. "During his tenure as chairman, they acquired several retransmission buoy services and communications commission licenses. His broadcast affiliates sprang from there."

"Morgan was back in uniform within five years, A. J. As deputy superintendent of the leadership academy over on Degoa-Earth, then, commanding the Fleet Strategic Studies Group, and retiring a second time in fifty-eight. He stays out of the limelight this time, until just before this war. Just in time for the war."

"What? What the hell does that mean?"

"Look, even before the war, but especially in the early months when the news was mostly bad; Commoners craved the escapism of their MV. We needed ever increasing variety in supernet entertainment media. GWM Cinematique's production companies, and their network of retransmission broadcast affiliates filled that need as well as, or better than, any of the others."

"Even the DIG's? But it's not G.W.'s profession. Those are, for him, just another series of hobbies at which he excels," A. J. quipped.

"The cinema productions are never his either. The military is the only real work the man has ever done. Yet, thanks to you, A. J. and networks like Capella Metro, his name is synonymous with so many iconic cultural events and locations, even beyond the Commonwealth. Six of his production studio releases were major hits last year," Maria mused.

A. J. grinned, reveling, but magnanimous with the temporary triumph. "But only one carried even a quasi-military theme."

"He played absolutely no part in their production, and yet, his name is permanently associated with them, more so than the producers, directors and actors." She sipped her wine.

"You have to admit though, Maria, Morgan did manage to have an actual hand in the production of this 'Praetor' presentation that's coming out. Most of the work went on during the height of the Trudan Campaign, and every Commoner knows Task Force Draken, under G.W. Morgan's command, were the ones who kicked in the door there and cleaned house."

"Okay, okay," Maria admitted. "How he managed to supervise the research effort, select the senior producers, and, it was said, interview the directors and lead actors, while fighting a major battle is beyond me."

"So, there is no doubt," A. J. pressed his advantage. "'The Praetor' is his product, and the Trudan and Aletia were his task force's victories. Your conclusion? Boss."

"None, yet."

She pulled her data pad from her handbag and brought up the small video of the incident in the CLA student discussion. It showed him clearly laughing and waving the thought off.

"My sources tell me, Morgan said, when called on the platform in front of the chief of staff, again, by the way, he was mocking a late night talk show host's comedic skit that had mocked him."

A. J. eased himself deep in his seat, he sipped his drink and wagged his finger. "Fortunately for him and for the Commonwealth, he's going back out on deployment. Where one can see the enemy more clearly than in the swamp of Commonwealth politics, where adversaries wear much more clever disguises. My sources say Morgan was ecstatic to receive orders for this mission. Whatever this mission may be."

"Nice oratory, A. J. But it doesn't tell John and Jane anything," she said with a grin. "We're not going to Vighandis. That much is certain," Maria assured him. "It's all over out there, except the crying, I've heard. Plus the Fleet Commodore there doesn't want him. She calls him the 'Glory Fellow'."

The bearded man spoke up from across the room. "Has it occurred to you, Miss Hardesty, that Morgan's supporters have a good chance of capturing majorities in their respective State Legislatures' upcoming elections?"

"John and Jane Commoner have long memories," another woman said. "In just two VET years, their new State delegates could force Morales to seat a Privy Council of their own ilk for the rest of his term."

"That's a frightening prospect, Candace," her companion joined in. "They could hold the Commonwealth Senate hostage, and force the constitutional amendment down everyone's throat, the Fleet expansion, and a permanent Praetorship to G.W. along with it."

A. J. sipped his aperitif, secure with a majority of support around the room.

The bearded man offered a parting comment, leaving for the dining room. "Miss Hardesty, opponents of the constitutional amendment to make the post of Praetor permanent know John and Jane, as always, will be thinking of their purses at polling time. And now, John and Jane know how, after Trudan, Morgan deliberately ignored long-standing Senate and Admiralty directives and liberated until then unknown, Aletia-Maranon, which had been forcibly enlightened by Alliance invasion and enslavement."

"You can't bear the thought he may be named Praetor someday, can you, Maria?"

"Myself, personally, I'll reserve judgement. I'll say this, the fifth century Denestri Information Group board of governors despised and lampooned the first Praetor. Here in the eighth century, their successors are no less opposed to the possibility of another."

"Hear, hear!" Someone across the room rapped a table in her support.

"You've gone after G.W. Morgan twice now, Miss Hardesty," the other industrialist matron asked. "What have you learned about him that makes your network so suspicious of him?"

"I haven't so much 'gone after him', as you say, madam," Maria answered. "I've investigated GWM Enterprises pleasure station operations. I went to determine if allegations of unsafe and coercive working conditions were true among the service personnel."

"And what did you find?" A. J. asked smiling.

"That those allegations were not only untrue but instigated by some of his competitors."

"Competitors where?" he asked, knowing the answer.

"Denestri, Boreali, and Eatoni," Maria answered in a huff.

The matrons and the young man grinned and nodded.

"Yes, 'gone after' is a little harsh for Miss Hardesty's investigations of G.W. Morgan, Aunt Harriet," the young industrialist chuckled. "Two former moguls and a fair number of ex-politicians she has 'gone after' are still in prison, if I'm not mistaken."

A. J. Mortimer raised his glass in toast to Maria at that. "Aye, lad. When she gets a scent of corruption, there's no stopping her."

"Why, A. J. Mortimer. Are you paying me a compliment? Thank you," she said smiling and nodding his way.

Servers made their rounds, another group of six departed. They were replaced by a group of four, led by a senator recognized by her Gabb'es Stellar State flag lapel pin and the silver Senate button of the state's secondary senate seat in the House.

The young industrialist's mother leaned forward a little and got Maria's attention. "And Batill'e?"

Maria burst out laughing. "Now that one was actually fun. The silly woman deserved what she got!"

"Batill'e? The Cesteran diva?" Drago asked Mitch.

A. J. heard him and looked up, recognizing their blue aviation branch Common Fleet uniform. One wore the shoulder boards of a Lieutenant Commander. Aviator wings and three rows of campaign ribbons decorated his class B waist jacket. The other sported two and one half cuff stripes similar to the officer's shoulder boards. Intrigued, he nodded his head in their direction. Maria spotted the head nod.

"What's that?" she asked, turning out of the high-backed upholstered chair to see who was talking.

"Oh, we're sorry, Miss Hardesty," Mitch spoke up, standing. "We, couldn't help overhearing."

Maria looked him over, smiling. Her heart thumped, she tried to speak, but couldn't draw a breath for a second or so.

"That's quite alright, Commander." A. J. said. "That's what happens here at Nicky's. We journalists are fair game to our bosses."

Drago was confused at that and turned as Mitch sat back down. "You wanna run that past me again, sir."

"Ha, ha. That's you, sir. John Q. and Jane A. Commoner." A. J. chuckled, noticing the warrant officer's uniform jacket was as decorated as the officer. "It's a part of what you in the fleet call the Kratari Code. We journalists have one too. It's printed on the backs of our press cards."

"Oh, no Kratari before dinner please, A. J. We were discussing Morgan," Maria said after catching her breath.

"What happened to Batill'e, ma'am?"

"Miss please."

"Oh, sorry miss. What happened to her?"

"A few months before the war, mister, mister, ahh."

"Mise, miss. Drago Mise."

"How nice. And you sir?"

"Me? Ah, Mitchell Pulke, miss."

"Mitchell, I like that." She felt warm. "Batill'e had a contract with GWM Cinematique. They gave her a house near the studio on Moktar-Sandor where she, on at least two confirmed occasions, verbally and physically abused at least one of the household staff members."

Drago was intrigued. "What does that have to do with Commodore Morgan?"

"GWM Cinematique, Mr. Mise."

"G.W. Morgan is GWM Cinematique?"

"Actually GWM Enterprises owns Cinematique," A. J. said. "You didn't know?"

"He's well above our pay grade," Mitch joined in, smiling at Maria. "We don't talk much. He orders, we do."

"He's well above the pay grades of most of us in this room, Commander," The senator from Gabb'es said.

Maria continued. "Anyway, Batill'e refused to apologize and compensate the staff member, and later made callous jokes on the matter on a Sandoran talk show before a live audience. This incensed Morgan. He travelled from his home in Sperieus to Moktar-Sandor to personally fire and escort the diva off company property."

Drago's eyes widened. Mitch leaned forward, fascinated. His eyes locked on Maria's as she spoke. Her slit serape sleeves shimmered ever so slightly with each movement of her arms.

I knew I smelled orchids. Mitch thought. *It's her. Beautiful, brilliant, dangerous, the Dragon Lady, in person.*

"Well, the Batill'e Corporation sued GWM Cinematique for breach of contract. In fact, they filed in four separate jurisdictions. They lost. They were all considered retaliatory and were summarily dismissed in every one."

Mise nodded, then chuckled.

"May I ask, where you're stationed, Commander. And what is your rank, Mr. Mise?"

"We're under Commodore Morgan's command, Mr. Mortimer," Mitch answered. "We're both assigned to CBC Draken."

"I see you're an aviator."

"Yes sir. I command a vortex squadron. Mr. Mise here is my Senior Warrant Officer, that's his rank. We're actually symbiots."

"Excuse me?" Maria didn't understand that.

"It's a fleet term, miss," Drago said. "We're interrelated. One has no purpose without the other. The commander flies and fights the squadron, I keep them maintained, armed and fueled."

Mitch added. "We're classmates, miss," CLA 'Fifty-six. I trained on the command and general staff track. Mise on the Logistics and Combat Support track. We're equals, drawing the same pay and benefits."

"That's very interesting. We're going to be shipmates then," A. J. announced.

"Oh really, are you joining our media embeds?"

"More like replacing them, Mitchell," Maria quipped.

"Miss Hardesty here stole my job as senior embed to your task force, Commander."

"Hey!"

"No, I'm kidding. She was, how do I describe what happened, boss?"

"The hell if I know. How about press-ganged?"

The conversation stopped as a host led a Common Fleet Provost Marshal Lieutenant into the salon from the main hall. The officer recognized LCdr Pulke from the attachment to the message he carried in his hand. He stepped forward and gladial saluted.

"I beg pardon for disturbing your evening, sir," he said.

Both Mitch and Drago stood and came to attention. Mitch gave the man his best parade ground return salute for the high-society types' entertainment.

"What can I do for you, Lieutenant?"

"Sir, this message arrived at our duty desk for you from Task Force Draken command shuttle about an hour ago. The billeting office informed us of your reservation here." The lieutenant handed the small envelope to Mitch and stood at ease,

161

awaiting a response. Across from them, Maria and A. J. exchanged glances and watched him open it and read the text.

Mitch nodded and handed it to Drago. "Thank you, Lieutenant, no response is necessary. It's a simple heads up."

"That's for damned sure," Mise chortled, handing the message back. The lieutenant snapped to attention and saluted.

"Yes, sir. Have a pleasant evening, sir. Chief."

"You too, Lieutenant." Mitch returned his salute and exhaled heavily, exchanging glances with Mise. He sat back down as the lieutenant faced about and left the room.

"Bad news, Commander?" Maria asked.

"Uh, oh no. Just a coincidence. I've received an invitation to discuss history."

"With Commodore Morgan I assume?"

"Uh, yes."

"So you're an historian and a fighter pilot, Mitchell?"

"He sure as hell is, miss. And good at both."

"Really?" Maria said, nodding and looking Mitch over approvingly. "Were you called in for the hearings, Mitchell?"

"Yes, miss, we were. You can call me Mitch."

"I like Mitchell. So you were there?"

Call me anything you want. "Yes."

"You don't sound very enthusiastic, Commander."

"It's been a long war, Senator."

The industrialist matron spoke up as a host gestured for her and her party. "One of my companies manufactures ejection cocoons and ambu-bags for the Common fleet and our State Guard units, Commander. I hope you never need either one, but if you do, it'll do its job. I can assure you."

"Actually, ma'am," Mise stood respectfully and gestured towards Mitch. If you mean Mas-Dilim of Epirus-Serianis, ma'am, one already has. Kept the fella here safe in the Trudan Corridor, for seventeen hours until we found him. We got lucky. Thanks for that."

The three of them changed direction and strode over to Mitch and Drago, Mitch stood immediately. They traded hugs with them all. "Bless you both," the mother said.

Maria's eyes widened in amazement. "Mitchell. You had to eject from your fighter into the void?"

162

"It gave me no choice ma'am. The system knew it was fatally hit before I did. It spat my ass out before she blew up. The cocoon did exactly what it was supposed to do."

"What happened then?" A. J. asked. His voice raised noticeably.

"Like I said, the cocoon did its job. Put me right to sleep. I don't remember a thing until our search and rescue guys cut me out inside the shuttle."

The young industrialist snickered at that. A. J. saw Mise's face harden.

"The same thing happens to me, mother, when I test prototypes," the young man said.

Mise lightened up. He reached out and shook the man's hand. "Being tossed around in an ejection cocoon once is bad enough," Mise said, nodding in admiration.

"They got the better of you, Mitchell?" Maria asked, eyeing Mitch.

"Well, miss, it was five v one, the hard way. I was the one. I got four."

"And damaged the fifth," Mise added. "She ejected too. Our guys brought her, Mitch and two of the others in."

The industrialists gave all in the salon a 'we'll see you later' wave and headed off towards their table.

A. J. saw Maria had not taken her eyes off Mitch for more than a few seconds, since she first turned to look at him. He saw an opportunity and took it. "Why don't you gentlemen join us, Commander," he offered, surprising Maria. "I'm sure the DIG can spring for dinner for two technical consultants preparing their media embeds for their basic training experience. Right, boss?"

Maria gave his arm a playful slap. "I hate you, A. J., of course, you're both welcome to join us," she said sweetly to Mitch and Drago. The two looked at each other and shrugged, smiling.

"Thank you. We'd be happy to," Mitch nodded.

"Fantastic." A. J. stood and moved over, offering his seat across from Maria to Mitch. He gestured to Drago to sit across from him on Maria's right. Hearing and seeing the goings on, a host made a quick table and seating change notation on her wrist pad, updating the restaurant.

"You seem to know a lot about our Commodore, Mr. Mortimer," Drago said, settling into this new unexpected situation.

"As much as he lets us know. He's actually a very private man. Did you know he was named for his fifth century ancestral grandfathers?"

"Actually, yes, that I know. Field Marshal Webster Gaven, and Fleet Command Sergeant Major Julius Morgan the fourth," Drago answered proudly.

"Webster Gaven?" Maria turned to him. "I've never heard of him."

"He was the first marine to be named Chief of Staff," Mitch answered. "A dragoon to be exact, both he and CSM Morgan were second war dragoons."

Maria shook her head. "Falling through the atmosphere like a meteorite with just a few centimeters of asteroidal alloy between you and eternity. Not for me. We don't have to do anything like that do we?"

Mitch saw the look of real trepidation on her face. His first instinct was to treat Maria like a civvie and fill her head with a lot of nonsense. But she was beautiful, her scent had reached out and grabbed him. The regulations were clear about media embeds. Plus an expensive dinner was on the line.

"Oh no, miss. That's well beyond basic training. You'll see a lot of dragoons around though."

"Especially the PT instructors," Mise said with a sly grin.

"That's one thing I don't understand about the ground forces," A. J. said, waving for a passing host. He exchanged an empty aperitif for another. Another host set a small tray of finger foods on the table between them.

"The restaurant will have your table for four ready in just a few moments more, Miss Hardesty."

"Thank you, that's quite alright."

"What's that, sir?"

"They've had skeletal muscular enhanced battle suits for centuries now. Why the continued emphasis on such brutal physical training."

Mitch laughed. "I wouldn't call it brutal. It's tough, for sure. I went through dragoon school and was an aviation liaison officer, or ALO, with a fusilier battalion. The SME is kinetic," he said. "It requires body movement to function. It only enhances an individual's strength. It doesn't provide it. The SME allows troops to bear the weight of their battle suits while carrying heavy loads

164

over distances and rough terrain, and in varying gravity. It prevents long-term orthopedic problems, but they still need to be physically fit."

"You're a pilot, Mitchell. Why'd you go to dragoon school?" Maria asked.

"To learn how they and the other ground pounders operate. It helps me to fight my squadron better in support of them. Every branch exists, ultimately, miss, to support the infantry on the surface. All the way out to the battle cruisers."

Drago saw the senior host, an older gentleman, with a distinct military bearing, standing nearby surveying his crew. He made a slight affirmative nod at Mitch's comment.

"I don't understand why we can't use robots for that kind of fighting. It's so, ugh, brutal and dirty."

"That's right, miss," Drago said. "War has to be, otherwise people would come to love watching it, like a game."

"But so many fine men and women are sacrificed as cannon fodder, often on some nameless asteroid or uninhabitable world. I mean, you pilots have your cocoons, vessel crews and passengers have life pods, we all have a hope for rescue. But those poor, bloody fusiliers and dragoons. We should replace them with robots."

"No, Maria," A. J. said. I understand what Warrant Officer Mise said. It must be sons and daughters on the pointy end of the gladius. Because fathers and mothers have failed to keep the peace."

"But that's the military's job, A. J., keeping the peace."

"No, miss. It isn't," Mitch said firmly. "Diplomats make peace, politicians and constables maintain it, when those fail, the military fights battles to win conditions favorable for the diplomats to restore the peace."

Maria was stunned. "Where did you hear that, Mitchell?"

"It's from the Sandoran military ethics manual, which was adopted as political ethics three-oh-one at the CLA, miss."

"Bang, Maria," A. J. chuckled.

"Not cannon fodder either," Mise said. "They're very well-trained and well-equipped. They're sent in to do specific jobs no one else can. In Trudan, Mitch covered marines securing armed habitats on asteroids. They were being used as bases from which the Alliance was interdicting our lines of commerce." Mise saw he

165

was drawing attention from around the salon. *Fine by me*, he thought.

"Well, those asteroids were key terrain. I know that sounds odd in a void battle, but whoever held those, how many was it, Mitch? Seven of 'em, controlled the Trudan corridor and all the commercial traffic between Baktimur and Epirus. Destroying them with heavy weapons was not an option."

"If we had blasted those rocks to dust and all the people and equipment with them, the primary debris would have been drawn inward and would have bombarded the Trudan home worlds. That would have been a real mess."

"It's a principal of war, Maria." A.J. said. "Economy of force."

Maria nodded.

"That would have created a nasty navigation hazard for us as well, miss." Mitch joined in. "We would have had to station a fleet of ore ships and octophages there to keep the trans-stellar transit lanes clear of the secondary debris."

"Yes, indeed," Mise continued. "Commodore Morgan wanted those habitats captured intact. The capital ships defeated the Trudan destroyer force, then covered the marines' shuttles and assault landers approach to the surfaces. The grunts seized three of the seven on the first day."

"And the others?" Maria asked, fascinated.

"We used the first three as additional staging bases to attack the remainder. It took a few more days," Mitch answered.

"That's putting it mildly, Commander," A. J. nodded.

"And that's what restored the refined fuel flow from Baktimur?"

"That's right," Drago said, nodding.

The senior host stepped up to Maria's left and made the familiar salutary gesture.

"Miss Hardesty, your table is ready. If you and your party care to follow me, please."

**

Maria took a beaming Mise's arm for the walk along Bursuq Hall towards the main dining room. "So, Drago, where's your home?"

"Cestere, in Borealis, miss. Same as Batill'e. Same provincial region. I always heard she was a prima donna."

166

"After fourteen years in the fleet, don't you feel it's time to think about settling down?"

"If you mean wife and kids, I'm way ahead on that." He pulled his PtC from his jacket inner pocket and scrolled through to his family album. "That's my wife Kadesh, the handsome fella there, that's Drago junior, he's seven," Mise announced proudly. "Those are the twins, Mitchell and Michelle, they're three."

"Twins! How wonderful," Maria said. She turned and looked back at Mitch. "Interesting names, Drago."

"Yep, Kadesh was saying just the other day, she hopes the kids' Uncle Mitch doesn't wait too long to bring them some cousins to play with."

Mitch grinned at the never subtle dig at his continued bachelorhood. Walking with A. J. behind Maria and Drago, Maria's scent filled his nostrils, her shapely, swaying body filled his eyes.

Maria felt warm. "Do you intend to settle down and raise a family someday, Mitchell?" she asked over her shoulder.

"Me? Well Miss Hardesty, to be honest, I don't give it much thought, except when I'm at Drago's house. What about you?"

Something in Mitch's smooth voice made Maria a little breathless. She didn't answer. She felt her face flush when she looked at him.

"Ha, I can see you now, Maria," A.J. burst out laughing. "A settled matron, raising little dragons."

The industrialists and senators acknowledged the four as they entered and were seated. Mitch stood across from Maria. Her skin looked aglow. *It's that dress,* Mitch thought. *The way it catches the light.*

As the host seated Maria, Mitch whispered in Drago's ear. "Do you smell orchids?"

Drago shrugged, I smell steak. You okay? You look a little flushed."

"So, let's make this official, gentlemen," Maria said as the three men sat down. "As our basic training consultants, is there anything special or dangerous we need to be aware of on Sestria."

Menu pads in the table illuminated.

"What do you mean, miss?"

"I've heard the enlistees are not to be trusted, that I, or we, rather should stay close to the officers."

"Who told you that?" Mitch asked with a hint of incredulity on his face.

She leaned in close and whispered. "My editor."

Her scent was intoxicating to Mitch. He inhaled so deeply he was sure she heard him.

"Don't you worry about that, Miss Hardesty," Mise interjected. "I'll tell you plain. The trainees are gonna love you both, because half the cadre will be afraid of you. Especially you, miss. But the other half are already quoting passages of your literaries while trainees do pushups."

Their table, and several others erupted in laughter.

"And where is your home, Mitch?" A. J. asked with a new aperitif in one hand. He reached into the finger food tray and picked up a fowlon nugget with the other and took a bite.

"Julespa, in the Trinovan."

"Julespa?" Maria looked at him, surprised. "How is it you're in the Commonwealth Fleet? Julespa's still a Valerian protectorate."

"Family ties, such as they are with us," Mitch answered. "It turns out I have kinsmen in Barat. That was enough for a special circumstance visa. The admissions exams did the rest."

"Call me Maria. Kinsmen? From the slave trade?"

I'll call you anything you want. "Yes."

Maria's soft skin and green eyes beckoned. They weren't the fierce and piercing ones like on her photos and interviews. A part of Mitch opened up to her that he never thought should, at least as long as the war was going on. *What is it about her?*

"How are the Julespians progressing reassembling your history?"

"I haven't really paid attention in the last few years, Maria," Mitch said, grinning. "I was a little busy."

"Something to do with fighting a war, eh?" A. J. quipped.

Their table host stepped up next to Maria.

"But you are interested in recovering more of your people's history, aren't you?" She raised a hand slightly for Mitch to hold his answer and turned to deal with the host.

"I'd like a small cut bovine, with a center of nephropidae with it, and sprouts, and breads please."

A. J. and Drago watched Mitch watch Maria. They exchanged glances, knowing what was happening.

"Yes, Miss Hardesty," the host said smiling. "May I recommend the house's vin rose' with your meal?"

"Yes, thank you."

The host turned to Mitch. "And for you, sir?"

"Nephropidae? That's boiled lobster, right? Is it prepared any differently where you're from, Maria?"

"No, I don't think so. Just drop the little bastards in boiling water and wait."

Mitch grinned. "I'd like your strip steak, medium, and nephropidae meat as well," he said. "I'd like sliced fries and greens on the side. With a dark ale, please."

The host grinned and nodded. "Yes, sir! And for you, sir?" he asked Drago.

"I'll have what he's having," he answered, pointing at Mitch. "Except make the steak rare, please."

"Yes, sir. And for you, Mr. Mortimer? You're usual?"

"My usual indeed, Terrence," A. J. boomed. "In fact, better add one of those lobsters for me too."

"Have you done any research among your people, Mitchell?" Maria asked.

"Actually, yes. Before the war, I did some on-site translating for a team at a dig near my home town. We didn't find much of major significance, but we got a pretty good insight into daily life in that part of the world, just before the Kuniean invasion. We were unenlightened, that much is certain, we probably thought we were alone in the universe. Our people never knew what hit them. To me, our liberation from the Kunieans by Commoners is the beginning of our history. "

"That's fascinating," A. J. said. "But why didn't you join the Valerian Armed Forces? They're very well respected."

"Interesting enough, it was a VAF recruiter who suggested I apply to the CLA."

"Really?" Maria asked, intrigued.

"Yes, indeed. I always wondered why the Commoners left after the war and let the Valerians move in. I was talking to this recruiting officer and the subject came up. He told me the gist of the story and gave me some source links. That's where I learned more about Kratari. What impressed me most was his return of the Gladius to the Senate. I read that most every government was stunned that he surrendered so much power. Everyone that is, except Khan Julian the Sixth of Valeria."

"Really?"

"That's right," A. J. interrupted. "In fact, when the Khan heard the news, he ordered the Fortress Danikui orbital battery above Krylein to launch a salute in Kratari's honor. That's the salute battery of the Khan's Own Guard. They still launch those salutes too, to mark the event. Just on the lustrum now. You've gotten a direct benefit of Kratari's invasion of the Trinovan, Maria," A. J. said.

"Oh lord. Kratari. Before dinner," Maria answered, picking up a finger of bread and biting into it.

"Mr. Mortimer, you said earlier you had a Kratari Code for journalists on your press card."

"Yes, yes indeed. Here, I'll show you." A. J. pulled his passport folder from his jacket pocket and pulled out the small, green press credential with his photo and handed it across the table to Mitch.

Mitch turned it around and immediately broke into a wide grin. "Well, well, well."

"What's it say, Mitch?"

Mitch handed the card to Drago on his left. He flipped it over and read it.

'**...an open, conductive news media, held responsible for its completeness, accuracy, timeliness, and security awareness by the Commoner. A news media that is a conduit for, and not a filter of, the information Commoners need every day to maintain the one true triumvirate, that is, the bond of trust between the free people, the peoples' government, and the peoples' armies.**'

"Sure sounds like something the old man would have said," Mise said, handing the card back to A. J.

Mitch turned to Maria. "Would it be safe to say the DIG doesn't exactly share the sentiment on their press credentials, Maria?"

"Oh of course it does, here, I'll show you."

Maria's press credential held the same admonition.

"I'm glad to see the system still works," Drago said, raising a tumbler.

"It takes a lot of maintenance, but we've managed to hold it all together."

"I can understand your point of view, Mitchell," Maria said. "And, to a lesser extent I understand A. J.'s, with Vizio's experience with the Alliance. But you have to see the Denestri point of view and that of the other central region tribes."

"What do you mean, miss?" Drago asked.

"You're from Borealis in the mid-zone. The outer states like Poia where A. J. is from, form a shield for you. Your mid-zone states protect us in Denestri."

"Well, it's not like one has to pass through a state to get to another, Maria. Alliance ships still accelerate around many of our heliospheres to reach their own destinations."

"Not without our knowing about it, A. J. And civilian ships and freighters, not warships, and certainly not fleets."

"And not without transit fees," Mitch added. "I understand what she means, A. J., Denestri and the central states gained an additional security layer, as it were, at the end of the second war, when Poia and the Nursery Crescent states came into the Commonwealth. But, Maria, the central states were firmly against liberating Questri-Shontor and the outer Trinovan worlds which actually strengthened that security."

"Because it exposed the so-called indentured migrant visa system as a slave trade, Mitch," Drago said. "And that was a great big black eye to the centrals and in the mid-zone too, Maria. Denestri and Barat weren't alone."

"But they were in the majority. A lot of big wigs got caught up in that," A. J. said.

"It certainly tore the heart out of the Barati entertainment industry. They haven't produced a decent cinema since," Maria chuckled.

Her scent, her soft olive face and silken hair held Mitch in rapt attention to her every move. The conversation went on as their meal arrived.

"Kratari's strategic defense through tactical offense, was technically, illegal," Maria said. "The Questri-Shontor was neutral. And the Trinovan, well, the three Trinovan powers were Alliance surrogates."

"Kratari was right, the Trinovan Legions were the Alliance's staying power," A. J. responded. "But each of the three were mass breeding slaves on their shares of the eleven other Trinovan worlds."

"So he got them to fight among themselves by liberating a few of those eleven."

"Fifteen actually, counting the inhabited moons." Mitch added in a flippant tone to lighten the mood.

"Okay, fifteen, but how does that justify invading Questri-Shontor."

"To protect the flank of the move into the Trinovan, Maria."

"So they were just in the way?"

"They were under Alliance occupation, as well, Maria," A. J. reminded her. "The March of Lights."

"Oh please, A. J." Maria snorted. "More propaganda. That staged event with that crazy woman."

"The liberation of Contagor'e Mare was not a staged event, Maria," Mitch said. "That's where Officer Candidate Webster Gaven distinguished himself. Kratari awarded him a battlefield commission for his actions there."

"I've never heard that."

"It's not a widely known incident, it's certainly never been in any of the cinemas about the invasion. And it had no bearing on Manduleya Tagareesh's trial," Mitch said.

"Every cinema I've seen about it focuses on B. I. Mikhailovich and Vane'a Munciy," A. J. remarked over his huge leafy green salad with fowlon bits after cutting and distributing the side of lobster across it.

"'Thirty Seven Hours' was excellent," Drago said, picking up a vegetable crisp. "Why hasn't Morgan's studios ever done that cine I wonder."

"They just did, Drago. Or they just finished one."

"Is the March of Lights going to be a part of that Praetor series?" Maria asked.

"Oh, yes," A. J. said. "Not only that, but I hear some major revelations are coming out about the old planetary surveillance teams that went away about that time."

"You mean absorbed into the fleet," Maria said. She leaned back in her chair and stared into space.

"Something wrong?" Mitch asked.

"Huh, uhn, no. I just thought of something someone said," she answered softly. "Tell me." She leaned in close. "Have you ever heard of a thing called Recondo?"

172

Mitch and Drago stopped eating and looked at one another for a brief second. Drago put his head down and picked at his fries.

"It's not something we like to talk about in public," Mitch said finally.

Maria looked him in the eyes. "Then you can tell me in private," she said softly.

Mitch chuckled, he looked down and took a bite of his steak. When he looked up again her eyes were still locked on his.

"Do you like to dance, Mitchell?"

"Well, actually I don't really know how."

"Would you like me to teach you?"

You can teach me anything you want. "I'd like that."

Across the table, A. J. shook his head and grinned. "Drago, do you gamble?"

"I've been known to risk a credit or two, A. J."

"I suppose we'll see these two in a day or so. It was nice knowing your commander, Mr. Mise. You'll never see him again," A. J. only half whispered.

"It's the end of an era. My Kadesh may get her wish after all. The shuttle to Tresium leaves in thirty hours, Mitch."

Mitchell and Maria looked at A. J. and Drago, then at each other, and smiled.

****

Saturum night, 2320 hrs, Southeast Tresium local time. The Sunshine Lounge. 09-02 of 770CE.

Looking down on the Tribe's sound stage, tucked away in one of the darkened privacy booths that overlooked the main lounge, today was Hardisen Batiste's lucky day.

"Po me anudder glass of dat, schtuff, Harry."

"Sure, babe, I'll pour you a double shot so you," Hardisen Batiste stopped in mid-sentence to hiccup. "So you can, so you can't bother… me so much with it." He barely got the words out before hiccupping again.

Batiste caught a lucky break when an already tipsy Samantha Proudfoot, showing lots of skin, joined him at the bar and bought the next couple of rounds. She spoke admiringly of his Recon Constable reputation and his new drover hat. After a while, things got even better. The couple who had the booth before them decided to take things to the next level and moved on to rent a

173

brothel room. He bought a bottle of local mash and claimed the booth with a good view.

"Aww, don't be like dat. C'mon you're slowing down, drink up. We'es gone be good friends." Sam Proudfoot nudged tighter against Batiste.

"Call me Hardi, Hardisen. Like I told ya."

Sitting up, he poured a double shot into her tumbler and handed it to her, then poured a much shorter one for himself. He gulped it down and poured another short one.

"Oh, oh, okay baby. Don't get testy. Dat's some shit hot combo. Don't you think, Hardi-Hardisen?"

Sam poured the shot straight down a well-trained throat. Handing the empty tumbler back to an amazed Batiste for a refill.

"Wow. Well, the combo's alright. But they could use a real vocalist," he snorted, pouring her another.

"I think Terri is pretty good," Sam snuggled closer. She gently stroked the back of his neck and ran her fingers through his hair.

"She stinks. And don't call me Hardi. It's Hardisen."

"Oh, don't be so stuck up," Sam said, massaging his neck. Batiste's head swayed back and forth. "Have another drink. You only say that because she turned down your offer."

They clinked tumblers. Batiste sipped his, Sam downed hers and set the empty tumbler upside down on the table. She slid her hand along his thigh and into his crotch and squeezed. He gasped, almost choking on his mash. He arched himself deeper into her hand.

"Ooh, maybe ah will call you Hardi, ooh," Sam giggled, breathing mash into his face. "Ma girl turned all this down?"

"Her tough luck, I, I know peoples, I, I mean people. I could have made her a star. But that's in the past. I want to focus on you."

He set the tumbler down and turned towards her, laying a hand on her thigh above her knee-high boots. He slid it smoothly along her denim shorts to her ass, working his way up along her hip and bare mid-riff, up her side to her breast. He squeezed and caressed her breast through her short-sleeved, shoulder-less peasant blouse. She let go of his crotch and reached around, gripping his ass through his denims.

"Focus on me? Ah cain't sang."

174

"Can you blow?" He whispered into her ear.

"Blow what?"

"Me for starters, then we'll see what else you can do."

"Here? Now?"

"Why not? Nobody can see us up here."

"I'll do it, baby. But not here in front of my cohort. Let's take this bottle and go out to your POV."

"Okay. Hot mama."

*

'Let me hear ya' holla, Commoners, for Lil' Rick and The Tribe!' The Jock's voice was almost drowned out by cheers and applause. Rick kept his word to Tony. The Tribe had rocked the house since 1700 hours.

Almost all of the fully mustered Thunderin' Third Herd, 3rd Cohort of 2nd Fusilier Battalion, was there. Other elements of the battalion and the regiment, including a lot of pathfinders, IEX Cavalry scouts and a good number of gray-jackets from the battalion's dedicated *Long Range Transport Acre* were there as well.

Grunts welcomed the transport's crewbies into their home away from their home away from home. They mixed and partied with them, regaling them with stories. There was plenty of spill-over around the runways, the Hippodrome booths and the restaurant.

Family members, from near and far, who had accompanied their loved ones to Tresium for a little more time with them before muster, strolled the storied lounge, enjoying the show, often to the chagrin of a 'momma's little boy' or 'daddy's little girl'.

The Sunshine Lounge was rocking to the beat. 'Lil' Rick's tribute band, 'The Tribe' had a wide repertoire of the latest chart-topping thumpers that impressed the Jocks and drew in a good amount of street traffic. Though they rotated lead performers routinely, 'Lil' Rick Anders was clearly the combo's leader and star performer. Terri joined them and she and Rick dedicated a couple of old love songs to Coop and Sara, and all the couples.

"Hey Terri! Do Get on Yer Feet!" someone yelled. Others joined. "Yeah, belt it out!"

Rick and Jason picked up the rhythm and Marcus on the percs joined.

"No, not me," Terri said into the mike after catching her breath. She pointed into the crowd. "There's Sergeant Mainworthy. Come up here, Recon and help us!"

The mates made a hole amid repeated shouts of 'RECON' and let Pathfinder Sergeant Rebecca Mainworthy through and onto the stage. There, the short-haired, taciturn dragoon showed the cherries in Recon she was more than just a walking, talking field manual, whose sole function in life was to make theirs in the platoon miserable. She, Terri and the Tribe got everyone on their feet with the old favorite, then 'Hold On' and 'All I Want'.

The Jocks spelled the Tribe between sets, which kept the dancers up and rotating. It took every ounce of patience he had, but Rick stayed focused on playing music and let Sam Proudfoot work the plan. The Kushiro Street patio, the ballerum and the Hippodrome were filled with partying, paying customers, including Proudfoot and her 'date' Hardisen Batiste of the Law Enforcement Command.

For their finale, the lycos, perc and horn combo, debuted three new songs. Sully led 'Treat Her Like a Lady', Rick did 'I Can Dream About You'. For 'Uptown Funk', Rick and four of the eleven member group set their instruments to auto and displayed their choreographic talents as well. The crowd went wild and immediately started copying the already popular uptown funk stutter slide step and shoulder roll dance moves.

Racking his lycos, Lil' Rick and the Tribe bowed one last time and stepped down off the sound stage, to echoing cheering and applause. The jock in the observation booth started a new track and a new relief of dancers. Rick worked his way through the crowd to the patio bar and the open seats Tony saved for him and Terri for breaks through the evening. Tony set a mug of cold brew on the bar in front of him as he sat down.

"Ahh, thank ya, Tony. This is gonna go down good." Rick hoisted the mug in salute to Tony and took a long drink.

"You deserve it, young man. You got some moves," Tony said chuckling, wiping down the bar. "There's five cameras and mikes for that stage setup. The jocks upstairs are real good at editing video. I'll send you the rough cuts and you can decide how much you want them to go for."

"You mean like sell copies?" Terri asked excitedly.

"Certainly," Tony answered. "You pick the cuts you like, and I'll market them on the stellar web. Say, seventy thirty, your way."

"You think they'll sell, Tony?"

"Hell yeah! There's always been musically inclined troops in the fleet. And people have made money on the side selling copies of their jam sessions on the web since there's been a trans-stellar web. Lots of celebs have gotten their start playing morale rallies on the transports or in trooper bars like this. And youngsters," he pointed in turn to Rick and Terri. "You two sing real good together. Morgan owns a couple of recording studios, they're always looking for, what is it you kids call it?" Tony waved both hands in the air, rocking his head from side to side. "The new sound?"

Several of the Tribe players and others gathered around, drinks in hand.

"Aw man, I could see us playing one of those pleasure liners like the Pegasus Star, Terri," Rick said nodding, catching his breath after swallowing a mouthful of brew. Combo members around them nodded.

"You and me aboard a cruise liner? And me unarmed? Keep dreaming, horny goat," she grinned, sipping a spritzer.

"Did I tell y'all about the honey I met aboard her? People, she was something else," he snorted.

"Something else, like what?" Terri tilted her head towards him, knowing what was coming next.

"She was a chambermaid on the deck above mine. Big, golden skin girl. Real pretty too. She reminded me of those pictures of Nasty Nicholla, so I asked her to come over and pretend to be her for me when she got off duty that day."

"Asked or paid?!" Terri shook her head in comic disbelief. Half her friend's stories of his sexual conquests were fantasies or wild embellishments he enjoyed regaling her and the rest of the platoon with. The other half were real enough to make the fantasies believable.

"Okay, paid."

Terri and the mates laughed. "What did you do to her, Rick?" she asked.

"Well, first she shows up in this short sarape, which was fine as hell, but she had something on that looked like that

177

Madonna's headdress we always see Nicholla wearing. I tell ya, girl, she was something!"

"So what did you do?" a mate asked.

"I turned the heat down on the lamalar and let it start to frost. I had her press her butt up against it for a few minutes, until she got cold."

"I hate to ask. But I know you want me to," Terri said in mock resignation, she already knew what was coming next. "Why would you want a big, cold, golden butt?"

"To thaw it out," Rick said slyly. The mates burst out laughing around him. "It took a while. And that headdress stayed on the whole time. I tried my best to shake it off. But she was big, like I said, and had good rhythm."

Terri rolled her eyes and shook her head. She chuckled at Tony. "My mate, here is a horny goat, Tony."

"He is that. But you can tie him down, with the right girl. Like you did with those two over yonder. Nice job," Tony said pointing over to the guests of honor, strolling their way from the ballerum, arm in arm, looking into each other's eyes. "So, how'd you do it?"

"That one wasn't easy. But they were the right type I could tell."

Tony smiled.

"Anyway, my shipboard station is on the command bridge. Sara is one of the close defense coordinators there. And Coop, well, we went through basic together. His shipboard is a hundred millimeter gun on B deck, right below Sara's station."

"You're on the command bridge for every duty interval?"

"Yes," she said, sipping her spritzer.

Small wonder, Tony thought.

"When I introduced them, Coop broke out in a sweat, he couldn't talk, he just stammered. Sara said he was cute, she told him to come back when he got himself together. But he didn't come back."

"What?! Scared silly huh? I know the feeling."

"He got it together though," Rick said. "While we were transiting between Trudan and Aletia, they managed to spend some time together on the communal deck. At Maranon, before we deployed to the surface, Coop bagged a Kritt fighter headed straight for the bridge. Commander Tate came up on the net personally and thanked gun B one two."

"Classy."

"Good old Coop comes back with, 'Ah had to protect ma woman, suh,'" Terri grinned and shook her head.

"Well that's good."

"I don't think Tate even realized what he was asking next, because he asked, 'well, who is that, gunner?' and Coop proceeds to identify her by name, rank and duty position."

"On the open net, Tony. The whole ship's company heard it!" Rick said, laughing.

"I looked over at Sara, when I heard that. I never saw a copper-skinned girl blush like that."

The old soldier laughed, shaking his head. "Excellent. Third Cohort deployed to the surface after that?"

"Yes, sir, the next day."

"Don't call me sir, Trooper."

*

Batiste could barely contain himself lounging on the rear bench seat of his Util.

"You gotta take those boots off."

"Why? I'll just drop my denims."

"Baby, when I blow, I blow. I don't want you gettin' all excited and kickin' me with those things."

"Oh! You're that good, huh?"

"Pour us another drink, Hardisen. Let me take those damned boots off and I'll blow you away," Sam said grinning.

They clinked their tumblers and downed another shot. Sam slid off the seat between Batiste's knees. Batiste couldn't believe his luck. Forgetting he was in his Util he stood to strip his denims, bumping his head on the roof and almost fell over, but Sam steadied him, laughing.

"Don't get too excited till you get those pants and those shit-kickers off."

He dropped his denims and underpants and sat back down with a wide grin and let Sam pull off his boots. A silver chain clattered to the floor out of his right boot.

"Is that the notorious choke chain you captured?"

"Yea. Sure is."

"Put it around me."

179

"What?!"

"Put it on me. Make me service you. Like the Sacorsti make their slaves do."

"You a freak or something, woman?"

"I'm drunk and you done got me hot, lookin' at this big, beautiful thang of yours."

"Yeah? You like that?"

"Oooh, looks yummy," she said, fingering his balls and softly blowing on his penis. It quickly stiffened and rose, glistening in anticipation. Sam picked up the chain and slipped it over her head and down to her shoulders. She pulled her hair through, then took the chain's running end and pulled it taut around her throat, handing it up to Batiste.

"Make your slave service her master."

*

During their whirlwind leave, visiting both their families, Corporal Cooper Peres and Petty Officer 1st Class Sara Coyningham-Peres had married three weeks before on Gabb'es-Lustra, the third and most tropical world of the 'Resort State'. At the patio bar, Tony nodded in satisfaction, watching the couple exchange hugs and kisses of congratulations, appreciation and a welcome back to work with Terri and Rick. He knew the rigors of a honeymoon aboard a slow Gabb'es viewing liner well.

For the reception, Tony had placed them in a booth nearest the patio bar that he and a bar-back worked alone. Conchita, his manager, had called in the entire staff and spread them to cover the expanding crowd. Four teams of bartenders, bar-backs and their supporting hosts ran the Hippodrome and one handled the restaurant and privacy booths. The cooks set up a buffet for the entire house and kept the serving line filled.

Tony was happy to go all out for the 'back to work reception' as Teresa Faisal dubbed it. Lean times were coming, it was best to empty the refrigerated stores. The regiment would be departing with the task force for its PDRE within days, then starting its deployment for however long that might be. Tony had heard rumors that at least one of the Fifth Fleet battle groups was slated to be stationed at Tresium when it returned from Vighandis, but when that would happen was anyone's guess.

For now though, everywhere Tony looked there was laughter and good cheer, well lubricated by good drinks, good food and good entertainment. The credits were rolling in, every host, dancer and brotheler's purse made a hearty jingle.

Rick and Cooper Peres came back to the patio bar while Terri and Sara chatted with their girlfriends. Rick cast a glance up towards the privacy booth Sam and Batiste had occupied.

"Looking for somebody, Rick?" Peres asked.

"I got an appointment."

"With a girl?"

"That's classified this time, good buddy. Let's just say, I was thinking about a song."

Peres turned and looked at him. "So, that's why Doc Sam was working that poser provost who tried to work Terri," He whispered.

Rick turned to him. "I don't want you mixed up in this one, Coop."

"Sam got your back?"

"Yep."

"Okay. So you always got a tune on your mind?" Peres asked, changing the subject.

"Or a girl. So, how's married life?"

"I dunno yet. Once we get on a schedule, things will be different. So far, it's been one big party and one liner cabin after another."

"The real fun will start when we embark."

Rick's vibrating PtC interrupted them. Sam Proudfoot's image in the small screen made him grimace.

"Sam, you okay? You look terrible."

'Thanks," she said with a smirk. 'I gotta shower. I reek of booze.'

"Where are you?"

'Upstairs, I rented a B-room this afternoon. I changed into my, 'working clothes' here before I met him at the bar.'

"Smart, you were looking hot. You okay?"

'I'm fine. A half an epicat pill at the right time, and everything you drink comes back up. And no hangovers.'

"Did you get it?"

Sam held up the shiny silver choke chain. 'I got it. You want it?'

"Naw, I won't need it. Where is he?"

'He's out by his POV. It's still there, I can see it from the window. It's a beat-up brown Rambler Util with a Provost Marshal vanity plate on the front bumper. It's on the west side of the lot, last row, along the tree-line. He was pretty mad when I ran off, but he's wobbly. I see him now, trying to clean vomit off himself and out of his pants. He's not thinking very much about the chain.'

"Are you alright? You didn't, I mean you didn't, ah, drink too much did you?"

'Richard. There ain't that much mash in the whole Commonwealth," she grinned. 'Now go be a good brother.'

"With pleasure." Rick breathed a sigh of relief that Sam was safe and the pharmaceutical key to their plan from her aid-bag worked when and where she said it would.

'I'll see you back at the cohort.'

"Good-oh," he said. He turned the unit to standby and positioned it in his shirt pocket then turned to Peres and grinned.

"HA!" Tony roared in delight. He shook his head, smiling and wiping down the bar.

"Coop, will you see that Terri gets back to the barracks okay?"

"No worries. Terri's gonna ask where you went. What should I tell her?"

"Tell her I met a girl."

"That won't fly. Wait, what am I talking about? You're Lil' Rick."

**

The brown Util was right where Sam said. Weaving around parked POVs towards the back row, Rick was about half-way across when he heard familiar moaning and retching. He tensed; he willed himself to relax as he walked along the last row following the sound. He found Batiste, naked from the waist down, on his hands and knees, vomiting at the base of a tree behind his Util. His denims and one boot lay on the pavement beside the open passenger bay door. The whole scene reeked of cheap, sweet mash, as Rick moved around it.

"Hardisen Batiste. You alright over here?"

"That, that bitch vomited all over me and my ride, man!" He barely got the words out before heaving again. "I can't see somebody get sick. I, I get, get, siiicck!" He choked out the words, grabbing his stomach and retching again.

"So did you get your rocks off, Hardisen Batiste?" Rick moved slowly, upwind, grinning down on the pitiful sight. He stopped with the Util between himself and the Lounge. He stood there for a moment, looking down on Batiste.

"Naw, man. That whore was so drunk she blew her guts all over me as soon as I got her down."

Rick's eyes went wide in fury.

"She's No Whore, You Fuck!" Rick yelled, kicking the man in the stomach. Batiste doubled over into a puddle of vomit.

"GET UP, YOU PIECE OF SHIT!" Rick backed up and squared. He balanced, standing on flat, dry ground, slightly elevated from Batiste in the shrubs. He relaxed his body, keeping alert and aware of his surroundings. Batiste worked his way to his feet somehow, wiping his face with one hand and extending the other to ward off another blow.

"Alright, alright. I got no quarrel with you."

"I've got one with you."

"What?" Batiste gasped, still holding his stomach. His knees wobbled. He swayed, side to side and back to front. Rick wasn't sure if he was feigning.

"What did I do to you?"

"You put my sister out of this rattle-trap out on Carder Rock Creek Road when she wouldn't perform for you. Didn't you?"

"That's between me and her."

"Not anymore, ass wipe."

"Look man, don't give me that, 'my cohort, my family' shit," Batiste said, steadying himself. "All the bitch had to do was give up a little pussy. Maybe her ass. I didn't mean no harm. The other girls all gave it up, but your girl had to be all high and mighty about it. So what? She come crying to you! And now you gonna assault a Provost! Who the fuck do you think you are, marine? You're under arrest!"

"By a cook?"

Batiste's eyes bucked in shock. He staggered backwards, almost slipping in vomit. "What did you say?" he hissed, looking around. He stepped forward.

Rick stood his ground. He had the advantage and intended to make full use of it. "The other girls gave it up you say. Gave it up to what? I don't see much there."

"Fuck you. It's clear you ain't hittin' that ass, get out of the way and let me get it."

"You're pathetic. How many women have you done this to, Batiste? Tell me, I wanna know."

"Scores!" he laughed, sneering. "Every woman in the LEC galley, for starters." He hiccupped and gripped his stomach.

"Thanks, that's good to know. Should be good evidence at your trial."

"What da fuck are you talkin'? They gave themselves to me willingly, every one of 'em."

"Every one?"

"Yeah. So what."

"So every one of them is a felony, ass wipe.

"What da fuck you mean?"

"I looked it up. You were on a Common Fleet military reservation when you coerced civilians into having sex with your sorry ass or walk home, that's rape. At League-Level, rape's a capital crime. You should know that in the LEC." Rick grinned. "But oh, wait, you're a cook."

"Nobody's gonna press charges against me."

"You wanna gamble on that? That's fine with me. But the recording from my PtC on the municipal web may change a few women's minds."

"You Son Of A Bitch! You Set Me Up!"

"No shit, bitch."

"MOTHER FUCKER!" Batiste threw himself towards Rick, striking wildly with his left. Rick stutter-stepped into him. Keeping his balance, he parried Batiste's swing with his left forearm, cocking his right fist behind his ear. Pivoting on his left leg, he stepped around and focused the entire right side of his body into his right shoulder and upper arm and gained momentum from the slight elevation. At the precise angle, Rick unleashed a short, hammer blow right hook into the left side of Batiste's face, driving him to the ground. It was too much for Batiste. He lay there, groaning, sprawled in the dirt.

Rick backed away, watching Batiste stir, then rise to his knees, holding his head in his hands. After a moment, he groaned and vomited again. Rick left Batiste wailing and sobbing on his knees. He turned and walked the long way around the lounge, ensuring he wasn't followed. Along the way, he unfastened his shirt pocket and checked his PtC. He kept his word to Batiste. He replayed the recording, ensuring neither of his sisters' names were mentioned on it. Before walking into the Cisco Street entrance, Rick claimed the file as his own, and uploaded it to the Redfordsville municipal web.

***

The news about Batiste spread like wildfire around town the next day. On the Depot, the 2nd Battalion, 7th Marines, and especially 3rd Cohort buzzed with speculation. There was talk of retribution by Law Enforcement Command provosts for an assault against one of their own. Rumors abounded all that day of a rumble in the works between some of the LEC and the Thunderin' Third Herd, including some Recon people. Battalion NCOs flooded into their barracks squelching rumors and calming everybody down.

Platoon Sergeant Crowder and Staff Sergeant Mixon spent most of the day in the barracks with Corporal Anders. By midafternoon, the rumors had been dispelled and tempers cooled. Troopers told Sergeant Proudfoot and Corporal Faisal they saw Anders carrying an overnight bag and leaving the barracks with PSgt Crowder and SSgt Mixon just before sundown.

***

0710hrs Monrum morning, Southeast Tresium local time. Orderly Room, 3rd Cohort, 2nd Bn, 7th Marines, Fleet Marine Barracks, Piraeus-Tresium Depot, 11-02 of 770CE.

"Corporal Anders reports to the Sergeant Major as ordered," Rick sounded off at attention in front of Cohort Sergeant Major Greer's desk.

"Getting an early start are we, Corporal?" the sergeant major snarled. "We haven't been back two weeks yet, and already you're makin' admin work for me." He sat erect in his swivel behind the console desk with his arms folded. Rick cast a furtive glance downward and caught his icy stare, then looked straight ahead again.

"I didn't intend to cause a big fuss, Sergeant Major."

"The hell you didn't!" Greer snapped back. "All I wanna know is, did you entice a fellow non-commissioned officer to commit a sexual act in furtherance of this, this scheme of yours?"

Rick was surprised for a second, he glanced down at Greer, then at Crowder, standing behind Greer's right shoulder behind

185

the desk. He snapped his head and eyes to the front and flashed a slight grin. "No, Sergeant Major! I can assure you, no such act was either planned or conducted."

"Are you sure?" SSgt Mixon asked, standing behind Rick's right shoulder. "We saw her put down a lot of mash."

"She knew the epicat dosage she needed to tolerate it, Sergeant. And for how long. She knew what she was doing."

"Did you entice her to do it?" Crowder asked.

"No, Sergeant. I tried to talk her out of it, but, like I said yesterday..."

Crowder cut him off. "Yeah, yeah, she's her sister too. What do you think, Top?" he asked, looking down towards Greer.

"It's what the centurion thinks that matters," Greer said, his eyes still locked on Anders. "Your conduct was unbecoming that of one of my noncommissioned officers, Anders, and I won't stand for it. Report for duty. Crowder, have him back here ready to go before the centurion at seventeen hundred."

"Roger that, Top." Crowder gestured for Rick to leave. Mixon stepped back and opened the door behind him. Rick faced about and, seeing the door open and clerks scampering away, marched out into the hall, where Terri, Coop and Doc Sam were waiting. Rick heard the orderly room door shut behind him. He cast a forlorn look towards his friends, he shook his head and shrugged.

"Seventeen hundred, back to work in the meantime."

*

"So what do you really think, Top?" Benson Crowder asked after Mixon closed the door behind Anders.

Maxwell Thurman Greer unfolded his arms and relaxed, leaning back in his swivel.

"I've got a wife and three daughters at home, and fifty-seven here in this cohort, plus the female officers. I'm damned proud of him."

"You think she'll say anything about it in formation, Top?" Mixon asked.

"Naravanutu? Naw, she's waiting for guidance from the battalion adjutant, who is waiting for guidance from regiment. Who's waiting for task force to wake up and have tea and crumpets before they catch up on the news."

"Do they drink jave at Regiment?" Mixon mocked. "Remind me not to go up there."

"You're not going anywhere near regiment, Staff Sergeant." Greer barked. "Or battalion. Naravanutu said she'd fight it out all the way up to Morgan if she has to. She's got a heads up on our PDRE tasks and it's right up your alley. The three shop at battalion is working up some demonstration HG taskings for your squad. But You Are Not Leaving This Cohort! Is that clear, Staff Sergeant!"

"Clear as mud, Top," Mixon chuckled. "What are you talkin' about?"

"You ain't heard? Lang didn't tell you?"

"No, tell me what?"

"We're going to Lucainus-Phuong for PDRE. We've got Phuong-Yeuin."

Mixon stepped back in stunned surprise. "Wha?! Wow!"

"No shit?! Happy Valley?!" Crowder's arms dropped to his side. "And us with a cherry lieutenant. Damn! Any word on where we're deploying to after that? Andolusia is in the wrong direction for Vighandis."

"Not a word. And that's got the old lady concerned. Battalion and regiment too. Keep all this to yourselves for now. She'll put the word out in formation. Open the door, let the clerks back in. Tell the CQ to start hustling the platoons out, Mix."

SSgt Mixon opened the orderly room door, allowing it to swing wide. "Formation! Everybody outside! Mornin' Parade, Pass the word topside, Barrymore!"

*

At 0730hrs, CoSM Greer stood to attention facing 3rd Cohort.

"Fall In!"

The infantry green cohort guidon snapped to the order. One hundred eighty seven pair of booted heels came together in a single thud, as 3rd Cohort, 2nd Fusilier Battalion, of the 7th Regiment of Commonwealth Marines snapped to attention in its' barracks quadrangle formation area.

Corporal Fiasal stood in the front rank, the 1st Squad of the 2nd Fusilier Platoon. Corporal Anders stood behind her in the second rank. Doc Sam stood in the Headquarters Platoon ranks. They, and the rest of the cohort guided on the actions of Corporal

Cooper Peres, holding the staff and infantry green cohort guidon. Peres stood in front of the formation, one step in front of, and one step to the left of the sergeant major.

Greer issued his next directive. "Receive the report!"

The headquarters section sergeant and each of the four platoon sergeants turned their torso towards Greer and gladial saluted. Returning to the position of attention, they faced about, and issued their directive.

"Report!"

Rifle and weapons squad leaders in the three fusilier platoons, and the headquarters and heavy weapons platoon section sergeants, half-faced left towards their platoon sergeants. They gladial saluted as they reported in turn. "All Present!" Or they named troopers on linen, mess or other early cohort detail, then half-faced right.

Upon receiving each squad leader's report and returning their salutes, each platoon sergeant faced about towards the front. Once all were facing forward, Greer directed, "Re-port!"

Peres and the troopers in the ranks remained at attention as the platoon sergeants declared to Sergeant Major Greer their formal verbal daily report from their squad or section leaders.

"All present or accounted for."

It was an anachronistic drill and ceremonies tradition. Each platoon's status had already been updated, forwarded to the orderly room, collated, and transmitted on up the reporting chain, long before Morning Parade.

The senior non-commissioned officer of the cohort faced about and awaited his commander. Centurion Alanis Naravanutu marched forward from the orderly room door between the 3rd and Weapons platoons. She took the most direct route to her position, twelve steps in front of the front rank of troops and centered three steps in front of and facing Greer. The much shorter centurion received his gladial salute.

"Madam, the cohort is formed."

Returning his salute, she commanded. "Take your posts!"

Greer faced about and marched to the rear, staying centered on the cohort, next to the XO. Corporal Peres stepped forward to assume his position from his centurion, always one and one. The platoon sergeants faced to starboard in marching, they moved to a position three steps to the rear of and centered on their

188

units. Simultaneously, the platoon leaders moved around their platoons from the port side to positions six steps in front of, and centered on them. All now stood, facing the front at the position of attention.

"Stand at..." the centurion barked.

The guidon elevated.

"Stand at..." the platoon leaders echoed her preparatory command over their right shoulders.

"Ease!"

The guidon returned smartly to the order, then thrust forward forty-five degrees. Third Cohort moved their left foot shoulder width apart from their right. They centered their hands at the small of their backs, keeping their fingers extended and joined. They interlocked their thumbs so that the palm of their right hand faced outward. Each officer and every trooper in the ranks, and all troopers on details in the cohort area, standing at doors, turned their head and eyes in her direction to listen to their commander.

"Morning, Thunderin' Third Herd!"

"Morning, Madam!"

"It's another fine day in the infantry. Is it not?!"

"Hooooah!"

"I hope you had as much fun as I did at the Sunshine. Hubby and I left early, so we missed the, ah extra entertainment. Anyway, I'm glad to see all your old, ugly faces together, in uniform," she grinned amid laughter from the ranks. "You, new people, don't worry. You'll be as old and ugly as the rest of us soon enough."

That drew a major laugh from the cohort.

"I've just got off the line with battalion operations. You should hear it straight from me, so there's no doubt in anybody's mind. The war is still going on, though Vighandis is the sole remaining active battle area. During the last few days of our stand-down here, there has been, and I quote, 'minor patrol activity and subsequent skirmishing at several points around the pocket out there.' End quote." She paused for a moment and looked around.

"We know what that means. Anyway, peace talks are heating up. The Valerians are involved now somehow, you can check up on the web for yourselves."

Though short in stature, Naravanutu stood tall in her troopers' esteem. They respected and admired her for her precise military bearing, for her frankness, for her proven ability, her sense of humor, and above all, for never insulting their intelligence. They trusted her.

"The next few days is kit-out. We embark on the twenty-fourth and set to the wave on the twenty-sixth. You know the drill, veterans. Teach your new people. Don't leave them hangin'," she admonished them. "Remember, we were all cherries once."

Laughter rose from her fusiliers.

"Damn Right!" someone in third platoon shouted.

"Shut up, cherry," came from across the formation from somewhere in first platoon. Raucous laughter erupted to Naravanutu's left front, much to her delight. She was about to raise a hand to quiet the outburst when Lieutenant Cartier, in front of second platoon, turned to her right towards Ensign Bolling and first platoon.

"Control those unruly people, Ensign!" she shouted.

First platoon instantly quieted. Stunned, they looked towards second platoon and their new lieutenant, then to their veteran platoon leader. Bolling turned towards his squad leaders.

"Calm your puppies, Sergeants," he said softly. Facing back to the front he nodded towards Cartier, then towards Naravanutu.

"Very well," Naravanutu barked, regaining control. "You've got equipment issue and maintenance, medical examinations, legal and web security by platoons and sections," she said. "Make sure you have all your gear packed and ready to set to the wave. When we close out of these barracks we won't be coming back! Our deployment orders are sealed, as usual. But you can tell your families that we're headed to Andolusia for pre-deployment readiness exercises."

"Lucainus-Phuong." She heard from somewhere in weapons platoon on her far right.

"That's right. Lucainus-Phuong. By a show of hands, how many of you have been there?" She raised her own hand. Only Greer, Crowder, PSgt Pettis, Ensign Bolling and a few NCOs in the weapons platoon raised theirs.

"You veterans think the Tantorans were tough? You think the Kritt were devious? Well, let me tell you something. The Lucainans who are the opposing force for our scenario are tougher and cleverer. We're going up against the First Lucainan Light

Cavalry. Be glad those people are on our side. They're more than tough, they know the ground there and they've never been beaten on it."

Murmurs filled the air.

"At ease in the ranks, people," Greer admonished the cohort. He walked around slowly behind the formation as Naravanutu continued.

"We are going to assault into Phuong-Yeuin exo-drome range, we will secure the Happy Valley and make the initial breach into Phuong-Yeuin town in support of the task force's overall mission," she announced.

"Dayum!"

"That's what I said, Trooper!" Naravanutu chuckled. The laughter in the cohort was a little more subdued this time.

"Anyway, we've got a lot of work to do and just a few days to make things happen. I want every weapon test-fired and battle sight zeroed and their exercise chips calibrated and logged before we embark. Battle suits, comms, STANO devices, same-same. Our vehicles and hold baggage are being shuttled up to *Acre* starting this evening. So our gear will be there waiting for us. There's nothing we haven't done before, Thunderin' Third, so let's get it done smart. Maybe we'll get a few more licks in before Nasty Nicholla calls it quits. Are we on the straight?"

"Straight, Madam!"

"Another thing. I'm sure we all kept up our personal P-T program while we were on leave, right?" She said with a sly grin, to the cohorts' chuckles.

"Phuong is no joke," she said. "I want to see more cardio and a lot more upper body P-T during the transit. Ammunition potency for direct fire weaponry at the battle school is set at one to fifty. You've all been shot with one to one hundred twenty in basic training. We use one to sixty-five at the Infantry School on Istria and in our B-Sims aboard ship. You get shot here you know it, you feel it. You get shot on Phuong with a one to fifty rate pulse, you're gonna know it too."

Bolling and some NCOs laughed at that. Naravanutu grinned. The Third Herd all saw she was enjoying this. "What does a one to fifty hit do, Mr. Bolling?"

"It knocks you on your ass, ma'am!"

"Alright." She stood to attention. The guidon came to the order.

"Cohort," She barked. The guidon rose. 3rd Cohort went to parade rest, head and eyes to the front.

"Ahttennnshun."

"Thunderin' Third Herd, Rock Steady!" 187 pair of boot heels thudded together as one.

"Sergeant Major."

Greer marched forward, halting three paces in front of his commander and gladial saluted.

"Take charge, Sergeant Major." She returned his salute, turning the cohort over to her NCOs. Naravanutu marched to the rear of the formation, pausing next to her XO to wait on her platoon leaders. Sergeant Major Greer stepped to his position based on the guidon and faced about. He directed the cohort to stand easy; then began Thunderin' Third Herd's cluttered duty day.

*

"Ensign Bolling, a word please," Naravanutu said, walking away from the cohort. The other platoon leaders and the XO followed her towards the barracks. The ensign trotted up and quickly caught up to her.

"Yes, madam."

"I like the way you handled yourself back there. I'll speak to Cartier. There's no need for you to. Ya hear me?"

"Yes, madam. I didn't expect that, where does she get off, ranting like that?"

"Just be at ease, Ensign and let me handle it. You're an officer now, not a hot-headed buck sergeant."

"Loud and clear, madam. But if she didn't have a month's seniority over me, I'd punch her lights out."

"Just be good, till you get that next pip. At least, after Phuong."

"Roger that, madam," Bolling chuckled.

The six officers and two officer cadets gathered in the Centurion's office, entering through the Orderly Room.

"There's a commander's conference over at battalion in about an hour. While Theo and I are gone, Rusty, make sure everybody is moving along on the adjutant and logistics officers' schedules or there'll be hell to pay. Those people bitch like old grannies."

"Right," Russell De'Avest, the executive officer said nodding. "I'll keep 'em moving. You just gotta know how to talk to bureaucrats."

Lieutenant Theros, the weapons platoon leader joined in the impromptu coordinating meeting that was Naravanutu's usual style. "While we're up there, madam, I'll see what I can do at S-2 to scare up some extra Phuong maps. The reproducible kind we can copy to flexmet."

"Make that a priority, Theo. And don't let anybody see you do it. Don't make the copies at battalion, just get a couple of masters. I'll have Peters make the copies here."

"Roger that."

"Okay, Rusty, you and Cartier tag along with second and weapons. Bolling, you and Jasmine stay with your platoons. If I don't see you at the noon meal, we'll meet at the O-club at say, eighteen hundred."

"Clear, madam." Most of the officers said in unison.

Lt. Cartier spoke up. "Madam, why is the XO shadowing me? Wouldn't it be a better use of our rank if I took my platoon with first, and ...?"

"No. It would not, Lieutenant," Naravanutu cut her off. "You've never loaded out for a deployment. Watch Lieutenant De'Avest and learn. Unless you want to learn by watching Mr. Bolling or Miss Jasmine, they've done it a number of times."

"No, I have nothing against the ensigns, madam. But, I understand now."

"That's good. Lieutenant, lesson one, watch and learn. Stand by." Naravanutu turned towards her executive officer. "You all go on ahead, we'll catch up. I want to talk to Jeana here alone for a moment."

"Yes, madam."

De'Avest and the others quickly left the office via its corridor door without passing through the Orderly Room. Ensign Bolling cast a wink at Cartier as he turned to head out the door. Naravanutu sat on the corner of her desk and beckoned for Cartier to take a seat in front of her.

"Lieutenant, I don't ever want to see another performance like what you did in my formation just now. It was totally uncalled for."

"Ma'am, may I say a word in my defense?"

"You may not, Lieutenant," Naravanutu said coldly. She looked at Cartier and shook her head. "Look, Jeana, I know who you are. We all do. We know you graduated first in your class at Sandoran Military Academy, but that was just this time last year. This time last year, most of this cohort was sweating on Eras-Junile's equatorial region in Spice Alley. Jeana, this is not the Sandoran Fleet. This is the Common Fleet. A commoner marine platoon is a family, Jeana. With you as its mama bear. That's the way it has to be. All we have are the Five Freedoms and each other."

"Ma'am, I'm not asking for special treatment."

"And you're not getting any. One way or the other. I'll bitch you out the same as I would any other jack-assed lieutenant. As per your father's request, no one in this cohort knows you're royalty, except myself, the XO and the Sergeant Major. The thing is, you've been here in the cohort, what, ten days? And already the veterans in second platoon are calling you a power hungry martinet. And now, you've gone and demonstrated that to the entire cohort. Ensign Bolling is a fine officer, he has earned his troopers' respect. Something you have yet to do with second platoon. And you've just made that job tougher on yourself. Lesson two, lighten up and listen more than you speak. Is that clear?"

"Yes, ma'am. Ma'am has there been any word on my request for transfer?"

"It's just like I said when you put it in, Lieutenant. I forwarded it to the adjutant without my endorsement. You've just got here, Jeana. You may have gotten off on the wrong foot, but that can be fixed. Plus, recon platoon is a specialty platoon. It's reserved for the most experienced platoon leader in the battalion, and that ain't you! Not yet anyway. You listen to Bennie Crowder and you just might make it."

"If I don't get killed first, ma'am," Cartier huffed.

"I'm going to forget I heard that, Lieutenant." Naravanutu looked at her for a moment before she spoke again. "I'm giving you a professional development assignment. You don't know you're people yet. You make note of the different stellar state flags on the sleeves of the marines in your platoon, Lieutenant. And you learn a little about each one. You talk to each member of your platoon and memorize what they look like, and how they walk. Coming and going. In fact, start with Corporals Anders and Faisal."

"Madam, I don't understand why that is necessary."

"It's necessary if I say it is, Lieutenant," Naravanutu snapped.

"Yes, ma'am. Ma'am may I ask what's going to happen to Corporal Anders?"

"You can ask. But I don't know yet. I'm going to talk to him first."

"Ma'am, if it were me. I'd court-martial him."

"I'm sure you would. Now go on, go get processed. I'll see you here after recall formation with your leadership and Anders."

"Yes, Ma'am." Cartier snapped up to attention and gladial saluted. Not wanting to give her another reason to complain, Naravanutu stood to attention and smartly returned her salute.

***

1330 hrs, Monrum afternoon. Commodore Morgan's office, Building 1, Depot Headquarters. 11-02 of 770CE VET.

"I've seen the video, Mr. Mayor, and I agree with you," Morgan said to the Redfordsville mayor and city council president's HG. He stood, walked around and sat on the corner his desk, just a meter or so from their image.

"However, my task force is only a tenant unit here. The accused is not under my command. I have spoken to the depot commander and the LEC battalion commander. Their adjutants and the judge advocate's office are cooperating with the municipal attorney and the constabulary. I am sure the interests of justice will be served."

'Thank you, Commodore,' the Mayor said.

"Unfortunately for us, Task Force Draken won't be here to see the outcome. We are closing rapidly on our rotation date."

'Ahh, the life of adventure,' the Council President said whimsically. "Were I not so old and settled, I would travel the stars in search of danger right alongside you, Commodore.'

Morgan smiled and nodded. "Well, sir, your job is by far the more difficult, and no less rewarding."

'Good fortune to you, Commodore.'

"And to you, sir."

The HG image faded.

"Damn. We dodged a round of crap on that one."

"What do you think they're going to do, sir?" Colonel Rivas asked, sitting across the office in a straight-backed chair.

195

"I don't know. I'm just thankful we don't have to deal with it."

"Uh, yes we do, sir," CSM Morris spoke up.

"How? Oh, our valiant young Corporal. What's his name?"

"Anders, sir, Richard, C. He's in the three-two."

"Naravanutu's outfit?"

"Yes, sir."

"Humph, lovely. Keep this in the NCO channels as far as battalion level and above is concerned, Moe. I don't want any appearance of undue command influence."

"Yes, sir. Does that mean you want to stay out of it completely?"

"Hell no! Naravanutu has gotta bust him, but it's cohort grade, cohort commander's discretion. I trust her judgment and Greer's."

"Roger that, sir."

"Humph. I wish I could give him a medal, humph. Okay, Debra, is Pulke here?"

"Yes, sir. I have him in the conference room with Bertrim and Harris," Colonel Rivas answered.

"Ah, good. Let's go talk to him."

"If you don't need me, sir, I'll go talk to Mackenzie at the regiment and pass a little advice down to Greer."

"Good idea, Moe. Do your best to keep the fellow on the order of merit list. No sense wrecking his education because he did the right thing."

"No worries, sir. I'll make sure he can soldier his way back."

**

The three officers talking at the conference room table stood to attention as Morgan and Rivas entered. "Relax, everybody, relax. How was your leave, Commander?" Morgan asked, shaking Mitch's hand and patting his shoulder. "Have a seat."

"I enjoyed every minute of it, sir."

"How's your family?"

"Very well, sir. Thank you for asking."

"And your squadron?"

"One hundred percent present for duty, sir. My service and support will begin shuttling up to *Draken* and setting up in three days. I'll fly the squadron up on the twenty-fourth."

"In fact, Commodore," Commander Bertrim, the task force operations officer, the G-3, spoke up. "According to the march order, Mitch's squadron has the combat patrol coverage for our embarkation."

"Good, good. Don't worry, I'm not taking it away from you, yet." Morgan kept an arm around Mitch's shoulder and gestured for him to take the swivel closest to his at the head of the conference table.

"I'm happy to hear that, sir."

"I want to know what you know about Contagor'e Mare back in the second war, and Third Dragoon's seizure of it."

Mitch was surprised. He looked at Morgan as he sat down.

"That's interesting, sir. I just had a conversation about the March of Lights the other day on Demeos, the night I received your message."

"Really? With whom?"

"Uh," Mitch cleared his throat.

Morgan looked at him curiously.

"Uh, Maria Hardesty and A. J. Mortimer, sir."

Morgan leaned back in his swivel in surprise.

"Together? And they didn't kill one another?" Morgan chuckled, looking around at the equally surprised Colonel Rivas, Commander Bertrim and LCdr Harris, the task force intelligence officer, the G-2.

"Actually they were quite civil. They were a little loud for my taste, but I came to understand that is customary at Nicky's on the River."

"Ah, Nicky's. That explains a lot. Tell me, Commander, what do you think of her?"

"Maria, Hardesty, she's, ah," Mitch cleared his throat.

"Relax, Commander. She has that effect on a lot of people."

"Mitch, did she ask you anything about Maranon?" LCdr Harris asked.

"Only if I was there; and called for the hearings. We talked more about Trudan."

Morgan's smile dropped. "What about Recondo?" he asked.

Mitch grew nervous. "Yes, sir. She asked me if I knew of the unit."

"What did you tell her?"

197

"Only the standard fare, sir."

"How did she respond to that?" Colonel Rivas asked from her seat on Mitch's left.

Mitch turned to her. "She asked if I knew any Recondo operatives, I told her I didn't."

"How did you meet her, Commander? Did she approach you?"

Mitch turned back to face Morgan again. "I believed it was a chance encounter, Commodore. We were already there when they came in together. Everyone in the room overheard her and A. J. Mortimer debating, and even took part. We got drawn in."

"What were they debating, Mitch?" Colonel Rivas asked.

Mitch looked at Rivas, then back at Morgan.

"You, Commodore," he said, in his best, matter of fact tone.

"HAH!" Morgan laughed and slapped his thigh.

"Mortimer saw my warrant and I together, he invited us over. They told us they were replacing our media embeds and asked us about basic training."

Morgan leaned forward in his swivel.

"Hardesty is assigned to us?"

"That's what Mortimer said, sir. Maria, ah, Miss Hardesty didn't sound very happy about it. She said she was 'press-ganged' into it with almost no notice."

Morgan and his staffers exchanged a look of surprise.

"I knew Mortimer and a small team was assigned, but Hardesty? Lovely, just lovely," Morgan muttered.

"Allen, Commodore. She's behind this," Rivas chortled. "That bitch!"

"It's my own damned fault," Morgan huffed. "I should have known that Galen interview back home was a DIG setup."

"Sir, I didn't..."

"No, no, no, Mitch. You're fine," Morgan said. "We hadn't been informed yet, that's all."

Morgan saw a look of relief come over Mitch's face. *There's more to this story,* he thought. *She's been known to operate between the sheets. But she cuts both ways.*

"Debra, put the word out to give her all our cooperation."

"Yes, sir."

"We've got some political issues involved in this next deployment, Mitch. And they're gumming up the works."

"Yes, sir. May I ask what our next mission is, sir?"

"You may not, Commander."

"Understood, sir."

"Okay, down to business. Mitch, I want you to tell me what you think the most significant factor was in Third Dragoon Regiment's success at Contagor'e Mare."

Mitch put thoughts of a night and a day with Maria out of his mind as best he could and focused on Morgan's question. "Commodore, I have to say, orbital and air dominance from the onset of the operation."

"I agree, Commander. I want you to work with Major Davis in the three shop again and come up with a way to establish the same dominance at Lucainus-Phuong. We need to capture a trans-stellar transport sized vessel before it departs the Lucainus planetary group. That's our primary task. Our secondary task is to secure an asteroidal habitat near the moon. Tertiary, and this is where you come in, we are to conduct a forced surface entry into Phuong-Yeuin range. Bertrim will set you up with the mission statements and tactical data on Phuong-Yeuin and Phuong's orbital defense. Once we set to the wave on the twenty-sixth, we have an eight day transit to Andolusia. Keep in touch with Davis' strategy branch and feel free to come up and see me with your ideas."

"Yes, sir. But, sir, I don't quite understand. Are you sure you don't want me to focus on our primary?"

Morgan's grey eyes lit up. "As far as this task force is concerned, Phuong-Yeuin IS our primary," he said. He looked around the table, then at Mitch. "Welcome to political gamesmanship one oh one, Commander."

***

1640hrs, Monrum afternoon, 2nd Platoon CP, 3rd Cohort, 2nd Bn, 7th Marines.

"I don't care what your motivation was, Corporal," Lieutenant Cartier barked, seated at PSgt Crowder's desk, berating Rick Anders. "Your lewd behavior on stage at the Sunshine Lounge was bad enough, I heard. But drunkenness and public fighting is conduct unbecoming of a Commonwealth Marine, no less of a non-commissioned officer in my platoon. If the centurion asks for my recommendation, I'm tempted to suggest courts-martial and confinement or transfer to another unit!" she said.

"That's your prerogative, Lieutenant," Rick answered standing at ease in front of the desk in the converted troop billet room. "But ma'am, to set the record straight. There was no 'lewd behavior', despite what you may have heard. You were invited, ma'am, the whole cohort was. And I wasn't drunk, ma'am," he said forcefully.

"Mind your demeanor, Corporal. Officers don't socialize with enlisted personnel," Cartier snorted. "Despite the other officers attending, they should know better." She folded her arms and scowled at Rick.

Rick knew he had to stand there and take it. Standing at ease on either side of the desk, PSgt Crowder and SSgt Mixon silently allowed the new lieutenant to exercise her authority. But Bennie Crowder was only going to let her go so far.

"Another thing, Anders. I believe you and Corporal Faisal are copulating. No-Cop is impossible to enforce. I've never accepted the notion. The military is too coarse an environment for a sibling relationship between genders. The way I've heard of you two carrying on, I'm convinced you're knocking boots. If I ever get any evidence, both of you are going to be gone from here. As Privates! Do I make myself clear, marine?"

"Loud and clear, ma'am."

"Step out and wait for us, I want to talk to your sergeants."

"Yes, ma'am." Rick snapped to attention and saluted. He faced about and left the room, forcefully closing the door behind him.

*

"That wasn't necessary ma'am. Anders and Faisal ain't doin' nuthin'."

"Are you sure of that, Sergeant Mixon? Are you with them all day and all night?"

"For a good part of the last year and a half, yes, ma'am. You don't know them like we do."

"That tells me you're entirely too familiar with your junior NCOs and with the enlistees."

"Ma'am', I...," Mixon held up a hand, stopping himself before he went too far.

PSgt Crowder checked the time. "We should be heading downstairs, ma'am. Its sixteen fifty. Take him on down, Mix. We're right behind you."

"Okay, boss."

Cartier let him go. Crowder waited until he had closed the door behind him.

"Lieutenant, I'm gonna tell you something, and I don't want to hear your response. I've seen Anders and Faisal sleeping together."

Cartier's eyes widened.

"Yes ma'am, I saw 'em huddled up close, spoonin', we call it back home. Trouble was, they were in their battle suits with IHEA covers. It's hard to fuck in an asteroid crater, in a vacuum, in negligible gravity, but two exhausted marines can snuggle up and take a break. I let 'em sleep. You'll understand soon enough."

**

Rick waited in the orderly room while his chain of command went into the Centurion's office to discuss his fate. Reduced to Corporal by the regimental surgeon, Sam Proudfoot walked past the open door and saw him, looking downcast, sitting next to the Sergeant Major's desk.

"Pssst."

Rick looked up and, seeing her, smiled. She tapped her chevrons and gave him a thumbs up, then she winked at him and blew him a kiss.

*

"Did you get any, ah, 'guidance' from battalion, Sergeant Major?" Naravanutu asked Greer in her office.

"Yes, ma'am, I did. The word from Sergeant Major Mackenzie and from Morris at Task Force is this is a cohort matter. They're leaving it to us."

"Hmm. I got the same from Colonel Nix himself," Naravanutu said. "Did you know forty-seven women have come forward since that recording went live. The adjutant said the thing has gone viral."

Psgt Crowder snorted and shook his head. "Damn. That fella's gonna get fried."

"That's a good way to put it, Crowder," she said. "What I want to know from you is how far are you willing to go, going to bat for Anders." She paused and lifted a finger towards Cartier.

"I know your feelings, Lieutenant. Sergeant Mixon, I want to hear from you."

"Anders is the best maneuver team leader in this cohort, madam," Mixon said forcefully. "We all know this. He's smart, and he's loyal, sometimes to a fault. I don't hold that against him."

"Crowder."

"He's gonna make a damned good squad leader one day, if he sticks around. If not, hell, he'll be a star on the stage."

"Sergeant Major."

"You know my feelings, ma'am."

"Yea, I have a daughter too. I'm pretty proud of him too," she lamented. She sighed heavily and pulled the partially completed form from her desk drawer, where it had sat since just after the Commander's Call. "Alright, let's get this over with."

**

"Madam, Corporal Anders reports to the Centurion, as ordered."

"Stand at ease, Corporal," Naravanutu said, returning his salute.

Rick dropped his salute and stood to parade rest before his seated commander. CoSM Greer standing on her left, Lt. Cartier on her right, Crowder and SSgt Mixon standing behind Rick all went to parade rest as well.

"You've been a busy young marine since you've been back."

"Yes, madam. You can safely say that."

"Hmm."

It was clear to Rick and everyone in the room that Naravanutu did not want to be there, doing this. Rick braced himself for what was to come. It was best to get it over and done with.

"The sergeant major has read you your rights. Do you understand what your rights and my command prerogatives are in this matter?" she asked formally, partially reading from the Common Fleet Military Code Form 15, Non-Judicial Punishment – Cohort Grade.

"Yes, Madam."

"Are you familiar with the charges against you? Would you like me to read the charges and specifications?"

"No, Madam. I'm aware I'm accused of conduct unbecoming, entrapment and assault with battery on fellow fleet personnel."

"Are you aware of the maximum penalty for such charges according to the code of military justice?"

"Yes, Madam."

"You have the right to request a trial by courts-martial, Corporal. If you request such a trial, these proceedings will come to a screeching halt. You'll be transferred to the Depot Holding Barracks to await trial while the task force sets to the wave. At this time, Corporal, do you wish to formally request a trial by summary courts-martial?"

"No, Madam."

Rick heard an audible breath behind him. He saw Cartier scowl.

"Alright. Initial the form in this block indicating you are declining courts-martial and allowing me to adjudicate the matter," Naravanutu said.

She turned the form around and pushed it across the desk to Rick. Anders pulled a stylus from his left sleeve pocket and leaned forward to initial where she indicated. He returned the stylus then straightened back to attention. Centurion Naravanutu leaned back in her swivel and gave Anders a long look. Rick stared straight ahead, focused on the wide angle cohort photo taken just before they deployed for the Trudan, almost eight months ago.

"I've seen the recording you uploaded to the web. It's pretty clear what happened, but if there's anything more you want to tell me about it, this is your chance."

"Ah, no, madam."

"Very well," she said. "Before I pass judgement, do you have anything to say, in matters of mitigation or extenuation that may influence my decision?"

Rick thought for a second. For the first time, since discussing the idea with Sam, a real fear of the consequences should anything go wrong welled up inside him. He pondered the offer, then decided not to say anything Lt. Cartier could later use against him.

"No, madam. As you say, it's all pretty clear."

"One question, Corporal," Greer interrupted. "If I may, madam?"

"By all means, Sergeant Major," she answered without taking her eyes off Anders.

"Anders, knowing what you know now, would you do it again?"

Rick couldn't help but flash a grin, but quickly recovered his bearing. "In the same circumstances, Sergeant Major. Yes I would. In a heartbeat."

"Humph," Cartier mumbled under her breath. Everyone in the office heard it. Naravanutu ignored her.

"Very well, Corporal. I'm reducing you one grade, to lance corporal."

"Yes, madam."

"Don't think you're getting off easy, Anders. I am NOT relieving you of your maneuver team leader duties in your squad. Phuong is gonna be a bitch, and we need every good marine. I fully expect you to soldier you way through this. Phuong will show me if you've still got the spirit. You succeed there, and there's no doubt in my mind you can do that, you'll earn those chevrons back before our deployment is complete. Understood?"

"Yes, madam. Madam, is there any word on where we're deploying to after Phuong?"

"No, Lance Corporal, not a peep. But whatever it is, you and your team be ready for it."

"Yes, madam," Rick sighed and reached up to his collar to remove his chevrons.

"You're still at attention, Anders," Crowder said behind him.

Rick dropped his arms to his sides. "Yes, Sergeant."

"Very well. Sign the form, Anders, go on and get in the proper uniform and get back to work."

"Yes, madam."

"If anybody gives you any shit about your status, you let Sergeant Mixon, Sergeant Crowder or the Sergeant Major know. We'll take care of them."

Rick smiled. "Yes, Madam," he said with a cheerfulness that surprised them all as he pulled his stylus again and signed.

"Dismissed."

Anders stood to, he and his commander exchanged gladial salutes. Rick faced about as Mixon opened the office door. Feeling a tear welling up, he marched out.

***

23-02 of 770 CE. Tresium Common Fleet Exo-drome, Senior Bachelor Officers Housing, billet 29B.

The time on Mitchell Pulke's wrist pad read 2045hrs void equivalent time. Piraeus was setting, casting long shadows through the living room windows. The shadows and the three-hour change told him it was 1745hrs local time, this last night on Tresium, for him and the Task Force. Maria's text was 15 minutes old, meaning there were just a precious few minutes before her taxi arrived from the exo-drome. He turned completely around in his Common Fleet Family Housing Warehouse furnished living room, for one last look.

His fully packed, aviation blue, Common Fleet duffle bag bore his last name, first name, middle initial and service number stenciled in white block letters on the outside. It lay next to two stacked containers holding all but three of his literaries, his MV and other odds and ends he picked up during the block leave and the hearings, ready for Sergeant Potiest to pick up in the morning and bring up on the shuttle. His bedroom, bathroom, and kitchenette were clean, and the trash taken out.

One of the three literaries left out lay on the lounge lamp table where he put it down after finishing it the night before. The other two lay on the out of place writing desk with his data pad and flexmet maps of Phuong–Yeuin range. He still had a lot of study and work yet to do. He considered packing it away for the night. Looking down at his carpet distracted him.

"Batman, vacuum, please." The small remote cleaner emerged from its charger and quietly began its pattern across the floor. The buzz at the door startled him. *Damn, she's here!*

Walking to the door, he saw a shiny black two-seater roadster parked at the curb instead of a taxi. He reached for the handle and opened the door just as it buzzed again.

"Hiya, Mitch." A smiling Lieutenant Commander Jefferson Tieras stood at the door with a bottle of J Double K mash in one hand. "Up for a snort? No sense leaving it behind."

Mitch laughed. "Damn, I've got company coming over, but come on in for a bit." He stepped back and opened the door fully and let his shipmate in.

"Company, eh? Anybody I know?" Tieras asked, heading directly for the kitchenette cabinets for tumblers.

"I'll introduce you. You're all packed I take it? What are you gonna do with the ride?" Mitch looked out towards the tree-lined Dexter Loop, towards the intersection with Dexter Lane, the route most taxis took, bringing guests to this part of the exo-drome. He could only hope the driver knew the senior bachelor officers' billets were on the opposite side of the exo-drome from the senior officer family billets area.

"The garage service will pick it up at the MAC Passenger Terminal tomorrow about this time. They'll store it for me."

"You sure they won't drive it around themselves?"

Tieras chuckled. "Naw, they're on the straight. They've got a good quality management rating. Plus they're vets, mostly. They'll service and containerize it, so they can ship it to me at the next depot."

"Got it. Hey Jeff, is there a Dexter Road, Lane, Loop sequence on the family side?"

"I would know this because...?" Tieras asked, opening cabinet doors.

Mitch stepped back in and shut the door, he adjusted the living room window blinds to see the street better.

"Next one over, above the basin. My girl is coming in from Sestria. She landed about an hour ago. I got a text from her a few minutes ago saying she was aboard a taxi and enroute."

"Hit the batman panel and bring up the map," Jeff said, pouring a tall one for himself and a short round for lucky Mitch. "I'll let you off easy with this, since you gotta fly tomorrow. And it's not gentlemanly to greet a woman with a drink in your hand."

"I didn't know that. Really?"

"Damned if I know, but it sounds good. Here," he handed the short round to Mitch and clinked his with it and took a short first sip. "Relax, Carson Metro drivers know this base better than the people who run it. Especially these bachelor housing areas and the crew barracks. You just haven't spent any time around here."

Tieras took a seat in one of the lounge chairs near the writing desk, watching the remote going about its task. Mitch sat on the lounger, side on, so he could face Jeff and look out the window.

"I've been here since the tenth?"

"You've been shut up in this flop-house since the tenth. Stefan sent me to see if you were still alive."

"He saw me the other day, at the gym!"

"So what, we can catch up. The Stefan story will work."

Mitch chuckled. "You're weird, man."

"So, how's it coming? The plan that is?"

"That's what Stefan wants to know."

"You got it. He's worried. He knows G.W. said to wait till we set to the wave, but it's his butt on the line."

"Yeah, I feel for him."

Looking around, Tieras' focused on the literaries.

"So what'cha reading? Yes, I'm snooping. 'Battlespace Management in Trans-Planetary Regions', 'Heliospheric and Planetary Forced Entry Operations'. Colonel Castrada Vida, Valerian Armed Forces. Brother, you've gone old school."

"Vida's the best source. I'm going back to the fundamentals. We've got to be bold, Jeff. It's gonna be a cast iron bitch. I don't know any other way to say it."

"You're the master cylinder on this puppy, Junior. I want you to shine like new money." He lifted his tumbler in toast. "What are the challenges?"

"I've researched every Phuong-Yeuin scenario that any of our units or the Valerians have done. And some of the State Guard units as well, but they don't have battle cruisers."

"Find any patterns?"

"I certainly did."

"Annd, you can't wait to just blurt it out."

Mitch chuckled. "No matter what, once we attack the asteroid or even the transport, the ground forces at Yeuin

Exo-drome are alerted and are released to move to their defensive zones."

"Yeah, okay. Most of the units that have been there take a lot of dragoon casualties on the drop zones," Tieras lamented. "The Lucainans were always dug-in on the high ground overlooking the exo-drome, just waiting for them."

"That's right. If we take too long neutralizing the station, and they get their surface based fighters airborne, they could draw off enough of our escorts to get into the shuttle stream. We start losing combat shuttles each filled with eighty dragoons, or a heavy lift shuttle. Or even worse, an assault lander. It'll be a disaster."

"Not what Stefan nor G.W. want, Mitch."

"Me neither. Surprise is key. We have to jam their ESR and their comms long enough to make the advance to contact. And we have to assault all three objectives simultaneously."

"The hell you say?"

"Our orbital bombardment and aviation has to catch the Lucainan mechanized units in their assembly areas or on the move, before they get into their positions in Happy Valley and in town."

"Or the marines will have to grind their way up that damned road through a gauntlet of fire."

"And clear a fortified town after that."

"While taking no more casualties than, what's the fleet average?"

"Forty-percent. No one has done it without taking at least thirty-four over the two day exercise time period. G.W. will accept thirty, but he wants to keep as close to twenty percent as we can get."

"Don't we all?"

"Yeah, but there's something else. It's political. Something that has to do with the fact we've had no information on our mission." Mitch sipped his mash and looked out, checking the street.

"What is going on with that? Everybody's spooked."

"Waste of time speculating. We'll know something after Phuong. You've got a big deal coming up yourself, professor. You all set?"

Tieras smiled at the thought. "I wonder who thought of a stunt like that. The war is still going on. You get pegged to plan our PDRE. And I, your classmate and best buddy, get what? I ask you?

I get wet nosing a bunch of middle school kids through basic cosmography on the stellar web. Morgan hates me."

Mitch sipped his mash and laughed at his friend. "You're an adjunct professor of cosmography."

"Yeah, so?"

"You were requested by the Osiri state school board. By name, I might add," Mitch said, pointing to him. "So. Are you ready?"

"Ready? The entire ESR anchor watch sat on a murder board for me to rehearse in front of. You ever been murder boarded?"

"Ohh, yes," Mitch grinned. "Fighter weapons instructor certification board."

"Then you know what I mean."

"Your crew murdered you? That means a lot, buddy." Mitch sipped again and checked outside.

"You should have heard Chief Mateo bellow. 'It's the first time it's ever been done from a Ship of the Line!' she said."

"Little Chief Mateo can bellow?"

"Like a volcano. 'It'll be a feather in the cap of THIS SHIP!' she said."

"And the crew couldn't wait to sign up, huh? Speaks well." Mitch raised his tumbler in toast. "When's the class?"

Tieras sipped his tall boy before answering. "Day after tomorrow."

"Well at least they gave you a chance to get back aboard ship," Mitch laughed, shaking his head. "Wow, the day before we set to the wave? As if you haven't got enough to do?"

"The way Mateo puts it, it gets me out of her way." Mitch shook a finger at him. "She has a point."

Tieras chuckled and sipped his tall boy. "Have you heard the news about our media embeds?"

Mitch perked up. "What about them?"

"They arrived today, we only got four, plus videographers, but two are heavyweights."

Mitch turned his head to look out the window again, more to hide his smirk. But it didn't work.

"What's that shit eating grin you got there, fella? You know something about that too. Don't you?"

"Do you know who the heavies are?" Mitch asked, feigning nonchalance.

"Maria Hardesty and A. J. Mortimer, Rivas put the word out that Hardesty was a last minute attachment. They don't know why, but to handle her with care. That she could go off like a bomb at any time."

Mitch smiled, he sipped his mash and chuckled.

"They're going with my chalk on the command group's second shuttle tomorrow. I saw their names on the manifest. Damn, Mitch. The Dragon Lady. She's something else. She's a looker for sure. I've seen her on some of those MV news shows. I hear her investigations have gotten people sent to prison. Rivas says she's looking for information on the Recondos. As well as wanting a shot at Morgan."

"Another shot. What did she say about Mortimer?" Mitch asked.

"He's a big editorialist out in the Nursery Crescent, a big shill for Morgan. That's what I hear. He had some kind of syndicated editorial show. We picked it up on Thesis. You know the kind? Political stuff, the talking heads type."

The remote cleaner finished its task and returned to its charger.

"Yeah," Mitch answered, searching the street again. "He's taking a sabbatical to accompany us on this deployment."

"Damn. You got all the inside poop in that one meeting with Morgan. Then you became a near-hermit. Must be big. I wonder what...," Jeff waved off the thought. "What's the other lit there, Mitch? 'Never Let the Bastards See You Cry'. You're reading Hardesty's personal self-help lits? Friend, the woman you're expecting is all the help you need. As for me, I'll have to help myself. Whatever. So what about this woman you got coming from Sestria? She must have been on the same shuttle with the embeds."

"Oh, no doubt," Mitch said with a grin.

"Keeping secrets, huh?" Jeff sat forward in his chair and took another sip. "Is she married or something?"

"What?! No! Well she was. Some asshole left her a few years ago, but no," Mitch said.

A white Carson Metropolitan Taxi Company Util rolled to a stop in front of his window. Mitch got up, walked over and opened the door.

"This must be my cue to disappear," Jeff said. He craned his head up to see out the window, then stood, to get a better look. A familiar looking woman emerged from the passenger bay wearing a Common Fleet issue gray crewmember's deck-duty uniform and boots. She wasn't wearing her cover, her black and streaked silver hair was bunted back to regulation. Her crew members' soft cap cover was rolled and stuffed partially in a cargo pocket of her uniform trousers, like any off-duty trooper.

The driver got out and walked to the rear towards the opening cargo hatch, but the woman got there first and hefted the Common Issue gray crewbie bag out for herself and onto her shoulder.

Tieras nodded in approval as she reached into her pocket with her free hand and tipped the driver anyway. The driver tipped his hat to her and turned back to remount his vehicle.

"Nice, but I thought you liked them taller, Mitch. Remember you said you would introduce me, maybe she's got a..." Jeff stopped in mid-sentence seeing Mitch stride out the door and down the walk towards her. He started to follow, then remembered what he had said and set his tumbler down, then headed out the door.

*

Maria Hardesty set her kitbag down. She stood to a perfect position of attention and gladial saluted a grinning Mitch.

"Media embed Hardesty reports to the Squadron Commander for booty duty, sir!" she announced as the taxi pulled off.

Mitch stopped in front of her and played along. He snapped to and returned her salute, he barely got his arm back down to his side before she had thrown herself into him, wrapping her arms around his neck and kissing him.

Orchids, oh man, those orchids.

*

Hardesty? Did I hear right? Jeff thought. *Holy shit! My buddy is riding the dragon lady. My Hero.*

*

Mitch picked up Maria's kit-bag, he put his arm around her and walked her up to the door where Jeff stood just outside.

"Maria, I'd like you to meet my classmate and my good friend Lieutenant Commander Jefferson Tieras of Epirus-Thesis.

211

Jeff this is my girl, this is Maria Joanna Hardesty of Denestri-Comar."

Jeff clicked the heels of his running shoes coming to the position of attention and extended his hand. "'Never let the Bastards See You Sweat, Cry, Run,' Maria Hardesty?" he asked, grinning.

"Yes!" Maria said shaking Tieras' hand. "The Dragon Lady herself. I'm very happy to meet another of Mitchell's friends, Jeff. Where are you stationed?"

"Aboard Draken with us, babe. Jeff commands the third watch. He's a professor of cosmography. So he's a lot smarter than me."

Mitchell? Hmmm. Tieras thought. "Hey, let me get that for ya, bud. It's the least I can do, I'll leave that JdK for you two."

"No problem." Mitch hefted the kit-bag to him without hesitation. "You and your team are on Jeff's shuttle chalk tomorrow, Maria."

"Excellent, we'll get to have a nice talk about Mitchell on the way up. But oh, you don't have to go on my account, Jeff. Not yet anyway." She looked up at Mitch and winked.

"I'm ordering from the steak house at the main exchange mall, have dinner with us, Jeff. Then disappear," Mitch offered.

"You sure?"

"Certainly," Maria said. "I insist. I love picking brains for dinner."

"I beg your pardon?!"

Maria gave him a mischievous laugh for an answer as they filed inside and closed the door."

***

Battle Group departure rendezvous zone Charlie, 3,000 kilometers beyond Fleet orbital anchorage 19C, 4,300 kilometers above Tresium. 1859hrs, 24-02 of 770CE.

This is not going to work. Mitch thought. *There's still a war on, I've got a job to do. I can't get married.*

After lifting off at 0800hrs, LCdr Pulke's Delta Squadron of *CBC Draken* flew cover for the task force's embarkation. The battle groups and transports formed at widely separated points above the planet's three main continental exo-dromes. On their last orbit, Mitch's finger four formation of vortexes, arced out of Piraeus to starboard of *CBC Draken's* direction of travel.

"Delta-zero-three-Alpha, this is Jaeger-zero-one, Tresium orbital squadron has assumed combat aviation patrol. Request approach vector, over."

Here, alone aboard his fighter, Mitch replayed last night's fight with Maria for the hundredth time and still couldn't make sense of it. He scanned his canopy displays and panel instruments between watching the transponders of the last group of shuttles and assault landers begin their approach to *CBC Draken,* the transports *Acre* and *Moncrief,* and the supply ship *Sabra,* as the preceding groups merged with those of the capital ships.

Five hundred kilometers off the *Draken's* port bow, Pulke's fighters decelerated approaching *Draken's* frigate picket zone. Passing within 50 kilometers of*DRP-2,* one of the *Predator*-class escort frigates, he slipped left a little, giving it a wider berth seeing a tanker shuttle from the orbital station backing off from the frigate's starboard fuel cells.

'Roger Jaeger-zero-one. Vector two-seven-zero, down, one-six, approach portside at zero point six, over.'

"Delta-zero-three-Alpha, confirmed vector, down-angle and approach velocity, All CAP reliefs are on station. Jaeger flight inbound. No hostile contacts. No friendly casualties, over."

'Roger, Jaeger, welcome home, out.'

CBC Draken is home. Mitch thought. *Anywhere else was what Jeff Tieras said, a flophouse.* He tried last night and this morning to explain that to Maria. They had had such a good time, laughing and talking over dinner with Jeff and making love after he left. *Rivas is more right than she or Jeff thinks,* he thought. *She does go off like a bomb. Both when she makes love and when she gets mad. She went off both ways on me last night.*

One hundred kilometers from *CBC Draken's* aft landing ramp, the formation pirouetted and starboard down thrust, to level out. Stacked on the leader's flanks, Jaegers 2, 3 and 4 fell into staggered trail of their leader.

"Tresium Control this is Delta-zero-three-Alpha -Jaeger-zero-one. Be advised my four are inbound on final to Delta-zero-three-Alpha, acknowledge, over."

The Tresium municipal office of Piraeus State traffic control acknowledged his flight was on final approach vector to *CBC Draken*. Pulke chopped power and lined the fighter up on the strobe lit center line of the ship's aft hangar launch/recovery ramp and lowered his landing gear. His wingman, Flight Sergeant Hermez followed, lining up on the starboard strobe line. In their wake, Lt. Orel and Ensign Jare, his second element, came in on the port strobe.

The vortexes stubby tricycle skid/wheels brusquely touched down one-third the distance up the runway. They rolled, still under internal power, through the magnetic screen into the semi-pressurized launch and recovery deck as the outer armored shutters began to close in preparation for pressurizing the outer bay. IHEA suited deck guides waving color coded hooded hand torches signaled the fighters off the runway onto the taxiway. The fighters steered toward crewmen driving 'Follow Me' carts which sallied forth from their pressurized squadron fighter park and maintenance gallery to marry up with their assigned craft and tow it to its bay.

Once the task force took to the wave and was no longer supported by Piraeus State Guard forces, the wings took up the CAP rotation as long as the three battle groups stayed together. A squadron from *CBC Dridantes* fighter wing took up the CAP, to be followed by *Drukar*, then Alpha, Bravo, and Charlie squadrons of his own wing, then on around again. The next squadron in the shift rotation stood to and was ready for launch as a reaction force in case of enemy contact.

Pulke shut his systems down and signaled the internal power was off to Chief Bascombe as his canopy retracted. His crew chief returned a thumbs up and waved a deck crewmember to maneuver the boarding scaffold over to DD-01's port side.

Bascombe squatted, surveying underneath the craft, then he waved the fuel handlers and weapons techs forward to re-fuel the bird and safe the missile systems prior to exchange. He strode around the vortex, looking it over with a seasoned eye, then he mounted the scaffold to assist his squadron commander.

"Welcome home, sir."

"Thanks, Chief. It was good to be back in the saddle. But now, it's good to be aboard."

Pulke unharnessed with Bascombe's help and climbed out of the cockpit. He removed his helmet and cradled it before climbing down the scaffold, a habit since taking an embarrassing tumble as a cocky ensign. He was met by his division leaders and the key members of his small administrative staff, all competing for his time. Helmet in hand, he headed through the squadron hangar bay towards the starboard access ramp to the mezzanine.

"We'll debrief in ten and get it done."

"Ten? Wow, sir. Don't you want to clean up? There's plenty of time. Right?"

"You people still drunk or something!" Mitch glared at them. "There's still a war going on out there, Lieutenant."

"Here, sir? In Piraeus?"

"Yes, Ensign. Even here, in the heart of the CAZ. Any of those commercial vessels we saw during our orbits. Any one of them could be paid Alliance informers. Any of the ore ships, or even their octophages maybe rigged as surveillance pods. Mise! I saw number eight's port nacelle's got a hiccup! Better check it out!" That was Mitch's way of saying, 'Hello, I'm back', to Mise. He had to bitch at him about something or he wouldn't think he cared.

"I'll have Chief Madow see to it, sir. But, sir, you gotta explain exactly what a hiccup is. I ain't ever seen such a word in the manual, Commander."

"You'll figure it out, Chief. Come by later. We need to talk."

"Roger, sir."

Mise broke away from the group grinning. All of his birds were home safe and fully functional. Every bird had a hiccup or floating whatchamacallit whenever Mitch got back after 'an easy one', meaning, 'No hostile contacts. No friendly casualties'.

Mitch turned towards the administrative. Mostly signing what the XO and Sergeant Potiest put in front of him. He headed

215

up the ramp towards his squadron administrative mezzanine, briefing area and billets, pursued by his pilots and headquarters personnel.

**

After debriefing, Mitch signed off on the last of the paper work in his ten meter square office/billet. He looked forward to a hot shower and a stiff drink. Then up to the mess for chow. *I gotta talk to Drago.*

"Anything else for me, Potts?"

"Nothing official, sir. Charlie squadron is in a pickle though, sir."

"Wing gossip already, Potts? What'cha' got?"

"Yes sir, last night. Get this, sir. Deck five's observation lounge is closed. Task force civil affairs claimed it for some kind of class being taught from there tomorrow. The lounge won't open till afterwards. Charlie's pilots didn't know. They got mad and complained to the XO."

"Yeah? What did they expect her to do?"

"No, sir. Not Lieutenant Warner. Commander Matese."

"What?! Those morons jumped their squadron AND the wing chain of command for a party?!"

"Commander McDonald was bagged out at the time, sir. Just coming off rotation. I guess they figured it was too trivial to wake him."

"That just goes to show ya, Potts. Even fighter pilots get a case of the dumb ass sometimes."

Potiest chuckled.

Potts' is a good man. Pulke had thought him too bookish looking when he first came aboard two years ago. *But he's the best clerk in the fleet.*

"Oh and, sir, the embed, Miss Hardesty, she's touring the hangars, since coming off the shuttle a bit ago. She'll be around for a few hours. Wing called down while you were in debrief to remind us to extend every courtesy."

She just came aboard today and she's already working? Damn. She must really be pissed. "Yeah, yeah. I'd keep out of sight when she's around, Potts. That woman's trouble."

"How so, sir?"

216

Pulke stood from behind his desk and went over to the lamalar panels overlooking the cavernous hangar a half deck below.

"I know the type," Mitch said. "She likes her life as a reporter, Potts," he said with a grin. He turned towards the clerk and wagged a forefinger for emphasis. "But she hates the fact she is single. She's looking for a story to blab and a husband to snag!"

Potiest grinned and shook his head. "Well, we're too smart for that, sir."

You maybe, Mitch thought. "Is there anything else? I see my stuff made it, thanks. Everybody's gear make it up okay?"

"No worries, sir. I haven't gotten any squawks from the inventories yet, No, sir, nothing else."

"Good, we've got another day, but put the word out, Sergeant, anything left behind on the surface after this time tomorrow gets left there," he warned.

"Yes, sir. I'll do that right now, sir."

Pulke turned back to look down on the hangar bay as Potiest closed the manway behind him.

Mises' warrants and sergeants directed small knots of maintenance crews working on his opened up fighters. Their panels were removed, exposing their engines and guns. Some of his squadron technicians' legs extended upwards, bracketing their fighter's canopies, their heads and upper torsos buried deep in the cockpits. Others were on their knees under the cockpits handing up replacement circuit boards and sensory nodes. Intelligence techs wearing sidearms, moved from craft to craft, removing filled Data Recording Devices from combat maneuver pods and replacing them with empty ones. Each DRD was accounted for, secured, and delivered to the wing S-2 for intelligence analysis and recycling.

Frame techs polarized void dust before vacuuming the hulls, thrusters, and nacelles. The weapons techs unloaded missile pods, inerting the AIM-3s and 4s before de-polarizing and vacuuming them. Then they maneuvered the lowered pods onto the handling carts. Each vortex's battle load of twelve each was safetied, vacuumed, and tagged before the cart was attached to a train of missile carts bound for the servicing magazine.

The reload train of serviced missiles, stored in the ready lockers, were brought forward and prepositioned under the craft's open missile bays. Red safety tags hung from pins inserted in

217

safety inter-locks on the four missile warheads in each of the magazines. Armorers serviced the M200 and M212 IEX auto-cannon, removing ammunition drums, de-polarizing and vacuuming their internal feed trays.

Mitch caught sight of Maria Hardesty and her videographer across the hangar bay in Bravo Squadron area. He watched her chatting with techies, taking photos, and even posing for some with crewmembers. They would have to work their way around through the vixen squadron to get back to his vortexes.

They looked like any other crewmember in their deck duties. *Rivas was right,* he thought. *That's why they call them embeds. Orchids, dammit. Whenever I see her. Ninety-four hours before rotation.*

Pulke turned and took a step towards his shower cubicle just as Drago Mise buzzed at his manway.

"Enter."

Drago stepped through the sliding manway before it opened fully. The device hesitated, then slid back to the closed position.

"I love fucking with the machine's heads," Drago snorted. "What's got you bug-eyed, fella? I saw that landing. It, in a word, sucked. Don't fuck up my lead bird. What's the matter?"

"I need a drink," Mitch grumbled.

"Really? Maria wants to get married and you stuttered."

Mitch chin dropped as his head rolled in his friend's direction. "How the hell did you know that?"

"Easy, you got the Phuong plan done early and uploaded it to the three shop. I hear Morgan is happy as a schoolgirl. And after a flawless squadron screen, you almost scrape my brand new bird's ass on the ramp. Had to be a woman. Seen it before. Saw it coming. Just not this soon," Drago chuckled taking a seat in one of the straight backed chairs in front of Mitch's desk. "Big fight?"

"It was a discussion."

"Did you get any before this, 'discussion'?"

"Sure."

"As good as the first time? And then came the, 'discussion', right?"

"Well, yeah. What are you getting at?"

"Hang on. This is an important lesson for you. Did you get any after this, discussion?"

"Uhn, no."

"Your, 'discussion' my boy, was a fight."

"And I lost."

"Men lose every fight with their wives. It's in some manual somewhere."

"You're enjoying this?! I, I..."

"You love her?"

"Yes."

"And there you are. That's the easy part. Got any booze?"

"There's half a bottle of JdK in the top box, over there. Dammit."

"What's the real problem, Mitch?"

"She wants me to resign my commission and go to work for her father. He's some big-time trial advocate on Comar."

"One of the most sought after in the whole Denestri stellar state actually."

"How'd you know?"

"Kadesh told me. She watches a lot of talk shows from there. It'll be one hell of an opportunity."

"Not for me, I couldn't do it."

"What? And leave all this?"

Mitch snorted and shook his head. "Actually, that's exactly what I told her. She didn't take it well."

"Did she cry?"

"Yes."

"Wow. Yeah, we both need a drink. You made the Dragon Lady cry? You're my hero."

"You don't like her?"

"Are you kidding? I love her to death. Kadesh is already regarding her as a sister-in-law. Marry that woman, Mitch. But be strong. Her asking you to leave the fleet is the same as you asking her to give up investigative reporting, seein' crooked motha fuckahs go to jail! That's what she does. It's in her blood as much as flyin' and fightin' is in yours, and there's still a war on. And that's what scares her."

"How'd you get to be so smart?"

"Drill Sergeants. You go shower. I'll go get us some chow and bring it down."

"And another bottle."

*

219

The pilots and flight crews of *CBC Draken's* fighter-bomber wing were busy settling into their billets. The deck officers, maintenance warrants, NCOs, and techies were more than happy to give Maria Hardesty and Nick Kung the grand tour of the battle cruiser's mid-decks housing the fighter-bomber wing. The wing's Vortex3 fighter squadrons and vixen surface attack and bombardment squadrons protected the battle group by providing long range reconnaissance, interception, deep strike and interdiction missions. The wing's 90 craft provided close support to the fighting vessels in the void and to the fusiliers and dragoons on the surface.

Flexible armored doors protected the cruiser's upper and lower launch and recovery bays. Supported by secondary and tertiary magnetic wave shielding, the doors rolled down into place from the hangar bay ceiling. The hangar bays, set amidships, made up the mid-decks between the second and third main decks. The bay doors opened onto void exposed ramps, each one third the length of the ship. The port side ramp oriented aft, and the starboard ramp faced the bow.

Nick found good perches for his datacam and stayed close. Maria looked around in awe at the wide bays filled with Vortex3s, the Commonwealth's latest generation, single seat, indo-exo atmospheric (IEX) fighter. The Senior Warrant of Bravo Squadron guided her over to Bravo-01's maintenance bay, her squadron commander's vortex. Its two, model J-19 series fusion reactor powered engines hung suspended from a push-me–pull-you scaffold just behind their empty drive well.

"I don't see any moving parts, Chief," Maria remarked as she scanned the scene to her own recorder.

"You won't, ma'am. Actually there are very few. These engines are modularized for ease of replacement. We can order spare modules from the manufacturing center aboard the supply ship."

"I understand. How powerful are these engines, Chief?"

"They can each produce a thrust to mass ratio of twelve point eight to one, ma'am. They can achieve a planetary escape velocity of twelve point seven kilometers per second. The craft 'whips off' a planet's magnetic field, ma'am. The vortex can accelerate to a stellar escape velocity of thirty-two KPS."

Maria walked around the fighter bay, gaining a better appreciation of the craft's size.

Technicians stood to one side to let her get a good look. The maintenance chief didn't try to rush her, but it was clear to Maria, the woman wanted to move along.

"The crew's on a tight schedule here, ma'am. This is a re-install. It has to go below for test-run, before CAP rotation."

"Oh, no worries, Chief. Lead the way."

The chief led Maria to Bravo-09's bay, across from Bravo-01. Its crew kept busy staging the fighter's battle load as the two approached.

"The vortex, ma'am, is a non-stealth, single-seat, multi-gun and missile battle platform." The chief raised her hands framing the craft. "All of this ordinance you see here, ma'am, is internally housed.

"You can call me Maria if you like, Chief. And you are?"

"Chauvier, Julia, ma, uh, Maria."

"Where are you from, Julia? Your accent sounds familiar."

"Denestri-Chalon," the chief answered tapping the Denestri state flag patch they both wore on their right sleeve.

"Ahh, sister. We're neighbors!"

"I know, I've read all your books."

"Oh, so you're the one," Maria quipped.

The chief smiled and relaxed. *The Dragon Lady isn't so bad.* As they walked around the craft, Chief Chauvier explained the vortex's armaments for its interceptor-superiority missions, bomber escort, surface attack, and close support roles.

"Its primary magnetic rail IEX armament, is this nose-mounted automatic cannon." She pointed to the exposed M-212 60mm rail-gun that launched exploding HSPF ammunition at a rate of 300 projectiles per minute. Bravo 9's armorers opened the magazine wells allowing Maria to see its on-board load of 750 projectiles.

"There are two thirty-five millimeter weapons mounted in its wing roots along the fuselage."

With its panels removed, Chauvier pointed out the exposed port side M200 35mm auto-cannon with its rate of launch of 600 projectiles per minute and on-board load of 1,500 projectiles each.

"So your pilots just can't blaze away like in the cinemas," Maria concluded playfully.

"Oh, no. That wouldn't be smart."

They stood to one side and let the crew maneuver the carts of long and short-range, all-aspect, IEX missiles into their positions under the fighter.

"These inboard pods, ma'am are short-range, AIM-three Flaggons," Bravo-9's crew chief explained. "They're particle seekers, while the long-range, AIM-four Flapper is microwave guided." The crew chief pointed to the outboard pods.

"Both missiles hold disintegrating deuterium impregnated rod, HSPF warheads, Maria," Chief Chauvier added. "When we arm them for a ground attack role, we remove the missile magazines and replace them with ordinance. Primarily, we would load anti-vehicle guided missiles in the bays. But the ship can carry a pod of SK bombs. We can load ten, two CDB bombs or a single, one KDB bomb."

"Fascinating."

"Care to climb aboard?"

In a few moments, Chief Chauvier and Bravo-09's crew chief had a thoroughly impressed Maria seated in the cockpit.

Though smaller than previous versions of the 450 year old vortex design, it retained the classic, tapered nose, with short swept horizontal stabilizers below the cockpit. The triangular or delta wing, and the slight hourglass fuselage, each milled from single units of space-laminated, high-iron chondrite alloy armor, creating an extremely strong frame. For additional protection, the cockpit and primary systems' computers rested within an electro-magnetic pulse shielded cocoon.

The wing's trailing edge lay flush with the horizontal, variable angle drive nacelle. The craft's sliding, teardrop shaped, lamalar armored one-way canopy allowed the pilot excellent all-round visibility in conjunction with the helmet integrated tactical display. Though it was indistinguishable from the craft's roughened grey hull from the outside.

The fighter's 20-hour fuel capacity, with a 4-hour maneuvering thruster reservoir gave it an excellent range and exceptional combat endurance. Ninety-two maneuvering thrusters embedded around the craft gave it unmatched void maneuverability. A short vertical stabilizer and computerized control surfaces extended upon entering atmospheres, and provided primary attitude control, boosted by the thrusters.

"I've seen and serviced a lot of 'em Maria," Chauvier proclaimed. "Valerian Jaegers, Stealth Vespids, even some captured Alliance Dart nines and Daggers. Kilo for kilo, sister, the Vortex three is the most rugged, versatile, and deadly single-seat fighter yet fielded."

"Wow! Julia, can I quote you on that?!"

"You betcha!"

Mitch flies this, Maria thought. *I won't make him give this up.*

*

Pulke stepped back to his lamalar and magnified to find Maria again. He spotted her just as Bravo Squadron handed her over to the vixen squadrons.

*

Down on the deck, Maria felt like a fragile crystal doll being carefully received by the next squadron maintenance officer. This time she was surprised.

"Good day to you, Miss Hardesty. I'm Lieutenant Commander Edris, welcome to Bombardment Squadron one hundred eighty-seven. This is Mr. Carmello, my senior maintenance officer."

"Mr. Carmello. Commander, have we met?"

"Bob, please. No we haven't, Miss Hardesty," he said with a charming smile in Maria's native south Central Comario.

"Oh. Are you Comari?" She smiled. "Please, call me Maria."

*

"What the hell is he doing down there? Cockhound!" Pulke muttered. He watched as Roberto Edris gestured Hardesty towards Grim Reaper 1, his command bomber. Pulke noted how the vixen's deck crew and senior warrant gave the lothario room to operate.

*

This time the squadron commander himself escorted Maria towards his command craft. The vixen's odd shape caught the journalist's eye. Edris watched her turn back to compare them to the smaller, more conventional vortexes. The bulbous center of the craft gracefully gave way to tapered wings. Maria was impressed with its smooth lines despite its roughened outer hull.

"The design is called a flying wing, Miss Hardesty."

223

Edris led Maria to the flight deck access ladder from the open bomb bay in the belly of the craft. He extended a hand to help her cross into the surprisingly roomy cockpit.

"That's because the stations are opened up. In flight, all these panel nodes close in around the pilot and bombardier. The navigator is okay, but things get busy for them." Bob Edris smiled and winked. "I have always admired your work, Maria. I'm sure your family is very proud of you. Not many long-lineage second daughters are so; how shall I say? Resilient?"

Maria laughed and looked around the craft.

The vixen was larger than the vortex. It had thicker armor and a crew of 3.

"These indo-exo atmospheric bombers are designed to use its targeting computers from planetary orbit. We penetrate atmospheres in high-speed dives, level off, and skim the planet's surface using terrain following lidars to our target's proximity at high sonic speeds, Maria." Edris gestured with his hands as he spoke. "At the computed release point, my bombardier slings our ordinance towards the target from a stand-off distance while I accelerate in a zoom climb back into orbit. The navigator re-programs the targeting computer for the next attack.

"Vixens carry an array of SK bombs from three score of 1cdb munitions up to three bombs of two thousand decibel yields, the new 1.5kdb bombs are encased in an armored housing with a programmable delayed action fuse.

"They're designed to penetrate deep into the surface crust before the SK release. The release, amplified by the surface's tamping effect, collapses subsurface command centers and tunnels as in a shallow tectonic quake."

"You describe it thrillingly, Bob."

"Ah, the stories I could tell you," he said smiling. "Perhaps, miss, when you're free, I can regale you with my fanciful tales of daring do!"

"Well, yes. I'd like that."

"I carry a payload of cruise missiles and exo-torpedoes as my interdiction and attack tools, Maria. The vixen is liquid fueled, with only forty maneuvering thrusters, it has as a consequence, a relatively short range and limited maneuverability, compared to a vortex. My self-defense armament is a rear turret mounted, twin IEX automatic cannon. My main defense is speed, given a fourteen point three five to one thrust to mass ratio. Depending on the range to the target, my bombers carry enough fuel and ordinance to make on average three orbital dive attacks before having to return to the cruisers to refuel and rearm."

"I see. Oh, it may be a bit, Bob, before you can regale me. I'd like to get settled in on-board first."

"It'll be well worth the wait, Maria."

He had a charming smile and an interesting machine. *A Comaro man. Interesting he mentions my lineage so quickly. Caution light. Yes, Papa. Oh, why was I so aggressive with Mitchell? We were having such a wonderful time. Aunt Zinnia will know what to do.*

Edris helped Hardesty climb down through the bomb-bay access from behind the navigator's station, into the open bomb-bay and step down to the maintenance deck.

*

Mitch watched Edris holding Maria's hand and standing close as they emerged from below Grim Reaper 1. He normalized the lamalar. "Shower!"

****

Departure plus one day. 1623hrs, 25-02 of 770CE. Starboard observation Lounge, Deck 5 CBC Draken.

LCdr Tieras was having a grand time of it. So were two hundred students, thousands of trans-stellar astronomic units away. They sat transfixed on the image of the battle cruiser senior officer just in front of them, standing on the deck of his warship against an endless stellar back-drop. Behind him, other vessels appeared in the distance as small bright objects, gliding silently at great speed across sections of the lamalar observation port in the shipboard lounge projecting from their home station HG.

"Our galaxy is approximately one hundred thousand light-years, or thirty point six kilo-parsec, or kpc, in diameter. Our Central Metropolitan Region and the Outer Metropolitan Region make up the approximate forty-five thousand light-years, or thirteen point eight kpc wide middle region of the galaxy. But we don't use light-years in our navigation and propulsion computations or gunnery. Instead, we use the parseci system relative to a fixed stellar and trans-stellar astronomic unit of one hundred fifty million and one hundred fifty billion kilometers respectively. The simple reason for that is none of our years are ever exactly the same, because of our different planetary rotation speeds, and our different stellar orbital durations.

"My home, Epirus-Theshis, for example, has a four hundred eight day stellar orbit, a year at home for me is four hundred eight days across ten cycles, what you call months. On your home, Osiri-Vesta, a year is three hundred forty three days, across, what, thirteen months? Our daily sub-units of time; hours, minutes, and seconds are also slightly different. Therefore our concept of how far light can travel in a day or a year is relative to what a day or a year means to each of us. This is why we use the standardized Commonwealth year in trans-stellar communications. Does that answer your question, Mr. Phifster?"

"Yes, Commander, it does. But what I don't understand are the components of the Commonwealth calendar, I, I...that's the closest I can frame it, sir. I'm sorry."

"No worries, Mister, I think I know what you're reaching for."

These Academic Level-11 students were progressing through their municipal system where Academic Level 12 standards equate to the third year of their tribes' pre-Commonwealth baccalaureate under-graduate work. Most of the students in the primary attendance were already contracted. They were out of reach of the Fleet Recruiting Command, but they still needed the general cosmography credits to meet their matriculation in time to start their contracted baccalaureate year. They must matriculate within the contractual year to ensure the job they wanted would be waiting for them.

The Recruiting Command was far more interested in impressing the many more thousands of other younger, non-contracted students within the broadcast arc. Students across 17 states had logged into the Stellar Web transmission in their labs, archives, campus kiosks, and home terminals to receive the lecture credit.

The two hundred in Tieras' audience were from four vocational schools in the Sarnova Provincial district on Osiri-Vesta. Their student and instructor consoles synched with the Stellar Web HVD system in Void Equivalent Time from their particular institution's classrooms. Sarnova was slightly above average of Commonwealth municipal school districts. Their year round instruction accelerated per capita academic progress along the

Standardized Progression Model for Academic Performance by upwards of 7% per year. Their academic and fitness performances paralleled one another, with every student required to participate in at least one team and one individual competitive sport.

Tieras noted the several officer cadets in the uniform of the Vestian Home Guard were a little more relaxed after they saw their images had been dispersed among the other students. They sat erect and attentive, but they smiled and interacted with the civvies. Pre-enlistment military training was an alternative to team sports in most every state, and many young students opted for both.

Tieras knew Osiri-Vestian industry-sponsored academic institutions were as highly competitive across the educational spectrum as anywhere else in the Commonwealth. These young people were all highly motivated; ingrained since childhood with the spirit of creativity in their own self-interest in order to contribute to symbiosis and the Common Good. With less than two years of mid-school left, to fall behind now, meant the baccalaureate slot went to somebody else, and with it, the job contract the year after that. There were other jobs for sure, but not THE job.

Commercial, governmental, and military organizations sponsored the Osiri baccalaureate level institutions as in all the Common states and the Valerian systems. The institutions conducted highly specialized academic, vocational, and technical courses as the norm for post middle school institutions. These awarded baccalaureate and higher level degrees after intense, competitive courses of typically less than one year in duration.

The alignment problem at the beginning of the lecture was quickly resolved. Students were recovered from their initial disorientation as their seating was rearranged. Their image collection and positioning in the HG photonic streams in their classrooms had their shipboard images appearing inside the bulkhead, the outer hull, and in the void. One student actually hyper-ventilated and asked to be excused, but he swiftly returned. The signals petty officer on the observation deck with Commander Tieras solved the issue by shifting and rotating the class, student by student, within his photonic stream into the lounge chairs and sofas of the three-tiered observation deck and crew lounge.

For a bit of fun, the petty officer placed a number of the youngest looking students at the lounge bar, which was, of course, closed for the occasion. All this gave Tieras a chance to think about that 'light-year' question that came right away as the session began, that had the students confused. He had not thought about light-years since he was their age. He was surprised the Vestians still emphasized it so much.

Tieras stood in front of the lamalar observation panel displaying his graphics projection. He was always slightly disoriented in a photon stream, but the techies were on their game and synchronized. He felt comfortable walking up to the second tier among the students. As they turned to follow him, he turned back to face the lamalar and shifted the projection to the next display.

The image reformed to the broad extent of the galaxy as seen from well out in the trans-galactic void. There were 'oohs' and 'ahhs' from the students as its bright white center and great spirals swirling out in kaleidoscopic arms came into crystal clarity and close enough to touch. An octagonal grid pattern emerged, overlaid onto the image. The vast cosmopolitan stellar regions began to slowly rotate towards the oblique, then to on-plane, and on, slowly completing a 360 degree rotation.

"Our Commonwealth calendar is a hybrid. The Common, or VET day is based on the speed of rotation of Macillus-Saluri of twenty-four hours. A Common year is based on the orbital duration of Degoa around Hatu of three hundred sixty Saluri days divided into twelve months of thirty days. This 'Void Equivalent Time' was adopted as base meridian for ships to adjust to when operating throughout the void. Our stellar chart grid systems have standardized the distance between Saluri and its parent star, Macillus, one hundred fifty million kilometers, as the standard stellar astronomic unit or SAU."

Whenever Tieras touched a particular stellar cluster or star, an expanded inset appeared naming the body and highlighting the planets in its orbit. Data points in Angylis and Vestian displayed the angle of view and direction towards the singularity. The rotation halted briefly at 136 degrees, then continued to slowly rotate as the view narrowed to the CMR/OMR known boundaries.

"Our two regions are collectively known as the optimum evolutionary zone. It is the optimal distance from the active galactic core for the creation of planetary systems capable of supporting life as we know it. We call this region the galactic habitable zone."

"The galactic core consists of a super massive singularity, serving essentially the same purpose as a star's nuclear core. You can't see the singularity as it is surrounded by the globular cluster, this inner-most region of densely packed stars you see here. They are the oldest, or generation one, star systems and are the source, the parents as it were, of the generation two stars here in the CMR and OMR.

"According to Chein cosmographic data, when looking inward from the galaxy's outer rim, the generation two stars of our region appear indistinguishable from the outer edge of the great globular cluster of generation one stars. This is entirely an optical illusion. The stellar systems in the CMR are close enough to explain the ease of contact between our stellar tribes, much closer compared to those in the outer regions including newly identified systems in the spiral regions. But we are far enough apart that there is no threat of mass stellar collisions.

"Our fleet's stellar cartography corps applied a multidimensional transverse mercator grid system to the known galaxy, which they divided into octodrants centered on the singularity. We use eight cardinal directions in the Osiri-Angylis language, north, northeast, east, southeast, south, southwest, west and northwest. These directions are based on the polar and equatorial axes radiating from the singularity outward via intersecting lateral, longitudinal, and diagonal bands in parsec units. Parsec units are divided into trans-stellar astronomic unit grid squares of one hundred fifty billion kilometers or TSAU.

"They applied the grid to multi-dimensional star charts and identified each square in each band by an alpha-numeric sequence. Each band's designation sequence is the opposite of its adjacent bands. The only repeat designations occur at the ninth or central axis of the singularity, where nothing manmade can survive.

"Points within the non-central axis grids are located by intersecting designations to a point within ten thousand kilometers. Improvements in navigation buoys have allowed measurement of locations to within one thousand kilometers. With precision plotting to within one hundred kilometers possible by triangulation using star charts and sextant, marker beacons, and navigation buoys."

Tieras scaled the display inward, bringing into clarity the outlines of the metropolitan regions. Tightening the display revealed the green outline of the boundaries of Commonwealth member states, and the color code denoting political alignments among the known stellar regions. Blue designated non-Aligns, white identified Valerian Monarchial League's stellar provinces. Red lines denoted the Alliance of Stellar Republics. The Patruscan League realms were yellow, with brown representing the Asigi Collective.

Rapidly pulsating black and white lines coursed through each stellar state. Thicker, black and gold lines snaked their way through each region between the stellar systems. Both sets denoted the interlocking webs of trans-planetary, stellar state, and trans-stellar retransmission and navigation supernets, like the one TF Draken was traveling.

The display shifted from the stellar map to smaller scale depicting the Osiri Stellar State and its immediate neighbors. Tieras highlighted Osiri-Vesta and his own home world, Epirus-Theshis, 1,543 TSAU distant and laid in a sample course. The enormous linear distances and transit durations flashed red in the data sections.

"In the early days of trans-stellar travel; crews navigated primarily by star chart and sextant. It was very slow, and travel was limited by the orbital position of the point of origin in one heliosphere relative to that of the destination in another. But we've learned to map and interact with planetary gravity waves within a star's heliosphere and the faster trans-stellar waves they travel on, that originate from the singularity," he said.

"We chart celestial magnetic fields using an alpha-numeric pattern and the multidimensional transverse mercator grid. For the last eight hundred fifty years or so we have ridden those waves. They are always there with constant and near constant accelerative and deccelerative change factors or deltas."

Tieras minimized the direct lay course and raised Osiri-Vesta's planetary wave overlay. The display came alive with pulsating yellow lines emanating from both Vesta's poles, encircling the planet and flowing in a teardrop shaped barrier tapering behind it along its orbital plane of her mother star. The display morphed, revealing blue stellar gravity waves emanating similarly from Osiri. The outer edge of Vesta's yellow planetary magnetic field lines interacted with Osiri's blue stellar waves, creating a faint greenish glowing halo around the students' home world.

"What you see here are countervailances, the interactions between the star's magnetic field and the planet's called the magnetopause."

The display morphed a third time. Expanding again, Tieras highlighted the outer edge of Osiri's heliopause where her blue grav-wave field lines interacted with green trans-stellar waves from the singularity. Some of them extended well out into the trans-galactic void.

"This greenish-blue area of plasma is the effect of the interaction between your heliopause and the trans-stellar wave band designated CX three seven."

"That's turquoise in Vestrinari, sir."

"Thank you."

Tieras was glad to hear that, and by the soft chuckles from all around, he knew he was reaching them. They were relaxed and having fun. He completed the teaching point on countervailances and linked his point to navigation and propulsion by raising the Vesta to Theshis direct lay course plot again.

"We maintain standardized trans-stellar and trans-planetary courses that we lay into navigation and propulsion computers from continually updated databases. We establish a navigational fix on our vessel while at a station keeping position by triangulating our destination, our home port or depot, and the singularity at the galactic center. We plot a series of intervening countervailances, or sling points, and program hyper-meron sprint and inertial drift durations along them to reach a designated deceleration point outside our destination's heliosphere."

The display highlighted each point of Tieras' explanation resulting in a looping track of several points, each depicting a steady green linear distance and transit duration. The longer total distance appeared on the side panel in steady green, above the flashing red initial course. Below the distance, however, Tieras pointed out the total transit duration of a few days, where the straight line interception method required several weeks. This led him to propulsion systems.

"Our transit times are steadily decreasing. This is driven by our symbiotic research into meron and hyper-meron technology, magnetic field mapping, and other research contracts awarded by global governments, nations and city-states, and venture capitalists. Design firms like Marchase & Martin right there on Vesta introduce new engine designs to markets almost every decade. In fact, Marchase & Martin designed CBC Draken's hyper-meron drive units. Many of her components come from your factories."

The students loved hearing that. Many had contracts with the Marchase & Martin conglomerate. They burst into applause and gave a short school cheer, but their advisors quickly calmed them back down. It was just a few seconds, but the transmission window was only open for ninety minutes.

"There is a symbiotic effect of two separate factors. Our magnetic field generator creates a magneto-pause. Civilians call it a bubble, we call it the cocoon, which actually meshes with and carries us along the wave. Our hyper-meron accelerator enhances our ionic particle fusion drive system. Hyper-meron acceleration units provide our ships the ability to sprint across the trans-stellar voids at what you would call hyper-light speeds relative to VET, riding singularity waves from, and to points outside stellar systems.

"The vessel, within its magnetic cocoon, or HLS capable bubble, uses short hyper-meron pulses while riding a planetary, stellar, or trans-stellar wave with a known AC DC-Delta. That is a quick way of saying accelerative or deccelerative velocity change factor. Grav-waves and the currents within them are plotted and changes are identifiable, so once we have fixed our location initially, we will know our location and velocity at all times.

"Once we decelerate and enter a stellar system we use those same sling and brake maneuvers and decelerate the vessel to slip into, and out of, the trans-planetary gravity waves of the planets. Our methods are incredibly fuel efficient and quite scenic. As we approach our destination, we can locate areas of wave interaction called…?" He extended an open palm towards the group.

"Countervailances!"

"…that's exactly right," Tieras said with a broad grin. "Countervailances… within trans-planetary magnetic fields to decelerate vessels to near station-keeping and turn the ship 'into the wave' to launch and recover papoosed vessels."

He saw a hand go up one level down from the bar.

"… yes, question Miss, ah, Miss Hashemi."

"Hashemia, sir. Karleah. You mentioned an HLS bubble; considering the accelerative interaction with the wave, how long will it take to get to your destination?"

"Ahh yes, my favorite question, how fast can we go? Well, miss, the short answer regarding VET relative hyper-light is, we don't really know our trans-stellar speed limit. The reason we don't know is the AC DC delta factor of grav-waves vary, with distance and attitude, or angle, from their source. Typically, the closer we are to the source of the magnetic field, the greater the change or delta. Also the farthest point; that area where the wave reverses on itself and returns towards its source, is another region where the delta factor can be very high and very turbulent. Our two primary systems interact with the wave to achieve the velocities we need.

"Keeping the base in mind at all times, meron, or m equals twenty-one kilometers per second. Even the big modular ore carriers, moving as slow as m-two when towing a complement of octophages, can still traverse the width of the Commonwealth Administrative Zone on well mapped wave schedules in about twelve weeks. Our destination is classified for now, but we arrive at our first sling point tomorrow. We've only been underway for about twenty-six hours, averaging m-six with an average AC DC delta of five point seven four. We're taking our time, and plan to arrive outside our first port of call in about nine days. Does that help?"

After a few more minutes of questions and answers, the lecture concluded at 1730hrs with rousing applause and cheers from the students and their accompanying faculty advisers. They cheerfully endorsed the coordinating adviser's expressed thanks to LCdr Tieras and the crew of *CBC Draken* for their service and her blessing for their safety, and that of the Fleet. Tieras snapped to attention and gladial saluted his fellow Commoners' fading images.

Maria's applause from the back of the lounge surprised him.

"Maria, ah, Miss Hardesty. I didn't know you were there. How long have you been there?"

"Just about half. I'm going to tap into this and watch the whole thing and get the credit myself, Jeff. You were marvelous."

"Thank you," Tieras said. "Are you finding your way around okay?"

"So far so good. But I haven't found Mitchell's squadron. We need to talk, we had a terrible fight."

"When?"

"The night before last, at his billet after you left."

"Ahh. That explains a lot, Maria. He's working on the Phuong exercise with the strategy branch up in operations. But I see you have got my brother all confused and crawling back into his shell. C'mon, we'll go around to the Wing Ratzkeller. We'll grab a bite to eat and have a talk."

"Ohh, thank you, Jeff." *Mitchell has a shell, too.*

***

Departure plus two days. Billet 3-4A5, aboard CBC Draken. Vicinity of Nav-buoy NG-8391K, within the Commonwealth Administrative Zone. 0630hrs, 28-02 of 770CE.

'Child, don't crawl back into that shell. You're on a great big ship, you supposed to be interviewing people and such, baby.'

"Yes Aunt Zinnia, I've been out among the crew. Some of them are very nice. But, I was glad to meet that Comaro man, yesterday. It was so pleasant to talk to someone flesh to flesh in our native language, without earpieces. It was, just refreshing, that's all."

'Child, you don't need some Comaro man on the make. He wants to add your family legacy to his own. Like Malcom. He'll spend it if he gets it or he'll run away when he sees he can't get it. Like Malcom did.'

"Yes, Aunt Zinnia."

'You've got your man. The Omens gave him to you, and you don't have the power to drive him away. So stop trying. You and he gon' raise babies together, but he will always be what he is.'

"Yes, Aunt Zinnia."

'And so must you, child. He will never ask you to give up what makes you what he loves. You must never ask him to give up what makes him what you love.'

"I love him, Aunt Zinnia. Not his lineage or his uniform."

'Then accept him with his uniform, child.'

"Yes, Aunt Zinnia. I have to go now."

Her great-aunt's image blew her a kiss and waved goodbye as it faded. She buzzed her videographer Nick, billeted next door.

234

'Yes, Miss Hardesty.'

"I'm coming out, Nick. You ready?"

'I'm squared away, miss. I'll meet you in the circuit.'

Maria checked her recorder and data pad in her side bag and left her billet.

Nikolay Kung, a DIG contractor from Perseaus, gravitated to Maria the day they all met on Sestria. Since then, he had barely left her side. He knew a good shot that enhanced a story when he saw one. Maria admired his unobtrusiveness, he knew how to shadow her without getting in the way. She often forgot the swarthy, dark-haired man and his little datacam was with her. Yet, as she learned on the rifle range, the veteran metro constabulary beat cameraman watched her like a guardian angel.

They walked slowly at first to get their bearings. They had no trouble finding the nearest deck locator panel and firmly fixed their billets on Deck 4, Section Alpha-5, near the upper amidships battery forward observation post. The closest deck lift abutted the aft bulkhead of the forward 68cm battery turret. Passing the lift, they followed the central passageway circuit corridor and headed aft, along the port side of the ship.

"So what's the plan, Miss Hardesty?" Nick asked.

"You don't have to be so formal, Nick. We're headed towards the second of my three favorite parts of the ship. What a battle cruiser is all about, if you have to have one, or fifty, with forty-five on active service."

"We've seen the fighting craft. The guns. Their twelve big sixty-eight centimeter guns."

"They're called 'rifles'. I still haven't quite figured that out."

"What's the third?"

"The command information and intelligence center, the CIC," she answered.

"I figured that. I'll sleep in when you go there. No datacams allowed."

"Journalists either unless escorted by the Chief of Staff or the Sergeant Major. And I think Sergeant Major Morris hates me."

"He hates everybody, except Morgan and Rivas," Nick quipped. "That's his job. Well, our billets are on the right deck for the guns. Deck four gives us access to three of the ship's four

Battery Direction Centers, and the mezzanine above the mid-deck hangar bays, where the vortex and vixen pilots are billeted."

"I'm glad you're with me, Nick. You know your way around."

"I studied the deck schematics on my viewer. You'll learn you way too, boss. Just remember to always check the deck panels."

"Gotcha. So where do the pilots hang out? You know to relax," Maria asked.

"Boss, if you're going to have any chance of catching up to Commander Boy Scout it's going to be at the fighter-bomber wing ratzkeller. It's aft of the mezzanine overlooking the amidships shuttle bay where we came aboard. I'll show you."

"I know where that is. Hmmph. Who doesn't know about me and Commander Pulke?"

"The DIG, boss. But I think they would like it."

Hardesty and Nick smiled, nodded, and happily exchanged morning pleasantries with crewmembers in these first hours aboard a Common Fleet battle cruiser. The informal atmosphere of the corridors struck her as odd. *They're not like Jordan said, and there are no Drill Sergeants.*

Commonly called 'the circuit', the softly illuminated central passageway corridors traversed the entire vessel on each deck, from the aft bulkhead of the forward battery turret, to the forward bulkhead of the aft battery turret. Segmented during action stations by armored blast doors and emergency mag-shielding and connected to other decks by sealable access ramps, each deck circuit held numerous small curves and sharp turns as it followed the configurations of compartments on either side.

Walking along, ahead of Nick, with her recorder in hand, crewmembers came and went from the outer compartments and work areas in the same disciplined manner Hardesty expected but it seemed everyone had a smile.

Passing the distinctive black and yellow striped panel section in the bulkhead Maria self-consciously checked her left lower cargo pocket for her evac suit.

Stop being so scared! It's a life-pod, learn to recognize them. Remember what Drill Sergeant Bodette said. 'Every set of DDs has an evac suit in the lower left cargo pocket. That's why there is a lower left cargo pocket. It's not a stash for pogey bait! Troop.' Only Papa had ever talked to me like that. Mitchell comes close. Mitchell comes. Stop it.

She turned around towards Nick's datacam.

"No battle stations drill has been called yet, but everyone knows one can be, at any time. 'No more Task Force Liberty's!' is an adage every Commonwealth trooper takes to heart. It has been three hundred fifty-five years since the Task Force Liberty disaster. But the pain of it has never died within our common fleet. *CBC Liberty's* berth at the Gabb'es-Sestria anchorage remains sealed in her perpetual memory. The one thousand two hundred thirty-nine officers and crewmembers that went into Poia aboard her, remain listed on active duty to this very day."

Jordan must have heard wrong, she thought as she walked along. *He said Common Fleet ships and fighters were old and dirty, their crews rough and mean.* She stopped at an intersection and, stepping to one side, she observed crewmembers moving purposefully along the circuit, coming and going from various compartments. Each compartment's address, denoting the deck, an abbreviation of its function and the major section of the deck, was stenciled in 3cm block letters on the bulkhead centered above the manway.

"I have to admit, I was a little concerned about what I had heard about the age of our ships before I arrived at the Sestria depot," Maria said towards Nick's datacam as she walked along. "However, since then and since I came aboard *CBC Draken* just over forty-eight hours ago, I've concluded the regular fleet ships I've seen don't appear to be very old. The vessel familiarization instructors on Sestria said our battle cruisers and destroyers are the latest versions of 450 year old Moktari designs. The Chein design of our Predator class frigate is even older."

These regular fleet crews are so polite, they are so open, and willing to teach. That's a Kratari legacy.

*

Nick recorded all types of crew members, recognizable by the branch insignia beneath their rank on their sleeve, like his and Maria's two crossed avian quill styluses below the initials CME. They all wore the *CBC Draken* left cuff band and their home stellar state flag patch on their right sleeve. Nick felt a part of the team, as Kratari had envisioned so long ago.

*

"This crew is from all over the Commonwealth of Stellar States," Maria continued, making a broad sweep with her arm towards passing crewmembers. "The inboard translation circuits are here because they're required aboard every trans-stellar capable vessel and deep void station. Common fleet battle cruisers certainly fit that category. But the translation circuits are rarely challenged, because this crew, like the rest of the Common Fleet, is immersed in Osiri-Angylis from day one of basic training as the Commonwealth's technical language.

"This Denestri-Comari journalist, is not as proficient yet with Angylis, relying instead on the programmable translators embedded in my PtC and earpiece to synch with the translation circuits. The cinemas and interactives are full of numerous amorous encounters in bars and resort stations that often erupt into slapped faces, tossed drinks or missed opportunities over the 'three-percent exception'. No such excuses here."

Maria didn't especially appreciate the rah-rah history lessons back on Gabb'es-Sestria but as time went by, certain symbolisms she had regarded as anachronisms or even propaganda before took on new meaning. She began to gain a sense of the meaning behind the graduation ceremonies she and her team witnessed before departing the depot for Tresium. Looking around at passing crewbies she imagined them having been called forward by name, and standing alone before their officers, their mates, and their families and stating the oath to defend the Commoners and support the Constitution.

They put the people first, then the rule book. Interesting, she thought. *The Denestri oath says they'll support the Constitution. It doesn't say a word about people.*

"Stellar State military formations have managed to keep their pomp and circumstance and their unique shipboard traditions. These regulars though are an amalgam of ostensibly the best of the practices and traditions of all the Common States," she searched her mind for an appropriate phrase. *Something papa would say.* "This child of many fathers, however, looks nothing like any of them."

"Cutting. Nice one, boss."

"It felt good. Just roll whenever you get the urge."

"Miss Hardesty! Oh, Miss Hardesty!" A familiar voice carried up the corridor from behind her. Maria stopped and spun, looking past crewmembers moving along past her. Emerging from the sliding, tinted lamalar manway of Compartment 4ESR3MS, the tall, young astronomer, Ensign Hakshatram, CLA class of '69, a replacement telemetrics officer she sat next to on the shuttle, came striding towards her.

"Sharadas! Good morning! How are you?"

"I'm good, miss. You headed aft?"

"Yes. I'm starting a routine of daily rounds, to catch the mood of the crew. I was working my way towards the batteries, where're you headed?"

"Same, same me. They're putting me to work straight away, Miss. I'm taking these update disks over to the Wing, to update their extended sensory pods." The young officer announced.

"Well that's grand 'Das? Have you settled in? Have you talked to your mother?"

They had to stop, after passing the open armored blast door and emergency magnetic shield generator panels, at section 4 amidships. They and others had to move to the inner wall to allow one of the 100mm close defense gun crews, room to cross the circuit with load carriers holding crates of what Maria thought might be ammunition, from a cargo lift. A closer look at the tags and stenciling on the crates identified them as batteries coming up from the Deck 5 armories. With the gun mount's manway open, Nick managed to get a good view of the gunner's compartment and twin breech assemblies.

"Oh, no, Miss Hardesty. I've been so excited, I haven't thought about it. I'd better make a reservation to call home after I get off watch."

"A reservation? Can't you just call from your billet?" Maria asked with a broad curious smile.

The gun crew pushed their cart across the circuit and closed the compartment manway, clearing the circuit for traffic.

"Oh, no miss. All personal communications are blocked. Nobody has any CCC access."

"Really?"

"Oh no, miss. Operational security. With the war and all. The watch commander told us when he visited us in the wardroom."

"Hmm, that's interesting, Das, I hadn't heard that."

She tried not to sound worried. She didn't want the ensign to know she had inadvertently broken a major security rule on just her second full day aboard. *They must know, they must be able to monitor every transmission aboard. What will Colonel Rivas say? Mitchell, I'll ask Mitchell, it'll be a good way to break the ice. Stop it. Fight your own battles, Go to Rivas and Karen Stone up. No one told me. I didn't know.* "I heard the announcement, calling all the newly arriving officers to report there. I wondered if I was supposed to go, but I followed the enlisteds. So you must have found it okay?"

"Well, kind of. Some marines took us up, and crewbies from our divisions took us from there to our billets. How is your billet, miss?"

"Quiet. So they're breaking you in right away eh, 'Das. Old school."

"True enough I guess. I sure am getting to know my way around, and a lot of the chiefs really well!"

"And this just our second day aboard. So, that means there's a method to their madness, 'eh, Das?"

"I guess so, Miss Hardesty."

"Ahh, remember what Kratari said, mister. Never guess! Give your best estimate. But never guess!"

The two walked and talked along the length of the circuit with Nick close at hand at all times. It seemed to Maria he was always recording, documenting what they heard, saw and said about it.

She stopped in front of one of the stellar locator panels at a lateral intersection. One of many such along the circuit and in certain common use compartments throughout the ship that kept the crew informed of the vessel's current stellar location, course and speed within its Area of Operations.

"Das, if you have a second, can you orient Nick and me to where we are right now?"

"Certainly, miss. That's something else the WC said. 'Give the embeds all your cooperation.' Especially you, miss."

"Really?"

"Yes, miss. Well you see," he said stepping out of the flow of traffic. Nick stepped forward to get a clear shot as well. "We are presently in the coverage of Nav-buoy NG-8391K. Heading east by northeast at meron factor six. We are running in a subducted stellar wave, at an AC DC delta of 5.9, which gives us an m-35.4 forward velocity."

"So with the constant of Meron or m=21kps, they taught us in basic training, we are cruising at 743.4 kilometers per second. Why such a slow, almost leisurely pace?"

"It's probably a programmed deceleration, to set us up, timing wise, for a loop to sprint, miss."

"Loop to Sprint?"

Hakshatram caught on and grinned. "Are we live? My family will faint seeing me with you!"

"We're not right now." Nick answered with a chuckle. "I'll give you a heads up a few days in advance so you can let them know."

"Great. Yes, Miss Hardesty, that's right. Vessels loop and sling around celestial bodies, while riding the magnetic waves that emanate from them with an accelerative boost from a meron or hyper meron sprint. Ships accelerate and decelerate in accordance with the data updated from the buoys and beacons."

Maria nodded. "So each buoy continuously charts and transmits gravity wave data on a specific region of the void, for a transiting vessel to pick up and interpret for their destination?" she asked.

"Yes, correct."

The panel depicted the flashing green task force unit symbol as it approached the steady orange Nav-buoy symbol, NG-8391K, labeled for the 100,000 astronomic unit grid zone designation NG and it's X, Y, Z, and Tier axes.

"In our direction of travel, NG-8391K links to NG-1912Y7, now just twenty TSAU distant," the ensign said.

"So, where are we now?"

Das grinned. "We're passing the lower region of the Kalfiairi Stellar State, thirty-four trans-stellar astronomic units to starboard, the middle region of Cestus, is here, fifty-six TSAU to port. We are domed by Barat. It's a massive star, miss, with a broad habitable zone. That state is huge. Whereas, we're doming, or passing over, Rowan, my home, for only for about the next three hours or so. The Betia Nebula is there in the distance off our port quarter below, and behind us, its outer edge at one hundred thirteen TSAU. Pirieus-Tresium and Depot Nineteen lay, now fourteen TSAU to the southwest, more or less sternward. Further down south there, lay Vighandis. That's the frontier region where the last of the Alliance units are trapped by our second, third and fifth fleets."

"I thought there were only two fleets fighting in Vighandis."

"Oh no, miss. Three, and elements of a fourth. It's hard to contain a force in the void, miss. The alliance units are all bunched together, damn near in a circle. Our people have to cover at least six times the area the Alliance phalanxes are occupying just to hold them in place."

"When will it end, Das?"

"Your guess is as good as mine, miss."

Maria looked towards Nick to cut, but he already had, and had turned to say hello to a cute crewbie girl.

"Das, earlier you said your watch commander mentioned me specifically?" Maria asked. "Is his name Tieras?"

"Her, miss. Lieutenant Commander Matulz."

"I don't know her. I've met Lieutenant Commander Tieras."

"The professor? Third watch. I heard he's great. Lieutenant Commander Harborn has second. Counting the XO, the wing commander and the squadron commanders, miss, the chiefs say the fleet grows Commanders aboard battle cruisers from seedlings called Lieutenant Commanders."

"Yes, there are quite a few, but with seven thousand or more for a crew. Interesting. You called Commander Tieras, the professor?"

"Yes, miss. He guest lectured at the academy a couple of years ago. I don't mind telling you, miss. Last year, three months before graduation, I was having trouble calculating wave velocities at strategic distances. Well, that's the most important part of our job in ESR, miss. My advisor suggested I view that lecture. It was a simple first day Cosmo one oh one lecture. I thought my advisor was telling me I was stupid or something but then I listened, and it all came clear. I was thrilled to hear he's our third watch commander. Maybe I'll get to work with him."

Arriving at the intersection with the upper amidships battery-turret access lateral, the two said a brief farewell for the day and parted company. Maria found she enjoyed talking with the handsome young officer, she thought briefly about how much more enjoyable he could be, but she quickly put it out of her mind. It would not be proper for her to sleep with so junior an officer. *Stop that!* She thought. *What would Aunt Zinnia say? The Omens say you've got your man.*

The marines at the entrance noted their arrival and buzzed she and Nick through the manway from the passageway into the lateral. The short corridor turned ninety degrees to the right and led past the long pictoral panels of earlier versions of *CBC Draaken* firing, or 'loosing' its massive ordinance towards some unfortunate Alliance vessel or surface installation. The *Drakens*, and her generations of crews had seen plenty of action.

The inner manway panels slid open as she approached, Maria knew she and Nick, were under constant marine surveillance in these sensitive areas of the ship, clearance or no clearance. It was the same aboard every Ship of the Line; gunners only trust other gunners, and even they must 'lay, lock, and verify'.

Master Gunnery Sergeant Josephus P. Barnes, 'Big Joe' to the crew, greeted Maria and Nick at the main manway into the BDC.

"Good morning, Sergeant Barnes. How are you?"

"Gettin' set for the next fight, Miss Hardesty. I hope it's a long wait. Good to see you again, Nick."

"You too, Master Gunnery Sergeant."

"You know each other?"

"We met at chow this morning. Incidentally, where were you?"

"Asleep."

"I'm going to start waking you up, for the gym and chow."

"Oh omens, Nick, not you too."

"Phuong's gonna be a bitch, Boss," Nick said. "If we go in on the ground, I don't want to have to drag your ass, plus Jolene here."

"I thought your D-cam's name was Jenny?"

"It was, I changed it. I ran into two women named Jenny during orientation and another in the MAC terminal on Tresium," Nick grunted, looking around for a good perch. "Too coincidental for me, weird."

The battery plotting table's photonic HG projection dominated the miniature command center. The illumination in the large circular compartment, behind and below the Deck 5 turret, was a constant mild blue that their eyes slowly adjusted to. The aura merged on the faces of head-setted crewmembers with the varying shades of green emanating from the consoles they sat in front of.

"You're just in time, miss. We were about to start tracking runs on some of the nearby shipping. All in simulation mode, of course."

"Oh, of course, Sergeant. You have any particular ships in mind?"

"I'm thinking something fairly large today to work the newbies with. There's an ore-ship with a brood of octophages about to cross our wake, to start with. Right now she's off our starboard quarter at about fifteen thousand kilometers. Care for some Jave' miss, Nick?"

"Sure, Gunny!"

"Ah, oh, certainly, thank you. How many newbies do you have, Sergeant?"

"Seventeen, miss."

"Is that a lot?"

"Not really, out of fifty. I had twenty newbies out of thirty aboard a destroyer in Spice Alley back in sixty-seven. Got real hairy. The Tantorans obliged, and made good training aids," Big Joe said with a smirk. He saw he had confused her. "The best training aids shoot back, miss," he added with a slow Lucainan drawl.

"I see."

Joe Barnes was born on the famous JKK Ranch on Andolusia-Lucainus, the Praetor's home. The J-double K as the locals called it. The sprawling sub-provincial farming conglomerate was Jana K. Kratari's most enduring physical legacy. Scores of communities, private and corporate farms, ranches, timber nurseries, and a vast forest preserve, called it home as well.

MGS Barnes took them to the jave' alcove, and shortly, after fixing them up with secure tumblers took them over to the Battery Turret Control Officer, who gave her a passing wave while she handled administrative duties of some sort. These were Big Joe's rifles during training, and he was more than capable of handling them, the simulation and the Embed, while she and the exec planned for Phuong.

Barnes placed Maria at one of the observer consoles close to his station so he could keep an eye on her while he supervised the drills. The console station went active with her presence, after he authenticated it for her. He controlled the distribution of all the data feeds from the outer ESR nodes, as well as streaming data from the surrounding ships and patrolling fighters. Barnes spooled up the tactical display from the plot board to her console. Maria synched her recorder to her earpiece, then held it up for Barnes to see. He shrugged and nodded as she set the active recorder back in her bag.

*

Task Force Draken's three semi-independent battle groups each consisted of a Delta–class battle cruiser, two Terrier-class escort destroyers and three Predator-class frigates. Each group took the cruiser's name. The plot showed Battle Group *Draken* and her two sister battle groups travelling in a loose wedge over-watch formation with the *Dridantes* group in the lead, *Draken* in echelon to starboard, and *Drukar* in echelon to port. Within the wedge, traveled four Long Range Transports, LRTs *Acre, Etar, Moncrief* and *Yulan*, embarking the 7th Marines and the task force surface support units. The transports formed an inner diamond protecting the fabrication and supply ship *Sabra* and the agro-carrier *Saffier*.

A destroyer flotilla of three *Taifun*-class Commonwealth Destroyers, six *Essex*-class frigates and a Raven-class escort carrier led by the destroyer, *CD Perseaus* maintained a loose pentagon formation above, below, and on plane of the capital ships. The vortex squadrons from the cruisers rotated shifts, maintaining a combat patrol extending the width and depth of the task force formation and the effective target identification range.

"The battle cruiser's main anti-ship weapons and bombardment assets are its four batteries of three each, 37.4 meter long, 68cm x 55 magnetic rail imbedded-SK rifles in four rotating turrets," Barnes said.

"Why do you call these guns rifles, Sergeant?"

"Damned good question, miss."

Barnes shifted the main display to a schematic of a battle cruiser targeting an installation on a planet's surface. An inset zoomed in on the lower amidships battery turret, while morphing into a schematic of the three decked battery system.

"They're guns because they're served by crews."

245

The display continued to change, devolving to a cut away view of the center, or number one gun. "But they are classified as rifles, because of the rifling, or grooves, in the barrel, from the barrel blank to the muzzle. These grooves are in-laid with the magnetic rails that propel the projectile. The barrel blank seals the barrel when the breach is open. When the breach locks, the blank unlocks. Always know your gun's BB lock status, gunners."

Each point highlighted and animated as Barnes spoke. An animation of the working of the weapon followed.

"As the projectile is propelled along the rails, their twists impart a spin to it, giving it a flatter trajectory. The projectile, or projoe itself is an oblong made of a high-iron chondrite asteroidal alloy, to survive atmospheric entry. It holds a recompressed sonic wave, the kinetic energy of which is equivalent to one point five kilotons of chemical based high explosive." Barnes turned to Maria. "Our term for that is sonic-kinetic or SK, miss."

"Oh, thanks." She smiled at him. She wasn't expecting that.

The animation continued to follow Barnes' narration.

"Gunners, we determine the physical shape of the charge based on the type of target. We can program them for point target mode, which focuses the charge's kinetic energy directly against a small radius of a target vessels' outer hull. Or, a proximity fused round shot for use against a wide area target. We also use that to make an omni-directional effect on, or just above surfaces."

The battery image faded, replaced by the battle cruiser standing off in geo-synchronized orbit of its target on the fictitious planet. The targeting image zoomed in, green cross-hairs followed the track of a river to a dam, with hydro-electric power generation plants on either side. A small red cross-hair settled and highlighted on each structure in turn. Columns of ranging and targeting data lit up below and flanking each target.

Barnes left his station to walk around the direction center, explaining as he went. Maria watched the crew, the shifting display and MGS Barnes in fascination.

"Our rifles achieve planetary bombardment against specific surface targets via direct atmospheric entry flight profile, from greater range, and with extreme accuracy. An illumine-coated band covers the rear third of the casing to allow observers to visually follow the shot to the target. Number one gun! Identify your target and state your range!"

A young, head-setted woman in the first, or lower tier sat bolt upright in her swivel in front of her terminal screen.

"Uhn, uhn,"

"Today! Johansen."

"Target is the dam, Master Gunnery Sergeant. Range, one million six hundred forty seven thousand kilometers."

"Very good," Barnes grinned. "Adjust your resolution. Plot the structure's dimensions. Gunners, a battery turret is capable of loosing its rifles singly, or all three, in battery volley."

The display shifted again, this time depicting the view of one of the power generation complexes next to the dam. Two concentric circles illuminated, encompassing the target. The inner circle highlighted in red. The outer circle highlighted yellow.

"On atmospheric surfaces, the secondary kinetic wave carries varying destructive effects far beyond the immediate blast, or release radius of the primary wave. The cruiser's turret arrangements allow maximum fires to be brought to bear in virtually any direction against either surface or void targets."

The display morphed again. This time the battle cruiser laid its aft battery turret toward the ore ship Barnes spoke of earlier.

"They are equally effective against point type void targets, such as other vessels and void platforms."

Another target identification brought the ore carrier into clear view on Maria's and the BDC crew's screens at 15,321 kilometers.

"The muzzle velocity, and maximum targeting range of SK rifle models remain classified, people. Your systems know what they are. All you need to know, on that score at least, is your range to target," Barnes continued. "However, the longest recorded engagement was in the third war, where a third round hit, loosed into the wave against a moving destroyer sized target, that's about four hundred meters by one fifty, was at a range of point six eight SAU, or a hundred and two million kilometers, after a three minute time of flight."

The cross-hairs moved in front of the ore-carrier. The outer targeting ring rested amidships. As the inner ring aligned with the bow, the cross-hairs flashed red. Confused, Maria looked up at Barnes standing directly in front of her, grinning.

"In the void, gunners, everything is in motion. You, your target, the waves in between. Our projoes don't ride the wave like the howitzers. Our projoes power through grav-waves. Consequently, we lead the target. So that the projoe and the target meet at the same point in the void."

A simulated projectile struck the ore-carrier's bow, forward of and below the flight deck. A second struck the amidships papoose rack, rupturing octophages and obscuring the vessel behind a glittering rainbow of vaporizing molten ore. A third projectile detonated above and just beyond the crippled carrier's starboard quarter, but still within range of its shockwave.

"Upon impact, gunners, or High Speed Programmable Fuse failsafe activation, the alloy casing ruptures, releasing, rather than detonating the SK charge. In the void's vacuum, the SK wave's kinetic effect shoves and buckles sections of outer hull plating.

"An effective series of hits on a target causes sufficient buckling to penetrate the outer hull and rupture the inner hull, causing a decompression. Crew-members without hearing protection aboard the target vessel are subjected, with each impact, to noise of gargantuan proportions throughout their pressurized compartments.

"I want you to learn the difference between a moving ship, like this ore-carrier, and a maneuvering ship, like this one."

The innocent ore ship became a menacing Tantoran *Trian* class destroyer bearing down on them bow-on, its port and starboard gun turrets ablaze. In an instant, the brute pivoted left and climbed out of sight. But two Ajax-3 anti-ship missiles bored in before the display dropped. Leaving Maria, Nick and the BDC crew stunned.

"We've got archival footage of Sacorsti battle cruisers too. But don't worry too much about them."

Maria, Nick and the gunners looked around at each other in confusion.

"A Trinovan general once said, 'Sacorsti battle cruisers are only frightening to the uninitiated. But a Tantoran destroyer will kill you!' He was damned right! You remember that."

"Yes, Master Gunnery Sergeant."

The display shifted to an expansive view of the task force formation. Then again to a tactical plot of the task force's current location relative to Barat's heliosphere.

"Gunners, significant battles rarely take place where we are now, in the deep trans-stellar regions. Battle areas traditionally begin near the stellar heliopause where fleets plot their deceleration points or anticipated enemy deceleration points. That's where vessels transit the plasma shock to enter the heliosphere."

The display re-oriented, highlighting an area along Rowan's helio-pause.

"This is also where fleets and task force units generally deploy from the approach march to a traveling overwatch formation. Units adopt a bounding overwatch as the likelihood of enemy contact increases.

"We'll be running battle drills, using archived targets, starting tomorrow all the way to the time we cross the line of departure into Andolusia. From that point on people, we are at ExCon five. That is, exercise condition five. You can expect contact with an Opfor vessel at any time. How do you know you are at ExCon, people?"

"Orange illumination, Master Gunnery Sergeant!!"

He grinned at Maria and Nick. "Simulation condition?"

"Blue illumination, Master Gunnery Sergeant!!"

"Defense condition?"

"Battle red illumination, Master Gunnery Sergeant!!"

"Gunnery Sergeant Barnes, you said your guns shoot in a different manner than the howitzers. How are they different?"

"Yes, miss. Those are smooth bore howitzers aboard the transports' bombardment platforms and the bombardment ships. They loose volleys into the wave against wide area targets across sections of the void, and, via orbital insertion, onto surfaces. I don't have footage keyed up of any, but you'll see them launched once the show starts at Phuong. It's gonna be a bitch of a show. Uhm, Pardon my language," Barnes said immediately.

Maria chuckled. "Oh that's alright, Gunnery Sergeant. I've been hearing Phuong referred to as a bitch so often I'm beginning to think she's a relative."

Barnes and Nick both burst out laughing.

****

Departure plus four days. Orderly Room of 3rd Cohort, 2nd Bn, 7th Marines. E Deck, LRT Acre. 0830hrs, 28-02 of 770 VET.

"Have I said today how much I hate these damned things, Top?"

"Too many times to count, Tony. It could be a lot worse." CoSM Greer handed headsets to each of his platoon sergeants. He had headsets as well, for his headquarters section sergeant, his motor sergeant, senior medico, and his bombardment support team sergeant. The cohort's senior NCOs had been dreading the assignment since he informed them last night, or what passed for night once embarked, after the Battalion Command Sergeant Major's meeting. Their squad and section leaders knew their assignments, leaving the platoon sergeants to gather in the orderly room to receive theirs.

"We got reporters snooping around and now we have to play nursemaid to a bunch of clerks back on Degoa-Earth too, Top?" PSgt Roxanne Pettis complained. "Damn, are we the only cohort in this task force today, or what?"

"Embrace the suck, people. You're all so adorable, everybody is drawn to you," Greer said with a grin. "As it happens, with such astonishing regularity around the regiment, a confluence of random events have coalesced in our laps."

"Huh?"

"Damn thing looks like a toy!" Weapons Platoon Sergeant Antony Brock examined the slender head harness with its short, semi-rigid fibroptic extension.

"It's real sensitive, I was playing with one last night," Greer confessed.

"So, who exactly are we entertaining with these things, Top?"

"A team from Fleet Personnel Management at Admiralty on D-E."

The Motor Sergeant, Technical Sergeant Andrea Michener got down to basics. "Why, Top? And why us?"

"Because we're here, lassie! Because it's almost time to submit next year's budget. On the straight, Top?"

"You're on the straight, Bennie. It's all part of a big manpower utilization study. The fleet's expanding over the next couple of years, and Personnel Command is trying to get ready for it.

"Think of it this way," Crowder said. "Finally somebody at the puzzle palace is going to ask you what you think and write your answer down."

"I like that. These here things are simple," the sergeant major continued, holding up a headset and putting it on. "Once you put it on, they activate on a standard voice command. The fibroptic is the transceiver. You just talk to them and they can see and hear what you do."

"Everything, Top?!"

"Yeah, everything, Roxanne. So mind yer manners!"

"You know me, Top. I'm the soul of patience." First Platoon's PSgt Pettis' sarcasm brought a chuckle to the group.

"Okay," he chuckled. "But if you want to see your counterpart, you have to come back here and HG on the pad. Clear? Otherwise go about your day, answer their questions, and bring the headsets back in one piece at recall formation, hooah?!"

"Hooah, Sergeant Major!"

"What about the embed, Top?"

"What about him?"

"Oh, well, nothing I guess."

**

The motor pool bustled as fusiliers deck guided armored vehicles moving between charging bays and the main diagnostic station or the range simulator. Walking the 2nd platoon's vehicle line with A. J. Mortimer and his videographer, Lieutenant De'Avest saw Sergeant Michener walk out onto the mezzanine above the headquarters vehicle bay through the manway from the orderly room area. He saw the curious headset she was wearing, but he had to contend with A. J.'s questions walking with him and his officer candidate shadow on his walk around of the motor pool.

"The Code of Kratari the Andolusian runs strong in the Fleet, A. J," De'Avest said, scanning the bumper number of the next squad carrier in line with his stylus and making notes on his wrist pad. "Especially among the noncommissioned officer corps. They're the backbone of the Fleet. No matter if one wears the platinum stars of the admiralty or is a smooth collar recruit, every man or woman in uniform is a trooper first," he said. "No matter their rank or duty assignment, every trooper has a sergeant or a petty officer. It's sergeant's business to keep troopers, crewmembers, things, ships, and units running. Sergeants keep

251

troopers trained and motivated. They keep them informed, on time and on target. My, our sergeants' train, maintain, and nurture the outfit, even though Centurion Naravanutu commands it. Ya hear me, Mr. Ymarh?"

"Loud and clear, sir."

"And you're her exec?" A. J. asked with a smile.

"That's right."

"Are you hoping for a cohort of your own someday, Lieutenant?"

"Hope is not really the word for that, sir. I'd use plan and aspire, but, yes."

The bays were filled with the cohort's battle complement of eighteen M109 Chariot squad battle carriers and six each, M38 armored fighting vehicles, M19 Skorpion mortar carriers, and M4 Viper anti-vehicle guided missile launcher carriers. Third Cohort's service support vehicle package of two light and three medium utils, an armored carrier recovery vehicle, and a front-line ambulance occupied two large charging/service bays under the mezzanine.

*

Tech Sergeant Michener stood on the mezzanine overlooking the motor pool.

"We re-embarked back at Depot one nine at Pirieus-Tresium. First Fusiliers aboard *Etar* is set up like we are. I've got what you see here on this deck. Every fusilier cohort motor pool is configured the same with charging and maintenance bays for each squad battle carrier, the mortars, AFV platoon, and AVGM carriers. We're standing on the mezzanine, above the headquarters vehicles' bays."

'Those armored fighting vehicles have turreted main guns. You have Leopard chars, not assault guns?'

"Yeah, that's right, sharp eye! Some people call them tanks. Us and First Cohort. Second Cohort, above us, they have AGs."

'Where are the dragoons?'

"They're aboard Yulan."

'Oh, that's right, there are three transports.'

"Four, troop transports actually, plus a supply/fab ship and an agro."

*

"So, who am I talkin' to? What's yer name?" PSgt Benson Crowder asked, walking his troop billet compartments.

'Call me Bob, and you're Sergeant Crowder, correct?'

"Bennie. Are you a machine, Bob?" Crowder opened the manway of a team billet chamber. The four bunks were configured to allow each trooper a modicum of personal space. The bunks were made, their wardrobes closed and locked, panel viewer turned off, latrine clean and dry.

'Me? No, I'm from Berrelli-Giffar. I've been in the AG here for about eight months.'

"Oh, ok, where were you before that?" Crowder passed through the connecting anteroom into the next team's chamber.

'CBC Intrepid's surface depot on Gabb'es-Sestria. This chamber's configuration is a little different.'

"Gabb'es-Sestria?! My condolences. Yea, we let 'em set their rooms up pretty much how they want. They're the ones who have to live here. The squads are in the battle simulators, I'm headed there now. We call it B-Sim. The troops call it the playhouse. It's just aft of us, down the cohort street."

'Did your whole cohort fight in Trudan and Maranon, Bennie?'

"Most of 'em, we've got about fifty replacements all told."

'You lost fifty troopers?'

"No. Twenty-one, six dead. The others didn't extend their tours after we got back. Everybody needed three years remaining on their enlistments to make this cruise. Those that didn't have it either had to extend or reenlist or get reassigned."

'Okay, now I understand. Our preliminary data wasn't clear on that.'

"Oh? What else does your 'preliminary data' say about us?"

Crowder exited the platoon billets, stepping into the main corridor, he turned left, heading aft towards the B-Sim.

'Oh my. Where are we?'

Startled, Crowder looked around. "Huh? Oh, the cohort street, like I said. You've never seen the inside of a troop transport before?"

'Never. Can you orient me briefly?'

"Sure. Let's see. We're here on E-deck in section five actually." Sections four through twelve of E-Deck are dedicated to us, third cohort. This open quad here is our formation area. The same sections of D and C decks are allocated to second and first cohorts respectively. While embarked, E-deck is the bulk of our world." He scanned around slowly. "It's our enlisted billets, orderly room, mess hall, aid station, gymnasium, battle simulators, ratzkeller, supply and arms rooms, carrier pool and maintenance shed."

Crowder started aft towards the B-Sim. "Though manways access various ladder-wells, the lifts provide the primary access to the other decks. Most important to the troops, me too, the lift accesses the communal deck, that's between B and C decks. The lifts also serve as terminuses for the deck trolleys. That's a vital commodity for the crew, especially the Ready Cohort. Clear as mud?"

Bob chuckled, then sighed. 'I hate to ask, Bennie, but it's on the agenda. What do you think of the idea of putting the infantry and other non-flight essential personnel in stasis until they are needed?'

"Like the Alliance tried with those implanted slaves back in the second war?! Real dumb! Imagine the disorienting effects of being awakened from stasis after a month or a year, then being sent into combat with no idea where you are or how you got there. Then at the completion of an operation, being put back to sleep. How many campaigns would it take to develop a psychotic killer from a rational, thinking human being? Then what do you do with them? They won't all be dead you know.

"The Alliance automatons had a kill-switch in their implants. I read where, when they pulled back from Gigantus-Himalia, the Alliance controllers simply euthanized the survivors left behind on the surface, instead of trying to withdraw and re-embark them. They just flipped a switch and fried their brains. I couldn't do that. I don't know anybody who could."

'Like I said, I had to ask.'

"No worries, mate. Every now and then someone asks the same question. And besides, how would we pay the troopers? For their time asleep? Or just for their time in combat? Or not pay them at all, again, like the Alliance tried."

There were few people in the corridor and none outside the B-Sim. Crowder keyed in the access unlocking the manway and hesitated. "This will be a new experience for you, Bob. So don't be scared by what you see. I try not to be, but I have some pretty imaginative squad leaders. Second squad, under Staff Sergeant Mixon is running a battle drill. He's running it without battle suit refraction, so you'll be able to see everybody. Fair warning, Bob. Mix can get pretty realistic. I'll stay in the observer lane, don't worry. Ready?"

'Ready.'

Crowder opened the manway and stepped into a darkened antechamber. He walked a few steps and passed through a meshed screen, into another world.

*

The crrumpp of mortar rounds and ripping high velocity cannon shells enveloped a wood line to Crowder's front, merging into an evil maelstrom of noise, pressure and ripping frag. Dirt, rocks and tree limbs danced and twirled with iron and SK wobbles across the sloping ground in front and into the tree-line from the combined fires of other weapons streaking in from the road below. Breaking past Crowder's right shoulder, the rolling bush that was Chariot 3-2-2 lurched to a halt behind a slight rise in the ground, nearly disappearing in the dense surrounding vegetation. They were on the slope of a forested hill, with a highway well downslope to the vehicle's right. An open column of battle carriers, AFVs, and other vehicles stretched along the road below them and to the rear, fading in the distance.

'What's happening here?'

"Happy Valley. Actions on contact. He's working flank protection."

The Chariot launched a vapor grenade and released its rear doors. 3-2-2's auto-cannon barrel lowered to level with the slope and launched short bursts of 30mm cannon and 12mm coaxial machine gun projoes into the line of trees and bushes in front of it. They shimmered in wobbling detonations, as its rear doors swung open.

"Dismount Left! Follow Me!" A battle-suited marine dashed from the troop compartment and sprinted through trees and underbrush upslope, the name tag across the back of his shoulders read 'Anders'. His intranet voice came through loud and clear over the room speakers. The eight fusilier maneuver team poured out of 3-2-2's troop doors in the leader's wake. Anders threw himself to the ground behind a thick tree, upslope of the carrier. Shouldering his M9G battle rifle/grenade launcher he launched two quick bursts of 12mm exploding projoes through the trees in the enemy's direction.

"On line, on me," he yelled, thrusting out arm and hand signals while keeping close to the ground. Ander's team dashed to cover, spreading out on either side of him. They slammed their bodies to the ground and opened fire. Looking at his people, he projected clear commands, first to one flank, then the other.

"Guide on my illumines. Light 'em up! Distribute your fire across our front. Right limit! Godwin mark left!"

Anders loaded and launched a 40mm grenade into the tree line ahead, across the front of the Chariot. Its sparkling wobble blasted off tree limbs, sending them splintering in every direction. He put a burst of 12mm into the same point and shifted to the center of the target area. By the time Trooper Godwin's grenade marked the left limit, Anders had a second round loaded and launched towards the center.

Crawling forward to another firing position, he saw SSgt Mixon and his light machine gun team, exiting the chariot and coming up at a crouch between his number 7 and the carrier.

"Jones! Support the gun!" Seconds later, short streams of red lanced out from the LMG joining the maelstrom surging into the enemy held tree line.

2nd Squad's withering fire cut a murderous swath across their front. Their 12mm HSPF projectiles blasted into the bases of trees, ripped through rocks and tore logs apart.

"Mark your targets and squeeze the trigger bar. Maintain your spot weld and sight picture! Slow is smooth!"

'Smooth is Fast!' the team responded.

Anders and his team shot anywhere an enemy soldier would try to find protection from their exploding projectiles. Green-blue pulses of return fire streaked back at them cracking and popping overhead and all around.

"Shift your positions! Don't shoot from one spot for too long."

A projoe detonated off 3-2-2's sloping frontal armor, then another sparkling impact, and another. The driver, Kaleley, launched another vapor canister, Corporal Johan's cannon spat a stream of 30mm projoes back at their tormenter as 3-2-2 slid back to better cover. The move was not a second too soon as a Pygan's

Hammer swooshed across 3-2-2's bow and detonated in the open air just beyond, rocking the Chariot and peppering its starboard side with fragments.

Crowder saw the squad was in one of a series of erosion gullies cut by winter rains down the slope towards the highway. He could see three more between the squad and the contact. By the time Crowder looked left, upslope, Mixon had made his decision. His intranet voice overpowered the cacophony in 2nd Squad's headsets, as he moved left, upslope passing behind Anders.

"Peel left and follow me! Spot that damned launcher and kill it this time!"

"Peel left and move out, people!" Anders launched a 40mm grenade, he rolled left and sprang up. He and the maneuver team struggled following SSgt Mixon and the LMG diagonally up the slope.

"Damn, Mix. They're moving too slow," Crowder muttered. "What's wrong with them?"

'Is there a problem? I thought their battle suits were SME equipped.'

"They are." Crowder looked over at the simulation status and read down the margin.

"Oh. I see. No, there's no problem. My squad leader is running the scenario on a one point eight gravity surface. I'll bet he didn't tell them. Seen enough?"

'Can we stay a bit longer, this is exciting.'

"It is, actually," Crowder said smiling. He shifted positions, moving behind Anders.

The squad moved quickly, circling through the denser brush and thicker trees near the crest of the ridge to a point twenty meters above and seventy meters south of the enemy position.

Crowder saw battle-suited figures shooting in his direction, he jerked noticeably, but steadied himself and watched the show. The figures' heat signatures were distorted by live foliage as they darted between the trees. They shot downslope towards the road, upslope towards Mixon's maneuvering squad, and along the slope towards the Chariot, now just in front of Crowder, that was blasting away at the tree line and launching vapor grenades. Two of them were reloading an AVGM launcher and preparing to launch.

"Chariot's sitting in one spot too long, Mix. He can't maneuver well enough to support you without getting nailed."

'You say something, Benny?'

"Sorry."

SSgt Mixon dropped to one knee at the base of a tree and shot them down. His LMG team came up on his right, slammed their bodies to the prone and laid down bursts of covering fire. Three figures around the launcher shredded, the launcher collapsed, riddled by 12mm explosions.

"You won't flank 'em in time, Mix. Fuck it, go straight in!"

'You're enjoying yourself.'

"I love this shit, man."

Ander's people peeled off to Mixon's flanks, found cover and opened fire as more figures turned and shot uphill towards the squad. Illumines flashed by from seemingly every direction. Kinetic wobbles from projoes' banging detonations sent dirt, rocks and tree limbs showering and spinning savagely around them. 2nd Squad and the enemy exchanged fire for several seconds, but more and more Alliance shooters were being seen and shot down. The bushy figures popped vapor grenades and broke cover running to the north, more dropped.

"Gladius!"

Theo Mixon and his fusiliers drew and fixed their gladius to the g-stud on the right side of the launch rail cover forward of their M9's fore grip assembly.

"Grenades!"

Four 40mm and six hand grenades sailed downslope, releasing on impact or in the air around the remains of a wrecked utility vehicle and the AVGM launcher.

"Move out!"

2nd Squad assaulted the last seventy meters downhill centered on the Util. Battle buddies worked their way down the wooded slope alternating shooting and moving, covering each other, supported by the LMG.

Two legionnaires popped up to Anders left front, making a dash to escape towards the woods to the north, Anders swung his M9G left and cut them down with a long burst.

"Two six, Danger close; cease fire, cease fire!"

SSgt Mixon's puffing, disembodied voice came over the cohort net as he and his team closed on the enemy position. As the dust and vapor began to clear, the maneuver teams' visors detected only fading heat sources from the litter of broken bodies, blood and scrap metal. Another legionnaire, covered in mud and foliage rolled out from behind shattered logs, firing a burst skyward as he stumbled away towards the north. A cascade of 12mm explosions enveloped him, ripping the battle suited legionnaire to pieces.

"Consolidate!"

"Two-six, this is two-two, all clear, all clear. One Hammer AVGM launcher destroyed, I count about a score small arms, two light MGs looks like, over!"

"This is six, understood, search the immediate area, then charlie-mike, follow us, one-two is taking point, over.

"Endex, Endex, Endex. Lock and power down your weapons. Close over on me."

*

From his orderly room console, CoSM Greer displayed the regiment's organization chart to help his interviewer understand. "Our three maneuver battalions and the support battalion comprise the Task Force Marine Expeditionary Unit, or MEU. Technically, it's a regimental combat team that's capable of sustained surface combat operations in either a gravitated-atmospheric environment, or in low-gravity non-atmospheric environments.

"The weapons and equipment have improved over the years." Greer keyed up photos of his troopers, in various stages of battle dress, handling and maintaining weapons and equipment. "Mostly on the inside. Components are smaller, Mike, more durable, with greater operating speed and range. But, neither the regiments nor their missions have essentially changed since before the Praetor's time.

"What does combined arms mean, Sergeant Major?"

"There are surface bombardment, air-defense, signals, and medical troops assigned to the fusilier and dragoon battalions. Additionally, the *Acre* and *Yulan* each papooses a task force engineer cohort's vessels. The bombardment battery, the regimental headquarters and support battalion are aboard *Etar* and *Moncrief. Moncrief* also has the IEX-Cavalry recon troop."

"Where are the Recondos? I heard you have a unit attached to your force?"

"They're not my area of expertise, Mike. I prefer not to talk about them."

"Oh, I understand, Sergeant Major." The interviewer knew the Recondos were aboard Yulan, but he could tell CoSM Greer was old school, and old school marines didn't discuss Spetznax Recondos.

"So, where's your home, Sergeant Major?"

"Prosean-Kurel. At least that's where I put the family. I bought a ranch there before the war. I'm from Kulak originally. You?"

"Epirus-Serianis."

"Karen Stone's home. She was one of my heroes growing up."

"I've seen a cinema or two about her."

*

Seated at his desk in his platoon CP, Tony Brock displayed Weapons Platoon's training schedule form, CF form 1, on his panel.

"Just like the squad leaders in the fusilier platoons, my section leaders and I account for every minute of our troopers' time from embark to debark and back. Deployments are marked by one hundred seventy hour Duty Intervals, or DIs. You see, Leticia, over each interval, cohorts maintain thirty-six hour transport support rotations and seventy-four hours of training and administrative time allotted to them. The remaining sixty hours is commander's time; and is allotted to the troops for rest and personal time.

"I'm noting, Tony, that while embarked, it is the sergeant's job to see to it that their troopers are neither bored nor abused," the interviewer said. "As you said, most shipboard support details don't take very long. I'm certain your section leaders manage to wiggle an hour or so extra per day for some sort of reserve. I mean considering the number of vehicles in your platoon."

"That would be a fair assumption, Leticia," Brock chuckled. "Squad leaders' time for my crews is essentially maintenance, and crew drill. I like to follow that up with a liberal dose of more maintenance and crew drill with as much simulator and D-battery gun time as possible."

'D-battery?'

"Ship defense battery. They're essentially the same mag-rail launcher as on my tanks."

'Ahh, yes. Of course. They can shoot maneuvering drones.'

"Exactly. Not the same as another tank or a surface vehicle. But it's useful."

"How do you and the troopers spend your off-duty time, Sergeant?"

"Well, the mess hall is always open. After completion of training there's the gym and troops can relax in their billet compartments or the ratzkeller. Oh, and of course there's the communal deck. Remember that a troopers' free time can be restricted by training requirements or punishment. And cohort commanders maintain the option of issuing a call to billets and lights out."

"Ratzkeller?"

"The cohort ratzkeller is our dayroom, meeting room, and common media area. Troopers can relax there and have a cold brew after duty hours. It's a smoking area, too. Smoking areas include the ratzkeller, and the squad bays but not their inter-connecting corridors."

"Why'd you join the regulars, Tony?"

"Me?! Shoot, I'm from Kalfiairi, the metro district of North Kishner, on Palara. The Palaran army pays more. But it never leaves the state except in time of war. Metro Kishner is all steel and concrete. I had to get out and spread my horizons."

"You enlisted before the war?"

"Oh yea. I got twelve years next month."

*

PSgt Roxanne Pettis walked the cohort main corridor to the gymnasium, she opened the manway and stepped in. Troopers of two standby squads sweated and grunted on various strength circuit machines. Others worked through heavy punching bag drills; or paired off for mixed pugilism and grappling. Looking up and turning full circle, Pettis followed battle-suited troopers negotiating the encircling tread track above the gym floor.

"What the..." the troopers' short sprints and odd, jerky movements baffled the interviewer. "What are they doing, Sergeant?"

"Ha!" Pettis chortled. "That's a variable grav track. They're running an asteroidal HG in their visors. Probably about point seven surface gravity. You should try it sometime. Good cardio."

"I'll pass. I do like sports though. Do you organize games or sports for the troopers?"

"Certainly, chain dodge ball is a favorite platoon on squad sport, at least here aboard *Acre*, but there are hoops out in the quad and the Communal Deck can be converted into an arena for gridiron. Third Herd has the regimental grappling trophy and is in second place for gridiron."

"I hear you allow wagering on those games."

"Well, that's what you may hear back on the D-E. Out here, we don't worry too much about what a trooper does with their money."

*

The senior interviewer switched everyone to conference mode. "Sergeants, I've never been in the military, how do you track continual improvement? How does a trooper get promoted?"

Greer took the lead and spoke first. "It's the same Common concept of being creative in your own self-interest, Caspar. Only it's manifested in what we call Proficiency or Pro-Pay. Troopers, corporals, junior sergeants, ensigns, and junior lieutenants are authorized the individual monthly bonus of up to twenty-five percent of their base pay for achieving the proficiency requirements set by the regimental commander. That was amended when the war started to include participation in surface combat or boarding party against a hostile force within the previous ninety days.

"Squad leaders are responsible for maintaining each trooper's training records and ensuring the trooper is prepared for promotion and greater responsibility. The trooper's TR documents their latest performance to standard of the individual skills and battle tasks they must demonstrate mastery of before consideration for proficiency."

Roxanne continued. "We look for a trooper to demonstrate consistency before they're considered for promotion. A trail of PB's on a trooper's finance record is a good first indicator of leadership potential. Once a trooper makes lance corporal, we start prepping them for the NCO education system starting with the primary course back on Sestria. Ugh."

"You sound like you don't like Gabb'es-Sestria, Roxanne."

Several sergeants answered in unison. "Nobody likes Gabb'es-Sestria!"

"So who manages your training records and the senior officers of the cohort?"

"We manage our own. The Centurion can inspect them anytime," Tony added. "Understand, Caspar. Pro-pay is targeted

262

specifically for the lower ranks. Platoon sergeants and above, and officers above the rank of senior lieutenant, maintain their own records and are not authorized bonuses."

"Really?! I truly didn't know that, so what's your incentive, prize money?"

"Damn straight!" Roxanne couldn't help herself; everyone on the conference got a laugh out of that.

"I still don't understand how that works." Another interviewer lamented.

Greer explained. "Ever since the Praetor's time, a portion of the commercial value of captured ships and their cargoes is awarded to participating marines, pilots, and crewmembers, as prize disbursements. That's in addition to the old tradition of prize disbursements for the capture of surface installations.

"Basically, a lance corporal, skill level one-A, pay grade E-three, staying proficient as a machine gunner during the previous year, stands to earn as much as the base pay of a senior lieutenant at pay grade O-two, that's more than triple the lance corporal's base salary. Add to that, taking part in a boarding party action during that same year. Now what they earn from that, of course, depends on the estimated value of the prize ship at auction, or the annual output of the installation."

"Are any other specialties granted bonuses?"

"Certainly!" Gunnery Sergeant Jackson, the bombardment support team sergeant answered. "All crewmembers get it. Search and rescue folks get a great annual bonus for verified saves."

****

Flags.

Departure plus seven days. 0320hrs, 03-03 of 770CE. Vicinity of Nav-buoy NG-763A, within the Commonwealth Administrative Zone.

"Oh my good Creator!"

The signals chief petty officer on duty on the bridge aboard *CBC Draken* pulled the message from the printer at her station and circled the time of receipt. Querying the authentication of the sender into the line item identifier, she compared the displayed set of digits to the message authentication and verified the identifier code for Vice Admiral Vicente' Oshermeyer, deputy chief of staff for operations.

Lt. Commander Tieras, technicians and staff officers around the bridge turned to see CPO J.T. Bailey giddy with joy as she initialed the upper right hand corner of the printout. Typing in *CBC Draken's* authentication code, she acknowledged receipt of the message, and forwarded it to the staff journal log archive for the chief of the watch.

"Flash priority traffic for all commodores from DCSOPS, Commander."

"Must be good news the way you're dancin' there, Chief," Tieras chuckled.

"It's hard to beat, sir. You're gonna want to wake the Old Man for it," the NCO replied, handing the printout to her watch commander. Grinning, she followed his eyes as he scanned the text.

"Ho-oh-lee shit! You got that right!" Tieras spun on his heels and stabbed Commodore Morgan's stateroom intercom button on his command console. Morgan's disembodied voice responded immediately.

'What is it, Commander?'

"I beg pardon to wake you, sir."

'It's ok, I wasn't asleep.'

"Flash traffic from Admiral Oshermeyer, sir. The cease fire is in effect! It's just like you said, Commodore. Including the egress windows for the Alliance units in the Vighandis Pocket."

There was silence for a second or so. Tieras was about to read the text when the commodore spoke again.

'What front-line trace time is in effect?'

"Zero six hundred hours of zero nine zero one void equivalent time, sir."

'Hot damn! We did it, Tieras! We really got it done this time!'

"Yes, sir," Tieras replied with a broad grin. "Shall I alert the commanders, or would you prefer to advise them personally?"

'No, no. The last thing anybody wants now is a speech from me! The troopers deserve to know straight away. Use the boomer and let the whole damned task force know at once!'

Hearing that, Bailey swiveled back to her console and set to work.

"Will do, sir! Will there be any changes for the morning briefing?"

'No, no changes. Put the good word out, Commander. I'll see you at the brief.'

"Very good, sir!" Tieras turned off the intercom and waved a hand to quiet the growing chatter in the command center. The word had spread fast. Techies and staff officers stood, shaking hands, fist-bumping or hugging one another.

"Settle down, people! Nobody told you to stop working!" Tieras trusted his Master Chief to maintain discipline. "Keep your mind on your stations!" But not even she could stifle a small grin.

"The boomer is spooled up task force wide, sir." Chief Bailey handed Tieras the rarely used ship-to-ship intranet. "All vessels, all decks show green."

"Would you like to do the honors, Chief?"

"The troopers will appreciate it more coming from you, sir."

Tieras smiled, he took a deep breath and took the big microphone in hand. Even after fourteen years commissioned service he had never used the boomer before. He pressed the push to talk switch. The boomer resounded with three high-pitched chirps, and the mechanical,

'Now Hear This, Now Hear This. CBC Draken to all task force vessels. Standby for message.'

With a tear of joy streaming down his cheek, Tieras read the text of the message into the active microphone.

Priority: <u>Flash. 0315hrs 03 - 03 of 770CE VET.</u>
From: <u>CFJ-3.</u>
To: <u>All Task Force Commodores, Station and Separate Unit Commanders.</u>
Subject: <u>Cease Fire.</u>
Message:

1.   ROE Level 2 is in effect upon receipt of this message. Fleet elements are to cease offensive operations and assume defensive positions at the nearest defensible celestial grouping.

2.   Fleet unit commanders in contact with the enemy are AUTHORIZED TO WITHDRAW.

3.   Alliance of Stellar Republic combat and commercial vessels under escort of Valerian Armed Forces vessels and showing no hostile intent, will be granted safe passage while on trajectories to Alliance-controlled territory as depicted on the telemetric front line trace as of, 0600hrs 09-01 of 770CE.

4.   Alliance safe passage transit window is 0400hrs 03-03 of 770CE through 0359hrs 05-03 of 770CE. Alliance vessels detected within the Commonwealth Administrative Zone as of 0400hrs 05-03 of 770CE are to be intercepted, boarded, and diverted to the nearest Fleet Depot.

5.   Covenants of Safe Passage and Response to Distress for neutral shipping is in effect in <u>ALL</u> Commonwealth administered trans-stellar regions.

6.   Administrative and recreational use of active navigation beacons is authorized as of 0600hrs 03-03 of 770CE.

7.   Authenticated acknowledgement required.

Signed: VO, VADM, CCF, J-3.
Distribution: Alpha.
<u>Authentication Follows:</u> Zulu-Kilo-Alpha-393-Quito-19.
<u>End of Message.</u>

*

Cheering erupted in every section aboard every ship in the task force.

**

Off-duty marine fusiliers and crewbies started partying straight away. A crewbie combo's impromptu concert vibrated across the strobe-lit lounge areas and ballerum. Corporal Faisal spotted Anders in the middle of the dance floor, his lycos slung at his back, surrounded by women, as usual. Terri worked her way through the thickening crowd of celebrating crewbies and marines to get to him. Rick looked relieved to see Terri making her way through the crowd to rescue him. He had laid it on a little too thick on stage during their rehearsal hour. Too many girls got too clingy, too quickly.

"C'mon, Rick, we gotta go. We got time to shower and get breakfast before formation. C'mon!" Terri tugged him away from the two crewbie girls he was dancing with.

"Okay, okay, I'm coming. This is bummin', girl. Hey ladies, I'll be back in forty hours!"

Two more women, a marine from another cohort, and another crewbie dancing close by, awaited their turn at Faisal's popular friend. They threw their arms out towards Anders in disappointment.

"We love you, Ricki! We love you!!"

"Yeah, yeah. Let's go, Terri." Lance Corporal Anders let himself be led away to the lift.

"Damn, Terri. The deck is gonna be jumpin', and we're goin' on the guns, that's bummin, girl. Bummin'."

"I'm not worried, Rick. They're gonna party for a good while. It's been four and a half years since anybody's had any real fun."

"They were all on leave, twelve weeks. You know me, girl. I partied my ass off! I don't know what you sayin'."

With his lycos secure behind his back, Lil' Rick put on one more dance move for Terri and the twenty odd marines and crewbies in his lift audience.

"It wasn't the same, guy. Things were still tough at home when we got back from Maranon. Prices were still high. Everybody was called up, or working extra shifts damned near all the time. That was no fun."

The lift halted at D-Deck and a couple of marines got off. The 2nd Cohort quad was a mass of cheering, excited troopers spilled out from their billets and ratzkeller. A pair of grinning

267

crewbie ventilation techs boarded with their tool kits and filter cart. The lift gate raised, and the car slid smoothly downward.

"You should've gone with me on the Pegasus Star. Did I tell you 'bout the honey I met aboard her?"

"About a hundred times, sweetpea. The big golden chambermaid you paid to pretend to be Nasty Nicholla, so you could bang her in the ass. Yeah, you told me. Not me, baby. After any kind of time out here, on any kind of ship, I want terra-firma. The natural kind, with wide open spaces..."

"We get that on every surface, Terri." Rick snapped his fingers softly to a beat he kept in his head.

"...with nobody shooting at me, and every surface except home. I like home."

Having had the same conversation at one time or another, others in the lift, even the ventilation techies, grinned or nodded, agreeing with one or the other.

*

The lift stopped on E-Deck in Section 09. The quadrangle was filled with joyous Third Herders milling about, crossing between the ratzkeller and the billets. Most were in deck duty uniform, but a few newbies were actually in Battle Dress Ensemble. Terri, Rick, and other Third Herders stepped off the lift, turning towards their respective billets compartments. With no PT this duty interval, there was time to shower and change, then get a leisurely breakfast before formation and work call.

"Check out the cherries, Rick. BDE and everything. All they need is to power-up and disappear."

"They're expecting a battle drill. They wanna be first in muster. As if it makes 'em look good."

"A couple of those new girls need to stay in BDE. At least the helmet."

"You're cold, Corporal," Rick grinned.

"At least I'm not a horny goat, Lance Corporal." Terri instantly regretted saying that. But Rick didn't seem to mind. She knew he would never admit it, losing that chevron really hurt his pride. But he did it for her, and after what Sam had told her, she knew she loved him. Centurion let him keep his fire team leader position, during surface or boarding actions, that was a good sign. Though she didn't intervene when Lt. Cartier assigned his shipboard gun station to Corporal Johan.

"I'll get it back. Sam too, you watch, maybe before this cruise ends, you'll see." Rick was quick to snap out of the rut.

"You gonna rehearse with us again after duty, Terri?"

"We can access the CCC after duty hours. Maybe we can catch some shows with Peres and Sara in their billet. Let's make a date of it."

"Oh? Yeaah!"

"Down, boy."

"You think you need a chaperone with me, girlie?"

"More like a bodyguard! I wonder if Sara got her sonogram yet."

"Damn, girl! You roped Cooper and tied him to a wife. Give the man time to enjoy married life. They been hitched, for what? Six weeks? Now you wanna nail him down with a kid!"

"Cooper was easy," Terri laughed as they entered the 2nd platoon billets. "He's the type. You, my friend, you are a long term project. I'll find somebody special and lock you down too. Horny goat." Terri waved at her friend and turned away towards her 1st squad billet. "I'll meet you here in the Common in twenty, we can go get chow."

"Roger that, Corporal. I'm starvin', now that ya mention it."

"Keep up your strength, horny goat."

Rick stood in front of 2nd Squad's billet manway, enjoying his second favorite pastime. Watching Terri walk away. *You're the special one for me.*

*

Hearing the announcement aboard *LRT Etar*, SSgt Lang, Sgt. Mainworthy, a battalion rigger sergeant named Purvis, and their CS-119 tactical shuttle crew chief shook hands and congratulated one another on their good fortune. They then went back to work inspecting the shuttle's retro-pods. Sergeant Purvis' data pad contained the manufacturing history of each retro-pod installed in the shuttle drop tubes. His data included the manufacturers' verification of the chemical composition of the production alloy that made up the inner and outer protective layers, the material's production heat number, the in-process assembly inspection signed by the operators and their supervisors verifying their workmanship at each stage of manufacturing, and the signed final inspection and acceptance record.

Every dragoon was aware their chosen profession was inherently dangerous enough, being ejected from a shuttle at sub-orbital altitude to hurtle through the atmosphere like a meteorite, without the fear of a tube malfunction, or worse, a pod burn-through.

Every dragoon's training records and those of every production worker's in the retro-pod supplier chain, included the semi-annual viewing of the video of the test simulator's personal ammunition cooking off inside a substandard pod, before it burns through and the simulator, camera and everything else burns away. A post-pod ejection parachute malfunction is more gruesome, but at least there was a body to recover.

Together, the NCOs inspected the mounting points, safeties, clearances, and interactives and matched material heat numbers to pod serial numbers. Lang signed SSgt Purvis' pad verifying his rigger's installation of the retro-pods, M311A6, Sub-Orbital Delivered, Direct Atmospheric Entry Pod, Personnel and Light Equipment-80 each. Sergeants trust The Creator, everyone else must sign their name on the blame line.

***

Aglifhate Command Cruiser Sacremoran; at the Bavat-Fera anchorage in the Alliance of Stellar Republics. 6:00pm Janus 7ᵗʰ, 469PCE.

First Admiral of the Shield, Ngier Mathilda vin Flavius stood at the forward rail of the mezzanine. Seething, she stared in silence out at the pathetic scene, her arms folded at her breasts. Tow-ships sheparded battle cruisers and destroyers past her lamalars on their way to berthing bays that were already accommodating two or three previous arrivals. Shuttles transported crews to the support platforms and on to the surface of Fera.

Every vessel showed some level of battle damage. These were from the trailing phalanx, the one caught by surprise when the commies sprung their trap. From then on, they held the sector of the Vighandis pocket closest to Bavat. But it had made no real difference, all the units suffered heavily. *The commies were waiting for them,* she thought. *They never had a chance. Tribune vin Galeio's heroic sacrifice achieved nothing, neither did Tribune vin Waxnar's. Heroic sacrifice, my ass.*

Commander vin Karanus, on the plot deck three meters below her, pressed his earpiece as he turned and looked solemnly up towards her. "Admiral, the phalanx's damage and casualty reports are coming in."

"Tell me later. Where are the Valerians?"

"There are three squadrons standing off just beyond the asteroid barrier, Admiral. Two more are transiting Bavat, they appear to be vectoring towards Madera."

"Humph, they're putting a ring around us to watch all our movements. Maintain a running track on all their movements, Commander. I want to know where all their ships and sentinel drones are at all times!"

"Yes, Admiral. We are tracking every Valerian and Patruscan drive signature in range."

"And get some people working on monitoring their signals. I want to know what they're saying to each other. Signal New Laconia, I wish to speak to the Madonna. I'll be in my stateroom."

"Yes, Admiral!"

Mathilda dropped her arms. She clasped her hands behind her back as she turned to face her assembled commanders, the ones she had held back, the fortunate ones.

"The Madonna's orders are to give the monitoring forces all our cooperation. But I tell you, no foreigner is to set foot on any of your ships without my permission. This is Alliance territory! As far as I am concerned, their right to board ends once any of our Vighandis ships enter the trans-stellar void. Put all codes and ciphers in security lock-down. Communications will be handled only by category one security clearance personnel. I shall have marching orders for you on the morrow. In the meantime, ladies and gentlemen, you may see to your divisions."

"Yes, Admiral!" they all replied in unison and gladial saluted.

Mathilda stood to attention and returned their salute. Again, as a group, they faced about and marched away.

"Mendoza, send me Cyrus and a carafe of wine," Mathilda commanded as she strode off towards her stateroom.

"At once, Admiral!"

**

The sisters thought alike, both wanted nothing more than a hot bath, a goblet of wine, and a caresser for the night. Nicholla was in her bath, one of her attendants stood behind her, gently washing and massaging her back. Mathilda removed her tunic and sat on the edge of a chaise to allow her man-servant, Cyrus, to remove her boots.

"Are you well, sister?"

'Yes, Matti, I'll be alright. You look exhausted.'

"They are allowing only division size units and smaller to gather, sister. Still, all of Phalanx Bordeaux has arrived. The divisions of Waxnar and Galeio's Phalanxes should be out of Vighandis by twelve hundred hours local time here tomorrow. That's about eighteen hours from now. But Phalanx Galeio's losses are so severe, sister. They had to abandon six ships and transfer the crews."

Nicholla looked on in sympathy. She waited as her exhausted sister paused to sip from her goblet and clear her throat.

"Fortunately, the crews destroyed their signals equipment and purged their cipher databases. Valerian tugs are hauling ships too badly damaged to make the transit to assembly areas, but they will still be in commie territory when the safe passage window closes. The Valerian admiral will make no guarantees for their security. The bastard!"

'Fret not, sister, you will have your revenge, on both the Commies and the Valerians in due time. For now, Mother tells us to be patient and cooperative.'

"Yes, sister. I have not issued any orders to my commanders yet, the Valerians are suspicious of any moves I make from here. What should I tell them if they ask for any re-deployment information?"

'Give them the minimum, Matti. We have the right to defend our realm and our interests. You can use your reserve forces to spread out across the interior and establish a cordon along our borders.'

"I shall instruct the commanders to march at best speed to the frontiers, except Vighandis and Shafir. And I'm watching the Tantorans. As the balance of the fleet is refitted, I will spread them out from here. They should drive the renegades towards the frontier units."

Her boots removed, Mathilda stood before her sister, allowing Cyrus to undress her as she sipped from her goblet.

'That will please Mother, Matti. I will tell her when she next visits.'

"How are you resting, Nicky?"

'Last night I dreamt of Lokia. I saw it through Mother's eyes. It was so beautiful!'

Again?! "I shall rebuild Lokia for you, Nicky."

'Mother will be pleased.'

"Yes, Nicky. Finish your bath, sister. I will see you again on the morrow."

'Go with Mother's blessings, Matti.' The Madonna's image faded.

"And you, dear sister." *She's getting worse.*

Matilda unpinned and shook her luxurious black hair. It fell obediently to its full length in the middle of her back. With her goblet in hand, she walked naked over to her hot, swirling bath and stepped down into it. "Intercom, bridge."

'Commander Karanus here, Admiral.'

*

273

The beast's different disembodied voices, fascinated, and frightened the servant.

Cyrus no longer remembered the name his mother gave him. He only knew his mistress spoke directly to the beast that swallowed them all and held them safe in its belly as it travelled across heaven. The gods had come to his village from the sky and taken him and many others to serve them. First they were taken into the belly of a beast and into lower heaven where they stared down in awe on their mountains and seas. Then, they were scourged, and then cleaned, inspected, and selected by other gods to serve them.

Cyrus considered himself fortunate. His mistress was the goddess of war for all these gods. They all bowed to her. His mistress bowed only to the spirit goddess, her sister, who appeared to her out of the very air. They looked alike, they were both beautiful. But the spirit goddess looked older and her hair was brown. *What a strange and wonderful people they are,* he thought. The mistress was good to him. He had one purpose, to serve and satisfy his mistress.

The god-steward, Mendoza, told him he must never try to learn where the beast took them, nor must he ever try to leave the mistress' home in this beast's belly without wearing the tight grey undergarment made from the stones of his home. Mendoza said they were not in the beast's belly but in its head. Cyrus didn't understand that, but he didn't care. The beast had not eaten him. In fact, he had never eaten better. And the harder he pleasured the mistress, the more the mistress pleasured him.

*

"Commander, contact Baron vin Ma'lese's office. Send the message, 'Noviest nine'. Then contact Colonel Mitre, remind him of my standing order regarding my sister's guards."

'At once, Admiral!'

Mathilda turned and looked up at Cyrus. "Take your clothes off, boy, and come here."

"Yes, Mistress."

**

Commonwealth Leadership Academy, Degoa-Earth in the Commonwealth Capital District. 0930hrs 03-03 of 770CE.

Chiming temple carillons could be heard all over the capital province long before Hatu rose. They continued with Macillus' rising. *With the end of this war, they may chime all day,* thought Doctor Enoch Wixom Jr. The end of the war would only scarcely affect one of his three jobs. He was running out of time in his consultant position with the Fleet Strategic Studies Group. He had to make a decision about the new Recondo selectees.

"The data transfer to Fleet Intelligence is complete, Doctor."

"Archie. Very good. That should keep them busy for a while," Wixom quipped. "Set up the rehearsal, please. Place the selectees' in the classroom one setting."

"Confirmed, Doctor."

"Archie. Start rehearsal at section two, please."

"Confirmed, Doctor."

Classroom one, the amphitheater lecture hall overlooking the archives, emerged from the walls and filled Wixom's office. The 100 selectees would soon come to know those cavernous archives well. The selectees were actually resting at Camp Red Devil. Archie superimposed their multi-dimensional personnel file images over those of last year's selectees but retained the expressions and body movements of that last class.

Dr. Wixom only needed to make a simple gesture towards a selectee's image, to bring up their name, home world and former occupation. This was to be the only formal lecture they would receive. Colonel Sachs' Instructor/Observers were to have the selectees seated around him at 0830hrs, Tage Moon morning, 3 days hence, to begin their first phase of Strategic Observation, Analysis, and Reconnaissance training. Wixom was responsible for informing them that they had made it through the selection process, and they were under his care and subject to his evaluation until further notice.

Wixom knew well from his own 31 years as a dragoon, a Recondo operative, and the last 15 years as FSSG's senior consultant, the extensive training that lay in store for them. He would never tell them how long they would be there, or how many times they will come back. Old Wix, as past classes referred to him, held the selectees as interns for 120 days to evaluate, and train, on the similarities of structure and development of societies and tribes.

Dr. Wixom checked his notes out of habit before beginning. He didn't have to, he knew precisely where he was. The old Sacor stellar system graphic rose from the holograph pad in front of his desk. He took a deep breath and began, once again, to practice the lecture that he could deliver in his sleep.

"The Sacorsti trans-stellar exploration program was still in its infancy when their combined science collective determined Sacor was already in stage three of supernovae evolution. They accelerated their void exploration into a colonization program to evacuate their populations."

The Sacor system shrank away as the image expanded, replaced by a wider image of its surrounding trans-stellar region.

"It was also around this point in time," he said. "Their science collective determined Sacor's intense stellar radiation created the generally monotone golden skin hue of all the Sacorsti. As they reached out beyond Sacor, they immediately discovered and confronted tribes with diverse tonal features in neighboring systems. The Sacorsti Aglifhate found this situation politically useful. Government control of mass media information allowed the Aglifhate barons and their chamberlains to influence their gentry to instinctively view diverse tonal tribes as inferior, deserving only conquest and exploitation for the prosperity of Pygan's Chosen, the Golden Sacorsti tribes."

He stood and walked around his desk. He sat partially on its corner before folding his arms.

Why now, Retnec? Why now?

Since the *Retnec* situation developed into this long range guessing game, Doctor Wixom had spent more time in the stacks than he had at home. Urgent requests for deep background information streamed in from the Admiralty, the Senate, the Chief Executive's offices, and from DOP 297, beginning the day the vessel began its extraordinary maneuvers. At least his wife understood something unusual was happening that he couldn't talk about. Which, even before the war, was not unusual. Enoch just had one of those types of jobs.

"The Sacorsti refined their hierarchies," he continued. "They attached skin hue and tone to ethnic and cultural attributes, establishing their tonal-racial-ethnic concepts for the known tribes

276

of humans. They established relative levels of intelligence, physical strength and agility, capacity for self-government, and several other categories for each. They were crafted to scientifically justify golden racial superiority. Many global tribes fought to retain their freedom, but were easily subdued as most were unenlightened, non-void faring societies with considerably less developed technologies."

The selectees were all outstanding specimens, but as with every class, some still stood out. Wixom had to be thorough and stick to the fundamentals to keep the talent uniformly spread across the entire group. There was also new information gleaned from TF Draken's operations on Aletia-Maranon to be incorporated. The more he learned of the Alliance's tactics there, the less convinced he was of the wisdom of the strategy behind it.

Maranon may not be the standard Sacorsti practice, he thought. *They may not have a standard practice. Stick to the basics.* The old life-searcher knew from experience that the real truth lay in the fundamentals. Beyond that, there was only interpretation and speculation.

"Then they met the Tantorans, a six world, newly solidified stellar tribe to use the Sacorsti term." The HG stellar image shifted showing the outward Sacorsti expansion encompassing the Tantori stellar group. Several selectees, from stellar states near Tantori shifted uncomfortably in their seats.

"They're what we simply call a stellar state. Though not as sophisticated as the Sacorsti, they were, in their own right, as technically capable. After three relatively indecisive battles within their heliosphere, the Tantorans were coerced into working with, or more accurately, for, the Sacorsti. The so-called Alliance of Stellar Republics elevated the multi-toned Tantoran tribes to a status equal to Sacorsti Periolaikoi. They do that for all their allies."

He became aware of a growing commotion outside and went over to have a look. "Archie, go to stand-by."

"Complying, Doctor." The selectees' images and stellar graphics froze.

From his fifth floor Cloister office, he saw the main Forum filling with students pouring out of the Old Main and the Cloister, even officer cadets and no small number of faculty members. The biting late winter wind and snow did nothing to chill their ardor at the news of the ceasefire. Earth was coming out of Degoa's shadow, and the vernal equinox was just days away. The morning's bitter cold was winter's last gasp for seven months. Still, they danced and twirled, throwing snow clouds in celebration.

Wixom was as elated as everyone else with the end of the war. But a wave of concern came over the First Deputy Superintendent of the Commonwealth Leadership Academy.

He stepped to his desk and pressed his intercom. He had to buzz his office manager twice before he heard her response amid close laughter and banter.

'Good morning, Doctor Wixom. You're up from the stacks! Have you heard the news? The war's over! It's finally over!'

"Yes, it's a great day, Agathia. I know."

The shooting part is over. For now. The war never really ends with those people. "I heard on the radio downstairs. Can you reach Madam Sullivan and ask her to please ensure our little darlings aren't taking our scrolls outside with them. I don't want them to think they can start a bonfire with flexmet."

'I'll try to reach her, Doctor, but it's pretty crazy down there.'

The archives were the tribal property of their home world and national governments. Dr. Wixom, Chief Custodian of the Commonwealth Archive, was directly responsible for their safekeeping. At times, he considered them his own. He wasn't afraid of losing his manuscripts and data scrolls from 336 home worlds and colonies that make up the 161 Common Stellar States, as Enoch preferred the constitutional name of the league, and the 5,617 nations and city-states, from those worlds. They were all exact, but level three duplicates. The original documents, or as close to the originals as the tribes were willing to provide, were safely secured in the vast, controlled environment of the stack vaults in the salt mine extensions that began seventy meters beneath his feet.

The vaults would stretch for 50 kilometers, if laid end to end. Instead they lay in tiers of concentric circles, with connecting laterals extending in each of the eight cardinal directions. Antechambers extend from, and between the laterals holding the documented histories of all of the Commonwealth member worlds.

"Call Chief Dalveen. Tell him to get some constables in the area, just in case."

'Yes, sir. Right away, sir.'

Enoch smiled, shaking his head at the students' exuberance. *Good for them. The Commoners have earned this peace. The last three classes had nothing to look forward to but crises and war.*

Still, a ceasefire celebratory riot on the training ground for the Commonwealth's future leadership would not look good on the evening news. Such a thing would have represented a lack of discipline on the students' part, and a loss of control on his part, and the faculty. Some of whom were as exuberant in the celebrations as the students, like the hedonist Earther, Gina Mateoni, from the Cultural Relations department. Enoch saw her, down there dancing and twirling with the male students like a showgirl. She was just asking for another reprimand. The Superintendent had vowed to fire her if another incident like the one last year was reported to her. Wixom decided Chief Dalveen would handle things.

But the selectees at Red Devil. Damn. "Agathia!"

Archival Integrated Extension routed E-wixom9's voice through the intercom Enoch had forgotten to engage. The system updated as quickly as possible adjusting to E-wixom9's deteriorating physiologic processes and responses.

'Yes, Doctor.'

"Agathia, get Colonel Sachs on the line, please. Tell him to ensure the selectees are not informed of the cease fire. Is that clear?"

'Doctor?'

"That's right, Agathia. The selectees are NOT to be informed of the cease fire. I will tell them myself during the lecture Tage-Moon."

'Yes, Doctor. But the news is spreading like wildfire, even Camp Red Devil should know by now. I'll call Felix there straight away.'

"Thank you, Agathia. It's for the evaluation. Have Sachs call me right back."

'Yes, Doctor.'

Wixom watched the joyous, hopeful scene in the Forum for a few more moments. As usual though, the sight to the southeast of the long abandoned home world, Hatu-Degoa, brought him back to his harsh reality. The Persean academician from eastern Manera wouldn't have been here, nor would any of this magnificent academy campus and archive complex, were it not for another war long ago.

Among his many accolades, Dr. Enoch Wixom Jr., Professor Emeritus of Trans-stellar History, at Hamun State University on Perseaus-Manera, was recognized as the Commonwealth's leading expert on the history of the Saluri and the Degoan people, the events that led them to destroy each other, and the cobbled together, ultra-secret force sent to put a stop to the fighting. The utterly foolish, sixteen year long, Saluri-Degoan War, destroyed the habitats of both home worlds, yet gave birth to the seat of the Commonwealth's Senate, and governing apparatus, its leadership academies, advanced military training, and repository of its combined histories. Ending the war brought the Cooperative States out of obscurity, and into positions of prominence.

"Archie, resume rehearsal."

"Complying, Doctor." The images and graphics reanimated as Wixom turned away from the windows.

"The Alliance continued its march of conquest. More tribes acquiesced. To be honest, Recondos, we don't know how many they've conquered. Sacorsti Homostoioi clans were incentivized to move their families, businesses, and holdings, and the Periolaikoi families in their patronage to the newly acquired territories to establish what are called Economic Conformance and Co-Prosperity Spheres. They are required to set a proper example of service to Pygan for the indigenous populations. These colonies eventually control the entire world."

Wixom paused as the next graphic rose to give the selectees' time to read and absorb the three primaries of the 9 Sacorsti Canons of Conduct. The Canons, with their 27 verses and their volumes of Implications, proscribed every aspect of individual and community life in the Alliance.

1c 1v – 'All matter under heaven is the creation of Pygan. The Homostoioi Gentry are the administrators of Pygan's material worlds'.

1c 2v – 'Enlighten the heathen in your sight and in your hearing to the truth of Pygan by word, by deed and by the gladius'.

1c 3v – 'Lust not for the pleasures of the flesh or material reward. Rather, submit two thirds of thy wealth, thy concubines, and the fruits of thy levies' labors to succor the Gentry and the Aglifhate'.

Looking back out the windows, he saw the celebrations in the Forum were already starting to settle down, and participants were beginning to disperse. Most were probably driven back inside by the cold. Many on the outer edges of the crowd must have seen teams of security guards making their way towards the amphitheater, from several directions to establish a presence. Their instructions were to let the students blow off a little steam, but not to let them get out of hand.

Degoa rose, her swirling clouds covered a quarter of the horizon to the southeast. Enoch sighed at the sight. Even after nearly twelve hundred years, the Saluri-Degoan War's significance to the CMR/OMR in general, and the Commonwealth in particular, remain undiminished. Its story was unmatched by any war, anywhere in the combined histories beneath his feet. Wixom cared so deeply about the philosophical aspects of their war, he used the story as the first part of the Recondo lecture. After all, it was the selectees' earliest predecessors that had brought the madness to an end in the first wartime application of the Enlightenment Protocols.

He turned back to his animates.

"The Sacorsti designate conquered peoples as helots," Dr. Wixom continued. "They retain their own governments. But they are required to tithe up to two-thirds of their global gross domestic product to support the Sacorsti Periolaikoi colonists who control them. Their military and security apparatuses are assimilated and made responsible for managing the levy of their own people to be made available for export through Alliance commodities markets. Since the Sacorsti are exclusively of the golden hue, their Aglifhate abolished slavery of goldens, even goldens who are not Sacorsti. Slavery of all others is regulated through the annual levies. Never use the word slave on an operation."

A hand rose in the fifth row near the center aisle, the industrial engineer from Epirus. Enoch didn't expect this. "Yes, Miss Jonas?"

"Sir, if the war is over, why is Sacorsti history important to our life-search training?"

Enoch was stunned. *What is this damned machine doing? Think fast!*

"Our conflicts with the Sacorsti have been cyclical up to now; based on a centennial convergence between our administrative zone and Sacor. The Sacorsti migration has changed that for the most part. But Recondos, sometimes you think you know a story, you think you know how it ends. But it never ends, it just evolves. You must go back to the beginning to get to the true heart of a story."

'Very good, Doctor!'

"Archie. Thank you, I wasn't expecting that."

'This class is unique, Doctor."

It is that. Wixom mused. "Archie. Continue rehearsal. Recondos, with the exception of the Alliance of Stellar Republics, the leagues of stellar states, the Commonwealth, Asigi, the Patruscans, and the Valerians carefully scrutinize and assess the potential of unenlightened tribes as part of a codified process based on the established Enlightenment Protocols. The Sacorsti and their Alliance take what they want. They make helots of tribes that are useful to them and slaves of the rest."

Wixom couldn't help but compare how the Twin Tribes, were absorbed into what became the Commonwealth of Stellar States against the Alliance practice. The Saluri-Degoan people, share the binary star system, Macillus-Hatu. Where Saluri orbits Macillus, and Degoa orbits Hatu. A total of thirteen habitable moons orbit the two uninhabitable Home worlds. Before their war, the moons held national colonies, but since, they had grown into thirteen distinct provinces of the Saluri-Degoan stellar state.

The open, gregarious, Degoa-Earthers of Earth, the 1st moon of Degoa, host the CLA and Common Archive under the brooding eyes of the ghosts of Degoa. They are the complete opposite of their adopted cousins. The Saluri-Demeotian people of Demeos host the legations of the Common Stellar States in the House of the Thousand Flags, in perpetual sight of their dead mother Macillus-Saluri. Wixom was certain, they were among the most dour and melancholy of all the Commoners.

"Recondos, there are two types of human tribes, enlightened and unenlightened! The majority of the enlightened tribes speak with one global voice, even if they are divided on their surfaces by national or ethnic boundaries. Those that do not speak as one to other planetary tribes risk becoming the victims of exploitation by others through the establishment of foreign spheres of influence on their Home worlds. Some of which begin to act more like colonies than nation-states. These situations nearly always lead to conflict."

He looked across their faces and waved an arm across the group. Anticipating their reactions to what he was about to say.

"You need to know Recondos. You have a price on your heads," he said matter-of-factly. "There's a big reward in gold for your dead body and equipment, and an even bigger one in platinum if you're alive with your equipment."

At that, the images exchanged expressions of surprise and apprehension, just as they did last year, and every year before.

"They haven't got a Recondo yet, dead or alive! But we've grabbed a few of theirs, and they've talked. We now recognize that infiltration and manipulation of information is a standard tactic of your Sacorsti counterparts. Your opposite numbers don't operate like we do. Waffen-Strelski Infiltration Unit operatives establish cover identities on targeted worlds. The I U, as their teams are called, use different techniques depending on the planetary tribe. They often conduct a simple military recon, as a prelude to overt invasion of mostly pre and low industrial tribes. But, they also use a subtle, long term infiltration called a 'soft awakening' for near void-capable tribes."

He collapsed the stellar map holograph and took a seat again at the corner of his desk, watching his charges as he spoke.

"The 'soft awakening' is where the I U manipulates the tribes' social and technological development. They like to set themselves up as rich, reclusive industrialists or financiers, staying out of the public eye. The I U operatives select and train surrogates from the targeted tribes. They provide them with information and assistance that gives their surrogate influence within the tribe, or even political or military power. Or, some technical innovation that propels the surrogate to prominence and draws large numbers of followers. The surrogates eventually establish control over the tribe economically and culturally.

Selectees sat forward. Some leaned back folding their arms, others cocked an ear towards him. All were listening intently.

"Using their surrogates, they use an infiltration technique that involves establishing cultural concepts within the tribe, that their human race and their world are unique. They implant the notion that other worlds which may be capable of sustaining life, would not necessarily hold human tribes. They gradually allow the tribe to learn of other habitable worlds, and then, by some so-called innovation, to establish 'contact' with what are actually the team's support and communications elements. They are basically feeding the tribe carefully selected bits of information about the universe around them the I U wants them to know."

Enoch was himself intrigued by this tactic. The universe, at least as far as the CMR/OMR and the extended spirals of the galaxy, teemed with life, especially human. There were expressions of intrigue, understanding, and critical analysis across the majority of selectees. There were a few questioning looks as well. Another hand raised on the left side, fifth row, a marine dragoon from Unar.

"Mr. Rochemount, you have a question?"

'Doctor, wouldn't a technique like that take years?'

"Yes, Mister. Decades even, but remember an unenlightened tribe's average life-span, in most cases, may be less than half our own. When their occupation fleets arrive, bringing 'advanced' medicines and technologies, the tribe receives them as great benefactors. Of course, after this initial enlightenment, the Sacorsti racial codes and levies are imposed."

Rochemount's image nodded.

"Keep in mind, ladies and gentlemen, we have yet to find any of these worlds. But based on information we've gleaned from intelligence captured during an operation called Little River, you can expect to find yourselves in situations where a supposedly unenlightened tribes' popular culture paints a very limited picture of the galaxy, and is reinforced by scientific evidence filtered by the I U. During the soft awakening, the tribe is only allowed to learn of other inhabited worlds and tribes the I U, or rather the Alliance, wants them to learn of."

The geologist from Andolusia, in the top right row raised a hand. "Yes, Mr. Jackson."

'Sir, isn't it too late by then to do anything to break the Alliance's hold on the tribe?'

"It certainly makes it a challenge, mister. We have an additional challenge. Our own Commonwealth's fundamentalist party manifesto includes a plank calling for universal enlightenment and prosperity by any necessary means. Fundamentalist policymakers work continually to expand and promote an entrepreneurial life search policy. They have lobbied several times, without success, to legislate fleet protection for certain ventures. In fact, the Fundamentalist Party organization has actively encouraged independent expeditions in the past even without such protection, or with hired soldiers. Civilian groups have been known to acquire vessels and travel to unenlightened worlds in attempts to establish contacts."

The murmurs began.

"We now believe that at least some of these unsanctioned civilian life-searchers have observed tribes they only thought were unenlightened. They may have, in fact, stumbled upon some of these I U infiltrated worlds. Many civilian searchers have been killed, some captured. But there are survivor reports that speak of national governments maintaining secret labs, where so-called 'crashed alien ships' are stored, and crewmember's bodies are dissected."

Enoch shuddered at the thought. He bristled at the word 'alien'. Every Commoner does.

"We know now that foreigners who are not of the Alliance are easily identified on an infiltrated world. Because they don't know how to recognize the Sacorsti fingerprint, as it were, in the tribe's information media and culture. Such fingerprints include monetary rewards for information proving the existence of so-called 'extra-terrestrials', and government investigations of 'unidentified flying objects'."

He stood and walked around, crossing the room. The images' heads and eyes followed him attentively.

"Commonwealth law continues to ban all such ventures and requires member states to report the location of unknowns, or 'bricks' to the Admiralty. The law requires due diligence reconnaissance and surveillance before initial, and finally, formal contact is established and the tribe enlightened. Such is your mission as Recondo Planetary Surveillance Teams, and your league, and even your Sacorsti counterparts.

"The Asigi Collective has no stated policy towards unenlighteneds. For our part, no global tribe, without at least a functioning, viable global coordinating body, is eligible for consideration for enlightenment by our member tribes. Even then, Recondos, the potential material contribution of the tribe to the League is always the deciding factor. The Patruscans and the Valerian Monarchial League have similar policies. After all, money talks, and business is business."

The intercom interrupted him.

"Yes, Agathia."

'I'm sorry to disturb you, Doctor, but Admiral Pol is on the secure HG with Admiral Oshermeyer for you. They say it's Dragoon urgent.'

"It's always urgent. Put 'em through."

'Yes, Doctor, coming through now.'

'Shall I stand down, Doctor?'

"Archie. Uh, no I may need you, stand by.

'Enoch, oh, I didn't mean to interrupt training, I thought...,' Admiral Pol didn't like disturbing Old Wix. Undue stress aggravated his condition.

"No worries, Admiral, these are just images. I'm rehearsing, the kids are still at Red Devil, asleep by now."

'Oh, okay, well here's the thing. We were running an audit of last month's batches of DOP two nine seven's intercepts when our search algorithm picked up on a personal communique from a known officer aboard *Retnec,* to a relative on Shafir-Alboa. It was dated fifteen Deciem, by the Sacor calendar, with an indirect reference to an Acquiescence Era diplomatic defector named Denisha Tinoch. We want to send it along to *Draken,* but we'd like you to take a look at it first.'

"Sure, I'll take a look. Where'd this person defect to, Andora?"

'Yes, as a matter of fact, Andora-Miso. How'd you know?'

"Almost fifty thousand got out through Poia, to Andora in the last days before the Acquiescence vote. You think the officer is Egalitarian?"

'Unknown. It's certain the recipient on Alboa is though, the thread is the thing. It reads like siblings. CCID says it's been a routine contact since *Retnec*'s signature was identified," Admiral Pol said. "There are ongoing funds transfers, levies, package shipments and the like.'

Admiral Oshermeyer joined in. 'But, the last five sets of exchanges establishes a familial link between the officer, ah, Tinor, and this Denisha Tinoch, and a sense of urgency.'

"Are you thinking she's telling her family to defect? Or warning them that she intends to defect?"

'That's what we'd like you to look into, Doctor,' Pol answered.

"Yea, it shouldn't take too long. But you really should bring the Valerians in on this one. They were a lot better at handling escaping Shafirans in those days than we were."

'Morales won't go for it, yet,' Oshermeyer admitted. 'The Privy Council doesn't like the idea of relying so much on the Valerians. I have a feeling you may be right, Wix. But the council will take it better coming from you.'

"I'll look into it this afternoon, Admiral. Give my best to Morgan and Ottwell. Tell them not to strangle Hardesty. Tell them I know she's a pain in the ass, but she's good people deep down. It'll all be up to her when they get back."

Both admirals chuckled. 'Will do,' Oshermeyer said. 'How are you getting on, Wix? They're gonna want to know.'

"I'll still be here when they get back, Admiral." Enoch grinned.

'Okay Wix, Demeos clear.' The two Admirals faded.

"Archie. Sub search Andora-Miso, circa four fourteen to four fifteen CE. Subject Shafiran defectors. Sub paragraph Celia Morginari."

'Searching.'

"Archie. Continue rehearsal."

The graphic extended to the known Alliance of Stellar Republic borders. The intercom buzzed again.

'Excuse me, Doctor. I have Colonel Sachs on line two.'

"Oh yea, okay, Agathia. Archie. End rehearsal for now. Time for my meds anyway."

'An excellent session, Doctor. The search for Denisha Tinoch is complete.'

"Archie. Good, bring it up."

***

Chambers of the Chief Executive and the Privy Council, House of the Thousand Flags, Commonwealth Capital District, Saluri-Demeos. 1930hrs VET.

"It's a reconnaissance! That is the only possible explanation. Edgar, why else would a ship like that be heading for such a remote sector of the galaxy?" Senator Hanash always ended his more forceful arguments with rhetorical questions. The Senior Senator of Navarist leaned back in his swivel and folded his arms. The other eighteen members of the Privy Council turned to look at Chief Executive Morales.

"You're speculating just like everyone else, Menelaeus," the Chief Executive shook his head as he spoke. "None of us will know *Retnec*'s intentions until Morgan's people get there and intercept her. And none of your arguments explain the vessel's maneuvers thus far," Morales warned.

"Directly behind my State!" Senator Richmond of Chein spoke up with a worried look. "Menelaeus may be right. It's a direct threat!"

Senator Cummings of Borealis wondered aloud. "Is it possible they are aware they are under observation and are trying to evade detection?"

"I've considered that, Brutus." Morales' answer was quick this time. "But it seems if they were aware of our deep observation, they would have made some mention of it during the negotiations. They would have introduced some 'stop spying on us' provision or other, but there was nothing."

"Wixom's data makes sense." Security Advisor Boyars was convinced. "The woman could have led a mutiny. That would explain the evasive maneuvers. *Retnec* is running and hiding from the Alliance. But why such an odd route?"

"The whole notion is utter nonsense!" Hanash was as confident in his conclusions as he was disdainful of others. "The crew of a vessel like that would be hand-picked, high Periolaikoi. They'd have too much to lose! These last communiques are totally innocuous, they could mean anything! No, brothers and sisters. Can you imagine the Strelski security that vessel must have onboard? Mutiny? Preposterous," he huffed with a flippant wave.

Senator Carsalis of Andora stood and stretched her tall, very pregnant, frame. She paced the aisle, deep in thought, between the senators seated at her section of the table and their close aides. Morales turned to watch her, Hanash and the others continued to scroll through the intelligence packets on their data pads.

"We have three issues, brothers and sisters. One, why is *Retnec* active now? Two, where is she going, and three, what are her intentions when she gets there?"

"You can add a fourth, Berniece," Morales added from his desk at the head of the table. "What forces are the Madonna going to send to follow *Retnec*, and what are their intentions?"

288

Senator Ngama of Prosean leaned forward, turning to Morales. "We know there are human tribes in the region. Perhaps Menelaeus is right and the Sacorsti are expanding in a new direction, using *Retnec* as an advanced scout," he offered. Everyone in the room noticed Senator Jamison perking up at hearing this, they knew what to expect.

"My point is," Carsalis, the senior Pragmatist Party member continued. "Until the task force arrives in the sector and makes contact with *Retnec*, we know nothing. Our speculation does Morgan no good. Edgar, I say we have given him his orders. Let him carry them out. For our part, we just have to wait."

*

Minimizing, or at least managing, G.W. Morgan's political antics had become a stumbling block for the Combined Fleet Command, the Senate Committee for Military Affairs, and for Edgar Morales' Privy Council. Even before the cease fire, the strategic situation had vastly improved over the course of 769CE. The military emergency, similar to that which, in 416CE, gave rise to the first Praetor, had been relieved; admittedly by TF Draken's brilliantly executed Operation Jagged Canyon in the Trudan Corridor. That action eliminated the major strategic threat and restored the flow of uniformly refined T_2H HE_3 fuels to the bulk of the Commonwealth.

As Morgan predicted, the widespread benefits of that successful campaign were immediately appreciated by the commodities markets, transport firms, and the Commoners in general. The campaign drove away the specter of economic recession, and even fuel rationing, which would have been catastrophic, as it turned out to be in the Alliance. It brought about the Tantoran Solidarity's defection from the Alliance camp, which forced the Sacorsti Aglifhate to the negotiating table.

Further, the Maranon Campaign; Operation Little River, the Spetznax-Recondo direct action and military assistance to the Maranite Rangers, and Operation Mighty River, the invasion of Maranon and subsequent clearing operations by the 7th Marines, had served to break the back of the Aglifhate Information Ministry's all-important media disinformation campaign towards enlightened stellar states across the CMR/OMR.

With Senate pollings fast approaching, the question of the constitutional amendment making permanent the post of Praetor was drawing the oxygen from the conference rooms. The matter prevented serious discussions of appropriations to bring the Commonwealth Fleet up to a post-war strength of twenty regular, and fifteen reserve task forces. This vast increase was a complete about-face from the three previous wars. In the past, there had been a traditional ceiling of fifteen regular task forces augmented by the defense forces of the Stellar States.

Senator Jamison's proposal to expand to ten Commonwealth Fleets, plus a reinforced fleet sized training infrastructure sent shivers down the spines of Pacifists, Liberons and Communals. The notion made Statists and Fundamentalists ecstatic and stirred the patriotism of some Conservatives. Yet, it left the majority of Conservatives and the Pragmatists somewhat lukewarm. Morales and the Senate knew this would be a tectonic shift in Commonwealth policy. The very thought of building a first strike, or forced entry capability to the minds of many, demanded its use to crush the Sacorsti Alliance once and for all.

The problem was the Commonwealth had always fought defensive wars. For good or ill, hostilities had always been initiated by the Sacorsti or their proxies, which, despite initial losses and tactical setbacks, had played well in the end for the Commonwealth in the Leagues and non-Aligned capitals and public opinion.

Spokespersons for the information and entertainment guilds, including several well-known actors employed by one of Morgan's own studios had asked the most pertinent question of all. Once such a capability is developed, and the Alliance threat is eliminated, what guarantees were there of either a return to a more normal capability or to civilian leadership? And no one in the common stellar states, to include any senator, had an answer.

The thought of maintaining large standing armies in peace-time under a military dictator was more than a solid majority of Senators and Commoners were willing to accept. Consequently, the Combined Fleet Command and the Admiralty was convinced the most effective way to regain some measure of control over the appropriations talks and to dampen the increasingly vitriolic rhetoric reference Commodore G.W. Morgan, was to redeploy his task force.

Technically, the war was still going on, Vighandis was considered, but the Fleet Commander there did not want the 'Glory

Fellow'. The Commonwealth still had open flanks and far flung outposts that needed resupply. Such outposts were far removed from the battle area and the Commonwealth's political turmoil. The *Retnec*'s activation after more than 350 years, and its recent odd behavior, was the perfect scenario to take him out of the public eye for several months.

*

"Eight months, at least. Berniece that leaves us less than a month to act before the Senate session ends. We will all suffer a detrimental for incomplete legislative processes. We will all be ineligible for re-election."

"And we all have pension trials to think about. Yes, Menelaeus, I know. It's a risk we all share."

"Which is exactly why we need a flexible general strategy now, Edgar." Senator Jamison of Chapuri leaned forward. "Task Force Draken has a full Recondo cohort. That is more than enough to establish firm contacts among whatever tribes they find."

"Once again you go too far, Nathan!" The Chief Executive regretted giving the Fundamentalist another opening. "We will not enlighten the tribes there without a thorough assessment and a vote. Here!" Morales stabbed a finger at the desk. "No field commander has the authority to initiate diplomatic relations. Not even Morgan! You yourself wanted to court-martial him over Maranon."

Senator Carsalis stopped pacing and folded her arms. Every senator around the table, and all their close aides knew what was coming next.

"Maranon must be the new normal! We must face facts, brothers and sisters, we may have won the battles, but the Sacorsti have won the war!" Jamison rapped a knuckle on the table for emphasis. "We have failed to halt their migration, whoever is left on the original Sacorsti worlds can't be of much concern now to Nicholla and her Aglifhate. Since we refuse to expand our fleet and suppress them, now that we have a chance, we either have to out-colonize and surround them or accept the eventual fact they will continue to spread and surround us!"

Chief Executive Morales got up from his desk and stepped to the windows overlooking the south forum. As usual it was filled with clerks and other staffers moving to and fro in the warm spring weather. Overhead, Saluri's swirling, radioactive clouds continued to inspire frank, open and effective deliberation in the seat of Common trans-stellar government, though not totally free of political demagoguery. Every Privy Council member had a say, the leaders of the seven major trans-stellar political parties, even the Pacifists. He himself was required to sever all party ties for his time in office. Here, all the Commoners were represented, not just the interests of any temporary political majority.

The Kratari 'suggestion' to Vaughn Nadrew had been standard practice since just after the second war. Like Nadrew then and every Chief Executive since, Morales did not have a vote, but the decisions and the responsibility was his, and his alone.

"Poia, Mai, and Perseaus, your silence is the thunderous, brothers. What say you?" Carsalis asked for the pacifist Morales, her old friend.

The three primary senators of the traditional frontline states looked at one another across the table. Senator Nash of Poia spoke for them.

"We've held the line in the Nursery Crescent for three hundred years, while the Aglifhate has pecked at the peripheries. They've tried, and failed, now to the south in Vighandis. It makes sense they are preparing for the next attempt. Why not continue to probe for a strategic outpost in our rear? To counter that, I say give Morgan the flexibility in his orders to take appropriate action regarding any suitable tribes he may find. He already has sufficient force to deter, or at least delay, any force that follows *Retnec*.

"Remember, the bulk of the Shield is in Vighandis and Bavat, and under Valerian surveillance. At best, they may follow *Retnec* with an ad hoc force, but we haven't detected any such movement. No, brothers and sisters, Berniece is right. We can afford to wait and let Morgan do his job."

"Hear, hear!" Maxis of Perseaus rapped the table endorsing the Poian.

"Kalen is right, Edgar. We have domestic issues to deal with, in the meantime. In addition, we own all of Vighandis now. We are responsible for re-construction on Kepi' and development on Ku'ffar and Karelis, and the re-education of the populaces there. The Asigi are going to be watching us closely on this! We can significantly lower the prime rates, but we have to maintain the income tax structure they currently have in place on the majority of the worlds within the state, that is, Ku'ffar and Karelis; and we must centrally manage the Commoner investment on the three worlds. We can committee it, and have it done and in place in a month." The Maian, Senator Kostar, agreed with the Poian, but never failed to let all present know that Statist Mai is not Liberon Poia.

"There you go again with the income tax, Kostar." Kalen Nash chastised his friend. "Always the income tax!"

Morales appreciated the distraction of the ancient debate between the two old allies. Permanently capped at 15%, the value-added tax, collected at the municipal level and apportioned upwards across the levels of government with the majority retained by the municipality, is always under assault. Its perpetual defense remains in their vibrant economies. The Common governments, at all levels, have the funds they need to operate and a small reserve. Base line budgeting with their 'end of fiscal period mad dash' to exhaust their budgets and reserves to justify automatic increases were specifically banned in the Constitution. Their forced frugality made excellent credit risks of Commoner governments at every level.

No Commoner had ever questioned the fundamental role of government, only the extent of its power. That power was controlled by its authority to tax. Though there were Statists, Communals, and some Fundamentalists who worked at every turn to impose at least a base levy on income as a source of guaranteed revenue. The other parties, the Pragmatists, the Conservatives, the Pacifists, and the majority Liberons held as sacrosanct, the freedom to be creative in one's own self-interest was immediately stifled by a government tax on income. Such a levy restricts freedom of enterprise, the fifth and inevitable result of the preceding four; thought, speech, association, and assembly. To the liberon mind, of which all the representatives in front of Morales were, though to varying degree, it was the freedom from such taxation that ensured the individual remained sovereign over the state.

*

Sacor II-New Laconia, the Plantation vin Ma'lese, residence of the First Baron of the Aglifhate. 7:37pm Janus 7th, 469PCE.

The message was not what Siegfried vin Ma'lese wanted to hear, but it was not unexpected.

"Mathilda is doing what she must to protect the Madonna and the realm, as well as her Clan, Stanley," he mused to his secretary. "If the Borigai learn of the increasing frequency of Nicholla's so-called visitations, their cronies among the Chamberlains can bottle up administrative affairs with endless investigations. This is no time for such nonsense. No. Of course she is perfectly sane. Nicholla and Mathilda were never allowed to see their helot mother. Their father was Homostoioi and so, by law, is his issue."

"Yes, sir. Of course. Homostoioi are to be raised by Homostoioi. Nicholas vin Flavius did his duty to breed inferiors out of existence, sire. The fact Nicholla selected Indira vin as a role model is perfectly understandable."

"Indira vin's appeasements saved the realm, Stanley. The old regimes wasted the talents of half the Homostoioi population simply because they were women. The Lady Annabella Ruecheuski of old Mandan, and Mistress Borigai Indira vin Ngier of old Laconia changed all that and brought stability and progress."

The First Baron turned and pondered out the broad picture window of his study, gazing across the sprawling metropolis in the valley below.

How did you control those two, Tiberius? I wonder. Perhaps your legacies should have included some of Indira vin's herbal tea recipes. Then I, too, could pretend my thoughts come from you, eh, old boy?

The lights of New Lokia were just beginning to sparkle as Sacor II set. Barons and Chamberlains had proposed many times to eliminate the references between the old and new star, home worlds and cities. But he and every other First Baron, the majority of Barons of each of the three tiers of two score and five, as well as the vast majority of the Gentry, have always vigorously opposed such a thing.

"Old vin Hutiar didn't do so badly," he muttered. "Our heritage is of old Sacor. We are here only out of necessity. To propagate Pygan's universes with right thinking, pious, Homostoioi, we must survive. We must have living space. And we must have servants!"

"I beg your pardon, my lord?" the secretary inquired. The baron had been brooding out the window again, lost in thought.

"I was just quoting First Baron vin Hutiar when he claimed his plantation here. It's there on the north ridge across the valley. It's a museum now, Stanley. Did you know that?"

"Yes, sire. I have taken my children there many times. My parents took me as a child."

"Excellent, Stanley. Pygan chose Old Sacor to supernova to spread the building blocks of the next Eon of Life. So it is that we are Pygan's chosen to spread our rule over the material universes. We must preserve the Homostoioi heritage, in museums, in literature and cinema, from the conquest of Laconia on through to unifying the fourteen worlds, to the creation of this grand realm. Is this not so, Stanley?"

"Indeed, my lord. That is what I tell my brood as I tuck them in at night. Though, I am never so eloquent, sire."

The first baron took the flattery with a smile as he turned and walked towards his desk. "You're a good man, Stanley."

The secretary smiled and bowed, keeping his head and eyes on the First Baron.

"Thank you, my lord. I have my father's example, and yours, to follow."

"How is your father, by the way? The old snapper!" Baron vin Maltese gestured a fighting stance in honor of his secretary's father's celebrated victories in the fighting ring.

"He is well, sire. I spoke to him just this morning."

"Good, good, give him my best when next you speak." The old baron had thought about Mathilda's message long enough.

"Instruct Admiral vin Flavius. 'Return to your sister's side as soon as possible, she needs the comfort of family in this difficult time for her.' Send that immediately."

"At once. Should I order your supper, sire?"

"Oh, well? Yes! Why not? And ask my wife and brood to come down, I think we should all dine together."

"Sire." The secretary bowed and backed away three steps before turning towards the door.

****

Stout Ships, Hot Pilots, and a Few Good Marines.

Cohort Sergeant Major Greer saw his guidon bearer was pre-occupied. "How's your wife, Peres? Any news yet?

"They postponed her sonogram, Sergeant Major. But she's feeling real good. Thank you for asking."

"Good. My Gertie felt faint and had morning sickness straight away too, so don't fret, Corporal. It's only just beginning. Ready?"

"Yes, Sergeant Major." The corporal grinned at the thought.

"Fall In!" Greer's command voice boomed. With no shipboard details this Duty Interval, all 210 assigned officers and troopers thudded to attention in front of him and the Guidon.

"Receive the Report."

The platoon sergeants saluted, they faced about, performed their time-honored daily ritual and faced back to the front.

"Report."

"All Present." Each platoon sergeant reported in numerical sequence from headquarters section, first through third, and weapons platoons. No trooper was out of ranks to be accounted for. Greer faced about. Centurion Naravanutu marched forward to her position.

"Madam, the cohort is formed."

"Take your posts," she commanded.

Greer faced about and marched to his position as the platoon sergeants and platoon leaders exchanged control.

"How's your wife? Any news yet?" Naravanutu whispered.

"She's fine, ma'am. Thank you for asking. Her appointment got postponed," Peres said.

"Ah, that's a good sign." She cleared her throat and surveyed the line of platoons.

"Stand at…" the centurion barked.

The guidon elevated.

"Stand at…" the platoon leaders echoed her preparatory command over their right shoulders.

"Ease!"

The guidon returned smartly to the order, then thrust forward forty-five degrees.

"Rest! Morning, Thunderin' Third Herd!"

"Morning, Madam!"

"It's another fine day in the infantry. Is it not?!"

"Hooooah!"

"I've just got off the line with the battalion adjutant. Yes, troopers, a general cease fire went into effect between our Commonwealth and Nasty Nicholla's Alliance about fifteen VET hours ago in the Vighandis Pocket. Fifth Fleet was really puttin' a hurt on 'em. So now the Valerians are valeting the darlin's out of our territory. The official word came down...well, you all heard it.

"There's a commander's conference over on the flagship in about an hour, after that, there may be some additional info. But so far as anyone at battalion or regiment can tell me; the cease fire appears to be holding, and yes, this looks like the real deal."

She allowed the hooahs and the applause for a few seconds before waving her hand to quiet them down.

"At ease in the ranks, people," Sergeant Major Greer bellowed. Naravanutu continued.

"As of now, this task force is approaching the Andolusian stellar state, for our next opportunity to excel!"

Peres nodded, recognizing Centurion Naravanutu's sly grin when she used that old term. He heard her say once it reminded her of Kratari.

"Exercise Dragon Slayer begins once our lead elements reach a point one TSAU from the Andolusian heliopause. That's one hundred fifty billion kilometers. We should reach that point by this time tomorrow. Thunderin' Third, expect a stand-to alert around that time, and don't expect much sleep for the next several days either. We're going to a real school, ladies and gentlemen! I shit you not! The opposing force there are the best of the regular Andolusian Defense Force. Since Kratari's time, it's a singular honor in the ADF to be selected to take a place in the ranks of the First Lucainan Light Cavalry. They copied the practice the Valerians use to fill their Khan's Own Guard. And Phuong is their home base.

"I've had supply generate some posters of Field Marshal Cantu's dedication of the Phuong Battle School. You'll see them around the cohort area, but here's what they look like."

She gestured to the supply sergeant in headquarters section. "Bring that poster up here please, Sergeant Barnette."

"On the way, ma'am."

Sergeant Barnette hoisted the poster board and trotted up next to Peres. Naravanutu stepped forward thrusting a knife-edge right hand at the poster.

"Burn this into your mind, troopers!" she said. "For over four hundred years, people, every Andolusian soldier entering the Phuong Training Area has had to pass this dedication. Our purpose there is to hone our skills against the very best. We don't use the word 'kill' at Phuong Battle School. It's a competition. We count coup against fellow warriors who, in recognition of their skills, are there to test ours." She read the text aloud to her cohort.

'The oath to protect your people did not include a contract for normal luxury and comforts enjoyed within our societies. On the contrary, it implied hardship, loyalty and devotion to duty, regardless of your rank. This Battle School is here to remind you of that oath!'"

A palpable hush fell over the formation.

"Okay, Sergeant Barnette, thanks."

Barnette hustled back into the ranks with the poster.

Naravanutu stepped back to her position and nodded at Peres, they snapped to attention.

"Cohort!"

The guidon elevated, 3rd Cohort went to parade rest, head and eyes to the front. The platoon leaders stood to attention, then barked over their right shoulder.

"Platoon!"

"Ahttennnshun!" The guidon returned to the order.

"Thunderin', Third Herd, Rock Steady!" All 210 pair of boot heels thudded together as one.

"Sergeant Major."

Greer marched forward, halting three paces in front of his commander and gladial saluted.

"Take charge, Sergeant Major." She returned his salute, turning the cohort over to her NCOs, then turned to starboard and marched away, followed by her officers. Peres and the cohort stood in place, Sergeant Major Greer and the platoon sergeants took their positions. Greer directed the cohort to stand easy and began Thunderin' Third Herd's duty interval.

298

*

The centurion and her officers walked to the command lifts and headed up to the observation and conference room on B Deck for Officer's Call.

*

Officer Candidate Ymarh's eager question rose from the rear of the lift as it started upward. "Has there been any further word, ma'am, about our mission now that the war's over?"

Naravanutu smiled. "Are you expecting an 'over the hill and far away' order, Mr. Ymarh?"

"Actually, ma'am, yes!" the young man responded eagerly, evoking the officers' chuckles.

"Don't you worry, mister, the Sacorsti are like bad cooking." Lieutenant De'Avest schooled his young shadow and Cartier. "They always come back with a bad taste. Their colonies are closer now. They'll regroup, have another coup, and come back at us again. The good thing is the Tantorans are out of the Alliance now. They were the real talent."

Centurion Naravanutu nodded in agreement.

"In the meantime, we drill, we watch, and we stay ready," She said. "You're going to get a real education shadowing the XO for an assault landing load out, Leon. Pay attention to battle loading. What we need on the ground first, gets loaded last. Got it?"

"Got it, ma'am."

"Mr. Fatovo, you stick with me."

"Yes, ma'am."

Lieutenant Cartier cleared her throat.

"Something on your mind, Lieutenant?" Naravanutu turned towards her.

"Ma'am, the training schedule has Mr. Fatova shadowing me this duty interval."

"I'm changing it, Lieutenant. Mr. FATOVO will accompany me as my primary signaler from now until the exercise is endexed."

"Madame, I must protest! I wish to speak to the battalion commander."

"As you wish, Lieutenant. We ARE heading to his officer's call." She struggled, and failed, to not sound sarcastic.

"It was Colonel Nix's order, all candidates will shadow their commanders and XOs. Colonel Allenby put the word out to the Cohort Commanders, but you can take it up with him if you like."

"No, ma'am. I understand. I," she sighed. "I, withdraw my protest, ma'am."

"Noted, Lieutenant."

On arriving at the observation deck, 3rd Cohort's officers and their fellows found the MV players already accessing regional news. The networks had announced the cease fire, and were already displaying the Sacorsti Aglifhate, or rather the AIM's simple cease fire announcement, which was carefully worded, as usual, to say nothing.

"The Shield of the Alliance Republics will always defend the Aglifhate and its sacred tribal states in Pygan's name against aggressors, usurpers, and non-conformists! The Mistress, and First Admiral of the Shield, will sheath her Golden gladius, for now; and take her place on the right of the Madonna of the Aglifhate."

**

Maria Hardesty's billet on CBC Draken. 0715hrs 03-03 VET.

"Mother, I had to take a quick moment to call you with the wonderful news!"

'You're getting married?!' Zara's excited image clasped her hands together in joyous expectation.

Maria was taken aback. "Mother, no. The war. The war is over!"

"Oh, that! Yes dear, that's very nice. It's almost bedtime. We heard the announcement yesterday. I thought you knew that."

"Uh, well, yes. But, well. Good then. It's a great day, mother."

'Of course it is, dear. My dear son Mitchell is out of the way of hurt, harm and danger. Now you two can marry,' she said. 'Wasn't that what he was hesitant about?'

"Mother, we had a terrible fight when I said I wanted to marry him. He said we haven't known each other that long. And now, I haven't even seen him since we came aboard, seven days ago. He's a busy man, and I've got a job too!"

'Child, I'm not getting any younger.'

300

"Mother?!" Exasperated, Maria buried her face in her hands and shook her head before looking up again.

'Leave that child alone.' Maria heard Aunt Zinnia's voice come to her rescue. 'Let her and that boy have fun bouncing each other. They got plenty of time. She betta not rush that boy. He'll come to her, he busy. Her job will bring them together.'

Maria blushed. "Oooh, you people. Listen, I gotta go, I just wanted to let you know, I'm safe. I love you all. Bye."

'Kiss my son-in-law for me, dear. Bye.' Zara's image faded. Maria leaned back in her swivel. She sighed in exasperation, then smiled at the thought of marrying Mitchell.

At least we're keeping in touch. Thank the Creator's Omens for Jeff. Maria scrolled through the apologetic text messages they had exchanged over the last few days. Including the one he sent to her from his fighter while on CAP rotation. She sniffled and wiped a tear, then got up and checked that her recorder and data pad were on standby in her sidebag before heading out. The visitor buzzer sounded as she was about to turn to leave.

"Enter."

The manway slid open, revealing Nick, A. J. Mortimer and her entire embed team standing in the corridor.

Maria scowled at them, thrusting her fists to her hips as A. J. led the other two journalists and four videographers in.

"What the hell are you people doing here?"

"Where else are we going to be, Maria? Every commander and operations officer in the task force converged here to hear the word personally from G.W., we followed our instincts and well, we bumped into each other."

"I figured you'd already be up on the command deck for the briefing, Hardesty," Yasmeena Odinot said. "I didn't see you there. I saw everybody except you and Nick, so I asked some marine where your billet was." The tall red-haired woman from the Osiri Stellar Post folded her arms, leaning against the bulkhead next to the manway.

"You're not holding up my wall, I mean, bulkhead, Odinot. Stand up straight. And its Miss Hardesty to you."

"What's gotten into you? We're not marines," the woman asked standing erect. "Oh, I'm sorry. Why would I ask that? Just a certain pilot I hear. Damn, woman. You work fast."

"That's enough, Yasmeena."

301

"You're defending her, A. J.? She stole your job!

"Nobody stole nothing, bitch. Show some professionalism and shut the hell up." The grey bearded videographer, Joe Malloy, from the same outlet, scolded Odinot to everyone's surprise, except Nick. "Don't y'all worry none about Miss Big Mouth here, the company sent me along to keep her in check."

Odinot folded her arms again and huffed but stayed quiet and stood up straight.

Maria stared at Odinot, still with her fists at her hips. She looked towards A. J., he knew what she was thinking and what was about to happen. Young Demetrius Lamphere of the Nevar Central States Herald-Tribune, from right here in Andolusia, stood with Julia Mack, his videographer and Michael Jones, all of whom were about the same age. Maria watched him, he was wisely staying out of the power struggle developing between herself and Odinot.

"You just keep on checking her, Joe. And we'll get along just fine. As it happens, I was just heading Topside. FYI, people. Journalists are not allowed in the commander's briefings unless invited," she said with authority, mimicking Drill Sergeant Bodette. *It works*, she thought. *It gets their attention and holds it.* "We're going to have to content ourselves with waiting in the wardroom lounge and comparing notes. C'mon, follow me."

She stepped towards the manway just as the visitor buzzer rang again.

"Omens, who is it now? Enter."

The manway slid open and Colonel Rivas stood there, smiling, seeing the entire team together.

"Am I interrupting?"

"No, Colonel," Maria said. "We were just coming out. What can I do for you, ma'am?"

"The Commodore has invited you all to the command brief. I was told you had all gathered here. I came down to escort you to the Topside conference room."

"Why, thank you, Colonel. It's a great day and a fine gesture by the Commodore." Maria smiled. "Let's go, people." She waved them out of her billet.

"Ah, may you and I have a quick word alone, Miss Hardesty?" Rivas asked as A. J. and the others filed past.

"Certainly, Colonel," Maria said.

As she stepped in, a different look came over Rivas' face. It wasn't the matronly, understanding one she had explaining the difference between the crew's personal communications protocols and those of the Embeds. Her expression turned stark, threatening.

Rivas waited, watching as the last of them left and the manway slid closed again. She turned to Maria with an icy stare.

"Look, Miss Hardesty. Maria. I'll make this fast. I'm only going to say this once."

Maria felt an icy grip in the pit of her stomach looking into the woman's cold, dark eyes.

"I heard you were sparking Mitch Pulke, back at Tresium. Before you say it's not my business, let me tell you, I make everything that happens in this task force my business. Especially when it concerns an officer of Mitch Pulke's caliber."

Maria eyes went wide. Her mouth dropped open to speak.

"I, I, yes. It's true."

"And you were cozy with Bob Edris in his bomber, the day you came aboard? And trolling the wing ratzkeller with Jeff Tieras the day after that?"

Maria gasped.

Rivas leaned in close. "I've got eyes and ears everywhere. I've heard about you. How you pump men for information and call them your 'sources'," she sneered.

"Don't deny it. I know everything. You and Edris are a lot alike, he's a dick-slinger. He likes to fuck n' dump as much as I heard you do."

Rivas kept up a relentless attack, her knife-edged hand gestures forced Maria back a step each time she thrust it towards her. Rivas saw the fear and confusion in Maria's face and pressed her attack home.

"Let me tell you something, sister. I don't care if you want to fuck Edris. Reputation wise you two are a match. But Jeff Tieras and Mitch Pulke are not your playthings! Especially Mitch Pulke. He's a big boy. He's free to bang who he wants. But we love him. Woman to woman, Maria Joana Hardesty, you hurt Mitch Pulke and every man-loving officer in this task force will be standing in line to scratch your eyes out. Standing in line behind me."

Maria was aghast. She didn't know what to say with Rivas' fierce brown eyes boring into hers. She pulled herself together and stood her ground.

"Colonel. Debra. I knew Bob Edris was not a good man as soon as I met him. I was trying to learn and do my job," Maria said, struggling to recover her senses. This was no time to be cordial and polite, all she had to respond with was the truth.

"Jeff is Mitchell's friend, which makes him my friend, because I love Mitchell. He's the man I'm going to marry. He just doesn't know it yet."

It was Debra Rivas' turn to be speechless.

***

Topside Conference Room, Deck 6, CBC Draken.

Rivas' whispered heads up to Morgan about Hardesty and Pulke made him smile, it didn't seem to bother him. The morning briefing began right on schedule. The assistant operations sergeant had to add chairs and open the extensions to accommodate the other task force vessel and unit commanders with their operations officers and the Embeds. There was no one on HG conference this morning, Morgan's commanders all wanted to hear in person his official word of the cease fire and its effect on their mission. The essential answer was none.

"The task force mission remains sealed, ladies and gentlemen," Morgan announced. "Until I say otherwise, all of our attention must focus on our PDRE, codenamed Operation Dragon Slayer."

Seated on Morgan's right, Rivas saw an annoyed look come over Hardesty's face across the conference room when Morgan said 'Dragon Slayer.' The journalist shot an accusatory stare towards Mitch Pulke, seated at the rear of the room at the aisle. Rivas watched him catch Hardesty's look and cringe. She watched Hardesty fidget with her recorder as Morgan continued.

"I assume our young replacement marines and cavalry troopers have mixed emotions at the cease fire news." Morgan's quip brought more than a few nods and quiet, pressure relieving laughter. G.W. leaned back in his swivel, tilting his head towards CSM Morris seated near the manway.

"How do you think it'll affect their morale, Sergeant Major?"

Everyone in the conference room turned towards Command Sergeant Major Morris. His voice barked even when he spoke in a moderate tone.

"They were real eager when we embarked, Commodore. They know they can do a lot with the equivalent of up to a year's salary and annuity for a few hours rifle and gladius work in an IHEA suit. They're probably a little let down. Their NCOs are going to have to make sure they don't get careless. But by the end of day one in Andolusia, they'll have snapped to."

The officers and senior NCOs in the conference room nodded in affirmation.

"Absolutely," Morgan said, endorsing his sergeant major. He stood and stepped away from his swivel towards the inactive HG floor pad. "Light a fire under your leaders down to the fire team leader level, and every symbiot team, commanders. Verify all weapons exercise chips' status are maintained blue at all times. That goes for everybody! Shipboard, aviation and surface. The last thing I want is a training fatality in Andolusia before we set off on our mission."

*

Is that what this is all about? Maria thought. *Seizing ships for the States to auction off and pay the fleet prize money? Maybe they are pirates like Senator Hanash said in the hearings? Just as the Board says. Bastards!*

*

Morgan stopped himself from revealing any information on their mission before rendezvousing with *CD Stone*. He hated having to withhold information from his commanders. *These are good people,* he thought. *They deserve to know.* The assembled group kept their attention focused on Morgan, waiting for him to finish his comments.

"There will be more information following, ladies and gents, but you can assure your people, this cruise will at least give them something to write home about." He felt a little better as another tension releasing round of laughter filled the conference room.

There was no use arguing. Colonel Rivas thought, looking around the assemblage of officers she knew so well. Morgan's battle group and support unit commanders knew he had his orders from the CE himself, and they were all just beginning one hell of a long deployment, one way or the other.

"I can tell you all this." Morgan looked around the room. "I see our place in the universe simply. You and I, and the troopers of

305

Task Force Draken are, with our brothers and sisters of the regular task forces, setting off to patrol the Commonwealth's far frontiers. Our job now is to face out and keep watch, while our State Guard and militia brothers and sisters go home to rebuild their lives in Common society."

*

Yeah, right, Maria thought.

*

"Bravo!" A. J. shouted and applauded. He stopped though, when the assemblage all turned and looked his way. *CD Perseaus'* commander next to him tapped his leg and shook his head slightly, mouthing the words, 'We don't do that here.'

"Oh, sorry."

"That's okay, Mr. Mortimer," Morgan said smiling.

I've got the resources to find Retnec and to haul it back. But the tribes in the region. Damn. Jamison may be right, for once. Lovely. And what if Mathilda follows Retnec with any kind of strength? I know I would. And what if they're already there? Behind us. Assume the worst and you'll never be disappointed. Assume Retnec is carrying technological reinforcement for another research planet, like Kafar-Ratab was in the second war. Stop it! Obey your own order.

"As you all know, I seconded *Draken* wing's Mitch Pulke to my ops staff for planning of Operation Dragon Slayer a couple of weeks ago and he's done a super job on it." Morgan looked around the conference room and found him. "Come on up, Commander."

"Yes, sir." Mitch's voice rose from the back of the conference room.

Rivas spoke up as Pulke stood and crossed the room under Maria's glare.

"Commodore, may I interject a quick word for the Embeds, before Commander Pulke begins?"

"Ah, certainly, Colonel. Uh, ladies and gentlemen of the press, anytime you have a question, Colonel Rivas is always happy to help you. Colonel."

"Just a quick lesson about code words, ladies and gentlemen. They are generated at random by an operational security algorithm. No one has any control over what codename is generated for an operation."

She gestured back to Morgan. "Thank you, sir."

"Ahh, yes. Quite."

Maria snorted, she smiled and nodded towards Rivas. Rivas winked and nodded back. Grateful for Rivas' covering for him, Mitch stepped up and stood to attention next to the HG projector control. Morgan stepped to the other side of the platform, close to his swivel.

"I want you all to know, when Commander Pulke briefed me on his concept I was as stunned as I was when I tapped him for Trudan. I fully endorse this plan, although I expect we will all have challenges to overcome. Normally, I'd keep my planners here in the CIC until the operation is complete, but once again, Mitch here has made me promise to let him get out there."

He turned to Mitch.

"We almost lost you in Trudan, Commander. But against my better judgement I'm going to allow you to go out one last time. You can come up to my command staff after you count coup against the Opfor with your squadron. Deal?"

"I'm at your service, of course, Commodore."

A burst of laughter and applause rose in the room.

Maria was proud of him. *My man is Morgan's master strategist.* Yet, she was concerned and confused about Morris' prize money comments. She looked around with anticipation.

"Go ahead, lay the fundamentals for us, Commander, and we'll take over," Morgan said, taking his seat.

"Yes, sir." Mitch activated the HG and raised the celestial plot of the Lucainus planetary group in the Andolusian Stellar State.

"Exercise, Exercise, Exercise. Hold your questions till the end of the brief. Ladies and gentlemen, a Totalitarian force known as Opfor seized control of the Andolusian-Lucainan colony on the moon, Phuong, approximately ten days ago. Phuong is the third and largest moon in the Lucainus planetary group, presently here, in the northeast octodrant of the Andolusian heliosphere. The colony has a population of approximately fifteen hundred Commoners including several families. The municipal infrastructure includes the primary exo-drome, industrial facilities and the town of Phuong–Yeuin.

"In addition, Opfor has seized the manufacturing and communications station on Phuong's Close Orbiting Asteroid, Phuong-Alpha. Lucainan ground monitoring, ADF reconnaissance and CCID long range telemetry have confirmed the Phuong-Alpha station is still operational. Communications intercepts suggest the Opfor intends to establish a base from which to conduct slave raids within Andolusia and in surrounding states.

"The Andolusian Stellar State emergency operations center reports local defense forces have been defeated attempting to suppress the Opfor. These actions constitute mayhem, slavery, and sedition under Lucainan, Andolusian and Commonwealth law, and pose a clear and present threat to the Peace and Sovereignty of Lucainan Citizens and to commerce in the Andolusian Stellar State. The Governor-Superior has therefore declared a state of emergency and has requested League level military assistance. As of zero five forty-five hours, day three of month three, the use of Common military force to neutralize the threat has been authorized by the Chief Executive, Common Stellar States, under the War Powers Act of One Hundred Four CE."

He picked up a photon rod and highlighted the celestial features in the region.

"At this point in its orbit, the moon Phuong is eight hundred thousand kilometers from Lucainus towards Andolusia, this makes it high summer on the surface. Phuong's orbital duration of Lucainus is fifty-four days fifteen hours, void equivalent time. The COA, Phuong-Alpha, has an elliptical orbit of the moon with a perihelion of nine hundred kilometers over its southern pole. As of now the COA is approaching its aphelion, northeast of the moon's equator at one thousand, six hundred kilometers.

"Currently, ADF intelligence reports the Opfor possesses void, aviation and ground combat capabilities, including one trans-stellar capable transport, the *Peltier Maru*, she is known to be in a low orbit of Phuong at this time. Intelligence has confirmed the citizens of Yeuin and ADF prisoners have been transferred to the transport. The Opfor's offensive void strength is confirmed to consist of one Jafir class, binary gas propellant rifle-armed destroyer, and three Predator class frigates. Opfor aviation includes one squadron of twelve to twenty tiger-five, indo-exo atmospheric fighters. The Opfor's surface force is confirmed to be one armored cavalry squadron combat team, consisting of three Troops of light armored cavalry including Puma Recce cars and Panther armored fighting vehicles, and one reinforced mechanized infantry company."

He saw the hand of one of Maria's journalists rise to ask a question.

"Hold your questions till the end of the brief, please."

The man quickly dropped his hand.

"In addition there are undetermined numbers of self-propelled mortar and artillery platforms and air defense units. CCID signals intercepts support the ADF Intelligence reports estimating the Opfor surface forces appear concentrated at and near the exo-drome. Here. And is ready to move, on order, to prepared positions in the high ground north and northwest of the exo-drome, particularly in this region running north along Highway one eight three, known locally as Joy Road and the Valley of Happiness, south of Hill three oh nine, here."

The plot shifted, centering on Lucainus-Phuong and Phuong-Alpha.

"Task Force Draken will conduct a heliospheric penetration of the Andolusian-Lucainan planetary group at
H-hour, zero five forty-five, of D-day, the fourth of oh three.
By no later than zero eight hundred hours, the sixth of oh three. Task Force Draken will, locate and seize the Opfor trans-stellar transport, *Peltier Maru* and liberate Commoners held aboard her with minimal loss of civilian life. Task Force Draken will destroy Opfor void forces in the region and secure Phuong-Alpha. Task Force Draken will secure the Phuong-Yeuin colony and exo-drome on the moon, Lucainus-Phuong, by planetary forced entry. The time is now zero seven forty-three hours, third of oh three."

Mitch stopped speaking and came to attention facing Morgan, who stood again and strode to the center of the room. Maria watched him take his cue and slip around the side, past Colonel Rivas' swivel and on to the rear of the conference room.

"My intent, ladies and gentlemen, is to effect a strategic and tactical surprise on the Opfor. We've got a wide exercise spectrum to play with and we're going to use it all. We will blind them with cyber-attacks, barrage jamming of their communications networks and ESR back-feed of false imagery to conceal our advance to contact through the Andolusian habitable zone. My concept of the operation is this."

The plot morphed, depicting separating axes of advance towards and investing Lucainus-Phuong.

"Major Cassidy, your IEX Cavalry squadron will lead the formation through the Andolusian heliopause, you will screen the battle groups' approach to Phuong and the entry. *CBC Draken* fighter-bomber wing and the Recondo *Condor* commanded by Master Sergeant Bittrich, will pass through your people and conduct Operation Bolo."

Maria perked up. *Bittrich, Recondo, Condor!*

Morgan continued. "Draken wing will draw the enemy fighter squadron away from the moon by electronic deception, ambush it and destroy it. Commander Simpson, take battle groups *Drukar* and *Dridantes* and follow one trans-planetary feature line behind the screen. Roy, you and Loraine will locate and destroy the Opfor void battle group.

"Phillipe will follow with the *Draken* group, the transports and *CD Perseaus* Flotilla. On my order, we will break off, Phillipe. We will approach Phuong via a separate route and simultaneously attack all three objectives by coup-de main assault! Colonel Romanov's Spetznax cohort, supported by a destroyer and two frigates, will intercept, board and seize the Opfor transport and secure the Yeuin citizens and prisoners."

Maria perked up again at hearing that name. *Bittrich is a master sergeant and Romanov is a colonel.* Morgan began assigning missions, and objectives before Maria had a chance to look around the room to attach a face to a name. Each commander nodded, studying the HG, and jotting notes on their wrist pads.

"One reinforced cohort of First Fusilier Battalion will land at LZ X-Ray on Phuong-Alpha, supported by a destroyer and a frigate and secure the station. The rest of the task force with attack and seize Phuong-Yeuin."

Morgan paused for moment to let the boldness of the operation sink in, before he continued.

"There, I intend to bypass and suppress the Opfor ground force, pinning them on or near the Phuong-Yeuin exo-drome by orbital gunfire and aviation. The main assault will not, I say again, will not go into Phuong-Yeuin Exo-drome."

Eyes widened in excitement around the room. Murmurs filled the air.

"Settle down, people," CSM Morris growled. The room went deathly silent.

"Instead, Colonel Nix will strike here, ladies and gentlemen. East of the town, well north of the exo-drome, outflanking those defenses covering the valley. The dragoon battalion and the regimental pathfinders will secure drop zone Greene, this two and one half by three kilometer prairie," Morgan said. "It's about fifteen hundred meters from the east edge of town. The dragoon battalion will expand the lodgment into the town and secure Hill three oh nine, here.

"The pathfinders will mark landing zone Greene for the regimental pioneer cohort with both gray-jacket construction platoons following by one nineteen tactical shuttles and begin construction of an assault landing strip for the second fusilier battalion and the support battalion. Second fusiliers, Allenby you're gonna get in on the Opfor's rear left flank! Harkness's dragoons and our guns will trap them in those prepared positions, and you will roll them up.

"First Fusiliers minus will remain in orbital reserve ready for commitment into any of the objective areas. Lieutenant Commander Harris is sending you the electronic warfare and deception plan. Commander Bertrim will upload your specific sub-units missions and fire support coordinations. Bertrim's people are uploading graphics, coordination times and points, comms, and logistical support to your operations data pads also. Check your pads and make sure you have all fourteen attachments before you depart on your shuttle."

The plot shifted outward, centering on their present position approaching Andolusia.

"We'll reach the deceleration zone here at zero, zero, three zero hours. That will serve as the attack position. We'll rendezvous with the controllers and evaluator's shuttles and take them aboard. We'll conference on the HG at that time for any frag orders. We'll go dark and advance by bounding overwatch to the line of departure, Andolusia's one TSAU line. Our penetration zone is here."

The point on the plot illuminated, its celestial coordinate rose and inset in the plot's marginal data. Seated behind Maria and scanning the room, Nick leaned forward, he tapped her shoulder and whispered in her ear.

"Check out Commander Bertrim. Watch him."

Maria nodded.

"The lead element will cross the line of departure at H-Hour, zero five forty-five," Morgan continued. "From there, take up the order of movement I specified. Operation Bolo of the deception plan will commence straight away. I'll be here aboard the Draken. What are your questions pertaining to the order?"

There were none.

"Lovely. Alright, ladies and gentlemen, I'm hungry. How about you, Sergeant Major? Join me in the mess, everybody. "

Bertrim walked over to Rivas' swivel after talking quietly with a signals chief and being handed a message, which he handed to Rivas. Maria watched Rivas scan the flexmet flimsy, then after a second or so, her eyes went wide as they all stood to attention and began filing out of the conference room.

Maria had her own job to do. She watched Rivas hand Morgan the message flimsy and whisper in his ear as she, A. J. and her crew walked out of the conference amid the 'brain trust', as she referred to the commanders and their primary staffers. Her head was spinning, but fortunately she had recorded the entire briefing. She lost track of Mitchell. Morgan read the message, he grimaced and handed it back to Rivas. Here was her first opportunity to talk to Morgan since being assigned to the team. And it was the worst possible time. She still smarted from her encounter with Rivas. She needed to at least talk to Mitchell.

The wardroom filled with officers and her own people. The ever-brooding, avenging angel, Command Sergeant Major Morris, stepped up to guard Morgan's open flank as usual. Guarding Morgan, Maria felt, from himself, and from her. They exchanged whispered comments which had Morris nodding, but the tombstone like expression on his face never changed that she could notice.

As the conferees moved on towards breakfast, Maria marveled at the officers' loyalty to G.W. Morgan. Individual commanders and senior staff officers approached him, offering their personal congratulations on being right about the ceasefire line the Alliance had to withdraw beyond.

"All in all it's a good thing, sir. The press would have loved to have used you as a punching bag. Good for their ratings," CBC Drukar's fighter-bomber wing commander offered as she shook his hand.

"That's very true, Jane. Besides, I like this job. Perhaps now that the war is over, maybe I'll see some of its perks once we get back. Lovely."

"Prerogatives of command, eh, sir?" *Drukar's* commanding officer chimed in.

"Yes indeed, Roy. Maybe after Phuong I can get some sleep and read a couple of good literaries. After you count coup on the Lucainans, there'll be plenty of downtime for me on the trip out this time. I'll be able to catch up."

Maria threaded her way through the group towards G.W., silently mocking the officers' lighthearted banter. It was obvious they were trying to ease what she saw were other issues the man still had on his mind.

"This cease fire comes just in time, Commodore. Your project is being broadcast beginning next week. Running active here in the CCC we'll pick up each segment as clear as day!"

"That's grand!" Beaming with pride, Morgan's face visibly brightened. "They're going to broadcast one a day, over six VET days starting on the twelfth. They've put, what do they call them? Uh, prologues in front of each segment. I'd rather run it straight through. But Vaneta and her people are the experts. They don't want people's butts going to sleep. Eh, Sergeant Major?"

Maria actually saw the avenging angel grin; he let loose something that passed for a laugh.

Now. There's an opening.

"The troops are really looking forward to seeing it, sir. After Phuong, it's been all the talk on the transports," Colonel Nix, the 7th Regiment's commander proudly announced.

He saw the dragon lady was on the move from across the room. He signaled Debra Rivas with a slight tilt of his head in Maria's direction. Morgan took note of the signal.

"Now they're the real critics, Colonel," Morgan agreed. *The game is on.* "I thought about coming over to watch a segment in one of your cohort ratzkellers, but your people carry gladii and sidearms. I might not make it off the deck!"

The wardroom exploded in laughter.

"Ha, well, they're secured, sir. Most of 'em anyways!" The 1st Fusilier Battalion commander's reassurance was lost to most of the officers.

*

CSM Morris stepped back and let G.W. and Colonel Rivas go a few steps ahead. Keeping one eye on Hardesty, he saw her coming. There was no need to stop her.

G.W. can handle her. The journalist is within her rights, and Rivas is there.

He watched Hardesty walk up to the rear of the small knot of officers drinking jave' surrounding Morgan, where she hesitated. Looking around he caught sight of Mortimer, Odinot and Lamphere and three of the videographers, their inactive datacams slung at their sides. The fourth, Kung, kept close behind Hardesty. *Good man*, Morris thought. *Watching her back, even here.*

Morris sensed the mood in the wardroom, the others waited, they were hungry, and expecting Morgan to authorize the mess service. Morris knew however, that G.W. Morgan hated ceremonies; except promotions, especially those of junior officers and NCOs.

He had often said. *'Recognizing a trooper's good effort with greater responsibility is the most fun a commander can have!'*

Commander Philippe Stefan, Officer Commanding, *CBC Draken*, looked over the heads of the officers and got a thumbs up from his chief steward.

"Commodore, would you like to authorize the mess?"

"Today is a marvelous and special day, Phillippe. You should do it. My staff and I are, after all, mere passengers aboard *Draken*."

Smiling, Stefan nodded towards the officers, and stepped away towards the 230 year-old silver ship's mess bell. The second such to serve aboard this fourth generation, or Delta class, of Commonwealth Battle Cruisers named *Draken*. The design of the fifth lay in storage awaiting funding debates in the Senate.

Ding-ding. Ding-ding. Ding-ding.

Everyone in the room stood to attention. "Steward, is the mess fit for my officers and guests?"

"Sir, the mess is the finest this ship has to offer."

"Very well, Steward. Commodore, ladies and gentlemen. Please, join me at the mess."

"My pleasure, Commander, Ladies and Gentlemen. Lovely, lovely."

CSS Sabra's commanding officer, the 1st Fusilier Battalion commander, and a vortex squadron commander from *CBC*

Dridantes stood aside to let Hardesty in. The banter around G.W. stifled itself noticeably.

"Good morning, ladies, gentlemen. Please, don't let me stop the revival. I just wanted to offer my congratulations, G.W., oh, pardon me. Commodore. It's not often one gets to make history twice in one lifetime." Hardesty extended a slender hand, which Morgan shook with a firm grip.

"I'll take that in the spirit in which it is given, Miss Hardes...eh, Maria."

"Ah, very good, Commodore. You remembered."

"How could I forget?"

"I'm glad we can let bygones be bygones, Commodore. After all, this is a great day, is it not?"

"It is indeed, Maria. You should go talk to the troops and let the good folks back home know how they're doing."

"Manning the walls. Dedicated warriors keeping watch while we civilians go back home to celebrate the victory, eh?"

"That's exactly right, Maria. Except, well, you're here too."

Surrounded by polite chuckles, Hardesty smiled sweetly at Morgan's smirk. He towered over her. But she had him where she wanted him.

"Yes, you were right about the Alliance, yet again, Commodore. So does that imply the military affairs committee was wrong not to recommend you for an unconstitutional Praetorship?"

Morgan sipped his jave' and tilted his head in thought. Much of the close banter stopped, heads nearby turned to see his reaction. Not even Morris nor Debra Rivas could predict G.W. Morgan with one hundred percent accuracy. A. J. Mortimer and Odinot stood within earshot, listening and noting the several attention-getting tap and head nods from across the room in the direction of the meeting between two people that always held explosive potential.

"You're loaded for ursi early this morning, Maria," Morgan said. "Tell me, have you had your jave'?"

There were a few more polite chuckles from the knots of officers nearby. The Dragon Lady took her shot and missed. Odinot turned and looked out a lamalar making a quiet snort.

*

Morris shook his head, smiled and stepped up to the jave' bar.

That 'unconstitutional' crap went too far. The man's too sharp this morning.

*

Maria could have gotten a good remark to use. *No matter, it's early yet,* she thought. *It was going to be a long cruise and G.W. will give me an opening soon enough, when he's ready.* It was the one thing she could predict about him. She was surprised no one else in the news media could, not even A. J. *He actually likes the game. Commodore Morgan plays journalists as well as he plays the classics on that damned three-bar lycos.*

"I'm not a strategist, Commodore, but I detect a certain boldness in your plan of action for Andolusia. How do you expect the opposition to react?"

"As this is an exercise, I expect them to be dumbfounded, Maria."

"And if this were the real thing. What would you expect?"

"You're going to see, Maria, this is a real fight. But to answer your question, if the Opfor were a real enemy, I'd expect them to die, dumbfounded."

Maria gave him a quizzical look, then nodded. "I understand, Commodore."

Morgan grinned, he had the advantage. "Lovely. But don't take my word for it, Maria," Morgan huffed. "I think you will learn a great deal by discussing the plan with its author. Colonel Rivas, make Lieutenant Commander Pulke available for Maria to interview before things get rolling?"

"Most certainly, sir. I'll take care of it straight away."

"Have a nice talk with Commander Pulke today, Maria. Then join me in the CIC in the morning to watch the show," Morgan said with a smile.

Maria felt faint but maintained her bearing. "Thank you, Commodore."

"We aim to please." Morgan winked at her, then turned and gestured for Stefan, the commanders of CBC *Dridantes, Drukar,* the *Perseaus* Flotilla and Colonel Nix of the marines to join him at a table. The commodore, and his officers let their senior media embed withdraw, like the Alliance units in Vighandis. And like the Alliance, they knew she would try again later.

316

Hardesty excused herself and threaded her way through the clusters of vessel and embarked unit commanders and their senior staffs. She made her way through the open extension into the lounge where stewards began serving breakfast.

Mitchell is not a pirate. But I don't understand this prize money shit. She pondered it over breakfast and finally got it sorted out with A. J. over a steaming bowl of her new favorite, the southwest Istrian staple made popular fleet wide during the second war, cheese grits and ground sausage.

***

Task force attack position, near the northwest octodrant of the Andolusian heliosphere. 0520hrs, 04-03 VET.

Blue illumination cast a soft aura in *CBC Draken's* combat information center but did nothing to dampen the aire of tension. All around the circular chamber, below and off-set from the bridge, staff officers, communications and sensory technicians received and sifted information updating the multi-plot in front of Morgan's command chair. Incoming telemetry data from vessel IFF transponders, primary and secondary voice and data links with each task force ship were continuously monitored by teams of symbiot crewmembers at all times. Nick, for once without his datacam, stayed close to Maria, who looked around in awe, taking it all in. Maria stayed close to Morgan but watched Major Arlene Davis. As task force assistant operations officer, she was in constant motion, monitoring the action by listening in on the various command nets.

"Is it always this way, Commodore? I mean, so tense."

"We're at the tail end of the information flow, Maria. It's going to get worse."

"Oh my."

Morgan grinned, but never took his eyes off the multi-plot for more than a few seconds.

"Initiate Bolo, Major Davis," Morgan said with a calmness that surprised Maria.

The major turned to Morgan and responded. "Yes, sir." She turned back and pointed to the bank of signalers in front of her. "Signal all stations, Hammers."

"How was your interview last night, Maria?" Morgan asked with a sly grin.

"Oh, it was marvelous, Commodore, thank you for asking. Commander Pulke, is, a brilliant man." Maria smiled. She tried to hide her blushing as she answered.

"I agree."

*

As Task Force Draken slowed to wave speed nearing the Andolusian heliopause, *CBC Draken,* and the LRTs *Moncrief* and *Yulan* began launch operations.

Aboard the *Draken,* as on every other ship, the multi-plot dominated the CIC. As Morgan's window on the deep void, trans-planetary, and eventually the orbital, sea, air and land battle spheres, everyone and everything in the command center existed to feed it information.

The multi-plot base map showed the countervailances and AC/DC delta factors of the local gravity waves' currents encompassing the Lucainus planetary group's celestial bodies of significance, and their orbital or stellar stationary, commercial and industrial features.

Additional overlays showed Task Force Draken's primary ship symbols in approach march formation and an increasing number of smaller symbols as bombers, bombardment platforms, and scout ships launched and deployed under covering fighters. Tactical phase lines, bombardment support target reference points, and a hundred other codes and symbols it had taken the people around Maria and Nick years of training and experience to fully master, kept Morgan and his people informed of everything going on in the void around them.

The location, disposition and operational status of every ship and buoy, every refinery and commercial platform or station in the area of operations was plotted. Links with the Admiralty and Andolusian State Traffic Control meant any civilian vessel's flight plan near the exercise area and their identification code could, if necessary, be brought up on an operator's console or from a staff or watch officers' data pad.

As Major Davis reviewed reports, she made notations on her notepad, updating the multi-plot. The major dragged and dropped symbols at the correct grid location and by tapping the enter key, the data appeared on the central plot, in Morgan's command chair side panel, and every other display on her distribution list.

*

Phuong-Yeuin town, on Lucainus Phuong.

On the mezzanine overlooking the underground command post, Hollandia Allen and the Chief of Staff sat together watching ship symbols illuminate on the opposing force's multi-plot. Symbols indicating decelerating warships began to populate the heliopause at a point 14 stellar astronomic units from Narudis, on the extreme right flank of the exercise zone. The heliopause regions nearest Lucainus and Phuong remained clear. More ship symbols illuminated, revealing three wedge formations of capital ships in battle array, closely followed by another diamond formation of large vessels.

The Chief of Staff turned in his swivel to the Andolusian Defense Force colonel, standing, with his arms folded on Mrs. Allen's left.

"There's our vaunted Commodore, Colonel, right out of the slot, just as I figured."

"Yes sir, he's coming off the Borealis commercial loop, to accelerate around Narudis. Typical. That'll put him here in seven hours. Note the time, Centurion Serpa."

"You're familiar with this maneuver, Colonel?" Mrs. Allen asked without taking her eyes off the plot.

"Yes sir, the time is now zero five two one hours VET, sir. Zero two, two two local," Serpa answered from the floor.

"Very well. Yes, ma'am. Very familiar. It's the standard approach for anyone coming out from the Capital District, Piraeus or Gabb'es in the Zone of the Interior."

"He's routing for the Narudis commercial zone. What is the most advantageous approach to get here, Colonel?"

"Well ma'am, as with anywhere else, it depends on your point of entry to the heliosphere."

He lifted his wrist pad and tapped in an entry. A looped course encompassing an accelerative orbit of Narudis and a deccelerative orbit of Lucainus highlighted in dashed lines in the plot.

"He's paralleling the most commercially efficient route. Every other unit has done the same. From Narudis he'll decelerate behind Lucainus and loop his landing force around the northern polar region, into us from the south and west. Defensively, it's advantageous for me. It's slow, I can watch his every move as he deploys."

The colonel then illuminated a second, dashed route in the center of the exercise zone, ending in the Lucainan leading asteroid field.

"This is what I would do, ma'am. I would loop to the Andolusia nine-zulu inbound, here. It's a high speed funnel approach between the influences of these two outer gas giants. It skirts the asteroid fields between Narudis and Lucainus. I would decelerate into the Lucainus leading fields here, ma'am. That allows for a shorter, high-speed approach to drop dragoons on the exo-drome from the north, and for the follow-on landers and even a supporting drop, here, east of town. You see this prairie?"

"Never mind all that," the chief of staff huffed. "When is the most advantageous time for you to attack him?" he asked.

The colonel turned to him shaking his head. "Never, sir. If Commodore Morgan comes at us in the same old way, as this indicates, we will wait, sir." He grinned. "And we will beat him, in the same, old, way."

They watched as Task Force Draken advanced through the heliopause, crossing from the trans-stellar void into Andolusia, 47th, in order of admission, of the 161 Common Stellar States. The Colonel placed both hands on the mezzanine rail and leaned over.

"Centurion Serpa, initiate defense protocol one. Have the Black Widow Squadron stand-to in their revetments. Have the flotilla take up close orbital defense. Advise the Peltier-Maru to power her reactors and make all preparations for getting under way. Inform Lieutenant Yacoby, Phuong-Alpha will go to two-hour standby alert."

"Yes sir."

"What forces do you have on Phuong-Alpha, Colonel?"

"I've trimmed that force down considerably since our last exercise, Admiral. I only keep a Recon section on the surface, a cohort level command vehicle, two panther AFVs and four Puma recce cars."

"Mrs. Allen gave him a questioning look. "Those are the same vehicles you have here, they are IEX capable?"

The Colonel shrugged, a little surprised at such an odd question. "Unh, yes, ma'am. Of course. All of my vehicles and equipment are indo exo-atmospheric."

*

C Deck, LRT Etar, trailing CBC Draken.

Staff Sergeant Lang tapped his wrist pad and projected his Battlefield Information and Imagery System in HG, displaying the undulating, sparsely wooded plateau north of Hill 309 and east of the town.

"Signalers, synch up your comms packs, come up on your primaries and make a signal check with the TOC. Sayeed, make sure the homing transponders have the primary and alternate frequencies pre-set for the battalions, the shuttles, and the landers. Like I said before, people, don't worry about the town or getting into a fight. The whole battalion is coming in on one pass. They'll take care of the town and anybody on the drop zone. As soon as you hit the ground, secure your equipment bundles, move to the center line of the D Z and set up to guide in the engineer shuttles. Brewster, see that tree there, in the middle of the D Z? It has got to come down before the heavy lift shuttles come in, you straight for that?"

"Demo pack number one is ready to prime and pop, Sarge." Trooper Brewster held up one of his three demolition charges, a number 1 stenciled in stealth marker on both sides.

"Good to go. Don't waste time, they're gonna be coming in from the north, ten minutes behind us no matter what. Mainworthy, plant your primary beacons at south central. Sayeed, you've got north central. It's not landing zone Greene until our beacons are aligned and active for the heavy shuttles. I'll head up to Hill three oh nine and set the guidance beacons for the assault landers. No matter what, your job is to mark and control the LZ. Keep your secondaries primed and ready. If any beacon gets hit or breaks down, you've each got a spare to get the job done. Got it?"

"Roger that, Sarge."

"Alright." Lang checked his chrono. "The time is now, zero five twenty-three. Shuttle load time in twenty, we launch at zero six ten. Hit the heads and get suited. Check weapons, team leaders. Make sure your exercise chips are inserted, blue and locked."

"You heard him, dragoons," Sergeant Mainworthy barked. "Line up on your kit. Weapons up, let's see those battery packs!"

*

E Deck, LRT Acre, also trailing CBC Draken.

The HG of 3ʳᵈ Cohort's objective projected for Centurion Naravanutu's officers and senior NCOs from her map panel that she laid on the mezzanine deck.

"Our birds will be the first to touch down on the assault strip, LZ Greene, here. Expect a bumpy landing. Start your vehicles on the taxi. NOT BEFORE! Once the doors open and the ramps come down, haul ass off the bird, got that?"

"Yes, ma'am."

"Good. Miss Jasmine, you roll off the landers, guide on the hard-surface road here, on the right, it separates the landing zone from the town. Move south on that road to this collection of buildings here, northwest of the base of Hill three oh nine. Seize and hold those buildings and cover the road. Block any Opfor movement on that road up from the south and support the Second Dragoon Cohort on the hill. Lieutenant Cartier, you and second platoon are in reserve. Mr. Bolling, take first platoon across the road, into town. Guide on this central east to west road here but stay south of it and support First Dragoon Cohort on your right. Seize and hold the buildings fronting this open area that looks like a park. Center on this school looking building here with the courtyard fronting the park. See it?"

"Yes, ma'am, I got it. Good fields of observation and fire. Good protection in those buildings."

"Roger that. I'll be with second and weapons between the two of you. Once the whole battalion is on the ground be prepared to attack south along this road into Happy Valley. The best part about this is we're coming at them from their rear and left flank. Their primary and alternate positions are useless. But don't get cocky, these people are good, don't expect them to panic, they'll have supplementary positions. Watch out for AVGMs and hastily laid mines.

"We have priority of fires from battalion and regiment once we touch down. That's frigate gunfire support from DPR-two, that's also its call-sign. Danger close is six hundred meters, platoon leaders. Aviation same, same," she said, looking directly at Lieutenant Cartier.

"Don't expect much else beyond the dragoon mortars and our own, until our battalion mortars and the support battalion unload. I'll control the attack drones. Questions?"

323

"What's the enemy strength, ma'am?" PSgt Crowder asked.

"Battalion combat team, expect about fifty armored vehicles, at least ten AGs. There's some kind of deception plan in the works in the trans-planetary sphere that's supposed to draw off the Opfor's fighters. If it doesn't work, expect air attack, at any rate, expect bombardment from roving light and heavy mortars. Headquarters, I need you on the ball for counter-battery radars and controlling the attack drones."

"No worries, ma'am,"

"Right then. The time is now zero five three two. Rusty, supervise vehicle load and staging. Sergeant major, feed a hot meal at zero eight. I'll do a walk through at zero nine. We stand to the Y at ten hundred. Remember surface time on Phuong is three hours behind VET. It'll be just after sunrise when we touch down."

*

Precisely choreographed, organized chaos reigned aboard every ship in Task Force Draken. Equipment received another of an endless stream of 'final' checks, vehicles loaded into landers. Deck crews serviced and armed fighters and bombers. Scouts, pilots, navigators and gunners made calibration checks, they re-bore sighted weapons and quizzed one another on the minutest details of each other's jobs.

*

Commonwealth Sustainment Ship Sabra, near LRT Acre.

The launch and recovery deck hummed, echoing the purring of idling drive units. Construction specialist, PO 2nd Class Sharia Barker sat in the cramped driver's compartment of her paver and waited, like everyone else, sealed in their vehicles in the two construction platoons. Her D-7 paver was the last vehicle to load Heavy Lift Shuttle 01. Her last view outside had been her partner paver backing into Heavy Lift 02 as the ramp in front of her closed. Now sealed off completely from the 8,000 plus crewmembers aboard CSS Sabra, Sharia's only view beyond her lamalars was the large stenciled 01, just centimeters in front of her. Sharia tapped the screen at the right front of her controller panel and got her paver unit operator's attention.

Seated in his separate compartment with his back to hers, PO 1st Class Clyde Kulnev didn't have his helmet on. Instead, he was fidgeting with his helmet liner mesh. Looking up, he grinned at her and blew her a kiss.

"Clyde, are we actually going to do this to somebody's farm field? That's destruction of private property isn't it?"

'Naw, girlie. It's a prairie. That's all government land. That half of Phuong is military training area. Been that way for a long time. It's the other half that's divided up into farms and preserves and such.'

"The photos look pretty. I mean with the green hills and the sea and all."

'I heard that whole area was terra-formed. The sea is a man-made lake. They carved out the basin and used the spoil to build the hills and ridges that make Happy Valley.'

"Why the hell would they do something like that?"

'To make life miserable for the grunts. They've built all kinds of exercise areas on that side of the moon. Lots of 'em are live fire zones too.'

"And we're going into that grunt shit with the first wave? We're not grunts! Why do we have to drop in, on a shuttle no less, and carve a runway outta the dirt, when there's a perfectly good exo-drome not even thirty kilometers away. I still don't get it."

'That exo-drome is well defended. We'd get our asses kicked going into there. We've got an important job, us and Smiley. We're the only two D-seven pavers in the whole task force. You heard that commander from *Draken*, the fusilier battalions need this strip in place and leveled and we've got thirty minutes, at the max, to get it done. Or else the whole plan falls apart. We're important.'

"Why are we doing all this anyway? The war's over. We had a hell of a time getting the breather units off this beast. These pavers are designed for non-atmospheric grading, not terrestrial road building."

'Quit yer bitchin'. The breathers needed to come off, we wouldn't have fit in this shuttle otherwise.'

"We gotta put 'em back on after we get back."

'That's true. We do,' Clyde smiled.

'Now hear this. Now hear this. Set launch condition alpha throughout the ship. That is all.'

'This is it, girlie,' Clyde said, donning his helmet. 'We're in it, for sure.'

****

325

Count Coup.

LRT Yulan, trailing CSS Sabra and the agro-carrier Saffier.

The sleek, blunt-nosed, tri-decked craft decoupled from the big, bulky, unglamorous transport's starboard upper gantry but kept close station with her. Aboard *Condor* 2, Master Sergeant Tara Bittrich absent-mindedly swiveled from side to side, watching the *Draken's* squadrons launch and form up on her multi-plot. Watching the wing commander, Delta-Whisky 01's symbol illuminate from the *Draken* and draw steadily away, she reached over and tapped the corresponding symbol on her comms side-panel.

"Delta-Whisky zero one, this is *Condor* two, standing by, over."

'Roger *Condor*. Break, Delta, this is Delta-Whisky one, vector Lucainus three two six degrees direct, on my mark. Maintain station within a three zero degree arc of *Condor*. Time is now, zero five two three hours. Squadrons acknowledge.'

**

CBC Draken CIC.

Maria saw Mitchell's vortex's call sign light up on the plot at the head of the trail squadron of *Draken* wing. She edged close to CSM Morris, standing behind Morgan's command swivel.

"Excuse me, Sergeant Major," she whispered.

"Yes, miss."

"Who is *Condor*?"

"Recondo surveillance and cyber-warfare bird, miss. Sergeant Bittrich's people," he growled.

"All stations are standing by, Commodore."

"Execute," Commodore Morgan commanded.

"Signal all stations," Major Davis said. "Odyssey."

"Bittrich, I've heard that name before. At the Maranon hearings and at the CLA Archives."

"Yes, miss. I know," Morris said looking down at her. Then he turned back towards the plot, ignoring her.

His cryptic answer made her cringe.

**

"They're on the move, Colonel. Standard wedge of wedges formation, sir. They have a cavalry screen forward and on their flanks," the centurion announced looking up to the guest observer's mezzanine from the situation room floor.

The colonel stood at the rail with a jave' cup in hand. The civilian woman and the Chief of Staff were seated in swivels pointing at and discussing the plot.

"Yes, I see. Identify those drive signatures pulling ahead of the cavalry."

"Identification is coming through now, sir," a head-setted extended sensory and ranging technician, seated near the centurion announced.

Waiting for a positive identification in the now bustling situation room, the centurion watched as the civilian woman said something to the colonel, who took a seat next to her.

"Vixen IEX drive signatures, sir. Forty plus, inbound on the Lucainus Echo five two nine direct wave. AC-DC five point three."

Above on the mezzanine, the colonel folded his arms and rocked side to side with a smile.

"Well, well, he's no slouch after all. He's bold, I'll give him that much."

"What's happening, Colonel?" the Chief of Staff asked.

"He's got the wave gauge advantage, Admiral. He's launching bombers from well outside the habitable zone to get in as many strikes as possible while he closes the range. He wants to catch my fighters on the ground with this first strike, destroy them and get credit for cratering my runways."

Mrs. Allen perked up at that. "But if he craters your runways, Colonel, he can't land on them."

"He has pioneers and construction support platoons, ma'am. He can repair them in a few hours, once his dragoons secure the high ground around the exo-drome. But Major Malone's people will give them a hard time doing either."

Allen and the Chief of Staff exchanged a long look.

"Get your fighters into orbit, Colonel," the Chief of Staff ordered. "Don't take any chances."

"Sir? Admiral, I," the colonel stopped himself, seeing Mrs. Allen's soft expression harden. "Yes, Admiral."

"What are you thinking, Colonel?" Mrs. Allen asked.

The colonel hesitated, looking at the plot. "I believe it's too soon to respond, ma'am."

"Nonsense, Colonel," the chief of staff snorted. "Those vixens are less than three hours away from here on that vector. I know those craft, and their capabilities. They'll be on top of us before you know it. Get your fighters up and in position to intercept them before they reach the countervailance with Lucainus golf eight two, that's the obvious Initializing Point for a bomb run on the exo-drome. If you catch this first strike without their escorts, they'll be easy meat, and Morgan will be hesitant to try again until he's much closer. Make it happen, Colonel."

"Yes, sir," the colonel snapped. He turned to his centurion on the floor. "Serpa, scramble the Black Widows."

"Sir? Ah, yes, sir."

***

Lucainus inbound gravity wave E-529, 3.5 SAU from Lucainus-Phuong. 0730hrs, 04-03 VET.

The silence in his headset allowed Mitch Pulke to wargame the operation from start to finish in his head, for the hundredth time, it seemed, since launching almost two hours ago. Despite his mental gymnastics, he found his thoughts drifting back to Maria's warm and inviting body in her billet last night and their settling on a situation they both felt comfortable with. Mitch smiled at the thought of someday meeting Great Aunt Zinnia. He pushed the pleasant thought to the lower recesses of his mind however, when his receiver crackled.

'Delta, this is Delta Whisky. *Condor* says, bandits inbound. Eleven o'clock high at two three thousand kilometers, now.'

The Draken wing commander's alert flashed through the four fighter squadrons and was received on *CBC Draken's* bridge.

*

"Commander Stefan, Delta Whisky reports *Condor* has bandits approaching their location on the Lucainus foxtrot nine seven outbound, three point eight SAU forward of Lucainus on an intercept course." The contact illuminated on the plot before the technician finished her report.

"Very well, inform the Commodore, first contact, zero seven three zero hours. All units will Charlie Mike."

"Roger that, commander."

328

One deck below, in the CIC, Maria sat bolt upright in the small visitor's gallery upon hearing the contact report. Her sudden movement startled Nick, sitting beside her, waking him from his snooze. Looking around, she saw Morgan, sitting calmly in his command swivel with his eyes closed, but she knew he wasn't asleep. He just sat there, listening to reports. He scanned the plot occasionally and made quick comments to Rivas, or Morris, or Davis. Commander Bertrim had come in and spoken to him twice in the last hour, but Maria didn't want to pursue what their conversations may have been about right then. *Bertrim isn't very involved in this wargame,* she thought. *I bet he's focused on the actual mission.*

*

Phuong-Yeuin.

The command post buzzed with heightened activity. Everywhere Hollandia Allen looked, there were hurried conversations and consultations. Technicians scurried about, activating additional consoles and communicating with their units. The multi-plot displayed a region of the trans-planetary void between Lucainus and Narudis, near the Narudis lower leading asteroid field, where two groups of symbols were closing to merge.

"They should be within acquisition range any second now, Mrs. Allen," the colonel said in a low, cautious tone.

"You don't sound very confident, Colonel."

"I have to say, ma'am. I have a bad feeling about this. This is too easy. No one sends vixens in at this range, with no fighter support, and no frigates or destroyers. Something's not right."

"What's not right is G.W. Morgan believing he can deceive and outwit me!" The chief of staff snapped in a huff. We'll give him a dose of humility before we send him off to Chein."

Mrs. Allen forcefully cleared her throat.

"Yes, yes," the admiral said, acknowledging her. The colonel said nothing. Well aware of the political game playing out between the chief of staff and the TF Draken commodore, he never took his eyes off the plot.

"Colonel, the flotilla reports they are staged at Phuong outbound yankee six, and standing by for orders," Centurion Serpa announced from the floor.

"Very well."

"Sir, contact report from Black Widow one!" a technician in the signals bay shouted. The multi-plot lit up with active transponders as every pilot appeared to be talking at once.

"What's that report? Put it on speakers," the colonel shouted.

'...not vixens! I say again these are not vixens, they're...'

The transmission from Black Widow 01 stopped in mid-sentence. The transponder signal changed color from green to red. Several other transponders changed color almost simultaneously.

"Damnation!" The colonel almost screamed in frustration. "I knew it!"

"What's happening?!"

"It's a deception! It's an ambush! Damnation! Serpa, tell Benitez to break contact, withdraw back to Phuong, NOW!"

"Major Benitez is down, sir. Lieutenant Monroe is down, Carstaires, Pedon, Silcar, and Moore are gone."

*

Countervailance of E-529 inbound and Y-6 outbound gravity waves, 3.8 SAU from Lucainus-Phuong.

Draken vortex wing's opening volley of AIM-3 and 4 missiles 'destroyed' most of the lead Opfor tiger element and threw the rest of the squadron into confusion. Seconds later, the void between the outer edge of Lucainus' trailing asteroid field and the forward edge of the Narudis leading field swirled with jousting Commonwealth fighters.

Small, black and silver Tiger-5s from Phuong dueled with CBC Draken's black, roughened vortexes. The tigers were badly outnumbered and losing pilots as their machines, caught in the pulse streams of simulated vortex gun projoes and missiles, powered down their weapons systems. 'Destroyed' tigers' landing strobes went active, the craft defaulted to auto-pilot and turned about, towards Lansdowne Exo-drome on Lucainus.

'Delta One, this is Whisky, they're splitting up, trying to break contact. We'll take the main body. You get those six at two o'clock low.'

Looking down and to the right, Mitch Pulke's visor read through his fuselage, picking up the two flights of three craft.

"Tien Lien." Mitch checked the wave gauge. "Dawgs, come right and follow me." He thrust rolled and inverted, diving after the tigers. Flanking their leader, Delta Dawgs accelerated to M-9.5 and rapidly closed the distance.

At 5,600 kilometers, *thirteen seconds to closure,* Mitch lined a tiger squarely inside his inner targeting pipper ring. The flashing yellow ring changed to flashing blue, *ten seconds to closure.* His targeting computer fed the data stream through its inner missile magazine as its port and starboard launch rails deployed. *Eight seconds.* The now exposed numbers one and two AIM-3 seeker heads locked on. The targeting pipper went solid blue. The missiles' seekers' growling in his headset matured into a solid tone. *Six seconds.* Mitch checked his flanks and rear, then squeezed the trigger. His weapons display showed the number one particle seeker missile indicate 'launched', he released the controller trigger and re-squeezed, number two 'launched'.

One, one thousand, two, one thousand, three, one thousand.

Both missiles' targeting pulses flashed the tiger. The tone in his headset became a hard buzz. The tiger's flashing strobe told him all he needed to know. Mitch instinctively thrust-rolled left wing over right and accelerated to 'avoid debris'. The tiger's wingman was off-angle for him. "Take the shot, George," Mitch called out to his wingman, Flight Sergeant Hermez.

Delta-Delta-02, 'flashed' the tiger's wingman. 'Got him, boss.'

The retreating tigers pivoted, turning into the Delta Dawgs. In less than a second, the two groups of fighters merged into a swirling melee of jousting pairs. Mitch locked on to another tiger, and 'loosed' an AIM-3 particle seeker at its glowing aft stabilizer. The tiger launched distractors, vapored and pivoted, breaking the lock. The missile tracked into a distractor and 'flashed'. George Hermez stayed on Mitch's five o'clock, watching his back. High on Mitch's right, DD-06 'flashed' a third tiger.

Mid-range on Mitch's left, Lt. Wendy Orel, DD-03, lined up above and behind a tiger. Her sight pipper aligned, she got the blue at just 200 kilometers. Squeezing the trigger, the tiger's strobe lit up. Orel broke away left. Ensign Jare, DD-04, wing-rolled right over left staying with her.

"Get that guy at ten o'clock, Berniece."

'Tien Lien!' Jare lined up on Orel's tiger's wing man and 'loosed' a particle seeker. The fighter juked, made vapor and popped distractors, breaking missile lock. Jare stayed with it. The tiger leveled, then dipped its' left wing. Anticipating a left turn, Jare decelerated, winging left over right a full spiral, bleeding inertia to stay behind it. But the tiger corrected, and in a flash, reversed its turn and rolled right. Jare's vortex streaked past. The tiger reversed again, rolled left and decelerated, dropping onto Jare's tail.

'Break right and climb, Berniece!'

The tiger 'loosed' a long 60mm burst.

DD-04's landing strobe flashed twice.

'Berniece's been hit!'

Orel pitched over, she got tone and loosed an AIM-3 at minimum range. In an instant, the tiger 'flashed'. Jare's vortex defaulted and broke away, headed towards the controller's rendezvous point, joining four other vortexes.

Mitch stayed with his tiger, switching to mixed guns, His vortex nosed down, he quarter thrust to port and dropped in behind the craft. Closing to one hundred kilometers, he pitched up eight degrees to line up his shot and 'loosed' a short combined burst of 60mm and 30mm cannon. The tiger launched another vapor spread, it combat pivoted to starboard and down, diving through it, while launching distractors and circling away.

"Dammit!"

'Stay on him, boss!'

Mitch thrust-rolled left over right and pushed into a near-vertical dive relative to his prior direction of travel. Accelerating through the tiger's vapor, he immediately recognized his mistake. The tiger had leveled in the vapor cloud and circled, waiting to ambush Mitch's pursuit. And Mitch had stumbled right into it.

'BREAK, MITCH!!'

Mitch slammed the controller to the left, firing his entire starboard thruster bank. His attitude indicator spun wildly, stars, asteroids, and the planets in the distance switched positions in an instant. Mitch felt a sick feeling in the pit of his stomach as his buzzer chirped twice loudly in his headset, then stopped.

"Shit!" *Near miss. Get out of his gun line.*

He jerked the controller into his gut with his right hand, jamming the accelerator hand grip with his left to the forward wall, applying full military power. The vortex zoom climbed, but the loud chirping followed. He right thrust over left and chopped power, rapidly decelerating. The tiger overshot, streaking past.

Mitch made a full spiral. He lined up on the tiger, full on in his screen and squeezed the trigger. The tiger flashed but broke out of his gun line.

'Lead him, boss.'

"Stay out of this one, George. He's mine."

'Get that motha.'

'Burn his ass, Commander!'

'Get him, Mitch. We got your back!' Mitch recognized the Wing Commander's voice among the others cheering him on.

The tiger dived, accelerating for the Lucainus asteroid field's outer edges, Mitch stayed tight on its six o'clock. The two fighters twisted and turned, dueling among the small boulders. Again and again, each gained an advantage. The hunter got a tone and 'loosed' a missile, or a gun burst, near-missing because of their prey's defensive skills. Then the hunter lost their advantage, becoming the hunted, getting near-miss chirps in their cockpits, until by their skills they manage to regain dominance. On it went.

Mitch watched his ammunition count dwindle, 200 projoes each in the 30's, 80 left for the 60 and one AIM-4 microwave guided missile. Even with the cooling unit in his climate controlled suit, his eyes burned from sweat, blurring his vision. Blinking to clear them, he almost lost sight of the tiger until it banked right, in front of a large asteroid. Mitch almost shouted for joy.

Big mistake, buddy!

It's shiny, black and silver body silhouetted against the gray rock in a 40 degree down-angle turn.

You should've went around it.

Mitch slow rolled, banked right and lined up, his gunsight pipper flashed blue for what seemed like the thousandth time against this tiger. He switched his selector to Missile A4 M-W. Staying in the turn, he got his nose in front of the craft and 'loosed'. The strobe lit up in a red continuous flash.

'Hooyah, Nailed Him!' Flight Sergeant Hermez burst over the net.

**

"Contact report from Commander Stefan, Commodore."

"What is it?"

"Delta-Whisky one reports, 'Seventeen tiger-fives destroyed, three damaged, four to six survivors have broken contact and are retreating for Phuong. We are returning to cruiser

333

to rearm. Time now, zero seven three six hours.' End of message, sir."

"Yeess!"

The whole command center crew turned and grinned at Nick, including Maria and Morgan. Morris' expression never changed from its perpetual scowl.

"My sentiments exactly, Mr. Kung," Morgan quipped. "Signals, casualties?"

"Five vortexes, sir. Four destroyed, one damaged. One pilot is assessed dead, four are assessed ejected, sir. SAR is inbound. Twelve Opfor pilots are assessed dead, sir, eight are assessed ejected."

"Very well, Advise SAR to grab credit for as many of those 'ejected' pilots as they can. Account for drift, plot and run an intercept, launch and recover their sleds, the whole bit. Lovely," Morgan said smiling. "Lovely."

Maria thought about Mitch, being ejected into the void back in the Trudan and how, without those 'White Bird' Search and Rescue shuttles and their boarding sleds, they would never have met. She anxiously scanned the plot and found DD-01's blue transponder, streaking away from a flashing red Opfor fighter.

"Major Davis, Advise Stefan to break off as soon as he has recovered his available fighters and SAR," Morgan ordered. "Advise the *Condor*, 'Ringgold'. Tell Bittrich to concentrate on locating *Peltier Maru*."

"Yes, sir."

"It's working, Commodore," Morris grumbled.

"It sure the hell is. So far," Morgan said nodding. He scanned the plot and his side panel, seeing all of his units moving into place.

*

"What's happening, Admiral? Colonel?" Mrs. Allen shouted incredulously. "Somebody tell me what's happening!"

"They've overrun my Black Widows," the colonel answered in disgust. "Centurion Serpa, sortie the flotilla. Signal Major Malone, have her battalion Stand-To and move out. NOW!"

"Sir, ah, yes, sir!"

"What are you going to do, Colonel?"

"I'm going to try to salvage the situation before it gets too far out of hand, ma'am."

"I, I, don't understand," the chief of staff mumbled to himself. "Those were supposed to be vixens. Not vortexes."

"Colonel, the senior controllers are not permitting the ground forces to move until either the transport or Phuong-Alpha are engaged."

"What?!" Mrs. Allen stood to the rail.

"Damnation. Stand-to all air defense, Serpa. Tell Major Malone to mount her vehicles. Tell her to stage at the gates and to be ready to roll at a moment's notice!"

**

The Lucainus Planetary Group. 0846hrs, 04-03 VET.

The Opfor destroyer flotilla broke orbit and looped for the Y-6 gravity wave, towards the E529 to screen the *Peltier Maru's* pending escape, but they were already too late. The lead elements of 14th IEX Cavalry's screen were already closing on the countervailance via the high speed E529 inbound wave. Scouts picked up inbound Opfor frigates in line of battle at a center bearing of 12 degrees relative to Andolusia approaching up-angle from Phuong, at a range of 14.5 million kilometers.

The Fitter scout ship's spot report to his platoon leader relayed to the Bravo Troop commander aboard the Troop mother ship. The position, course, and speed of three identified Predator-class Opfor frigates were relayed to the cavalry squadron's bombardment platforms. The platforms pulled a hip-shoot. They dropped from the march and bled their inertia occupying a hasty launch position in a localized subduction in the wave. Within 3 minutes of the call for support they delivered their first immediate suppression bombardment mission to fix the Opfor formation.

The ready squadrons of vortex fighters from *Drukar* and *Dridantes*, and a *Dridantes* vixen bomber squadron launched to attack the group. A second scout's report identified the Jafir class destroyer, 15,000 kilometers behind and Phuong-ward of the Predators. The scouts slipped to the flanks and continued to march towards Phuong's flanks, as the advance guard of the Drukar/Dridantes force closed in.

The Opfor attack was a forlorn hope. Desperate to close the range, the Opfor frigates accelerated to flank speed and advanced in line abreast, zigzagging, making vapor and launching vapor shells in front of them. They 'launched' torpedoes at 4.5 million kilometers and continued to advance, closing to guided missile range. The Jafir, just slightly larger than the Predators, kept concealed, lurking in the Phuong-ward asteroid fields. She repeatedly emerged and loosed a salvo, then darted back into the fields.

Evenly matched, the fast, highly maneuverable, heavily armed and armored frigates 'launched' guided missiles at 3.8 million kilometers and began exchanging 100mm gunfire at 2 million kilometers. Closing on the countervailance first, the Commoners held a wave gauge advantage.

Aboard every frigate, gunnery officers put themselves into the minds of their opponents' navigation/propulsion officers and vice-versa. Neither side 'shot' directly at the other, rather, they led their targets and loosed proximity-fused projoes into their opponent's anticipated path. Predators pitched and yawed, making erratic changes in direction, behind screening vapor that spoiled the opponents' sensory locks, but reduced their own gunnery effectiveness as well. 'Hits' were recorded on both sides, navigation strobes flashed once or twice indicating near-misses or non-fatal damage.

The suppression bombardment and vixen torpedoes stalled the Opfor line, the ships bled inertia, maneuvering to avoid the sensor-blinding vapor blossoms and the effectiveness radii of flashing SK simulator salvos. The jousting went on for agonizing minutes, before the superior weight of shot from the Commoners began to tell.

The lead Terrier-class destroyer, CD *Malvern Hill* of the Drukar group joined the fray, 4.3 million kilometers from the Opfor line. Slowing to wave speed, her four battery turrets counter rotated as she turned to port. Her twelve, 30cm rail guns 'loosed' three broadsides into the Opfor, supporting the Commoner frigates and covering her sisters' advance. CDs *Mallory* and *Bagration* made vapor and climbed Phuong-ward, searching for the Opfor *Jafir*. CD *Komar* dove Lucainus-ward behind vapor and gave additional fire support, pinning the Opfor frigates.

'SK' flashes and blossoming vapor clouds bracketed the Opfor frigate line and erupted among the Phuong-ward asteroids in the distance behind them, searching for the *Jafir*.

Coordinated from *CBC Drukar's* upper battery turret bombardment direction center, the heavy ships split their bracket. *Drukar's* and

Dridantes' 68cm rifles and the bombardment platforms' 72cm howitzers delivered the first of three massive 'SK' salvos into the pocket.

Commoner frigate gunners clearly saw continuous flashing navigation strobes on two of the Opfor ships through the battle flash discriminators in their gunsights. Some gunners cheered, others cursed, deprived of credit for the coup after a mind-numbing, physically exhausting joust against worthy opponents.

*

Morgan followed the engagement with satisfaction. The fight wasn't over, but the Opfor was hurt, badly, and reeling in confusion. "Lovely. Time to drop the pretense, Major Davis," he said with a wide grin. "Signal Condor, 'Terminate Bolo, go Eyeball'. Advise Stefan he may close to close bombardment range and loose when ready."

"Yeess, Sir!"

"Maria, you may want to go down to the main battery observation post to watch this, Commander Tieras is on his way. He can answer any questions you may have."

"Yes, Sir!" Maria snapped instinctively, much to her surprise.

"Time to show Mrs. Allen exactly who she's dealing with," Colonel Rivas said, turning to Maria and smiling.

Who's Mrs. Allen, Colonel?" Maria asked.

**

Phuong-Yeuin. 0848hrs,

The Opfor multi-plot froze and pixelated in a kaleidoscope of color for several seconds. All around the command post, technicians' monitors went to test patterns or blue screens. Techs and NCOs threw their hands up at their consoles, looking around in confusion.

The chief of staff leapt to his feet. "What's happening, Colonel?"

"I, I don't know. Centurion! Stellar flares?"

"Negative, sir. Nothing forecasted. Sir, I think we're being jammed!" The plot reset as the Centurion spoke. He turned around, and after a second, he gasped. "Colonel, we are not being jammed. Not anymore."

"What the hell is he talking about?" the chief of staff snapped. "What the hell are you talking about, Centurion?"

The Colonel looked down at Serpa, then up at the plot. What he saw made him recoil in shock, but he quickly recovered. He turned to the chief of staff with a disdainful smirk.

"Admiral, we were being fed a false image. This is the actual ESR plot, sir."

"I don't understand." Mrs. Allen stood from her swivel, looking around in confusion.

"He has Recondos attached to his force, doesn't he, Admiral?" the Colonel asked with an accusatory stare.

"Well, yes."

Mrs. Allen's head turned first to one, then to the other, then to the plot. "There are two battle groups approaching from Narudis now, when all three were there before. That group standing off in front of Lucainus wasn't there before."

"Yes ma'am, it was. It was approaching on the Andolusian nine Zulu all the time. Under a looped projection from an EW warfare bird, that you never told me they had! Damnation!"

The chief of staff slumped into his swivel.

"That cruiser symbol sitting one hundred thousand kilometers away is *CBC Draken*, ma'am," the colonel sneered, stabbing a finger at the plot. "Morgan's command battle group and a destroyer flotilla are well within bombardment range of us. Right now! And he has his transports with him. Admiral, Mrs. Allen, he's not going to the exo-drome, his entire marine regiment is going to drop in right on top of us on that prairie just outside of town! He's going to flank my positions in Happy Valley. This exercise is programmed to take up to two days." The colonel rubbed his chin, massaged his neck and rubbed his bald head. "Now, I'm on the back foot in less than three hours. I'll be damned. Heh. I'll be damned." He turned towards his operations officer on the floor.

The centurion wasn't looking at him, he was furiously gesturing at the plot, arguing with a stoic controller.

"They'll be caught out in the open if we don't get them on the move, now."

The controller major's HG image from Lansdowne was firm. 'The rules of engagement require the surface force remain in place until the void objectives are attacked, Centurion.' Behind the major, conferring senior controllers and umpires nodded their heads in agreement.

"Serpa, have Malone get as much of her force up here into town as possible. She's got less than an hour before all hell breaks loose."

"We still can't move, sir!"

"What troops do you have here in the town already?"

"A rifle company and the battalion mortars, ma'am. Malone has a light tank section on Joy Road at the Route three bypass intersection, plus a few air defense squads on the hill. But most of the force is on the exo-drome, ma'am."

"Centurion Serpa, Colonel, inbound vixens, confirmed drive signatures, fifty thousand kilometers and closing!"

"Damnation! My cavalry!"

The plot showed the rapidly advancing bomber formation. Worse, groups of smaller illuminated craft began emerging from three of the transports, a small number from their bows, and a stream from aft.

"Bombardment platforms and shuttle launches! Dragoons inbound."

"The formation is separating, sir. Ships are breaking for Phuong-Alpha and for *Peltier Maru*. The other battle groups are forming a cordon around the planetary group."

"They've cut off the transport's escape."

"He hasn't won yet," the Admiral said. Get your fighters into the air! Intercept the group heading for *Peltier Maru*."

The colonel turned sharply but maintained his bearing.

"Admiral, Sir," he said calmly. "I don't have any fighters here anymore."

The admiral's eyes went wide. "I DON'T CARE!" He raised both clenched fists over his head and stomped his left boot.

"ADMIRAL! GET A HOLD OF YOURSELF! Mrs. Allen shouted at him. "He's beating us!"

The chief of staff slumped back in his swivel, he leaned forward and buried his face in his hands.

'Centurion, the controllers agree. You now have sufficient evidence to release your surface force.'

"Colonel, where is this prairie?" Mrs. Allen demanded. "Show me."

"Yes, ma'am. But you'll have to don hearing protection. In fact you should have a battle suit on to go to the surface," the colonel cautioned. "These training munitions still produce fragments."

"Very well, fetch a set for us, I want to see this for myself."

"Admiral."

"Never mind him."

***

8,000 kilometers above ground level of Lucainus-Phuong. 0850hrs.

Descending rapidly, the CS119 tactical shuttles' loadmasters and their crews helped Lang and the other dragoon leaders check and verify, as each dragoon set their mini-breather compensators to Phuong's 22% O^2 and grav to 0.9g surface gravity. They checked dragoons donning their main and reserve parachutes and securing weapons and equipment to their BDE equipment harnesses. The leaders tapped a fist with each trooper and sealed them, and their squad equipment walkers into their pods, starting the pod pressurization sequence. Leaders checked each other, then mounted their pods. The loadmaster crews secured them as the shuttle formation decelerated and vectored east by southeast towards the Phuong-Yeuin complex.

*

CD Perseus flotilla's vespid squadron launched from its escort carrier and covered the group and the transports as the *Draken's* vortex squadrons rearmed and refueled. The vespids then escorted *Draken's* Vixen squadron's strike against the exo-drome and Happy Valley.

*

The Taifun class *CD*s *Kerak* and *Kingston* engaged and 'destroyed' the air-defense missile battery emplacements on Phuong's southern polar cap with cruise missiles and 47.5cm gunfire. They dispatched their marine detachments to the surface via CS-112 tactical shuttles to secure the area. CFs *Fidelity* and *Warspite* dropped into low orbit and deployed eight hunter-killer retro-pods. Each retro-pod contained a pre-assembled Max-5 surveillance drone and two Ranger attack-drones to search for and attack Opfor electronic signatures.

*

At 0854hrs, LCdr Bob Edris piloting Grim Reaper 01, broached Phuong's mesosphere over its northern polar cap leading *Draken's* 24 Vixens, escorted by the *CD Perseaus'* flotilla Vespid fighters.

340

At Yeuin Exo-drome, Opfor Major Malone turned around in her command carrier cupola and looked down the column of idling armored vehicles formed up in march order behind her. Only the controller's Util sat in front of her vehicle, just inside the exo-drome's perimeter gate. She listened to the cross-talk from her three cavalry troops of 1st Lucainan Armored Cavalry (Light), and her rifle company in town, as her frustration mounted with continued silence from the command post. The flash of pre-dawn lightning across the summer sky to the north caught her eye. Such was not unusual on Phuong, neither were streaking meteorites.

*

Aboard CBC Draken, Maria and Nick, with his datacam, joined LCdr Tieras and observed the action from the forward battery observation post. The big guns' began their systematic program to rake the forested ridges and the plains surrounding the exo-drome with pinpoint accuracy. It wasn't going to be a live fire exercise, but it made no difference to the crews. The SK 'flashers' would still make for a spectacular light show.

At 0855hrs, all four of CBC Draken's battery turrets commenced 68cm gunfire on the south side of Hill 309 and Happy Valley. Her escort destroyer's 30 cm and 25cm guns and the flotilla frigate's 150mm guns loosed their initial bombardment against the north side of Hill 309 and the edge of Phuong-Yeuin town surrounding the drop zone.

**

The controller's Util moved to the road shoulder, clearing Major Malone's cavalry to move. She rocked in the open commander's hatch as her vehicle lurched forward. The first message from the Command Post since the Stand-To order began to crackle in her headset, as the lightning flashed all around her and all over Phuong-Yeuin Exo-drome.

*

Commander Edris' Vixens broached stratospheric, decelerating to Phuong sonic 5 and stayed in their dive. They broached tropospheric at sonic 3 and dropped to 300 meters above ground level. Streaking in from the north, Vixens made their high speed runs just above the undulating surface just as Andolusia's first rays broke over the eastern horizon. At 300 kilometers range, they popped up into an 81 degree climb at their release points,

341

slinging 1cdb SK cluster munitions to release directly over the slopes along Happy Valley, Joy Road, Hill 309 and the west side of the road separating the landing zone from the town. Their bombs 'detonations' joined the already sparkling display over the exodrome, Hill 309 and Happy Valley.

As the vixens broke away, their supporting vespids rolled in on Phuong-Yeuin itself, making repeated strafing runs. As the vespids broke away, the Max-5 surveillance drones vectored Ranger attack drones in to hunt down and suppress survivors and support the dragoon drop.

*

650 x 650 kilometers slant range north of Phuong-Yeuin. 0900hrs.

LRT Yulan's CS119 tactical shuttles lumbered in under heavy electronic counter-measure protection. They leveled into a wedge formation and bored in at a drop altitude of 650 kilometers above ground level. Aboard the lead shuttle, the individual iron-chondrite lamalar retro-pods slid down, rotated to starboard and locked in place. All eighty indicators showed green on the crew chief's display board; his load crew visually verified each pod in the eight ranks as secure. The crew chief transferred the pod power systems to the flight deck. He gladial saluted Lieutenant Colonel Harkness, the 3rd Dragoon battalion commander in Rack 1.

*

SSgt Lang's pod was in Rack 9, directly behind Colonel Harkness. He stood inside in ejection position. His feet and knees together, body bent slightly forward at the waist, elbows tucked in, hands on reserve, chin tucked into their chest. Lang felt the familiar pre-drop anxiety as his helmet visor fogged, then cleared, he flexed his knees and relaxed. Inert gas filled the interior, the pods rotated, engaging the launch-track release safeties into the ejection standby mode. From outboard to inboard, each rank of pods slid smoothly beneath the cargo deck to the launch tracks below. The floor of the cargo deck slid shut and re-sealed.

The lead CS119's pod extraction ramp slid open. The track section engaged, feeding the pods aft along the extraction ramp through the ejection channel. All 80 retro-pods streamed through her ejection ports and away from the shuttle.

**

342

Lang got the green for a safe ejection in his visor. Four seconds later his heart leapt into his throat as his pod's first stage retro package fired, forcing it downward. The black of the void swirled. It changed positions with tan and green Phuong and her azure blue atmosphere as the pod hurtled towards the surface.

The crushing g-force and roaring rush outside remained muffled inside the 10cm thick pressurized pod and his 1.5cm thick woven metal battle suit. Sparks flashed past him as the pod entered the upper atmosphere. Flame engulfed him as the pod's outer shell began to burn away. The sparkling brilliant, searing heat pattern looked oddly familiar to the dragoon. Its blue, white, orange, red, and black stack of super-heated air and outer layer pod material streamed away all around him.

*

Emerging from the command post bunker in the center of town, Mrs. Allen, the Opfor colonel, and Centurion Serpa were dumbstruck by the sights greeting them. Their side of town had been hit hard. Smoke and dust in the town's streets had an amber tint from the flashing exercise strobes on 'destroyed' or 'damaged' Opfor armored fighting vehicles. The distinctive odor of metallic powder explosives filtered through her suit's environmental wafer.

Mrs. Allen stood aghast, taking in the scene. The elite mechanized infantry company in the town had been brimming with confidence just hours ago. She looked around now at a despondent gaggle. The shocked and bewildered troopers sat or stood around aimlessly after being assessed. Their Battle Dress Ensemble transponders were deactivated, rendering their weapons useless.

She heard the screeching roar of SK projectiles streaking in from the northern and western sky through her hearing protective unit. They erupted in a brilliant flash. They detonated with terrific bangs, like drums beating in rapid pulses above the prairie outside of town, and in the range of high hills just beyond. The bombardment rent the pre-dawn darkness, spattering the prairie with instantaneous bursts as bright as mid-day. Then, scores of points of light streaking across the sky from the northeast caught her eye.

"They timed their bombardment with a meteorite shower, Colonel?"

The colonel followed her gaze. "Damnation," he muttered, shaking his head. He grinned in admiration.

"They're not meteorites, Mrs. Allen. They're dragoons."

"What?! Damn."

"Come with me to the Bank, it's the tallest building in town. You'll be able to see their landing."

*

All reports of assessed casualties and damages flowed in to the main controllers' stations beneath the Lansdowne exo-drome. The data routed to the controllers at the Opfor command post, their vessels, and the Phuong-Alpha communications station. Additionally, the Controller's Utils in the field on Phuong were part of the distribution chain throughout the exercise.

Lieutenant Colonel Marquis was enjoying the show. Grinning, stepping out of his Util in front of a frustrated, never before 'assessed', Major Malone. Marquis put his helmet on and activated his visor. Bringing up the assessments application, he unholstered his 'God-gun' and set off down the line cataloging 'destroyed' and 'damaged' vehicles, 'dead', 'wounded' and 'stunned or otherwise incapacitated' Lucainan grenadiers and cavalry.

*

Dragoon pod retro-packages fired at 4,500 meters AGL. Decelerating the pods and deploying their breaking streamers, further slowing them. At 1,400 meters, the screeching of the inner pod liner alerted Lang to the final micro-seconds before his pod's battered inner liner broke open.

The static lined attached Lang and his equipment bundle were expelled out and away from its' expended retro-package and streamer. Within a fraction of a second, the static line pulled taut, breaking the pack closing tie on his main parachute back pack, and extracting the drogue chute. Its deployment extracted his main parachute.

Instinctively, Lang, by this time at approximately 300 meters, reached up to grab his control risers and took manual control of his descent to the surface. His 9,000 kilometer descent and rapid deceleration from the deck of *LRT Etar* culminated in a comparatively soft five point of contact left side parachute landing fall, balls of the feet, calf, thigh, buttocks and back.

He lay on his back unbuckling his harness. The parachute fluttered softly to the surface just meters from him as he popped his harness and wriggled out. The parachute partially re-inflated from the rush of displaced air pushed from the impacts of the last 'SK' bombs.

Lang secured his M9. He inserted a thirty round magazine, chambered a round and rose to one knee. He slung his rucksack cross-armed over his head, the ensemble slipped over his arms and the harness shoulder pads came to rest on the shoulders of his battle suit. He grabbed its belly band and snapped the ends together. Lang set the wizard box linking his M9 and helmet interactives and scanned the immediate area to get his bearings. His re-calibrating helmet visor HUD shifted slightly, then cleared.

He tapped his wrist pad and the BIIS tactical overlay in his helmet visor lit up. The battalion was right on target. Dragoons were landing all over the prairie, securing their equipment, recovering equipment walkers and moving swiftly, refracted across the open terrain towards the 'SK' wobbles suppressing their objectives. He came up on the regimental tactical net.

"This is Greene. Hot Java, over."

'Roger, hot java, Charlie Mike, out.'

He tapped in another command and the six legged squad walker detached its parachute harness, unfolded its legs and rose. "Cameron, Watts, let's go. Walker, follow."

Moving south at the vault towards Hill 309, they joined a dragoon platoon and Colonel Harkness' command group also moving towards the hill. Lang was satisfied to see Mainworthy's transponder and those of her Alpha team moving south along the center line in his visor display. Corporal Sayeed and Bravo team's transponders headed north to site their beacon.

He breathed easily, shuffling with his M9 at the ready, around and over hummocks and folds in the earth. His team, Privates Cameron and Watts moved with him, close on his flanks and rear. The squad walker, loaded with ammunition and supplies easily kept pace five meters behind him through knee-high grass across the uneven ground.

'The D-sevens are gonna dig a runway through this, Sergeant?" Private Watts huffed over the intranet.

"Sure will, Troop." Lang answered. "Those pavers will chew right through this stuff, grind it, smelt it, and spit it back out its ass-end. Since we're atmospheric, it'll harden and cool quick. You'll see."

Shuffling along almost effortlessly, Lang let the micro-fiber, skeletal muscular enhancement body suit do the work under his BDE.

"What you huffin' for, Watts? I ain't tired. What's your problem?"

'I'm not tired, Sergeant. I'm right behind you.'

"Spread out, dammit! One grenade will kill us all."

'We really gonna use all this shit we're carrying, Sergeant?' Private Cameron tried valiantly not to sound as winded as Watts.

"It's not shit, cherry. It's vital. It's worth more than you or I wouldn't have you carry it. You break it or lose it. You done bought it. Understand?"

'Roger that, Sergeant.'

Suddenly, the earth shook. Lang looked over his left shoulder and caught a glimpse of the large tree in the middle of the prairie falling amidst a cloud of smoke. A stealth landing marker beacon, set for 3-second pulse strobe, lit up nearby. Lang switched to his primary squad net.

"Good job, Brewster. You and Antheil link up with Sayeed."

'Will do, Sarge. Damn, I thought it was a real tree. The damn thing was just a hollow shell. It's a training aid.'

After vaulting across the prairie, Lang started up the north slope of Hill 309 keeping behind and to the left of the dragoons. They were spreading out among scrub grass and saplings on the lower slopes towards the line of dark evergreens that began about 200 meters further upslope. As Lang, Cameron, Watts and the walker climbed the slope, Mainworthy's beacon lit up in his visor. Then Sayeed's on the north side, lit up in line with Brewster's and Mainworthy's. Lang tapped his wrist pad and came up on the Tac Net again.

"Steak and Eggs, zero nine zero seven. Steak and Eggs, zero nine zero seven!"

'Roger, Steak and Eggs.'

Lang and several other veterans heard the familiar swoosh and immediately yelled a warning across the intranet.

"Incoming!"

*

346

Aboard Condor 2.

Master Sergeant Bittrich maintained a vigilant scan of the battle area. The Opfor's *Jafir*, one *Predator* frigate and at least four tiger fighters remained unaccounted for. Any of them could inflict damage and casualties until it was converged upon and dealt with. Bittrich knew, if they managed to rendezvous, a coordinated attack could be devastating.

She watched from her highly specialized craft now as *Condor One*, carrying its full complement of 85 Spetznax operators, decoupled from *LRT Yulan* and rendezvoused with the *Draken's* second escort destroyer, *Latimer*, and the frigates, *DRP 1* and *2*.

With a lock on the *Peltier Maru's* transponder and her drive signature, Bittrich's EW crew gained access to the transport's engineering mainframe once they identified and interrogated its drive signature master codes. She then vectored the four ships towards her. The force traversed the battle area in close formation and inserted into the Phuong C-3 outbound wave. There they quickly gained their own lock on the transport, just 700 kilometers AGL of Phuong-Alpha.

*

Even before the war, the Spetznax Regiment had long experience in the type of work they were headed for. The regiment traced half its lineage to the Istrian Spetznax commandos of the second war. The Recondo half was far older. Without the Recondo arm of the regiment, the Commonwealth itself would never have existed.

The regiment was the one Commoner force with a record of near continuous direct action and strategic reconnaissance of enlightened tribes, and planetary surveillance of unenlighteneds across the Central Metropolitan Region since the Saluri-Degoan War, before the Commonwealth was founded. They were an open secret within the Fleet and the Common Senate's intelligence and security services, in certain strategic think-tanks, and in similar circles in the capitals of their foreign counterparts. Though neither they nor their counterparts were often mentioned outside those realms.

*

Condor 1 remained at Action Stations after decoupling from *Yulan*. She immediately powered up her inboard armaments, keeping all her primary decks and compartments sealed. With

Latimer in trail overwatch of the *Condor*, *DRPs 1* and *2* spread out and overtook *Peltier Maru* to starboard and above as she rode with the wave. Closing to 50 kilometers, the frigates 'loosed' 100mm gunfire into her drive nacelles and communications, ESR, and stellar collector arrays, blinding her and wrecking her propulsion systems.

Aboard *Condor 2*, as the transport's exterior systems were being neutralized, Master Sergeant Bittrich's crew scrammed the vessel's reactors. Peltier Maru's critical interior emanations went dark on Bittrich's panels. After a moment or so, the vessel's magnetic signature decreased significantly, indicating her interior magnetic field had collapsed. More than any other Common Fleet trooper, Spetznax operators knew well what went on aboard those ships. Bittrich smiled and signaled *Condor 1*.

*

Plunged into the cold and dark as in a meat locker, in zero gravity, the *Peltier Maru's* crew couldn't run. Most important, they couldn't operate systems to vent any of the 'levy-decks' as the Alliance called them.

*

Condor 1 closed on *Peltier Maru*. She fired forward braking thrusters and up-thrust 40 degrees to close on the transport at M-0.15. Lieutenant Colonel Madison 'the Mad Man' Romanov, commanding Alpha Cohort of the regiment's 1st Battalion, gestured for Operator Percy to keep her seat in the command observation compartment's cupola. He stepped up to the seat's side panel, tapped the ship's address system and spoke to his operators.

"I just want to remind you all," he said. "Commodore Morgan assigned us this mission for a reason. You all know, the controversy about what to do with us has been going on back on Demeos for a good while. Now that the war's over, some big changes are in the works. Not in the way we do things, rather, who we do them for. Spetznax and Recondo need to stay together, here, within the fleet.

"That's why Oshermeyer and Regiment has kept us attached to Draken for so long. To show the fleet we are a multi-faceted weapon supporting the regular forces. The word is we've got a hell of a job coming up after this. What it is, I don't know. G.W. does, but the other word is, he is gagged until we pee all over this here transport. Percy is sending down the latest from C-two. Man your sleds and get it done."

**

The 1st and 3rd platoons acknowledged from the aft and starboard shuttle bays. The 2nd platoon leader, Centurion Angelis Macnau acknowledged 'Mad Man' and Percy's latest update. He knew his orders. Conduct the same battle drill any Commoner or State Guard IEX capable marine platoon should be able to do in their sleep. And do it to perfection. He took another scrutinizing look down the centerline of his platoon's Ready Deck along the ranks of IHEA/BDE suited operators, from his position at the access ramp to the Sled Deck.

Satisfied, he re-joined them, making last minute checks from top to toe of their own and then each other's IHEA fittings and seals, and BDE interfaces. They checked and secured their weapons and battle packs; their gravity assist packs and grapnels. They checked their all-important breach and seal kits, called 'biscuits' throughout the Fleet. Then they rechecked everything from toe to top.

Macnau hopped 2 or 3 times and flex rotated as Operator Meta watched for missed seals or loose equipment. With none found, he checked Meta. Then he keyed the direct personnel link on his wrist pad and went two-way to his platoon sergeant, Sergeant Major Maxwell.

"Combat board, Max. Treat it like any slaver, they may try to eject cargo manually or use them as shields."

"Roger that, Angel." Maxwell then keyed over to the platoon intranet.

"Listen up people. That old tub out there was a real slaver before the second war. The Valerians captured it and sold it to us. Now it's a training aid. These Lucainans here play the game like we do. So go in hard! Shoot anybody in a uniform that looks like a threat, ask questions later! Secure your sleds!"

Condor 1's Ready and Sled Decks began to depressurize, extracting atmospheric gases from the troop and egress decks into the deck storage tanks. The operators felt their IHEA's familiar slow constriction around their BDE, compensating for the loss of external pressure.

Sergeant Major Maxwell walked the length of the troop bay, spot-checking operators' IHEA suit seals, life support settings

349

and weapons. In well-drilled sequence, the squad leaders shuffled their people down to the Sled Deck where the fire teams loaded onto and powered up their assigned boarding sleds. Maxwell descended the port access as Centurion Macnau descended starboard and mounted their sleds. Macnau mounted with bravo team of 1st Squad, Maxwell mounted with alpha team of 2nd Squad.

**

Operator Hasse Motua, leading alpha team, smoothly worked through the sled and weapon power-up, its function check and navigation pre-set sequences. Armed with a 20mm exospheric machinegun, their sled held seven IHEA-BDE suited operators, including the driver in its' open chassis.

"Secure your seats to the front. Lock your weapons. Set your visors to mag four. Stellar filters active. Standby for ramp separation."

Condor 1 maneuvered towards *Peltier Maru's* main L&R deck. *DRP 1* shifted fire, adjusting short bursts of 60mm auto cannon projoes into the deck 5 shuttle bay. *DRP 2* stood off, turning out to overwatch. *Condor 1* hove to 15 kilometers aft and below *Peltier Maru's* stern quarter. *Condor 1's* Sled Deck bay doors separated; each half retracted into their recess in the vessels' hull.

Broad, blue and green Lucainus spread away to port, the lights of the major southeastern hemisphere cities dotted the surface, diffused through scattered clouds. Out the starboard bay, less exotic, Lucainus-Phuong lay much closer. Sparkling pyrotechnics were clearly visible on her surface, east of Lake Yeuin.

"Cocoon is active! Hold on to your lunch, boys and girls, disengaging. Eighty-nine seventy-five kilometers AGL!"

Docking clamps released, *Condor 1's* six sleds hung motionless in the egress bay, then each slowly lowered level. Clearing the bay, they thrustered out to the oblique towards the port bow to clear the mother ship forward and moved into an echelon right formation.

'Eighty-seven ninety-five AGL of which one?'

'He said Eighty-nine seventy-five.'

'We going down or up? Never mind.'

'Keep bein' funny.'

"Cocoons' interfacing," Motua announced.

Maxwell always thought he could see the shimmer of the sled's magnetic cocoon as they passed through the *Condor's* into

350

open void. It was always an illusion, but the slate gray mass of Phuong-Alpha looming in front of them and the dark hull of *Peltier Maru* was very real. They grew in his visor as the rapidly accelerating sleds readily attracted towards the asteroid.

"Rotate seats and ready grapnels!"

Operator Motua released the grapnel locks as he steered with his thruster controls. The operators rotated their seats to face outboard to the open sides of the chassis. Operators Tyler and Farouk oriented their M9s outward. Maxwell, Operators Adma, Carter, and Mitchell, each pulled the 50cm diameter grapnel lode line from the bulkhead at their quarter of the sled.

The frigate ceased fire. Following their sledding operators at an oblique, *Condor's* 40mm and 60mm rapid-guns stood ready to suppress the outer hull on the flanks of the exterior maintenance manways and airlocks at the L&R deck at the boarding party leader's command.

Peltier Maru loomed closer. At Centurion Macnau's command, condor loosed a short burst into her to kill or drive enemy crew clear of interior passages near his access points. Operator Akers maneuvered her sled toward the port quarter of the L&R deck, now just 5 kilometers away as pulses streaked past. Below, to her right rear, 2nd squad's two sleds trailed her. Alpha team of 1st squad was above her, to the left front with 3rd squad in trail behind her.

Seated behind Akers, Centurion Macnau overlaid that tactical plot in his visor. He saw 1st and 2nd platoons' shuttles above him, swinging around from *Condor* under Mad Man and approaching the command shuttle bay as he controlled his platoon's final approach.

"Hold Two-one. Two-two come abreast. Two-three hold."

One kilometer out, Alpha team of 1st Squad fired braking thrusters and let the others come up on line to their starboard.

"Refract!" Macnau ordered. "Reduce to mag one and advance to the main L&R deck. First squad, secure the port access. Second squad secure the starboard. Third, follow me. Move out."

The sleds angled upwards, staying on line and well spread to broach the lip of the L&R deck at the same time from widely separate points. Broaching the L&R deck, 2nd platoon's boarding sleds surged forward across the 175 meter width of the landing platform to the bay doors on the port and starboard sides. Operator

Motua set his sled down well forward of the landing pads, getting as close as possible to the starboard exterior manway. He hovered the sled at three by three meters.

"Dismount! Deploy grapnels!"

With Tyson and Farouk over-watching, Maxwell, with Adma, Carter and Mitchell, their M9s slung across their front, flex-vaulted to the deck and secured their lodes to the outer hull in the quadrants around the manway. Staying inside the leads, they readied their weapons. Motua watched as his team took their ready positions.

"Set..., secure..., charging..., standby." Increasing the Portable Magnetic Field Generator output, Motua extended the sled's cocoon through the lode leads to the transport's outer hull and exterior manway. "...go!"

Carter went to work tapping the exterior manway lock controls.

'Internal power is dead. Circuit is free..., open.'

The upper, middle and lower latches slid away, clearing the manway. Their visors at Mag 01 in active low-light, Mitchell worked the center latch. Adma stepped forward with a concussion grenade. He and Mitchell made eye contact with the grenade between them at visor level, Adma pulled the release.

'One, one thousand, two one thousand.'

Mitchell swung the manway partially open just enough for Adma to hurl the grenade inside. He saw it ricochet off the interior bulkheads as Mitchell pushed the manway shut again.

'Three one thousand, four one thousand.'

Mitchell re-opened the manway as tiny wisps of smoke dissipated in the vacuum.

Motua led the way. The team and Maxwell followed securing the manway behind them. Carter moved forward again. He tapped and opened the inner airlock to the ready room. After a second and a third concussion grenade, Motua entered low left, Mitchell went high right, and the fire team followed. The operators encountered six uniformed 'bodies, apparently two women and four men. Massive 'blood globules', weapons, IHEA suit accoutrements and fragments floated throughout the compartment.

'Two-six this is two-five, entry complete, no resistance. Suppressive fire accounted for six. I say again, six down, over.'

352

'Roger that, two-five, no resistance here, five down in here. Be advised, one of the down has senior officer shoulder boards. Break, alpha-six, this is two-six, entry complete, no resistance over.'

'Roger two-six. One, make your approach.'

Alpha cohort's breaching team cleared the compromised compartments at their entry points then accessed the kinetic power assists to allow the shuttles carrying the Mad Man and the balance of the cohort to land, access the shuttle bays and dismount their operators with additional PMFGs. Seven biscuits had to be applied to seal the L&R deck manways and inner airlock. Once the first pressurized compartment was safely entered, Alpha cohort began encountering live Opfor crew members and exercise controllers. Weightless, cold, and totally disoriented in the unpowered transport, the Opfor immediately surrendered in section after section to the heavily armed and armored, IHEA-suited operators with grav pads.

Peltier Maru's holds were filled to capacity. Alpha cohort found and liberated one hundred fifty 'slaves' in the crew billets and found the town's population', manacled to body racks anchored to the levy decks. Securing the vessel compartment by compartment, Alpha cohort secured the crew and transferred the ship's officers to CD *Latimer* in manacles. Nothing needed to be done for the 'levy simulators' after medico operators scanned each training aid's bar code into a med-reader and passed their data up the reporting chain.

*

Phuong-Alpha.

Two assault landers from LRT *Etar* bearing 2nd Cohort, (Reinforced), of 1st Fusiliers surged towards the close orbiting asteroid. The cohort, with an additional fusilier platoon from 1st Cohort, the battalion scout platoon, two engineer squads and Demetrius Lamphere with his videographer, Julia Mack, began shuffling down from their troop decks to the vehicle decks within minutes of launch.

Working and living together for the last two years, Lamphere and Mack shared what they believed to be a perfect relationship. As an unmarried couple however, their situation was at odds with the marine's No-Cop policy. The marines let it slide, and they had, so far, managed to avoid any issues by not displaying open affection while among the troops.

353

Lamphere and Mack were unarmed, but otherwise fully outfitted in battle dress ensemble and IHEA covers.

'I like these suits, Demi,' Julia remarked, standing beside him and recording marines boarding their Chariots. 'We can talk on the direct personnel link without anybody hearing us.'

'We can argue too.'

'Not the way you gesture and gyrate, baby doll.'

The Cohort XO walked past them, spot checking squads when she stopped short. She turned towards them, and said something, but they couldn't hear her. Lamphere raised his right gauntleted hand towards the right side of his head, using the 'Say Again' hand and arm signal. The XO tapped her wrist pad and raised both hands towards her earpieces, 'Go Intranet.'

Julia tapped her man's arm and reset her own comms. The XO gave her a thumbs up.

'You people know which chariot you're riding in?'

'Uh, actually, Lieutenant, we don't know.'

'Follow me,' she said abruptly. She spun on her heels and strode off towards the bow, with Lamphere and Mack hot on her heels. The three walked past carriers closing their troop ramps as the bay illumination went to launch stand-by amber. They passed three chariots before the XO stopped at a buttoned up HQ-4, where she tapped her wrist pad. 'Head four, open up, I've got the Embeds for you.'

In a short moment the troop access door swung open and a helmeted head popped up over it.

'You found them, Lieutenant?'

'The Embed and videographer, Mason. Take care of 'em.'

'Yes, ma'am.' The tall marine's helmet visor cleared as he stepped out and gestured for Lamphere and Mack to board.

'This is the Boss. You'll be able to get a good view of everything from here. Enjoy the show, but don't touch anything, unless Mason says it's okay,' she cautioned. She waved and continued on to her vehicle and mounted.

'Your Chariot awaits, sir, madam.'

'What's your name, again, Trooper?' Lamphere asked.

'I'm Sergeant Mason, Lawrence T. And you two are?'

They introduced themselves as they climbed into the chariot's fighting compartment and Mason re-sealed the door. Instead of 14 fusiliers in sets of bucket seats normally facing side mounted external firing ports, the fighting compartment was crammed with sensory monitors and communications gear in front of four bucket seats surrounding a small observer stand and periscope in the center. A single seat with a firing port and roof hatch were present on either side of the rear ramp, and two were forward near the driver/gunner compartment bulkhead. A second marine gestured them towards the two empty firing port seats up forward and the two other marines let them squeeze by.

'Can we take our helmets off in here?' Julia asked, looking around.

'Not yet, ma'am. I wouldn't recommend it once we launch either. It's gonna be a short trip,' Mason advised.

'The XO called this a Boss, Sergeant. What does that mean?'

'Bombardment Support Section, Mr. Lamphere. We talk to the bombardment batteries, the ships, and everybody else putting steel on target for the grunts. We didn't see you at the order. I went out looking for you when we stood to the Y. I'm glad Tormasov found you.'

'We were supposed to be at the briefing?' Julia asked excitedly as the gripper pulled her into the seat.

'Yes, ma'am,' another marine answered her. 'The centurion's word is you get the grandstand view. The whole VIP treatment.'

'So spell our names right. Okay?'

'Sure, gotcha'.' Lamphere said with a nod. 'We didn't know we were supposed to be there. What did we miss?'

'You two stick with me.' Mason said. 'Us that is.' Pointing around to his crew. 'We'll keep ya up to speed. Tap the panel next to your firing port there. I'll show you where we're going.'

The 189 kilometer diameter asteroid displayed in both their screens. The more or less round, lumpy image zoomed into an area just north of its craggy middle zone. The asteroid, was actually three large, rock formations fused together, and covered in several layers of compacted regolith with a thin crust covering of loose regolith dunes caused by gravity drifts.

A relatively uncratered plain, or basin stretched generally east to west, fronting a wide range of rugged hills on the north side of the plain, and a larger stretch of heavily cratered basin to the south. The broad crater field extended below the equator to another jumbled chain of hills.

'This stretch here, running east to west, is our landing zone. LZ X-Ray.'

Mason zoomed in closer. Details of a network of roads radiating in the eight cardinal directions from a main road encircling the landing zone emerged. 'In fact it's the only LZ on this side of the whole rock. It's an administrative landing zone. So for safety reasons, the exercise actually begins once we off-load.'

'Yeah, we know. We've been here before. We've covered Home Guard training here.'

'No shit? Where y'all from?' a female named Peters asked.

'Nevar Central States Herald, on the other side of Andolusia. We're stellar opposite of Narudis.'

'So this is your neighborhood. You must know the ground here better than we do.'

'More or less,' Julia laughed.

'Which objective are we hitting?' Lamphere asked. 'The mine and smelter? The refinery?'

'No, the vacuum press plant and communications station, there, on the southeast track.'

Lamphere and Mack both traced the southeast radial, winding along a 10 kilometer long valley to another basin. There, an antenna field and a series of regolith domes marked vehicle and personnel accesses to the sub-surface habitat.

'Is the facility defended?'

'There's only one way we're gonna find out.'

'Now Hear This. Now Hear This. Stand by for Lander Launch Starboard.'

'That's us, folks,' Mason said. 'Switch your panel to channel 3 to get a pilot's view.'

'Yeah, it's sweet.'

***

0907hrs. Condor 2.

"Sergeant Bittrich, I've got a lock on the *Jafir*. Sending the plot."

"Way to go, Simpson." Bittrich rotated in her command chair towards her primary ESR scanner. The Opfor destroyer's symbol appeared on her console emerging from the dense asteroid zone below and behind Phuong.

"I've got them all,' Simpson shouted. That zone there must have been a rally point. I see lots of subduction pockets in there now, Sergeant."

"Coming out to die gloriously, huh?" Bittrich snarled, seeing her worst case scenario play out. She keyed her fleet net transmit selector to clear voice.

"Draken from Condor. Counterattack! One destroyer, one frigate, five tigers approaching Acre, ten o'clock low, five eight thousand kilometers, now, over!"

**

LRT Acre.

'BATTLE STATIONS. All hands! Man your battle stations!'

Shipboard illumination began to flash, klaxons blared. Blast doors and emergency magnetic shielding powered up, separating primary and secondary compartments throughout the ship. Everywhere aboard the transport, crewmembers reacted as if their lives were at stake, just as they had at Aletia-Maranon, in the Trudan before that, and Spice Alley before that.

'CLOSE DEFENSE WEAPONS FREE.'

'B one two up!'

"Roger, B one two up," PO1 Sara Coyningham Peres, the defensive fire control station operator replied from the command deck directly above the twin 100mm gun station.

'C three oh three up,' the C deck, triple barrel 30 mm machine gun turret's report crackled in her headset.

"Roger, C three oh three up!"

'Red zone, one o'clock low, to three abeam.'

On it went, for fifteen more seconds with each of eight defensive fire control sector operators receiving weapons' status reports by deck, caliber of the weapon, and number of barrels on the mount; from up to ten mounts and turrets in their sector of the transport's defensive fire zones. Each gunner's voice confirmed the

357

green status of the mount from its fire control assist computer to Sara's display, until, at 0828hrs and 53 seconds, the defensive network was fully operational, 7 seconds inside the 2-minute battle school standard.

The DF controllers scanned their sectors and adjacent sectors for incoming targets. Using order of battle classification assist software, they designated targets for the appropriate weapons system or combination of systems. The overlapping sectors covered the transport for 360 degrees, out to the maximum effective targeting range of its ordinance.

I gotta protect my man, Sara thought with a smile.

With her husband Cooper and the cohorts mounting their landers preparing to deploy to the surface, it was up to the gray-jackets to defend their ship. PO1 Yuan Ji and her crew manned the twin 100mm semi-automatic cannon at the B Deck starboard amidships section, below the command center.

Ji kept her body centered in the gunner's chair and her feet firmly settled on the loading paddles. The sighting display lit up as soon as she grabbed the port and starboard hand trigger grips. The sighting binocular smoothly telescoped towards her face and synched with her helmet visor.

Sara's voice filled Ji's headset. "B one two. Two crossing the bow, climbing towards one o'clock, one five hundred, crossing oblique."

"I see 'em!"

The display in the binocular showed the illuminated inner circle of two concentric circles and the target post, or 'pipper', representing the convergence point of the projectiles. Ji's body movement controlled the chair, anchored into the turret cradle represented by the outer circle in the display. Depending on its approach angle, she led the target with the pipper, or rested it on the target.

Aligning on the intruding tigers, vertical stadia lines flanking Ji's pipper displayed the range to her targets. Illumination changed from red, to amber, to green. Read-outs on her port and starboard visor panels displayed ammunition status, HSPF failsafe setting adjustment, target speed and exact range, gun elevation, target deflection, and sight magnification.

The IFF illuminated the Tiger-5 as Opfor blue. The safety interlocks disengaged and permitted the two-stage triggers to be fully depressed. The range-finder engaged at the half depressed or 1st stage position. The fire control assist computer queried her to visually confirm Commoner, or Opfor. It automatically adjusted the target magnification and queried the fleet database for the Tiger-5's silhouette and identification code.

Ji followed through on her trigger squeeze, she didn't hear the weapon's report in her gunner's pod, and Mark-6 100mm SD railguns had no recoil. The illumine tails of the two projectiles exiting their rail barrels lit up her sight reticle. The battle flash discriminator in the screen let her see the detonations as the tiger flashed. Her gun status blinked back to the ready. Ji laid onto the second tiger and squeezed her triggers. Its strobe winked. She loosed again, the fighter pivoted and streaked away downward across the bow.

"C three oh three. Torpedo at twelve o'clock, direct, one nine hundred. Torpedo at two o'clock, oblique at one six hundred. B one two, one at three o'clock, two thousand lateral." Sara's soft voice methodically guided Ji's kill of each intruder in turn.

"Nail 'em, Ji Girl! Nail 'em!" Her primary loader cheered her buddy and gunner on.

The weapon's loaders popped open their ammunition storage lockers and engaged the next ready packs of 100mm, disintegrating deuterium dust, 'flash' projectiles into the ammunition rack below and centered on the port and starboard breech assemblies.

The battle damage klaxon and flashing blue illumination startled everyone aboard.

"We've been hit!"

'Torpedo impact. Damage control, lay to deck five, port side launch track bays.'

3rd Cohort's port side loading bays! Sara's heart sank. *Wait, Cooper's is on the starboard side. Oh, thank the Creator.*

*

"Get out, get everybody out! Go, go! "CoSM Greer yelled across the intranet, shoving 1st Platoon marines from *Acre* Assault Lander Alpha 1's 'damaged' access gantry back to the Y intersection before it sealed off. Forward along the corridor, 3rd Platoon marines moving aft towards the gantry were met and bowled over by the rush. The tangle of battle laden troops along the narrow corridor from the Y intersection to the port assault landers could not back out to the Y before the inner blast doors sealed.

*

Bridge, CBC Draken. 0910hrs.
"*Acre's* been hit! Port side! Torpedo launch from the *Predator.*"

"Dammit!"

"Commander, *Kingston* and *Kerak* are engaging the *Jafir*. She's trying to slip back into the asteroid field. They are breaking orbit to pursue. *Mallory* and *Ba'gration* are closing on the *Jafir's* rear. *Mallory* reports the vessel is heavily damaged."

"Very well, finish her off. Where's that *Predator*?" Stefan demanded. "Find it! Signal *Sabra*. Delay your shuttle launch until we deal with this threat."

"Sir, I've got it. Three two five degrees, two zero degrees down, range one zero five thousand."

"Forward battery. Kill that ship! Helm, Come Left Forty-Five Degrees, Twenty Degrees Down, lower amidships battery free. Loose as Your Turrets Bear!"

"Commander, *Sabra* says HLS one and two are launching now!"

"Dammit! Kill that *Predator!*"

*

After donning their evac suits to standard in front of two of the exercise controllers infesting the capital ships, Maria, Nick, and LCdr Tieras folded down seats from the forward battery observation post aft bulkhead. They had a grandstand view of the gunfire support going into Yeuin being interrupted by the developing fight to protect the transports. The senior observer of the crew around them controlled a targeting circle, quartered by adjustable sets of cross-hairs superimposed on a standard octagonal grid in the lamalar. Tieras stopped his narration of the action for Maria and Nick and turned up the volume for the intercom link from the guns.

'Number one, base gun. Target, Predator frigate, Opfor Papa zero four, area suppression, standby battery volley. Range as your guns bear.'

Indicators on the wall panels in front of the observers and the live camera feeds of the action on the gun decks directly beneath Maria's feet preceded the turret officers' verbal acknowledgements.

'Stand-by, battery volley. Gun one, target Opfor Papa zero four. Loose!'

Maria saw IHEA suited crewmembers in the panel instinctively reach up to cover their ears despite their hearing protective units inside their helmets.

"Brace yourselves, watch the center barrel muzzle," Tieras almost shouted with excitement as the compartment began to vibrate. Terrified, Maria's eyes went wide.

Whirrrh, Phaaroon!!

Their compartment resounded with Number 1's thunderous report. Discriminators in the lamalar cleared the barrel flash. The star bright illumine band arced out and down, clearly visible in the continually magnifying lamalar until it burst in a brilliant spectral flash, below and to the left of the moon.

The observer keyed his mike. "This is OP one, shift left, one five mils. Up three, repeat," he said.

"Watch the little red light on the tip of the barrel, Maria."

'Left, one five mils. Up, three, repeat.'

The gunnery officer's number three panel flashed amber, then blue.

'Stand-by battery volley. Target Opfor Papa zero four. Loose!"

Whirrrh, Phaaroon!!

The second star bright illumine lanced out, arcing downward and flashed in the distance. This time the battle flash discriminator revealed a bright red flash moving slowly in the center of the cross-hairs.

"This is OP one. Target Hit! Amidships. Target is slowed to wave speed. Adjust for motion, and fire for effect. Fire for Effect!

'Forward and lower amidships batteries. Three rounds. Loose!'

*

"What's Acre's status?" Morgan demanded.

"We're getting conflicting reports, Commodore. I'm getting it sorted out," Major Davis snapped back without taking her eyes off her data pad or breaking her stride between signaler stations. "Sir, Acre took at least one torpedo in her port side L&R ramp. She cannot launch port side landers. She says losses are feared heavy among the lead cohort units on the port side."

"Just lovely," Morgan snorted. "Tell Tate to launch whatever he's got left. Alert First Battalion to launch into LZ Greene. What's happening on the drop zone? What's happening on X-Ray?"

*

LRT Acre Assault lander personnel gantry Bravo-1.

'Lieutenant, I only have a few seconds. First and third platoons are gone. You take over what's left of the cohort. When you get to the surface..," Centurion Naravanutu's wrist pad image blacked out. The words 'Battle Casualty- Shipboard' flashed across a shocked Lt. Cartier's screen.

"No time to worry about it, Lieutenant. We gotta board, now!" PSgt Crowder yelled, grabbing Cartier by the arm.

"Wait, wait! What do I do?" She hesitated at the head of the gantry to their assault lander, Acre Bravo1. She looked around, mesmerized by the flashing blue illumination and repeated three sharp klaxon blasts filling the air.

"Ma'am, that's the emergency launch warning! The lander hatches are gonna close and its leaving with or without us!" Crowder and Signaler Jackson shoved the dazed lieutenant the rest of the way along the gantry, towards the loadmaster and Mixon who grabbed her and hauled her in. Crowder dashed back up the gantry and forward, then down the gantry ramp to AALB-2. Seconds later, the illumination went to standard launch red and administrative launches of assault landers AALB-1, 2 and 3 were allowed by the controllers, followed by the bombardment platforms from the bow.

The shipboard BIIS went active as soon as they launched. Orbiting their transport, awaiting Landers 2 and 3, Mixon, Anders, 2nd squad, A. J. Mortimer and 2nd, Headquarters and Weapons platoon troopers looked on in dismay through their troop deck lamalars at the flashing blue strobes illuminating most of the port side of the L&R, E Deck, and D Deck from section10 to the launch bay.

"Dayum, must've been two or three torpedoes that got her."

"She's still serviceable."

362

"Yeah, but what about our guys?"

"I hear we got a lot of casualties."

*

'Knock it off!' PSgt Crowder's HG image yelled from aboard AALB-2. Fusiliers scurried out of his way as his image bounded the length of the troop bay.

'Listen up people. Forget first and third. We are the cohort! We have the cohort's mission.'

Crowder spun around, glaring into his platoon's stunned faces. His gaze fell on SSgt Mixon, standing next to battle-suited A. J. Mortimer and his videographer. Mixon looked Crowder in the eyes and tilted his head towards Cartier.

She sat with her shoulders and back slumped against the bulkhead, her hands in her lap, her helmet lay on the deck at her boots. Jackson, her primary signaler sat next to her, holding her M9 with his. The lander loadmaster stood over her, between her and the hatch that she, Crowder and Mixon had pulled and shoved the woman through just minutes before.

Her eyes were vacant, as if in a trance. Crowder and Mixon both knew, and so did the other squad leaders and veterans in the platoon, this was her Romeron, her make or break moment. She could become an effective member of the team, with their help. Or they could shut her out, get the job done and be stuck with a liability from the start of the deployment. The marines turned to look at their platoon sergeant.

'Lieutenant Cartier, ma'am,' Crowder called out to her from almost half-way down the troop compartment. She didn't look up. She just sat there, staring at the deck.

Her hushed, unsteady voice answered. "Yes?"

'What are your orders, ma'am?'

*

Phuong-Alpha. 0919hrs.

Three Recce cars from Scout platoon, 1st Fusiliers followed a Max-5 recon drone visual link along the winding road through the low hills south of LZ X-Ray. An M38 Leopard armored fighting vehicle followed them in close overwatch, keeping one road bend back behind the trail Recce. The Leopard led the five Chariots of the cohort's 3rd fusilier platoon. Two Leopards and half the cohort command group, H-1, the centurion's chariot, H-4, the Boss, and an engineer squad vehicle followed the fusiliers.

363

'What's that group moving along Huber Road, on our right, Sergeant Mason? Lamphere asked, pointing at the drone feed.

'That's second platoon, they're swinging round to come down on the site from the northwest. We're taking the direct approach from the north. The rest of the cohort is in reserve, just outside the LZ's admin zone.'

'I see.'

Lamphere sat there, swaying gently with the motion of the eight wheeled carrier on the undulating road in the asteroid's 0.697g surface gravity. He watched their green symbols moving slowly alone along the paved industrial road for another long moment.

Alone, he thought. *Wait a minute.* 'Sergeant Mason, where's the industrial traffic?'

'What industrial traffic?'

'This is an active mine. There are robotic haulers moving ore along these roads all the time to the smelters. That's how the place pays for itself.'

Mason gave Lamphere a suspicious look. Then he reached up and tapped a key on the signals panel next to his periscope perch.

'Six-seven, this is foxtrot.'

'Go ahead, foxtrot.'

'This is foxtrot, the Embed has been here before. He says this is an active mine. He is wondering where the auto-haulers are, over.'

There was silence for a long moment.

'Six, this is six-seven. Security halt. Stay on the road. Dismount walkers. Scan for mines before you herringbone. Out.'

'What the hell?'

'Foxtrot this is six-seven, I see your position, stay there. Monitor the Max feed, light up your TRPs.'

'This is fox, wilco, over.' Mason tapped commands on his panel and stepped onto his periscope. Without a word between them the other marines set to work on their scanners. Mason flipped the intranet on.

'All links are up,' the woman Peters said, but no one responded or stopped working their own systems.

Julia tapped Lamphere's arm and pointed to his battle view. 'What's happening, Demi? What did you start?'

'I don't know, babe.' Lamphere blew his girl a kiss and tapped the panel.

The view out the port side told him nothing. Only a seemingly endless expanse of rolling gray-black hills and stars stretched out in every direction.

'Check your seals, people. We're depressurizing. We'll pop the hatch if anything cuts loose, Mr. Lamphere. You can get a better view.'

'Thanks, Sergeant.'

'Demi, check it out,' Julia called out from the starboard side. Lamphere slid over and caught sight of squad walkers scurrying about along the road and the road shoulders. Each drone stopped, lowered its body to the surface and arced its seeker head twice from port to starboard. At which point it stood, advanced a distance into the dunes and repeated the action.

'What are those walkers doing, Mason?'

'Checking for mines,' he answered without turning to look. 'They're using the ground penetrating radar in their belly node.' Mason continued his impromptu lecture as he slowly rotated the periscope. 'They do a wide arcing scan, then move along.' Peters and the three marines manning their stations each gave the others a running account of their status and Mason coordinated their actions with the mortar crews back at the LZ, and the supporting warships.

'The two lead scouts are dismounting, Sarge. Number three is moving along the road.'

'Third platoon is deploying behind the Leopards. The lieutenant is about fifty meters behind the lead squad. Second squad carrier is breaking left, third and plat daddy to the right.'

'Movement to the front, Sergeant! Drone has mounted movement, both sides of the road. Two vehicles north at three hundred, forward of the scouts. There's three more, to the east at six five zero.'

'Six-seven, this is Foxtrot, drone reports vehicles ahead, both sides of the road, relaying feed.'

Lamphere and Mack watched the action unfold in the fire support team members' panels. Mason looked over their suits and, seeing everyone's master seals were green, stood and opened the periscope hatch.

'Hey, Julia, switch seats with me. Get a shot of this squad on the left.

'Here I come.'

Julia stepped across the compartment with her datacam at the ready. She tightened her view on Lamphere's firing port panel as he slid out of the way. Lamphere opened the hatch above Julia's seat and, keeping his feet on the deck, raised his head and shoulders into the open, between the already exposed gunner in the forward compartment and Mason.

Andolusia's light reflected off regolith dust particles suspended just above the surface like a light mist. The effect made the panorama of undulating gray and black regolith dunes shimmer as he looked around. Scanning to the south and southwest, Lamphere could see the upper warning strobes on the refinery cracking plant and the smelter's aggregate towers in the distance. The communications station's antenna fields to the northeast were ahead of him, but the gunner's cupola restricted his view to the front. He turned to see Julia come up out of the hatch on her side, recording the squad he told her about.

The squad dismounted its carrier and spread out in the dunes in front of it, about 150 meters to H-4's left. The carrier backed off and found a hull down position with only its 30mm auto cannon turret exposed. The squad's maneuver team separated into two fire teams with the team leaders carrying M9G grenade launchers. The auto gunners, carrying the M9R with canisters of ammunition belts securely attached to their BDE, took positions near their leaders. M9 mag rail battle rifle armed fusiliers took individual positions behind boulders and in folds in the surface on the flanks. Then, in full refraction, they all disappeared into the regolith.

'Roger Fox, we see dust clouds. Sit tight. Stay under cover. Advise the Embed, controllers say the ore hauling is on admin hold in this area based on their production schedule. Tell him I still owe him a brew, over.'

Lamphere turned and gave a grinning Mason a thumbs up.

*

Once off the road, dust clouds roiled everywhere a vehicle, or a walker moved in the light gravity. A fine, gray dust film quickly covered every vehicle and piece of equipment.

'Fox, this is scout lead, adjust bombardment. From TRP six, north three four zero, multiple surface vehicles moving through gullies, over.'

'Scout Lead this is Fox, adjust bombardment. From TRP six, north three four zero, multiple surface vehicles moving through gullies, out.'

Mason tapped a command key pulling up a firing solution for the mortars laagered behind them. Peters worked out a solution from her flexmet bombardment tables attached to her map board with a protractor. Mason looked up and got a 'ready' nod from Peters, before keying the mike to the mortars.

'Six-eight this is fox, bombardment mission. Platoon volleys three! From gun two as base gun, elevation five, eight, zero. Deflection fan center bearing two, three, five. Charge six. Braking thrusters at two three five six meters. Above surface burst at six meters.'

'Check,' Peters calmly endorsed him.

'This is six-eight. Bombardment mission. Platoon Volleys Three. One magazine, load. Standing By! Plat two, base. Elevation five, eight, zero. Deflection fan center bearing two, three, five. Charge six! Braking thrusters at two three five six meters! Above surface burst at six meters. Marked. Stand by.'

The silence over the cohort net shattered.

'Contact Front! Cobra, right side of the road, fifty meters! It's hull down in the shoulder. Shit! Shoot that damn thing!'

'What!' Peters swiveled from the map panel to the drone view and caught sight of Scout 3's Recce blasting away at one of the Opfor's notorious little, tracked, anti-vehicle guided missile launchers.

'Scout three's right on top of it.'

Two bursts of red pulses lanced out from the Recce's turret mounted 30mm auto cannon and 12mm bow machinegun. Two rockets struck out towards Scout 3 in retaliation. The two vehicles flashed one another. The fight was on.

The dunes lit up. Green-blue and red zipping 12mm and 30mm illumined auto-gun projoes crisscrossed the plain in front of H-4. Leopard AFVs and Chariot personnel carriers' silhouettes illuminated from weapons' muzzle flashes and obscured instantly in dust. Leopards and Recce scouts shot towards Lucainan Pumas scout vehicles and Panther AFVs working their way across the dunes.

The Panthers' 100mm main guns and coaxial machine guns supported the Puma's advance from hull defilade positions they knew well. Pumas worked their way through the maze of dunes, often raising little or no dust. The little scout then popped up over a dune and loosed burst after burst of 30mm projoes, suppressing sections of 2nd Cohort's hasty defense, while its mates and the panthers worked their way forward.

'Fox, six-eight, time of flight, zero eight, shot, over.'

'Shot, out. Break, scout lead, TRP six shot, over.'

The lead scout's response was delayed. When it came, it was accompanied by shouts and the staccato report of their weapons from inside their fighting compartment.

'Get mounted dammit! Roger shot! Fire for Effect, fire for effect. They're coming at us, across the dunes to my front. Three, correction, four, to my front. I see more dust clouds approaching from my right at two o'clock, southwest of my position, over!'

'This is six-seven. Scout lead, pull back through my line and swing west. Follow your drone feed, get around them. Link up with the deuce and charlie mike to the station. We'll deal with these people and push on. Break. Foxtrot, SK and vapor in effect, over.'

'Scout lead, wilco. Break, pop vapor, Kabir. Break contact!'

'Fox, SK and VP in effect. Spplassh, over.'

'Splash, out!'

Mason tapped Mack's arm, gesturing up and outward, following the arcing glow of tiny steering rockets, angling the next salvo of a magazine of eight SK mortar projectiles from each of the three semi-automatic platforms downward from their maximum height of rise. The bombardment erupted with flashes of shimmering wobbles amid the dust clouds where most of the Opfor illumines were coming from. The dunes lit up again with blue-green outgoing illumines. Not as many red came back at them. Red strobe flashes began to appear through the dust.

'Echo Four, this is six-seven. Panther and a Puma approaching the road, from your one o'clock, closing at five hundred. See them?'

'Roger, six-seven, stand-by.'

*

The Leopard section leader kept his targeting screen overlaid to his helmet visor. He rarely had to look down at the one in the cupola. He kept his head up and moving in places like the Trudan asteroids and here on Phuong, scanning for the target. He switched to the vehicle intercom.

'Gunner, panther, one o'clock, SKAV, load SKAV.'

The Leopard gunner responded with his visor firmly meshed against the main gun sight's wrap-around panel.

'SKAV up! Target, Panther AFV. Four nine three meters, I got his port bow. Target UP!'

'Loose!'

'On the waay!' The gunner depressed his foot pedal, launching a burst of 20mm coaxial machinegun projoes as he squeezed the main gun trigger, launching a 120mm SK anti-vehicular projoe into the Panther, just behind the driver's compartment. Flashing, the vehicle crunched to a halt amidst a cloud of dust.

In the Leopard turret, the barrel blank snapped shut, the breech block unlocked and dropped open to the half-lock. The loader shoved the next projoe into the open breech, tripping the breech lock and opening the barrel blank. 'SKAV up!' the loader yelled.

She spun around and rolled the next projoe from the ready rack into the gun breech feed path, getting the exercise blue high speed programmable fuse fail-safe set light.

'SKAV ready!' She stood by to ram her gunner's next shot home the second the breech opened.

'Gunner! From the Panther, Puma carrier at eleven o'clock, at five twenty. He's swinging to the right around the dune.'

Taking command of the turret, the gunner rotated, putting the gun in general alignment. He made minor corrections on the azimuth and elevation settings and lased the target, getting an instant return.

'Acquired, sarge, at five one eight. I see three antenna stubs. Company commander!'

'Loose!'

'On the Waay!!'

The Puma flashed.

'SKAV Up! SKAV Ready!'

*

LZ Greene.

Everywhere around the exo-drome, in Happy Valley and in Phuong-Yeuin town, Opfor survivors collected their wits and gathered what weapons and extra ammunition they could between orbital stonks, fighter-bomber sweeps, and the cursed attack drones. Fortunately, for the Opfor, the drones couldn't be everywhere, they couldn't see everything, and soon they would run out of ammunition. Individuals and groups escaping the valley, braved the gunfire suppressing the hills and made their way as best they could towards Hill 309 and the town from the exo-drome in the south.

Meanwhile, 3rd Dragoon Battalion marines were vaulting their way to the crest from the north and into town from the east. As SSgt Lang lit his beacon, in line with those on the prairie, SSgt Eduardo Berch led 2nd squad, 1st platoon of 2nd Cohort south from the drop zone.

Berch talked to himself, war gaming possible enemy reactions to every action his squad might take as they scaled a long finger ridge toward a rock outcrop to the left, or east, of 309's crest to secure the cohort's left flank. With the rest of the platoon moving up through the woods to his right, Berch scanned the slope ahead as he climbed. Since the drop, the veteran dragoon had heard spasmodic small arms fire and mortars from the direction of the town far to his right.

*

The northwest slope closest to town was dotted with orchards, that surrounded a group of stone houses along a dark, narrow, tree lined country lane that overlooked the town to the west, across the bypass road. Narrow logging trails extended through the dense woods above and east of the houses towards the crest of the hill, and down the south face towards the exo-drome. LtC Harkness' command group and a platoon of dragoons reached and occupied the group of houses and the woods around them, winning the race to secure the approach to the town and the landing zone to and from Happy Valley. But dragoons lost or tied many of the races to the crest to the northeast.

*

370

Berch kept his machinegun team in a loose diamond with him. Bravo Team brought up the rear 50 or so meters behind him and the walker, while Alpha Team, about 75 meters further upslope, approached the dark line of conifer trees two thirds of the way up the slope through thinning underbrush.

The walker's proximity threat alert chirped in his HPU. A threat arrow illuminated in his visor angling towards the rock outcrop at the same time his machine gunner's voice clicked over the intranet.

'I got movement, Sarge. Ten o'clock, left of the rocks in front of Alpha. Two, three guys, maybe more.'

Berch looked left and up. He saw heat sources of battle-suited figures emerging from the gloom beneath the trees and dropping to the ground.

"TOAST 'EM VIC! Boufar, Come up. Lay suppressive fire ten o'clock! Put a Komodo into those trees. Break, Rita, there's movement to your front, base of the tree line!"

The first muzzle flash came from the Opfor upslope. Illumined projoes zipped out from the trees a split second before Vickey's machinegun. Detonations popped all around Alpha team, driving them to ground. Baxter, on the right, closest to Berch flashed. The team instantly returned fire.

"Walker, Baxter is down!"

The hillside erupted with gunfire. At less than 400 meters range, the hypersonic mag rail launched projoes' detonations in their target areas preceded the cracking report of their exit from the muzzle of their weapons. The squad walker skittered past Berch on the left, vaulting over obstacles heading directly for the 'wounded' Private Baxter.

Vickey's 12mm MG42 light machine gun chattered off short bursts accompanied by the M9 rifles of Berch, Atkins, and Bravo Team's three fusiliers. Cpl Boufar and Trooper Meah pumped out 40mm SK grenades across the width of the target area as fast as they could load and acquire. The bases of the trees obscured in dust and SK wobbles. A streaking 84mm komodo rocket lanced into the trees one hundred meters in front of the Alpha team leader and detonated in a brilliant flash.

Even before the battle flash cleared, Berch could see Alpha Team's four green silhouettes assaulting the tree line. Corporal Slovene and her team flex vaulted the 100 meters through the underbrush and over deadfall under Bravo's covering fire. Berch held his fire and watched through his targeting grid as Alpha Team spread behind trees and stumps. They grenaded the area around where the komodo exploded and closed in, at the vault.

"Cease fire Bravo, Cease fire Vic!" Berch heard three more *Pow-Kraks* from M9s upslope before the ridge fell silent.

"Bravo, move out. Stay to the right, watch your ass," Corporal Slovene's excited, puffing voice cracked over the intranet.

'I got six down up here Sarge! One's an officer, a Major. They've got blowpipes up here too; I count five on their walker. I lost my cherry.'

Berch stood and vaulted forward, waving for his machine gunner to follow. "The walker's got him, Rita. We'll bag and mark him on the way up. Consolidate, there's probably more coming up behind them!"

The shoulder-fired air defense missiles are a major find.

'Roger that Sarge. Nice view. You sure can see a ways from up here.'

'Voice text. One six this is One two, contact report, six Opfor KIA, including one field grade officer. Five SLAD captured. One friendly wounded. Walker will upload status and coordinates inbound. We will Alpha and charlie-mike. Out.'

By the time he had spoken his text message to his platoon leader, Berch had reached the walker and Baxter. The walker's exercise chip searched Baxter's status. His olive drab green name tag across the top of his wizard box changed to bright orange.

'Well, well, Private, you get to take a nice long nap," Berch said with a mischievous smile. You're incapacitated. They gave you a sucking chest wound to challenge the medicos.'

'Aw shit, that hurts! What the fuck happened, Sergeant?'

'Now you know what a one to fifty pulse hit feels like, dragoon. Heh, you a member of an E-Lite club,' the sergeant said grinning as he transparented his visor. 'Game wise, you can't talk. You can't hardly breathe, according to the data,' Berch said with a smirk. Squatting next to him he pulled the ambu-bag from the marine's aid pouch on his battle suits lower right leg as the machine gunners came up.

'The bag's gonna put you into a coma,' he explained. 'They'll download the DRD in your suit. That'll tell the medicos how to treat you when they get you back to the aid station. They may not wake you up here on the surface. Don't be surprised if you wake up in sick bay back aboard Yulan.' He patted the young marine on the shoulder as he and Vickers' assistant gunner pulled the bag up over his body and closing it.

'The controllers will send the after action report once the exercise is over. We'll track back and see how you got hit. In the meantime, nighty night.'

*

Opfor survivors from the exo-drome bumped into the lead elements of 2nd and 3rd Dragoon cohorts. A score or more firefights erupted across the long, heavily wooded ridge of Hill 309. The Commoner dragoons, wearing mottled green armored battle suits, fought a steady stream of sharp contacts across their platoons' sectors with desperate individuals and small groups of Opfor grenadiers wearing black battle suits of woven metallic armor over microfiber SME chain mail. Contact reports flooded across the cohorts' and LtC Harkness' battalion tactical net.

*

Sharia Barker listened to the loadmaster's updates during the launch and the flight, but most of what she heard made no sense. The loadmaster's warnings and commands since they broached tropospheric and started the landing sequences were more interesting and exhilarating.

'One kilometer to touch!'

Finally, she thought. *Something is happening.*

*

Sabra Heavy Lift 01 guided in on Corporal Sayeed's beacon. At one thousand meters, it rotated its drive nacelles and slowed to a hover almost directly over the beacon.

*

'Seventy. Start your engines.'

That was what Sharia was waiting for. She depressed her left foot pedal and pressed the 'Start' button on the right side panel. The motor purred, her cab illumination went to exercise blue and Clyde's helmeted image appeared on her panel screen.

"You know I hate looking at those black visor eyes. Transparent. Let me see your eyes, dude."

'Oh, yeah,' Clyde answered, transparenting his visor.

*

373

The pilot followed the pathfinder's radioed instructions and his team member's arm and hand signals to the secondary beacon and, taking direction from the third dragoon in Sayeed's crew, spotted over the drop point for its inbound load.

*

'Forty. Stand-by, touchdown. Now.' SHL01settled to the surface. Sharia felt the bump. She saw Clyde's image rock with the motion.

'Ramps!'

The dark horizon crackled with flashes silhouetting hills in the distance in front of her as the ramp dropped. Her chrono read 0919hrs.

"Hey, it's still dark!"

'Drive, girl!'

Sharia shoved her controller forward. The D-7 rolled, the cab dipped down the short access ramp and the wheels beneath her bit into the earth. The right slipped a little but caught traction and the paver lurched forward.

"Hey, who's that? A marine?" Sharia switched her comms to intranet. "Hey you, get outta the way!"

'I'm your guide! Follow me!"

"Okay, I got ya! Don't slow down."

Sharia rolled off the shuttle behind the running marine. The battle-suited figure kept his M9 battle rifle tight against his body as he ran forward. After several meters, the marine turned sharply left, beckoning for her to follow.

"I don't turn that tight dear, but I'm coming." Sharia said, manipulating the controller and keeping behind the marine. Until he abruptly stopped and dropped to a knee pointing at a flashing BVLS beacon.

'See this marker?'

Sharia looked down and to the left and saw the flashing amber beacon the marine pointed towards. "Yes."

'This is your left limit. The other guy is gonna be working the other side. Follow the light line along the beacons to the perpendicular line to the south about twelve hundred meters. When you get there turn to the right. Towards the town.' The marine pointed to Sharia's right front, where sparkling wobbles danced among the silhouettes of buildings.

"What's going on over there?"

374

'Over there? Uhn, a fight!'

"You mean a battle?"

'There's a first-class row going on over there, baby!'

"I'm not goin' in there!"

'Of course not. Plow down to the other side, turn around to the right and follow that light line back here.'

"What if somebody shoots at me?"

'Don't worry. They will!'

"What?!"

Just then, four brilliant flashes lit up the middle of the prairie in rapid sequence. Sharia heard a roar and saw SHL01's underside pass overhead in the blink of an eye, as four sharp cracks from the middle of the prairie split the air. The big craft accelerated away to the southeast.

'They're shooting at us now!' The marine waved her forcefully on. 'Move out! Plow!"

Sharia shook her head and smirked in the panel towards Clyde. "Did you hear that? They're shooting at us!" She dropped her blades, opened her scoops, released the granulator break and manipulated the controller.

'Yeah, they do a lot of that here.' Clyde set the plow depth, bed and shoulder dimensions and makeup process control. Then he set the smelter temperature and the pattern feed.

'Smart-ass.' Sharia pressed her foot pedal, slipped the brake and drove forward.

*

From a corner window on the top floor of the 'Bank' building, Mrs. Allen watched the colonel and Centurion Serpa pull binoculars from protective pouches in their battle vests and scan the prairie to the east. Finding a pair in her own vest, she did the same.

"Oh, my!" she gasped. Faint heat shimmers moved about like advancing insects all across the open areas as the sky lightened. Forming into ever larger groups, she could easily see they were moving towards the town and the hill to her right. The images disappeared when she lowered her binoculars. "How many, do you estimate?"

'Battalion strength, at least. Eight hundred effectives, maybe more.'

Serpa stopped scanning and put his binoculars away, then tapped his wrist pad. The colonel saw his helmet jerk in surprise and turn towards him.

"Do you have ANY forces left, Colonel?"

"Odds and ends. Squads and crews we're scrapping together. Serpa, tell the command post to search the database. Find somebody alive down in the streets to get things organized here in town. Don't go yourself, I need you here."

'Already on it, sir,' Serpa called out over the intranet, even though neither the colonel nor Mrs. Allen had switched theirs on.

"Damnation. Heh," the colonel chuckled, shaking his head. "He did a good job catching us in the assembly area. But my people aren't gonna just give up, ma'am. You hear that shooting off to the right? My people are defending Hill three oh nine for as long as they can."

"You admire him, Colonel?"

"I don't know the man myself, ma'am. He's just another commie commodore to me. But he's got a hell of a staff."

"I'm beginning to understand that, Colonel," Mrs. Allen said, raising the binocular and sweeping the broad prairie across the highway towards the north.

'We've got three mortars working over the prairie, Colonel,' Centurion Serpa said. 'They're roving dismounted through town and loosing one half magazine at a time before they move again.'

"Very well."

"What good does that do, Centurion?"

'It lets 'em know we're still here, ma'am.'

Mrs. Allen could only chuckle, scanning the far north of the prairie.

'Colonel. Good news. The panther section at Joy Road and the Bypass is still intact. Sergeant Steiner has collected about forty grenadiers, with AVGM launchers and a couple of light mortars.'

"Excellent. Primo. Damnation. Tell Steiner to push scouts forward into town but not to bring his tanks up until I find out what's happening on three oh nine. Understand?"

'Understood, sir.'

Mrs. Allen pointed toward the north end of the prairie with her right hand, holding the binocular with her left. "Colonel. What's that steaming blob out there?" she asked.

Below the flickering, flashing slope of the ridge, Sharia Barker followed her orders as she did on any construction site. Aligning her plow and scoop units, her D-7 dug into the soil and ground its way forward at a remarkable 3 kilometers per hour.

"Oh shit, Clyde, this is easy!" She exclaimed, watching the readout at the base of the lamalar, left of Clyde's image in the screen panel. "I've never seen an intake rate this high before."

'We're atmospheric. There's lots of O-two and water. I gotta raise the process temperature range.'

"Do your thing, baby. I got this. You see Smiley?"

'On your left, just behind us, Clyde said smiling. 'Drive baby, drive. We're at one hundred meters.'

His eyes focused on the hot, grey, processed mixture spreading out in the wake of his smelter unit. Clyde monitored the mix of soil with the asteroidal rock aggregate in his reservoirs. He raised the temperature to account for the high moisture content raising a high steam plume, but their cameras easily penetrated the mist.

*

"Colonel, what is that?" Mrs. Allen asked. "What the hell is that?"

"It's a D-seven asteroidal paver, ma'am,' the colonel answered with a smirk and a nod. Two, in fact."

"How long before they have a serviceable landing strip in place?"

"Twenty minutes, maybe less."

"Put SK on those pavers, Colonel. As much SK as possible!"

"Ma'am. May I ask what level your authority is?"

"I have the Chief Executive's authority, Colonel. I'm going to be your next Admiralty Chief of Staff."

Centurion Serpa turned his head slightly in Mrs. Allen's direction. His eyes widened, he said nothing and stuck to his task.

"Yes, ma'am. Serpa."

'On it, sir.'

**

Flashes erupted in Clyde's screen all over the area around the newly surface strip. *No matter.* He thought. *At this density setting, it'll take an eighty centimeter solid rock to penetrate this here strip.* "Five hundred meters, Sharia baby, drive, girl," He said into his screen. *In this atmospheric pressure the mixture is bed hard in two minutes, and surface hard in four minutes, let them shoot.*

'What's that plinking and clanging?' Sharia's bouncing image asked.

"Micrometeoroids."

'Oh. What?! We're atmospheric you said. Ain't no micros hittin' us! They're shooting at us ain't they?'

"Drive baby. Six fifty. Drive."

'I hate this shit!'

'Sharia, this is Smiley, you see those flares?'

'What flares?'

'In the sky, shooting up from the ridge.'

Sharia looked up and caught a glimpse of a rising rocket, she watched it burst high overhead above the ridge she was rapidly closing on. "I saw it. Who is that? The enemy?"

'No. Those are our guys. The dragoons are signaling the assault landers. We've got maybe ten, or fifteen minutes.'

"Don't talk to me! Drive!"

*

'Colonel, the dragoons are launching signal flares. They're vectoring their assault landers.'

"What flares?" Mrs. Allen protested. "I don't see any flares."

"Your visor isn't fully tactical, ma'am," the colonel advised. "Those are BVLS flares, beyond visible light spectrum."

'With your permission, ma'am,' Centurion Serpa stepped close and took her left wrist. He tapped the visitor code into her wrist pad, activating Mrs. Allen's basic visor systems, her BIIS and intranet.

'Thank you, Centurion.'

'My pleasure, ma'am,' he said, pointing out and up. 'You can see over there to the east above the ridge, four flares. There goes another one.'

**

"The heights are secured." Acre Assault Lander Bravo-1's co-pilot announced.

"De-orbital burn in five, four, three, two, one, commencing de-orbital burn, come left four-zero, down one-six."

On the vehicle deck, half of 2nd platoon sat secured in three of their Chariots, one Leopard, one Viper AVGM carrier, two Skorpion mortars carriers, the Headquarters-3 supply Util and Cpl Proudfoot's frontline ambulance.

With her sisters at six minute intervals behind her, AALB-1 slowed. She extended her stub wings and rolled 40 degrees to port and 16 degrees down-angle. Already at 500 kilometers AGL, she immediately began to flare. Pilot Officer Markow kept the control yoke in her gut and worked the yoke triggers of the steering thrusters; PO Peters, the co-pilot, modulated the braking thrusters stopping the flaring.

Just below 200 kilometers, the full extent of Phuong's gravitational pull took effect on the 250 ton capacity lander. Each lander broke their spiral at 120 kilometers, extending their wings before broaching stratospheric over the moon's very real western ocean, still well north of the equator. Steering east by southeast, they buffeted through the tropopause, 20 kilometers over the west coast of the maneuver continent. The blunt-bowed, cylindrical landers broached tropospheric over the mountains north by northwest of Phuong-Yeuin under vortex escort.

'Six minutes out, Lieutenant. Rotating drive nacelles,' PO Markow's voice cracked in Lt. Cartier's HPU.

'Unh, roger,' she answered, shaking herself. She looked around behind her in Chariot 3-2-4's fighting compartment. Her veteran signaler, Jackson and her equally seasoned gunners, McElroy and Sulaske and their assistants looked back at her. Jackson nodded, unblinking, his jaw clenched, he reached his right gauntleted fist up towards her. Cartier bumped hers to his.

"Roger, Pilot," she repeated firmly. "Break, Six Minutes, Second. Secure your equipment! Check weapons exercise settings. Go intranets."

Jeana Cartier lifted her M9 and checked the indicator above the 1.15Kv battery pack latch cover, ensuring it had a steady deep blue glow, and verified hers with Jackson's. Then she tapped her code on her wrist pad. Looking around the compartment she saw fusiliers verifying their own, their mates and the crew-served weapons in the compartment and switching to the platoon net.

'We've got a good plan, remember the changes from the frag order,' she said. Transponders in her lower visor screen lit up, indicating every node in her net was receiving her. She didn't have to call for a net check as the manual said. She made her own, like Benny Crowder did.

'This is going to be tight, but, I couldn't ask for a finer group of brothers and sisters to count coup with, than Second Platoon. Those bitches down there are gonna hear from the Thunderin' Third Herd.'

'HOOOAHH!!!'

'Firing distractors!' PO Peters voice filled the intranet. 'Skid wheels down and locked. Touchdown imminent. Unlocking cargo doors. Ready ramp battery backups!'

'Ten Seconds! Launching vapor projoes. STAND-BY!'

*

AALB-1 swooped through vapor clouds, its engines roaring in full reverse thrust forty five degrees down angle to the front. Flaring at 200kph, the assault lander settled with a rolling thump 20 meters along on the still steaming runway. Corporal Sayeed watched wide-eyed as the lander's emergency drogue chute deployed, and its forward breaking thrusters fired. The skid/wheels' brakes smoked, but the big craft slowed and finally crunched to a halt at the 500 meter mark, shrouded in steam clouds. The drogue chute smoldered and flamed on the runway. Sharia Barker's D-7 Paver emerged from the cloud passing 10 meters from AALB-1's starboard wingtip, on her way to the north end.

AALB-1 powered her engines down two thirds, her nacelles began their rotation to primary, her vehicle deck side panels rose, and their ramps extended. The loadmasters saw the six gangway lamps turn green once the vehicle ramps meshed properly in full surface contact. They waved Private Osborne, Lieutenant Cartier's driver, and the others forward. With their squads and crews aboard, drivers eased the vehicles over the gangway aprons, down the ramp and onto the surface.

The roar of lander engines, the flat crrumpp and brilliant 'SK' wobbles of mortar projectiles greeted Chariot 3-2-2, Leopard 4, and Viper 6 exiting on the starboard side in line abreast. Flashes winked from silhouetted buildings in the distance on the right. Illumines streaked across their front, exploding among the trees along the highway, others into town, still more lanced out towards the ridge ahead to the left.

Chariot 3-2-4, 3-2-1, Skorpions 5 and 6 and the Front Line Ambulance exited on the port side, facing Andolusia breaking over the hills, but the roar of engines and the battle raging behind them and to their right was deafening, until HPUs compensated, absorbing and rechanneling soundwaves, reducing their relative impacts to below 80 decibels. Still, troopers shouted to make themselves heard, even across the intranet.

'Mind those pavers, drivers!' Cpl Kilgore, the Viper section leader cautioned.

'Damned straight. You don't want to have to pay for one of those,' Osborne quipped, but stopped talking abruptly. 'Sorry about the cross-talk, Lieutenant.'

'Relax and drive, Osborne. Get us into the fight,' Cartier answered, with a grin. She turned around in her cupola chair, spinning her monitor.

'Right then. Get away from the bird, people. It's gotta roll to clear the way for number two. We're it for the next six minutes! Port section pivot steer right. Follow me to the Bypass road. We'll link up with the dragoons on the hill. Starboard section advance to the town. Everybody get clear of this strip and maneuver rapidly, out.'

'This is two, Roger that, four,' SSgt Mixon answered, coming up out of his hatch and surveying the scene. 'Leopard four, Viper six, swing left, steer into the mist. Give that paver a wide berth and follow me. We're heading straight for that tall building in the center of town.'

The vehicles cleared their ramps and pivoted towards the ridge. Mixon waved and signaled his driver forward. Plunging into the mist, he turned around to see the leopard and the viper were following before everything turned gray. His visor was slow adjusting.

*

'Colonel, command post says commoner assault landers are on the ground in the prairie,' Centurion Serpa reported in a calm, matter-of-fact tone. 'They say they are no longer receiving transponder signals from the force on Phuong-Alpha.'

The colonel turned to Mrs. Allen. "Ma'am which of these missions is the task force's primary?"

She turned to him with a surprised look. 'You don't know?' her metallic intranet voice asked. She reached over and tapped the code the Centurion gave her. "You weren't told?!"

"Actually, we're never told what the priority is, ma'am. For us, they're all primary missions. But this, this is unprecedented. He has decisively won every engagement and I have inflicted very few casualties on him in any of them. May I ask, ma'am, for the sake of my troops' morale."

"You may not, Colonel!' she said sharply. "I haven't seen any evidence of assault landers on that prairie, just steam clouds. It could be another deception and not an assault strip being built."

'Ma'am, look there. In the middle of the prairie,' Centurion Serpa said, pointing to the northeast. Mrs. Allen turned that way and with her suit unpowered saw only the cloud. She re-keyed her wrist pad, her visor lowered and pixeled slightly then cleared.

*

AALB-1 emerged from the dense steam cloud taxing to the south end of the runway closest to the ridge. There, it turned right, advanced and turned right again facing to the north. Armored vehicles were already trundling rapidly south across the prairie.

*

Mrs. Allen watch in awe as the big craft powered its drive nacelles and accelerated. It surged along to the north through a cloud of steam and lifted smoothly off and away. Silhouetted against a golden sunrise, she caught the vapor and distractor bursts of another incoming lander.

The colonel and Centurion Serpa saw the controller Util turn the corner to their left and roll to a halt in the street below, in front of the main entrance. The front passenger door opened, and Lieutenant Colonel Marquis stepped out, looking around.

'We're up here in OP one, Colonel Marquis,' Serpa said into the intranet.

The controller turned and looked up. 'You've got dragoons clearing buildings two blocks that way,' he said pointing to his right, the way he had come. 'They own the hill and there's mech on the ground. How long are we going to let this go on? Lansdowne says this is tertiary, sir. General Hayworth says we're wasting ammo.'

"Stand by," the colonel shouted down. He turned to Mrs. Allen. "It's up to you ma'am."

'Damn! What's that term, Colonel? For end of exercise?'

"Endex, ma'am."

'Very well,' she said. She turned her intranet off once again. "Endex. Advise the admiral's barge crew to make all preparations for our return to Demeos as soon as possible," she said, removing her helmet.

"Yes, ma'am."

"Damn."

****

Task Force Draken.

1630 hrs. Ninth day of the third month of 770CE.

Maria uploaded her report of Operation Dragon Slayer to Jordan Mason, then walked with Nick to the starboard shuttle bay to board *Draken* CS 814 for a trip to *LRT Yulan*.

The Lucainans were magnanimous regarding their 'defeat'. To their mind they had done their jobs, and made Task Force Draken commanders, staffs and troops think and earn their pay.

The task force consolidated and counted noses in high orbit of Phuong over the 4th and 5th. Over the next three days, the Lucainans showed their sportsmanship by conducting a joint pilot debriefing and hosting the task force marines and many gray-jackets on their many excellent firing ranges. The capital ships cleared their throats with live fire exercises, at the orbital gunnery range at Mordred, the ice giant Tasco's outer moon.

The night before re-embarkation, the Lucainan cavalry invited their Common Fleet marine counterparts to a huge open-air banquet and regaled them with their versions of ancient warrior dances called Haka, which impressed and maybe even frightened the marines a little.

By 0800hrs, 09-03 the task force had departed the Andolusian heliosphere and set to the wave, enroute to, as the locator panels all stated, 'Port of Call-To be announced'.

Gazing out the port and upper lamalar portals, Maria Hardesty could clearly see two of the task force's destroyers in the distance. She caught a faint glimpse of one of the screening frigates, which one, she couldn't be sure of. She was about to turn to ask the shuttle's loadmaster a question about that when she was startled by the craft's bucking and shuddering.

"What was that bumping, Chief? Is there turbulence in the void?!"

"No, miss. We've passed through *Draken's* magneto-pause. Our cocoon is interacting with hers. We're in free void now and running with the wave. She'll buck a little every time we pass through a bigger ship's cocoon during
L and R ops. You fly mulies long enough you get used to it," the chief reassured her.

"L and R?"

"Launch and Recovery, miss."

"I see."

Maria chatted with the crew chief, the loadmaster, and some of the 10 member flight and cargo crew. The remaining 18 seats on the passenger deck were empty this trip. The craft's cargo was mostly recyclables from *Draken* to be sanitized and refilled aboard the supply ship *Sabra,* and rations restock on the return. They were twenty minutes out from landing on *LRT Yulan.* The shuttle would drop them off there, then re-launch to await *LRSS Sabra,* and pick them up again in twenty-four hours. The time gave her a chance to get a good look at the task force formation and gain a greater appreciation of its coverage. She also got her questions answered about the destroyers and frigates.

Maria knew from books and cinemas, that Praetor Kratari had effectively employed independent flotillas of destroyers, frigates and converted ore-ships called mini-carriers for fighters during the Second Alliance War. But it was Commodore Morgan who had the greatest success with three such flotilla, supported by two battle cruisers and 7,000 marines, when he cleared the Trudan corridor of Alliance forces and pirates beginning in the fourth month of 769CE. Like the majority of the crewmembers she had talked with, Chiefs Newton and Ma'reo, and the bulk of this crew were veterans of that campaign and were justifiably proud of their accomplishments.

Once again, these NCOs and crewmembers were proving themselves not to be as gruff and rough-hewn as Jordan Mason had made them out to be. Every conversation revealed more of a strategic and political savvy Hardesty had never before appreciated in military personnel. Information flowed easily from these regulars. *Another Kratari legacy,* she thought.

She found herself enjoying even more the symbiosis of equipment and tactical doctrine with political and economic facts and forming a broad strategic picture she had not fully appreciated before joining the task force. Maria admitted to herself, *I'm going to enjoy this assignment, even if I don't get any dirt on G.W. Morgan.*

Maria knew most of the Trudan story from the senate investigations. Her notes were, as usual, at her fingertips. A symbiosis developed as the journalist and the veterans filled in gaps in each other's perspective.

Gaseous $_3H$ and $_2H$, what most tribes called tritium and deuterium, and the helium isotope, He_3, were three of the most strategically vital raw products generated in every star and carried on stellar winds into the upper atmospheres of celestial bodies or into the regolith on the surfaces of bodies with no atmosphere. For centuries, every commodities market universally mined and traded these materials as the primary fuels for fusion reactors to produce electricity. Two other commonly traded natural materials, lithium and iridium, were also strategically vital for the manufacture of electronic components and various alloy metals.

In addition to their personal investments, for generations, every Commoner has shared in the wealth generated in their planetary group through their raw materials mining and commodities trading annuities from their Stellar State, or Home world government. The price of standard grade T_2H He_3 affected everything. Stellar state production rates and refining quality influenced their state's currency values, interest rates, and credit ratings.

No electrical power grid, no environmental system could function without fuel, no carrier could move. Manufacturers and transportation companies needed to power their own fleets of vessels, borers and asteroid grinding octophages. Most important, it was the primary fuel for the production of domestic electrical energy for hundreds of mundane apparatuses and appliances in offices, homes, and workspaces.

Located in the northeast of the CAZ, the Baktimur Stellar State contained 14 gas giants, 10 of which had escape velocities low enough as to allow the extraction of vast industrial quantities of tritium, deuterium, and He_3 from their upper atmospheres. These and other large fields were the primary sources of the uniform grade fuels for large commercial fleets and the military, freeing Stellar State sources for low-cost domestic use.

The Baktimur region was the fourth largest field in the Commonwealth, only the Mandalian and Osiri fields in the central metropolitan corridor were larger. No other war aim was as important as securing the lines of communication and supply from the outer mining complexes to Baktimur-Minoa, and then on to Epirus-Serianis and the rest of the Commonwealth.

Supported by the Kritt, Trudan void forces occupied and fortified habitats and their sentinel stations on three class-1 asteroids in the northeast Trudan's dense outer barrier. These provided Kritt forces good forward operating bases and numerous concealed routes of approach to cross the narrow gap of trans-stellar void to reach the equally dense fields in the south by southwest Baktimur and the transit lanes beyond. Trudan forces frequently raided mining platforms and convoys across the Baktimur border region and diverted captured cargoes to the Alliance.

Operating costs and insurance rates soared across the Commonwealth, affecting the Leagues and many
non-Aligns. Prices steadily rose, depressing productivity. The fear of a loss of projected revenue brought pressure from legislatures to raise VAT rates which, as the rate edged closer to the 15% ceiling, brought out the income tax advocates. Maria was in the press gallery the day the smooth talking Jayan Kabir, the secondary Gelesia Senator from Gelesia-Karilon, addressed the Senate. Most of the crew just shook their heads when she projected the video from her recorder.

'Surely, brothers and sisters, surely we can take the prudent measure of securing for the sake of the continual maintenance of the Common infrastructure a small yet steady stipend from the richest of us, for the collective good of the poorest of us.'

"He makes it sound so symbiotic, so helpful for poor people."

"That's just a sweet coating, Jasmine. It doesn't take long before we're all getting taxed like rich people. Straight to the poorhouse."

They would get no argument out of Maria or Nick on that point. The senator was just the current leading voice of minority Statists that had always been around.

The Statists had always sought to assert the power of the state over the individual, and to fuel that power by siphoning off revenue from the incoming worth of the individual rather than from what the individual spent.

During Operation Jagged Canyon, Task Force Draken located, bombarded, and assaulted the Trudan asteroid fortifications. The task force drove Kritt forces completely from the system and destroyed or captured the bulk of the Trudan destroyer flotilla, breaking their ability to continue the war. Eliminating the threat from the Trudan and reopening the T_2H He_3 flow was the turning point of the war. Its effects were immediate and widespread.

The T_2HHe_3 bubble burst as the price dropped by half overnight in Commonwealth and in non-Aligned commodities markets that trade with the Commoners. Pressure from industries to divert state production from domestic energy to vessel fuels disappeared. So too, diplomatic pressure to increase production and export was taken off the Leagues, especially the Asigi. Commonwealth interest rates plummeted, credit markets loosened as businesses began circulating hoarded reserves of cash metals in the form of new contracts and orders for durable goods. Correspondingly, fuel prices jumped by one-third virtually overnight in the Alliance and in Alliance leaning markets.

Even with the Common VAT locked at 10.3% for the next three years; government revenues increased by 11% over the first three weeks after Trudan, and stabilized at 13.23% after sixteen weeks, silencing income tax advocates once again.

"I hear there's talk of dropping the VAT a full two percent."

"Not bloody likely, mate."

"It sure would be nice."

Across the Commonwealth, consumer prices plummeted shortly after the refineries started back to full capacity. As the price of refined, standard grade T_2H He_3 fell, so in turn did those of other commodities where rising operating and transportation costs hampered their production or delivery.

"My speculator is predicting boom times," Chief Ma'reo announced. "She says it may exceed that even of the pre-war surge back in fifty-nine."

Within the fleet, it didn't take long for mail from home to become more upbeat. Care packages began to arrive with goodies that crewmembers and troopers hadn't seen in months. All of the crew had similar stories of the recall of laid-off workers back home. With labor disputes over wages and benefits settled, and longshoring parties unloading more civilian goods at the ports, constabularies were reporting rises in portside pilfering to almost pre-war levels. The quest for profit apparently assumed a slight advantage over patriotism once the end of the fighting was in sight.

"What do you think of their compromise for military funding?" Maria asked. "I understand the budget cleared the way for the construction of a sixth fleet to go ahead."

"More than that, miss. They're gonna go with the recruitment of five new marine regiments, plus three cavalry squadrons."

"That means more transports and their crews."

"I don't know if it's such a good idea, Miss Hardesty. The more task forces and fleets we keep in peacetime the more apt we are to use 'em on somebody that pisses us off."

"Besides the Alliance?"

"Yes, ma'am, any of the non-Aligns, maybe even the Tantorans."

"Don't even think it, Leah!"

"I'm just saying it's possible."

The conclusion of the three previous major wars had all resulted in rapid and massive fleet demobilizations. Each time, in the fleet's view, policy-makers had gone too far in their budget reductions, requiring draw-downs so severe and arbitrary they sapped the morale and effectiveness of fleet units.

Postwar draw-downs at home and concessions to the Alliance to achieve temporary deals, the fleet believed, sowed the seeds of the next war. In some cases to the point that severe consequences in its opening stages were inevitable. This time, however, the Liberon and Pragmatic majorities in the Senate seemed determined not to repeat their predecessors' mistakes.

In the days after TF Draken set into the wave, the Senate reached a compromise and appropriated funds to field three new regular task forces, increase funding to the Stellar State forces, and elevate the Recruiting and Training Command to Fleet status. This created six operational and one training fleet, every faction got something.

"I say it would be best to build up and just go in and kick the Shafirans' asses and get it over with! Damned backstabbin' bastards!" The lower deck loadmaster's aggressive attitude surprised Maria. Everyone else was hoping for a long peace.

"Don't mind her, miss. Veronica is Poian, from Vizio. They still hate the Shafirans from the second war."

"Wouldn't you? If it was your home world they bombarded and invaded?! Fuckin' bastards."

"It wasn't the Shafirans, they were pacifists. They had no choice but to acquiesce."

"For pacifists they sure took to fightin' pretty damned quick!"

The shudder of passing through *LRT Yulan's* cocoon, and word from the flight deck to prepare to land, broke the spell, but the conversation had been beneficial. Much more of what Hardesty had read and heard in the investigations made sense now that she saw more of the fleet's point of view.

*

Draken CS 814 landed under the watchful eyes of fully manned 100mm and 120mm auto cannon and close defense automatic guns. A taxi cart latched onto the forward tow pintle and drew the craft off the end of the active launch ramp and along the turn around. The shuttle rolled to a stop at the third bay. Ahead, two of *Yulan's* shuttles were loading recyclables for their own run to *Sabra*. The port-side passenger access parted as Maria and Nick removed their crew helmets and thanked the crew. The deck officer greeted her as she stepped down onto *LRT Yulan*.

"Welcome aboard the long range transport *Yulan*, Miss Hardesty. If you'll step this way, there's someone here to meet you."

"Thank you, lieutenant. Who might that be?"

"Her," Nick said, gesturing towards the tall, dark marine sergeant advancing on her.

"That would be me, Miss Hardesty." Master Sergeant Tara Bittrich said in their native south central Comario.

"I understand you've been asking questions about me."

****

CBC Draken.1828hrs 09-03 0f 770CE.

The intercom buzzed in Morgan's stateroom.

"Yes, Commander."

"Commodore, I have Lieutenant Colonel Romanov on your command channel."

"Good, put him through."

Colonel Rivas sat sullenly in the swivel before Morgan's desk. She still didn't like the plan, and she had raised her objections. Morgan noted and appreciated each, but he had made up his mind, and he had his own orders. The stoic CSM Morris sat on the sofa behind them.

"Lieutenant Colonel Romanov, sir."

"Madison, how are you feeling today?"

"Much better, Commodore. My apologies again for missing the Commander's Call this morning. I didn't want to be a distraction."

"No worries, Colonel. You didn't miss anything. The real fun won't start until after the Stone arrives."

"Ye.., ahhhh-choo ...argghh, I beg your pardon, sir."

"Have you tried that ocillocote I told Doc Kaiser about?"

"Yessir, arrggh, Yessir, you wouldn't know it but I'm actually breathing much better, thank you again."

"My pleasure, Colonel. It's good for whatever ails you. Is your visitor aboard?"

"Yes, sir. Ahh, excuse me, I sent Bittrich to meet her at the L&R bay. She took her up to the command deck to meet with Commander Hauptmeyer. They've got her a billet up there. Bittrich will feel her out, and Major Danston, my XO, is going to brief her in the morning, I should be ready to receive her by midday."

"Lovely. That's good. Treat her well, but don't coddle her. She can spot a load of crap in an instant!"

"Rest assured, sir. We'll give it to her straight. My folks are a little nervous though, especially Sergeant Bittrich."

"Bittrich?! She's got ice water in her veins. You tellin' me she's nervous?!"

"I've never met a Recondo who wasn't nervous about somethin', sir."

"Granted, but she can relate better to Hardesty than anyone. Same age, same home world and all. Two things are certain, Colonel. One, the fleet will publicly acknowledge your existence after the docu-drama premiers. Two, the facts about Little River are going to come out sooner or later. This woman is going to be our ticket! More so than A. J. Mortimer could ever be. There are near void capable unenlighteneds where we're headed. She's seen a small part of your capabilities; she's really going to see you in action when we get to where we're going. Maria Hardesty is our best wager for getting the truth out when we get back home. The DIG will run with what she says."

"Yes, sir. So your guidance remains the same?"

"Yes, Colonel. Your objections are noted. If it makes you feel any better, Colonel Rivas agrees with you, but the alternative is too terrible to contemplate. The Fleet needs the lead role in life-search, or the Alliance will achieve an advantage again."

"Understood, sir. No limits on info or access except training."

"More than that. Feed her information and data until she vomits! She's smart, no! She's extremely intelligent. Any hint of deception and the game is up."

"We'll make it happen, sir."

"Lovely. Good to go. Now go back to bed and feel better. Out here."

"Yes, sir. Thank you. Good day, sir."

The die was cast, John Q. and Jane A. Commoner were to be informed of the existence of Spetznax-Recondo PSTs and their basic functions in peace and war. A civilian, a journalist, the Dragon Lady herself, had already witnessed a small part of their capabilities. Now, she had almost unlimited access to participants and after-action reports on the most recent Spetznax-Recondo operations on Aletia-Maranon.

The selection process, training, and most operational information, was still classified Top-Secret, Need-to-Know. But official acknowledgement of the unit's existence and significant operational history as far back as the Saluri-Degoan War, was about to be revealed to a journalist whose media organization was, at that very moment, dedicated to tearing it down and dispersing its parts to as many as seventeen separate civilian directorates.

Such a move would, in the opinion of the Commodore and the Admiralty, lead to an unmitigated disaster. Morgan and the bulk of the Admiralty were in complete agreement. Maria Hardesty's assignment to TF Draken with its organic Recondo cohort would forestall the DIG and the CE's office until they heard from her.

"Go ahead, Debra. Get it off your chest."

Colonel Rivas had made her case but had one last arrow in her quiver.

"Commodore, we all know Senator Hanash and his hangars-on represent the big info media conglomerates more than their own constituencies', sir. We can't count on all the admirals to stand together, Commodore. If Hardesty doesn't come around, if she reports what the DIG wants her to report, half the platinums will fold like a cheap tent. If we hadn't won so big at Maranon, sir, they would have stood by and let Hanash's amendments railroad you into retirement and decommission a third of the fleet again! Phuong was just a sideshow for them."

"Debra, I'm glad you're making this more than just about me. There are more important things than recognition. Sometimes you just have to do the right thing, and sometimes you don't really want to remember the actions you've had to take. Keeping the fleet strong enough to do its job is what's important here."

Morgan stood and walked over to the bar. He stood there for a moment, squinting out the lamalar above it at the stars through the twisted whorls of its transparency, as the task force sped on towards its rendezvous with CD Stone. Morgan liked this view, displaying the void in a chiaroscuro of color and light. It was blurred and imperfect in the distance, only his ships close aboard were undistorted at mag 03. To him, that represented reality better than a totally transparent view at mag 05.

While people thought his business acumen was sound, Morgan remembered words of advice given him when he closed his first casino deal.

"Colonel, an uncle told me once, he said 'Boy, you may think you're smart, and many will say that you are, but you have to look at the heart of this choice. You are taking up a business that preys on people who are easily addicted. Every time someone that works for you earns a credit, they earn it on the backs of those who can't help themselves'.

"My old Uncle Paul was right about that. Some of my people make it look so damned glamorous. But those poor wretches who sit at my machines playing the odds, can't avoid the glitter and spectacle, but let's face it, Debra, you and I both know that I have every machine fixed to pay out based on timing and coin volume. As the coin volume rises the machine kicks out a percentage.Lovely, lovely. Hell, the gamers even know that themselves; but they won't stop!" G.W. turned towards his chief of staff. "When John and Jane Commoner learn about life search and what the Alliance did before, they won't be able to get enough. What do you think, Moe?"

Command Sergeant Major Morris didn't care for journalists in general. He didn't like Maria Hardesty, or the DIG, in particular, but he saw no useful alternative that would satisfy Praetor Kratari's triumvirate. They were still a conduit of information to the Commoner, not a filter. *They want to steer the Commoners towards Fundamentalism and universal prosperity by any means. This is dangerous.*

"Commodore, Colonel, I don't gamble, don't know anything about it. To me, reconnoitering unenlightens is the ultimate adventure. We need hard professionals to do it. Not bureaucrats who simply collect and store data, or ne'er do wells who would think to make themselves kings over some ignorant tribe. Senator Jamison and Senator Hanash haven't thought the thing through, sir. Imagine the chaos of independent agencies enlightening brick tribes whenever, and wherever, they come across them. Cultures turned upside down overnight. Suicides, and worse, competing enlightened tribes, and even conglomerates creating spheres of influence within a brick tribe. I can't imagine the wars such a thing would spark, Commodore."

"Well said, Sergeant Major." Colonel Rivas nodded in agreement.

"Damned right," Morgan said. He turned back to the bar and poured himself a tumbler of JK Ranch sour mash.

"We keep Hardesty on the straight, the PSTs will stay with the fleet, Debra. Our problem will be weeding out the volunteers who know they don't stand a chance at selection, but they're there applying anyway on the off chance of hitting a jackpot. Hell, Roberto and his crew are already suggesting a renegade Recondo sequel to 'Praetor'. I told him no way in hell."

He poured two more and handed one each to Rivas and Morris. He offered his favorite three toasts. They stood together.

"To the Fleet. To Task Force Liberty. To Jana Kratari, the Andolusian!"

"Hear, hear."

The intercom buzzed again.

"Yes, Commander."

"Destroyer contact with two frigates, sir. Three points off the starboard bow. IFF *indicates CD Karen L. Stone the Second*, with the frigates *Mallory* and *Stefania*."

"Lovely. Thank you, Commander. The task force will go to battle stations and remain there until further notice."

"Aye, sir. Battle stations. The time is eighteen thirty-three hours."

****

Guest billet 3-A, Command Deck, LRT Yulan. 1840hrs, 09-03 0f 770CE.

The billets and corridors were sealed. Maria Hardesty, Nick Kung and Master Sergeant Bittrich were accounted for. They watched through the lamalar view port as streaking illumines engaged and destroyed target drones during the drill.

"I got my orders," Tara Bittrich said, sitting down in one of the kitchenette bar stools facing Maria seated at the dinette table. "The Colonel and the Commodore say I have to talk to you, but I'd rather be dipped in shit."

"You want me to turn my Julien off, Master Sergeant?"

"Julien? Oh, the datacam. Distort our faces and voices and no last names. Just Operator Tara or whatever. Okay?"

"Sure thing, Tara." Maria nodded, turning to Nick, grinning. "Julien?"

*

Task Force Draken refit, resupplied, and rested at Depot 19 and stood down for eighteen weeks. It had been a welcome respite, for most, after operations in the Trudan and Aletia. For most, but not all.

Aletia-Maranon was the home of what was an unenlightened, non-void faring, outer region tribe. The early industrial tribe was a collection of almost one hundred sub-tribal nation-states and multiple ethnic groups. The Trudans knew they were there but left them alone until Kritt reconnaissance units evaluated them.

Aletia was classified a G type, yellow dwarf star, with a class three-sized habitable zone. The class-1 Alpha inhabited world, and two other class-1 Delta, habitable, un-peopled, worlds were excellent to fair candidates for agricultural and industrial work camps. The Aglifhate allowed the Kritt to invade and begin harvesting industrial and strategic minerals and levied slaves. Additionally, Aletia-Maranon gave the Alliance a second base from which to interdict the Baktimur fuel flow.

Few Maranites noticed the meteorites falling on the 12th night of Flandar of the Maranite year 1816, 06-01of 768CE in the Commonwealth. With no inkling of the celestial events taking place around them, what appeared to be a meteorite shower actually slowed and changed direction. They revealed themselves to be rough-hulled flying machines moving in formation as they descended to land on the outskirts of towns and cities at strategic points over several days on all four of the planet's inhabited continents. The craft disgorged humans in fully covered metal skins like armored knights, but with infinitely more powerful weapons and self-propelled vehicles. The invaders began rounding up whole villages, killing anyone who resisted.

Shocked and stunned, Maranite military units and civilians took up arms. The most sophisticated of Maranite tribal armies had fought one another in linear formations of massed ranks of soldiers' armed with single shot, muzzle loading weapons. These fusils fired lead projectiles via reactive solid propellant. They were ineffective beyond 400 meters against other Maranites. They were useless against the invaders' armored suits except at suicidal, point blank ranges. Maranites brought crew-served field guns forward into the firing ranks to deliver direct fire round shot and disintegrating canisters containing small iron projectiles. They used equine mounted cavalry units for scouting, raids, and staged massed charges in support of infantry attacks.

Maranite aerial forces provided only observation by tethered hot air balloons. Their naval forces operated multi-gunned, sail and steam powered ocean going ships. Surface forces communicated with horns, drums, signal flags and heliograph at the tactical level. They used conductive wire based, electro-mechanical code key transmitters between major commands.

Every Maranite army and navy fought the comparatively few invaders from the sky, basically the same way, once. That is, if they had a chance to form ranks or line of battle. Very shortly, few Maranites were in any position to offer further effective organized resistance. Those that did adopted far less formal, far less suicidal, but infinitely more effective tactics. The Maranites had never given up the fight. Surviving military units and civilian partisans formed groups of 'Rangers' and gave the Kritt and Waffen Strelski occupation forces pure hell in Maranon's mountains, deep forests and their littoral regions.

In the towns and cities, Maranite civilians and intelligence operatives made highly effective use of their unsophisticated, non-electronic communications to find local opportunities to strike back. The Maranites found unique ways of isolating individual invaders, they managed to kill some and take a few prisoners. They forced prisoners to teach them to use captured weapons and equipment.

When TF Draken bombarded and seized asteroid habitats in Trudan, clearing the Baktimur corridor, the Kritt and Sacorsti Waffen Strelski units abandoned the Trudans to their fate. But then, instead of withdrawing towards Krittar they went to the planetary group in the stellar region prisoners called Aletia, with TF Draken in hot pursuit. IEX-Cavalry scouts located Kritt drive unit and transponder signatures on the second planet's surface next to large concentrations of non-technical populations.

This revealed an unprecedented opportunity. In the past, Commonwealth forces had captured many individual helots from worlds forcibly enlightened by the Alliance but had always found they could provide little practical information, if any, about their home worlds' locations. Aletia-2, the inhabitants called Maranon, was the first forcibly enlightened helot world to be precisely located. Commodore Morgan pressed his pursuit. TF Draken established void superiority in the planetary group. Morgan ordered the Recondos to deploy to the surface and informed the Admiralty of the situation.

On 09-01 of 769CE, the third night after the first anniversary of the invasion of their home, the subjugated Maranites were treated to a spectacular display in their northern night skies. The flying craft that before, had come to rest on their soil in smooth silence, came screaming down to fiery crashes. The occupiers were thrown into panic.

Over the next few days, ranger units began meeting other technologically advanced peoples who immediately raised their visors revealing their faces. The Recondo Planetary Surveillance Teams lowered their weapons and spoke to the Rangers in unfamiliar languages. The more the suspicious Maranites spoke among themselves, the more the newcomers spoke to them in their own tongue.

"The Maranites called us 'Commoners of Draken'," Bittrich said. "We offered to help them attack the invaders, but they weren't easily convinced. We brought down the Spetznax platoons, made a few raids ourselves on Kritt installations on each continent, and liberated some Maranite prisoners. After that, the local ranger units started seeking us out. You want some tea or something? These billets all have kitchenettes." Bittrich thumbed over her shoulder.

Similar to her billet aboard *Draken*, Maria's billet aboard *Yulan* had all the looks and appearance of a standard cruise liner berth. The layout was similar enough, she felt at ease, and got up, heading for the kitchenette.

"Jave' would be good right now, I'll make some for us. Please, do continue," Maria said. "I'm fascinated."

*

The Recondos secured Maranite trust by bringing in medical supplies and treating wounded. They raised images from their communications packs and showed their cautious hosts where they, and their tormentors came from in the night sky. They allowed the Rangers of different nations to coordinate with one another in real time. Soon, with direct assistance from the Recondos and Spetznax platoons, Rangers conducted several major raids against Alliance surface installations. The most spectacular was the raid on the Waffen Strelski Civil Action Company headquarters in the central palace on the principal Maranite city of Conate'col, the capital of the planet's largest national power.

*

"That one was something, sister girl." Bittrich shook her head in admiration, recalling the sheer audacity of the Maranite plan. "They coordinated it so well. We learned a lot about working with non-technical indigenous tribes, Maria. We haven't had that much experience with pre-industrial bricks."

"What's a brick?"

"That's what we call an unenlightened tribe. It's not as derisive as the Alliance word for them, 'wog'."

"Hmmm, that's interesting. So what happened on the raid?"

"Anyway, they got us in through the city sewers. They took us straight to the utility cellar under the central palace. We took the Waffen Strelski there totally by surprise. We killed a few, but altogether we took about forty prisoners, mostly staff officers and personnel. We found a freaking gold mine of intel, all with no friendly casualties! The Rangers liberated over two hundred civilians." Tara Bittrich sipped her jave'. She nodded in approval at Maria's handiwork. "Yeah, sister girl, it was a good day." She smiled and took another sip.

*

Conate'col and the other raids disrupted Alliance communications and air defense systems, and secured landing zones to insert the 7th Marines in the well-publicized Operation Mighty River on 08-02 of 769CE. Commodore Morgan dispatched the cruiser *Drukar*, the destroyer *Carter Jackson*, and two frigates to suppress the installations on the uninhabited worlds until 3rd Battalion could be released from Maranon. The marines cleared the installations on Aletia-1 and IEX Cavalry units reconnoitered Aletia-3, which the Maranites called Malestra and Malevena.

The two unpeopled worlds were much more tectonically active than Maranon. The planets were thickly vegetated and populated with vast herds of assorted wildlife. Aletia-Malevena included significant numbers of large, powerful, reptilian predators. Cavalry scouts surveying the surface, detected disrupted drive signatures and emergency marker beacons.

The scouts were forced however to remain above five kilometers to avoid being attacked by swarms of feathered, flying reptiles. The fresh impact craters and trails of scarred and shattered trees held the remains of three Kritt shuttles, evidence enough of the creatures' numbers and ferocity. No Commonwealth vessel attempted a landing on Malevena, though scouts detected evidence of Kritt survivors.

The invading Kritt were defeated on Maranon within ten days of the marine landings, though acts of terror continued until the last Sacorsti Strelski holdouts were rooted out. The task force evacuated 200 Strelski, 50 Waffen Strelski, and over 5,300 Kritt prisoners were to Commonwealth prison camps in Baktimur. Task force engineers transported wrecks and captured military equipment to the secured Aletia-Malestra installation to await disposition, far out of reach of the inquisitive Maranites, who were not yet independently capable of powered atmospheric flight.

TF Draken S-5, civil affairs units worked with restored Maranite governments. They provided technical information and specifications to build networks to communicate more rapidly with one another. Commodore Morgan allowed the Maranites to keep certain captured Kritt non-military equipment and, medical information technology. He thought it a small gesture of compensation for the death, destruction, and the horror of occupation. Maranite language copies of The Central Metropolitan Region Census of the Commonwealth and Other Known Stellar States were distributed.

TF Draken's victory on Maranon produced a major intelligence coup. A significant number of the Waffen Strelski Civil Action Company assigned to catalog the Maranite populations were among the prisoners taken during Operation Little River, along with their vessel and their intact data-bases the night Operation Mighty River began, exposing the Aglifhate's entire forced enlightenment process.

The Maranon Campaign was a watershed event in Commonwealth history. The Alliance invasion and their defeat by TF Draken forced the Commonwealth Senate to acquiesce to the military requirement to invade an unenlightened tribe, exposing it to cultural contamination from which it could never recover. The campaign completely disrupted the Maranites' technological development.

"Maria, our civil action teams and contractors are gonna be there on Maranon for some years to come, attempting to clean up and assess the long-term societal effects on the population. They were invaded, people taken away as slaves, to Creator knows where. Then here we come, and fight battles over their heads and in their streets. Wreckage and weapons from societies advanced by fifty or more generations ahead of anything they had ever seen or imagined literally fell through their roofs."

Nick heard the sadness in her voice. He saw Maria had picked up on it as well.

"It's hard to get one's mind around it all, Tara. I couldn't imagine what that must have been like for them."

"To be honest, sister, neither could I, then. Now, it's all I think about. You don't mind if I smoke do you?"

Commodore Morgan, Colonel Rivas, the Operations Officer, Commander Bertrim, and several Spetznax officers, as well as Task Force CSM Morris, Bittrich, and other senior NCOs had been called to the House of the Thousand Flags on Saluri-Demeos to testify in classified Senate Foreign Relations and Military Affairs Committee hearings on the matter.

Senate charges were considered against senior Spetznax command staffers and the Recondo Team Sergeants for allegedly violating the rights of indigenous personnel, by involving them in unauthorized combat operations against the Kritt and the Waffen Strelski.

The most significant issue was the decision to conduct active combat operations in a region not then a part of, or a threat to, Commonwealth territory or Commoners. A second set of charges were raised resulting from the Spetznax Recondo Teams, on several occasions, handed Alliance prisoners, particularly Waffen Strelski soldiers, over to the tender mercies of the Maranites. Who had, to say the least, very imaginative and painful ways of settling scores.

The Operation Little River after action report was not revealed to the public. But the charge of treason was bandied about in contemporary issues opinion media by spokespersons of Morgan's political opponents, led by the DIG. The fact that he had ordered an overt assault on an unenlightened world, without the approval of the Combined Fleet or Senate Committee for Military Affairs, was, to his opponents, proof the man could not be trusted to respect the Constitution.

Aletia's strategic position as an Alliance base astride the Trudan Corridor, and the fact that the Maranites had already been forcibly enlightened by the Kritt, was conveniently left out of the opposition's media argument. That fact was not lost on the Commonwealth Senate or the Commoners.

*

"The intel we captured is gonna go a long way to figurin' out just how much reach the Alliance actually has. That's pretty much it, Maria."

"Well, not totally, Tara. When they reached the compromise, the Senate was able to shelve the constitutional

401

amendment question for now. And they dropped the charges pending against you and your team members. Right?

"Yeah, Admiral Pol said it was a gesture of no hard feelings. Fleet Command promoted me and a couple of others to Master Sergeant. They recommended to the Military Affairs Committee, that Major Romanov, our team leader, be promoted as well. Most of us are still together here with TF Draken, this is Spetznax Unit three. Romanov is here in command; you'll meet him tomorrow. A few rotated to the D E to work at Red Devil or the CLA."

"The CLA? What do you do there, Tara?"

"I suppose I can tell you. While we stand down between missions or retrain, some of us work for Doc Wixom in the archives. Others work in the other Institutes, professor's assistants and such, and some are faculty advisers."

"No shit?!"

"No shit, girl, but don't print that!"

"I won't. Well, I'll be damned! I spent all kinds of time in the archives' scrolling chambers during the investigations, and before we embarked, I never knew!"

"Yeah, I know. No one does, beyond Old Wix, the superintendent, and the department heads. I figured you'd be coming around sooner or later."

***

In the vicinity of Nav buoy NG-1912Y7. 1949hrs 09-03 0f 770CE.

Twenty seven civilian and thirteen Combined Fleet Operations passengers and several equipment bundles debarked from two of the *Karen L. Stone II's* shuttles aboard *CBC Draken's* command shuttle bay. Command Master Chief Zoupre' of the *Draken* personally saw to their billeting while TF CSM Morris escorted the leaders of the group to the Commodore's stateroom. Pleasantries were brief; they all knew each other.

"I understand we have a mutual pain in the ass aboard." DOP-297's CCID station chief warmly shook Morgan's hand and accepting a mash with the other.

"Yes we do, O-man," Morgan chuckled. "But she's presently occupied over on *Yulan* with the Recondos like you and Old Wix suggested. How is he anyway?"

"Not good, I hear, but he's still in there kickin', he sends his best. We had one hell of a time making him stay so he can be treated."

"Ol' gloomy Wix, I'm gonna miss him."

"Me too, G.W., we could sure use him on this. But he's sent everything he has, and we'll be able to reach him fairly clearly all the way there, if you have enough buoys."

"I've got twenty with me. Sabra's fabrication shops can build more if we need 'em. Comms wise we'll be okay." Morgan assured his friend.

The station chief took a seat on the lounger, next to the lamalar, and sipped his mash. "About Hardesty, do you think the Recondos will do any good? Do you think she'll come around to our side?"

"Oh, she'll come around, O-man. To be sure, she'll come around when we don't need her anymore. Like some damned bank that hounds you to loan you money when you're no longer in debt!"

"Who's gloomy now?" Both old friends chuckled and let their staffers in.

*

CBC Draken, in the Chein-Haeun Stellar State, near DOP 297.
0900hrs 10-03 0f 770CE.

Since 2330hrs 05-03, *AGRV Retnec* had continued moving erratically, halting and powering down, then resuming travel after several hours each time. The vessel's actions continually stirred consternation among the report recipients along the chain of CCID threat analysts and technical intelligence personnel.

The preceding 48 hours had been extremely busy for the team of planners, intelligence analysts, order of battle specialists, telemetry tracking teams and cosmographers that arrived aboard *CD K L Stone II*. Even though they had been hastily brought together from throughout the Intelligence Directorate and the Combined Fleet, their seemingly unrelated bits and pieces of odd information dating back to well before the Second Alliance War were falling into place.

The Shafiran neuro-surgeon, Salezar Ben-Ali, had been prominent in the Second Alliance War as Aglifhate Prince Borigai Advan vin Ngeir's chief of neurological research. He was retained in the position by the Madonna Borigai Indira vin Ngeir after her coup d'état. Whatever the relationship between the Prince and the doctor had been, the relationship between the first Madonna and the doctor must have been infinitely better.

Immediately after the war, CCID and the Valerian Intelligence Service identified the residents of the heavily guarded palatial estate on Shafir-Ailea which the doctor frequently visited and monitored the movements of the research ship *AGRV Retnec*. Enough was known of the doctor's activities to make him and the *Retnec* a high priority target.

The armistice in 417CE cancelled a plan to intercept *Retnec* with a cloaked cruise missile. However an independent attempt by rebels on Jodar-Primanar to assassinate the doctor while on a survey of that planet failed. Indira vin ordered three Primanar cities leveled in retribution. The surviving populations were branded and deported to mines and work camps throughout the Alliance, with instructions to camp commanders that they be starved and worked to death.

Dr. Ben-Ali continued to supervise Aglifhate research from the planet laboratory of Kafar-Ratab and travelled across the Alliance aboard *AGRV Retnec* finding new methods of applying his automatonization processes, and other research, enhancing slave productivity.

Both CCID and the Valerians lost track of the doctor after the death of Indira vin and the short reign of Madonna Annabella in 128PCE/429CE. *AGRV Retnec* was reported to have been decommissioned shortly thereafter.

***

The party of analysts updated the Commodore and his senior staff. Afterwards, the strategy branch of the operations center was sealed and placed under marine guard. At 2220hrs, Mitch Pulke, Arlene Davis, and the plans NCO reported to Morgan's stateroom wearing sidearms. At 2243hrs, the trio returned to the strategy branch with the Top Secret, Close Compartmented envelope containing the single data disc tucked and buttoned in Mitch's lower blouse pocket. By 0430hrs, 12-03, an 'aerie' message had gone out. The main mess dining area was commandeered and converted into a conference room to accommodate a large group of 230 officers, warrants, and senior NCOs.

Commodore Morgan didn't like to hold a lot of meetings or briefings when deployed. Most information and decisions could be made and transmitted without bringing commanders and their staffs from across the formation, away from their own ships and commands. Detailed operations orders were different. So when he called an aerie, it was a big deal.

**

Shuttles were stacked up out to 300 kilometers waiting to make their approach and disembark commanders and their staffs from all over the task force. Shuttle flight crews quizzed each other about what could be going on that is so important as to require an aerie for all commanders down to battalion and squadron level aboard *Draken* at 0930hrs. It was already 0900 and four shuttles were holding outside the port hangar, three off the starboard, and three at the command deck shuttle bay. Rumors circulated that the cease fire had broken down.

They competed with those of the Commodore's backdoor appointment to Praetor, and that the task force would come about and head to Saluri-Demeos to assume control of the government.

Worried ship and unit commanders aboard stalled shuttle craft were advised by Colonel Rivas that the operations order had

405

been delayed one hour, commencing at 1030hrs, to allow for safe shuttle operations. The task force intelligence and operations staffs were relieved, as well. Both sections needed the extra time to collate the intelligence databases' of *Retnec* images, information on its systems, and the latest telemetry from DOP 297, its outer beacon line now just three SAU to starboard.

No pre-briefing packs were generated, the video signals section routed co-axial cable to the projectors in the mess from the assistant operations sergeant's console in the command center plotting room. She would monitor the briefing from there while projecting images, references, and maps to the monitors. Mission packs were to be distributed by courier after the operations order.

*

Colonel Rivas' instructions to Maria and her team were clear, written, and unambiguous.

"All, I say again, all aspects of Oplan Dragoon and Dragoon two are classified Top Secret-Official Chronicles, until further notice. Is that clear?" she asked. "Please sign here."

Hardesty felt the same quiet tension that had settled in among the officers waiting in the dining area for the Commodore's entrance. She and Mitch exchanged a nod and a smile, but he didn't come over.

**

Things had settled down considerably by 1010hrs. All the commanders and at least their operations officers were aboard and seated in the converted mess. All exits had been sealed, and armed marines posted in the corridors. The task force went to battle stations at 1016hrs.

Morgan wanted to get this over with quickly and get underway, they had a long way to go. Despite the days and hours of analysis, interpretations, and staff work, they still didn't know anything definitive.

That's what they pay me for. Heh, I'm rich enough. I'd do this for nothing if they'd let me. Lovely. Lovely.

Morgan and his command group marched off the lift from Topside. They turned down the corridor towards the main mess. Command Sergeant Major Morris was one step to his left and rear, Colonel Rivas on his right, followed by the CCID station chief from DOP 297 and the rest of Morgan's primary staff officers. At the mess hall, the marines snapped to attention and made rifle salute, their sergeant released the lock on the p-e cell, allowing the one unlocked door to slide open as he and Morgan exchanged gladial salutes.

CSM Morris stepped in first and announced him. "Ladies and Gentlemen, the Task Force Commander!"

Subordinate commanders and staff officers all rose and stood to attention facing the podium flanked by portable monitors. Commodore Gaven Webster Morgan winked at the young sergeant, then strode forward into the mess. The sergeant nodded, standing to the side to allow G.W.'s brain trust to pass. He broke into a wide grin as the door slid shut and he faced about.

*

"Take your seats, folks. I want to make this short and get you out of here! If you're like me, you're going to want to sit down and watch the big show tonight. That'll give you time to process what we're about to put on you."

Morgan took the podium while his staff took chairs alongside the starboard bulkhead. The rows were occupied in a descending order; the cruiser, destroyer commanders and the marine regimental commander accompanied by their operations officers filled the front rows. The cavalry squadron and frigate commanders, the fighter-bomber wings, the marine battalion commanders, all with their primary staff officers and NCOs sat behind the primaries. The Spetznax and the other specialty unit commanders and members of their staffs sat behind the maneuver units, the remaining seats were filled with critical vessel division chiefs and staff personnel.

The Commodore didn't waste any time.

"I'm going to give it to you straight away so there's no doubt. Here's the situation. *AGRV Retnec* is on the loose again. She's fully operational, and you all know what that means!"

No one had expected anything like this.

There were expressions of utter shock on the faces of the assembled officers and staff. Maria gripped A. J.'s arm. He put a hand atop hers as she struggled to catch her breath. She scanned the room, and found Mitchell again, sitting stoic along the bulkhead with the planning staff. She saw Tara Bittrich and Romanov, just a few seats from Mitchell and an empty chair next to them. *I'll wait to move.*

"We know its point of origin, its present location, and its trajectory." Morgan continued. "She's headed for an unexplored region well behind our back door here in Chin-Haeun. Mr. Clarence Ottwell is here from DOP two niner seven. He and Commander Harris will give you the latest intelligence estimates. We know nothing of the populations of the region the *Retnec* seems to be headed for beyond the fact that there are void capable or near void capable tribes there. Our mission is simple, get there and find *Retnec*. Seize her, her data, and her crew, and bring them back to the Commonwealth Administrative Zone! Failing that, we will destroy her, and steer her wreck into the nearest star!"

Morgan paused, looking into the eyes of each of his veteran commanders to let that sink in. After a second or so, he continued.

"We are to conduct preliminary surveillance of the tribal populations in the region for enlightenment potential. Said tribes…" he bowed his head slightly and paused; he still could not believe what he was about to say.

"…said tribes are to be warned of the potential Alliance threat. How we do that is up to us and depends on who we actually find. We are to defend them, if necessary, or assist them in their own defense from any probable Alliance invasion force. Mr. Ottwell will fill in the details, then we'll talk routes, comms, and logistics. I don't want to go over this in open forum for any longer than necessary, so hold your questions 'til the end of the brief. Go ahead, Mr. Ottwell."

CPSIA information can be obtained
at www.ICGtesting.com
Printed in the USA
BVHW042143240920
589611BV00015B/645